Pokémon™ Alola Region Sticker Book

Over 300 species of Pokémon—including the Island Guardians and Ultra Beasts!—can be found in the Alola Region Sticker Book, and now you can collect and stick them all! From cute little Pokémon like Togedemaru and Rockruff to amazing Legendary Pokémon like Tapu Koko, Solgaleo, and Lunala, you'll find hundreds of different stickers featuring Pokémon of the Alola region, plus vital information including their type, size, and the island where each is first encountered. Take a tropical trip to the islands with the Alola Region Sticker Book!

$14.99 USA / $17.99 CAN

Pikachu Press

The Pokémon Company International

Gotta catch 'em all!™

Publisher: Heather Dalgleish
Art Director: Chris Franc
Design Manager: Kevin Lalli
Designers: Hiromi Kimura, Emily Safer, Chantal Trandafir, and Mark Pedini
Illustration: Mike Cressy
Merchandise Development Manager: Eoin Sanders
Merchandise Development: Trish Ledoux
Project Manager: Emily Luty
Editors: Wolfgang Baur, Hollie Beg

Published in the United States by

The Pokémon Company International
10400 NE 4th Street, Suite 2800
Bellevue, WA 98004 USA

Visit us on the web at www.pokemon.com

Printed in Shenzhen, China

17 18 19 20 21 6 5 4 3 2 1

ISBN 978-1-604-38196-2

WELCOME TO THE ALOLA REGION STICKER BOOK!

You'll find that each Pokémon here has a colorful sticker and listing that includes its name and how to pronounce it, its Pokémon type, height, weight, and Category—plus a mention of where it is first encountered in the Alola region. Legendary and Mythical Pokémon, plus the Ultra Beasts, are noted as well. Now get out there and catch some Pokémon stickers!

PSYCHIC
ABRA

PRONUNCIATION: AB-ra

HEIGHT:	WEIGHT:	CATEGORY:
0.9 m	19.5 kg	Psi Pokémon
2'11"	43.0 lbs.	

Melemele Island

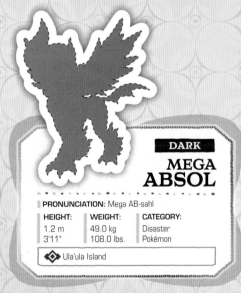

DARK
ABSOL

PRONUNCIATION: AB-sahl

HEIGHT:	WEIGHT:	CATEGORY:
1.2 m	47.0 kg	Disaster
3'11"	103.6 lbs.	Pokémon

Ula'ula Island

ABSOLITE

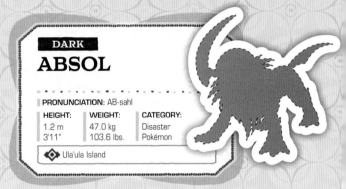

DARK
MEGA ABSOL

PRONUNCIATION: Mega AB-sahl

HEIGHT:	WEIGHT:	CATEGORY:
1.2 m	49.0 kg	Disaster
3'11"	108.0 lbs.	Pokémon

Ula'ula Island

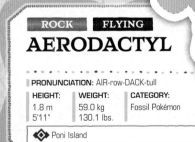

ROCK **FLYING**
AERODACTYL

PRONUNCIATION: AIR-row-DACK-tull

HEIGHT:	WEIGHT:	CATEGORY:
1.8 m	59.0 kg	Fossil Pokémon
5'11"	130.1 lbs.	

Poni Island

AERODACTYLITE

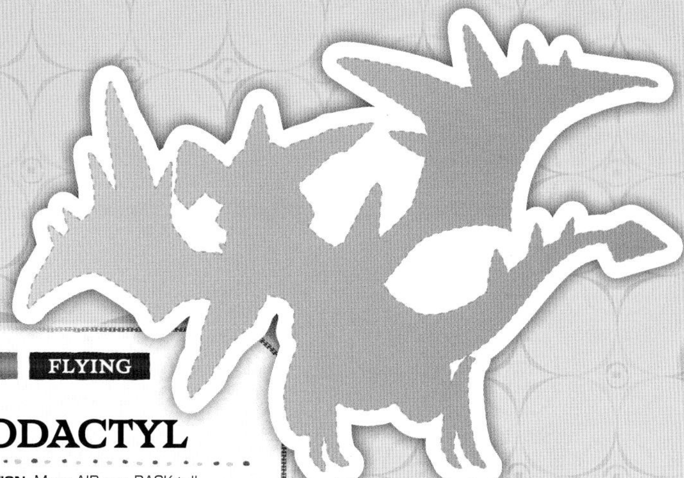

ROCK FLYING

MEGA AERODACTYL

PRONUNCIATION: Mega AIR-row-DACK-tull

HEIGHT:	WEIGHT:	CATEGORY:
2.1 m 6'11"	79.0 kg 174.2 lbs.	Fossil Pokémon

Poni Island

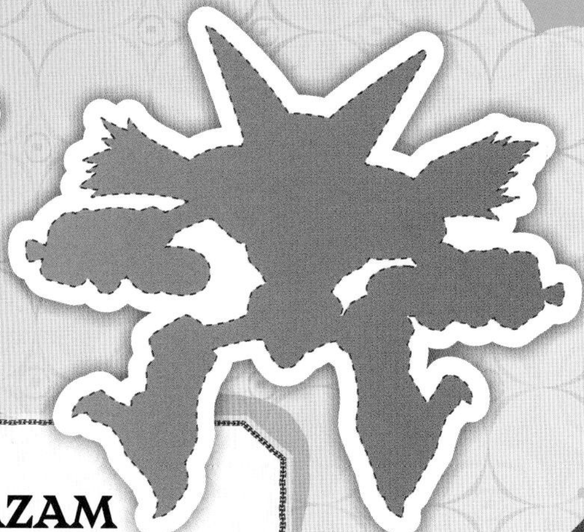

PSYCHIC

ALAKAZAM

PRONUNCIATION: AL-a-kuh-ZAM

HEIGHT:	WEIGHT:	CATEGORY:
1.5 m 4'11"	48.0 kg 105.8 lbs.	Psi Pokémon

Melemele Island

PSYCHIC

MEGA ALAKAZAM

PRONUNCIATION: Mega AL-a-kuh-ZAM

HEIGHT:	WEIGHT:	CATEGORY:
1.2 m 3'11"	48.0 kg 105.8 lbs.	Psi Pokémon

Melemele Island

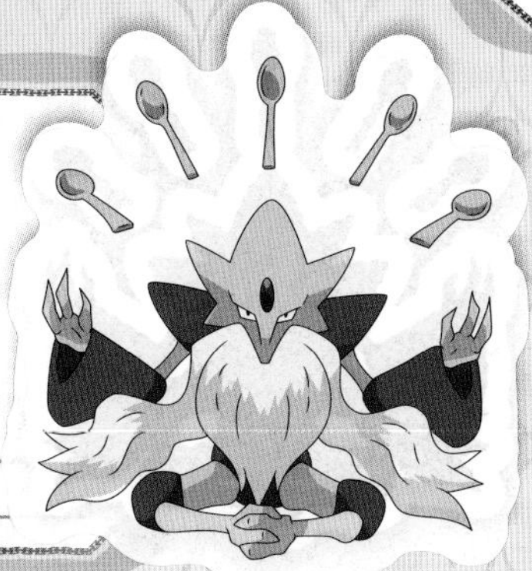

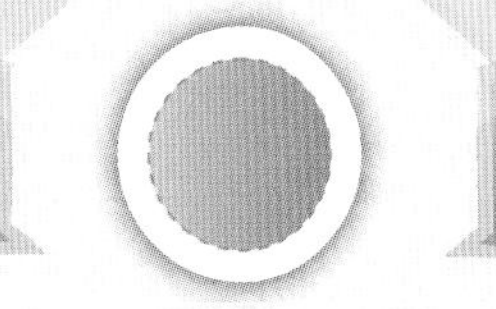

ALAKAZITE

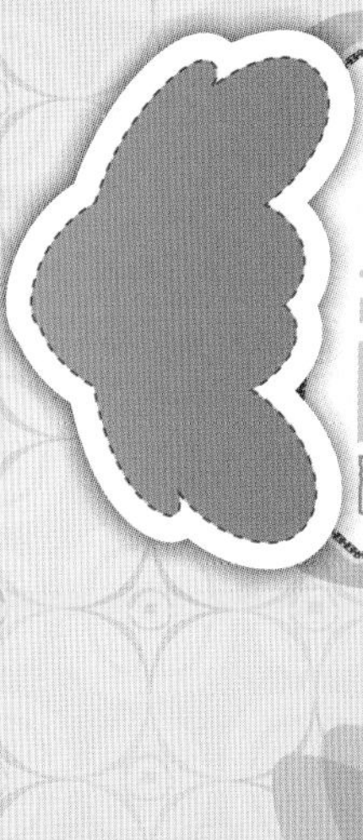

WATER

ALOMOMOLA

PRONUNCIATION: uh-LOH-muh-MOH-luh

HEIGHT:	WEIGHT:	CATEGORY:
1.2 m 3'11"	31.6 kg 69.7 lbs.	Caring Pokémon

Akala Island

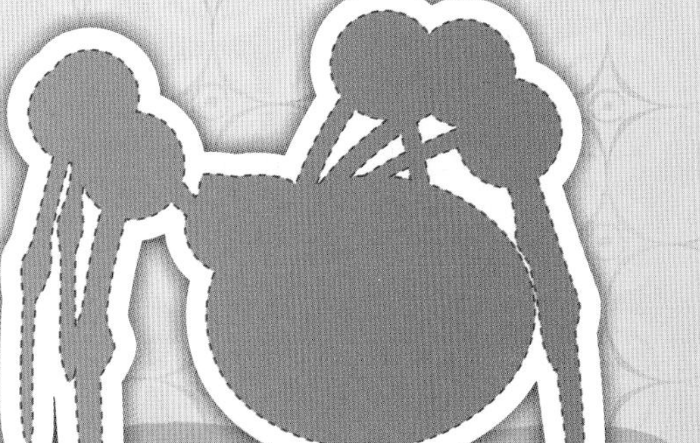

WATER BUG

ARAQUANID

PRONUNCIATION: uh-RACK-wuh-nid

HEIGHT:	WEIGHT:	CATEGORY:
1.8 m 5'11"	82.0 kg 180.8 lbs.	Water Bubble Pokémon

Akala Island

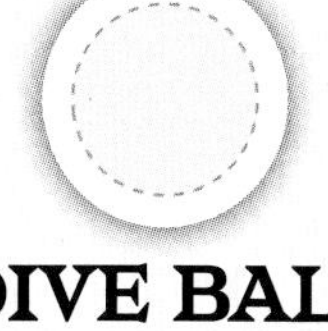

DIVE BALL

FIRE
ARCANINE

PRONUNCIATION: ARE-ka-nine

HEIGHT:
1.9 m
6'03"

WEIGHT:
155.0 kg
341.7 lbs.

CATEGORY:
Legendary
Pokémon

Melemele Island

ROCK FLYING
ARCHEN

PRONUNCIATION: AR-ken

HEIGHT:
0.5 m
1'08"

WEIGHT:
9.5 kg
20.9 lbs.

CATEGORY:
First Bird
Pokémon

Akala Island

ROCK FLYING
ARCHEOPS

PRONUNCIATION: AR-kee-ops

HEIGHT:
1.4 m
4'07"

WEIGHT:
32.0 kg
70.5 lbs.

CATEGORY:
First Bird
Pokémon

Akala Island

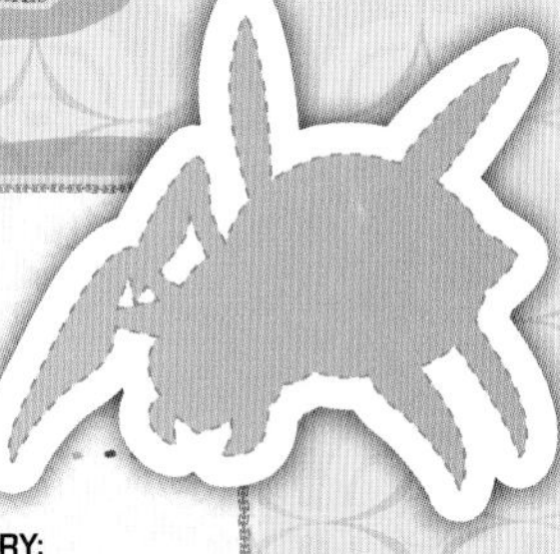

BUG POISON
ARIADOS

PRONUNCIATION: AIR-ree-uh-dose

HEIGHT:
1.1 m
3'07"

WEIGHT:
33.5 kg
73.9 lbs.

CATEGORY:
Long Leg
Pokémon

Melemele Island

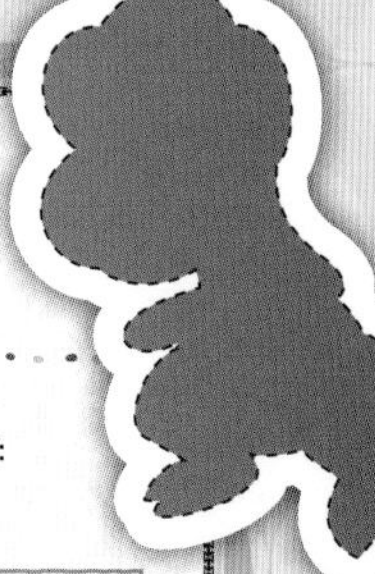

DRAGON
BAGON

PRONUNCIATION: BAY-gon

HEIGHT:
0.6 m
2'00"

WEIGHT:
42.1 kg
92.8 lbs.

CATEGORY:
Rock Head
Pokémon

Melemele Island

WATER GROUND
BARBOACH

PRONUNCIATION: bar-BOACH

HEIGHT:
0.4 m
1'04"

WEIGHT:
1.9 kg
4.2 lbs.

CATEGORY:
Whiskers
Pokémon

Melemele Island

ROCK STEEL
BASTIODON

PRONUNCIATION: BAS-tee-oh-DON

HEIGHT:
1.3 m
4'03"

WEIGHT:
149.5 kg
329.6 lbs.

CATEGORY:
Shield Pokémon

Akala Island

STEEL **PSYCHIC**
BELDUM

PRONUNCIATION: BELL-dum

HEIGHT:	WEIGHT:	CATEGORY:
0.6 m	95.2 kg	Iron Ball
2'00"	209.9 lbs.	Pokémon

 Ula'ula Island

NORMAL **FIGHTING**
BEWEAR

PRONUNCIATION: beh-WARE

HEIGHT:	WEIGHT:	CATEGORY:
2.1 m	135.0 kg	Strong Arm
6'11"	297.6 lbs.	Pokémon

Akala Island

NORMAL
BLISSEY

PRONUNCIATION: BLISS-sey

HEIGHT:	WEIGHT:	CATEGORY:
1.5 m	46.8 kg	Happiness
4'11"	103.2 lbs.	Pokémon

Melemele Island

ROCK
BOLDORE

PRONUNCIATION: BOHL-dohr

HEIGHT:	WEIGHT:	CATEGORY:
0.9 m	102.0 kg	Ore Pokémon
2'11"	224.9 lbs.	

Melemele Island

ROCK
BONSLY

PRONUNCIATION: BON-slye

HEIGHT:	WEIGHT:	CATEGORY:
0.5 m	15.0 kg	Bonsai Pokémon
1'08"	33.1 lbs.	

Melemele Island

GRASS
BOUNSWEET

PRONUNCIATION: BOWN-sweet

HEIGHT:	WEIGHT:	CATEGORY:
0.3 m	3.2 kg	Fruit Pokémon
1'00"	7.1 lbs.	

Akala Island

NORMAL **FLYING**
BRAVIARY

PRONUNCIATION: BRAY-vee-air-ee

HEIGHT:	WEIGHT:	CATEGORY:
1.5 m	41.0 kg	Valiant Pokémon
4'11"	90.4 lbs.	

Melemele Island

B | ALOLA REGION STICKER BOOK

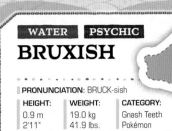

WATER PSYCHIC
BRUXISH

PRONUNCIATION: BRUCK-sish

HEIGHT:	WEIGHT:	CATEGORY:
0.9 m	19.0 kg	Gnash Teeth
2'11"	41.9 lbs.	Pokémon

◈ Ula'ula Island

WATER
BRIONNE

PRONUNCIATION: bree-AHN

HEIGHT:	WEIGHT:	CATEGORY:
0.6 m	17.5 kg	Pop Star
2'00"	38.6 lbs.	Pokémon

◈ Melemele Island

ROCK FAIRY
CARBINK

PRONUNCIATION: CAR-bink

HEIGHT:	WEIGHT:	CATEGORY:
0.3 m	5.7 kg	Jewel Pokémon
1'00"	12.6 lbs.	

◈ Melemele Island

BUG FLYING
BUTTERFREE

PRONUNCIATION: BUT-er-free

HEIGHT:	WEIGHT:	CATEGORY:
1.1 m	32.0 kg	Butterfly
3'07"	70.5 lbs.	Pokémon

◈ Melemele Island

WATER DARK
CARVANHA

PRONUNCIATION: car-VAH-na

HEIGHT:	WEIGHT:	CATEGORY:
0.8 m	20.8 kg	Savage Pokémon
2'07"	45.9 lbs.	

◈ Poni Island

DUSK BALL

WATER ROCK
CARRACOSTA

PRONUNCIATION: care-a-KOSS-tah

HEIGHT:	WEIGHT:	CATEGORY:
1.2 m	81.0 kg	Prototurtle
3'11"	178.6 lbs.	Pokémon

◈ Akala Island

NORMAL
CASTFORM
NORMAL FORM

PRONUNCIATION: CAST-form

HEIGHT:	WEIGHT:	CATEGORY:
0.3 m	0.8 kg	Weather
1'00"	1.8 lbs.	Pokémon

◈ Akala Island

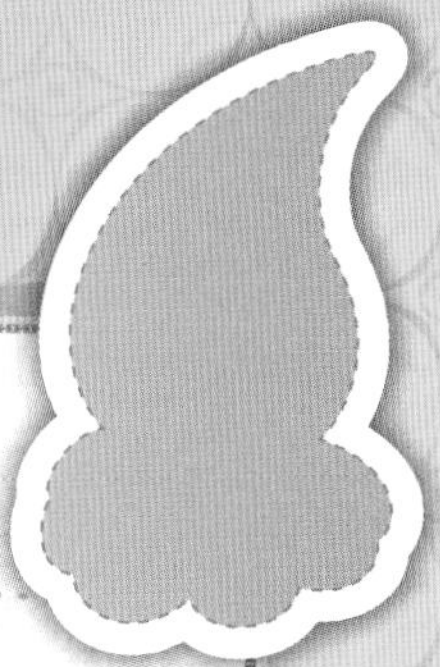

NORMAL
CASTFORM
RAINY FORM

PRONUNCIATION: CAST-form

HEIGHT:	WEIGHT:	CATEGORY:
0.3 m	0.8 kg	Weather
1'00"	1.8 lbs.	Pokémon

Akala Island

NORMAL
CASTFORM
SNOWY FORM

PRONUNCIATION: CAST-form

HEIGHT:	WEIGHT:	CATEGORY:
0.3 m	0.8 kg	Weather
1'00"	1.8 lbs.	Pokémon

Akala Island

NORMAL
CASTFORM
SUNNY FORM

PRONUNCIATION: CAST-form

HEIGHT:	WEIGHT:	CATEGORY:
0.3 m	0.8 kg	Weather
1'00"	1.8 lbs.	Pokémon

Akala Island

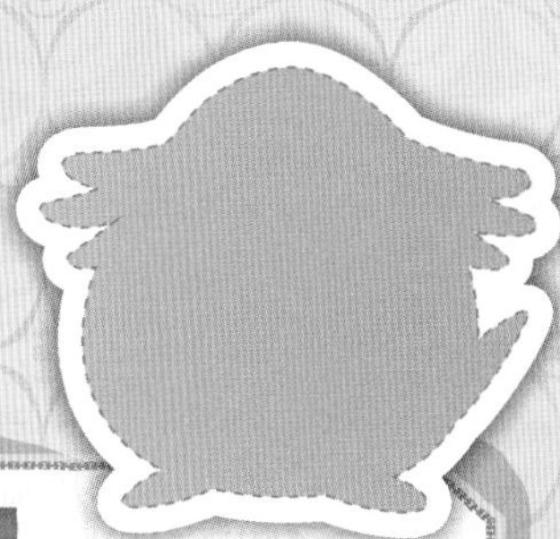

NORMAL
CHANSEY

PRONUNCIATION: CHAN-see

HEIGHT:	WEIGHT:	CATEGORY:
1.1 m	34.6 kg	Egg Pokémon
3'07"	76.3 lbs.	

Melemele Island

BUG
CATERPIE

PRONUNCIATION: CAT-ur-pee

HEIGHT:	WEIGHT:	CATEGORY:
0.3 m	2.9 kg	Worm Pokémon
1'00"	6.4 lbs.	

Melemele Island

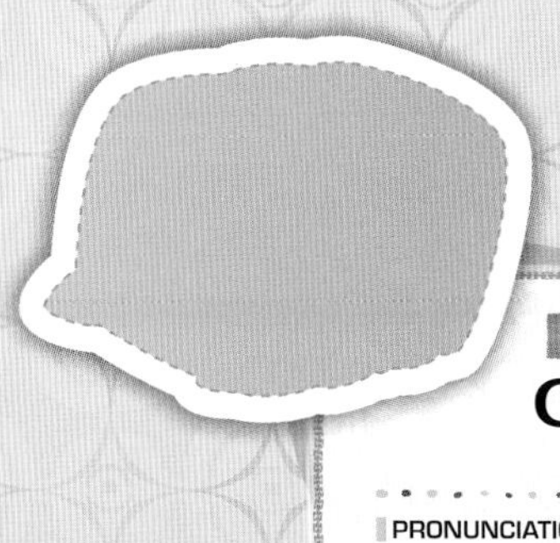

BUG ELECTRIC
CHARJABUG

PRONUNCIATION: CHAR-juh-bug

HEIGHT:	WEIGHT:	CATEGORY:
0.5 m	10.5 kg	Battery Pokémon
1'08"	23.1 lbs.	

Melemele Island

WATER ELECTRIC
CHINCHOU

PRONUNCIATION: CHIN-chow

HEIGHT:	WEIGHT:	CATEGORY:
0.5 m	12.0 kg	Angler Pokémon
1'08"	26.5 lbs.	

Akala Island

C | ALOLA REGION STICKER BOOK

FAIRY

CLEFABLE

PRONUNCIATION: kleh-FAY-bull

HEIGHT:	WEIGHT:	CATEGORY:
1.3 m 4'03"	40.0 kg 88.2 lbs.	Fairy Pokémon

Ula'ula Island

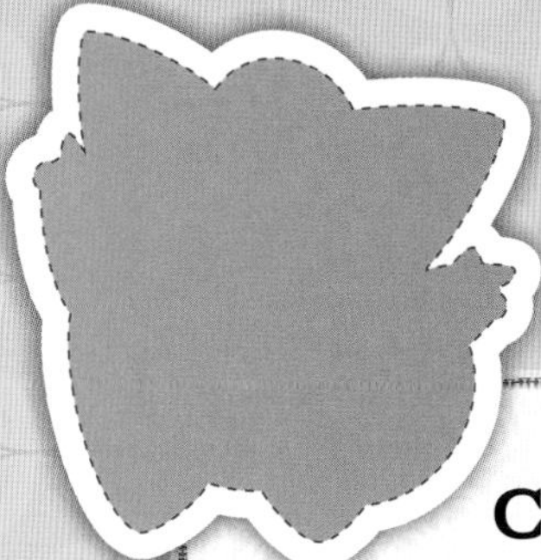

FAIRY

CLEFAIRY

PRONUNCIATION: kleh-FAIR-ee

HEIGHT:	WEIGHT:	CATEGORY:
0.6 m 2'00"	7.5 kg 16.5 lbs.	Fairy Pokémon

Ula'ula Island

FAIRY

CLEFFA

PRONUNCIATION: CLEFF-uh

HEIGHT:	WEIGHT:	CATEGORY:
0.3 m 1'00"	3.0 kg 6.6 lbs.	Star Shape Pokémon

Ula'ula Island

WATER ICE

CLOYSTER

PRONUNCIATION: CLOY-stur

HEIGHT:	WEIGHT:	CATEGORY:
1.5 m 4'11"	132.5 kg 292.1 lbs.	Bivalve Pokémon

Melemele Island

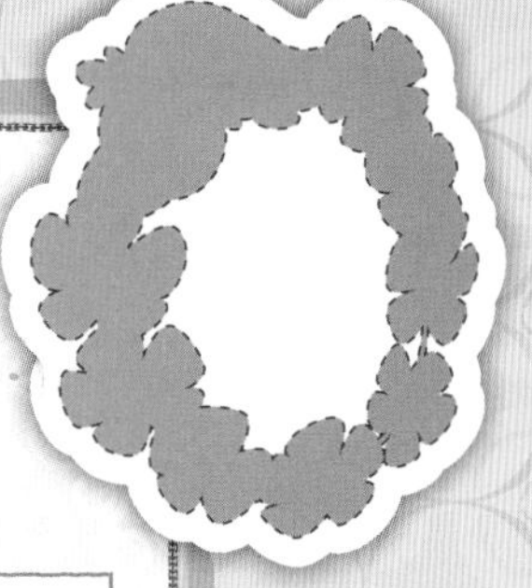

FAIRY

COMFEY

PRONUNCIATION: KUM-fay

HEIGHT:	WEIGHT:	CATEGORY:
0.1 m 0'04"	0.3 kg 0.7 lbs.	Posy Picker Pokémon

Akala Island

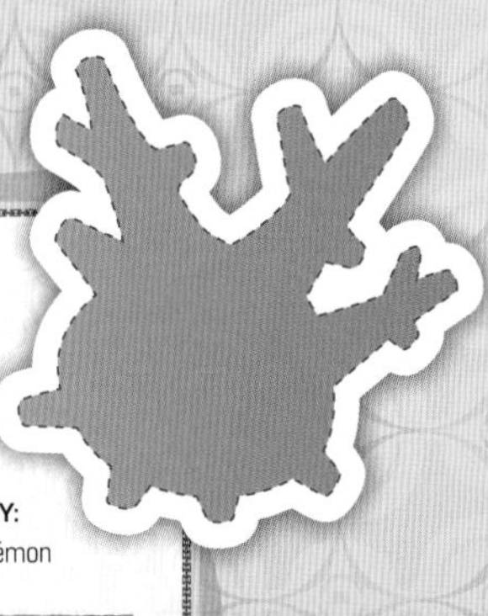

WATER ROCK

CORSOLA

PRONUNCIATION: COR-soh-la

HEIGHT:	WEIGHT:	CATEGORY:
0.6 m 2'00"	5.0 kg 11.0 lbs.	Coral Pokémon

Melemele Island

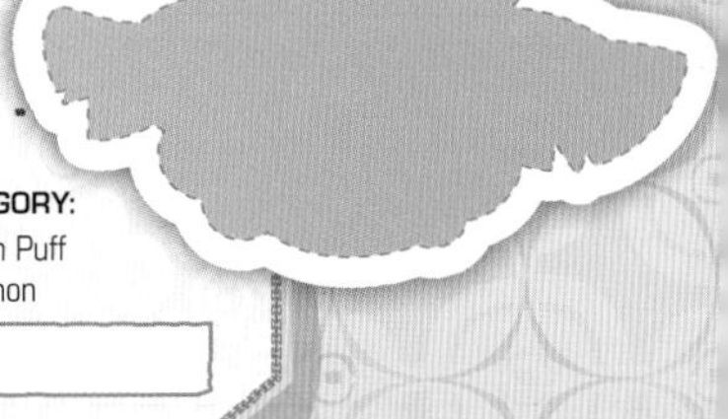

GRASS FAIRY

COTTONEE

PRONUNCIATION: KAHT-ton-ee

HEIGHT:	WEIGHT:	CATEGORY:
0.3 m 1'00"	0.6 kg 1.3 lbs.	Cotton Puff Pokémon

Melemele Island

FIGHTING ICE
CRABOMINABLE

PRONUNCIATION: crab-BAH-min-uh-bull

HEIGHT:	WEIGHT:	CATEGORY:
1.7 m	180.0 kg	Woolly Crab
5'07"	396.8 lbs.	Pokémon

 Melemele Island

ROCK
CRANIDOS

PRONUNCIATION: CRANE-ee-dose

HEIGHT:	WEIGHT:	CATEGORY:
0.9 m	31.5 kg	Head Butt
2'11"	69.4 lbs.	Pokémon

Akala Island

FIGHTING
CRABRAWLER

PRONUNCIATION: crab-BRAW-ler

HEIGHT:	WEIGHT:	CATEGORY:
0.6 m	7.0 kg	Boxing Pokémon
2'00"	15.4 lbs.	

Melemele Island

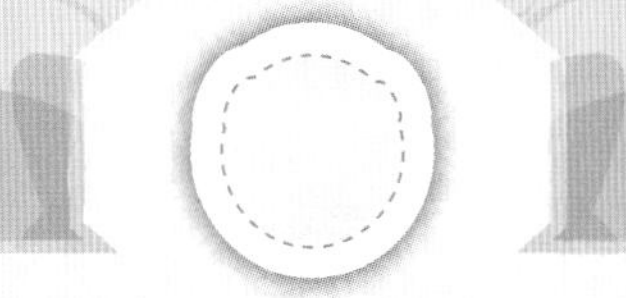

GREAT BALL

POISON FLYING
CROBAT

PRONUNCIATION: CROW-bat

HEIGHT:	WEIGHT:	CATEGORY:
1.8 m	75.0 kg	Bat Pokémon
5'11"	165.3 lbs.	

Melemele Island

GROUND
CUBONE

PRONUNCIATION: CUE-bone

HEIGHT:	WEIGHT:	CATEGORY:
0.4 m	6.5 kg	Lonely Pokémon
1'04"	14.3 lbs.	

Akala Island

BUG FAIRY
CUTIEFLY

PRONUNCIATION: KYOO-tee-fly

HEIGHT:	WEIGHT:	CATEGORY:
0.1 m	0.2 kg	Bee Fly Pokémon
0'04"	0.4 lbs.	

Melemele Island

C | ALOLA REGION STICKER BOOK

GRASS **FLYING**

DARTRIX

PRONUNCIATION: DAR-trix

HEIGHT:	WEIGHT:	CATEGORY:
0.7 m	16.0 kg	Blade Quill
2'04"	35.3 lbs.	Pokémon

Melemele Island

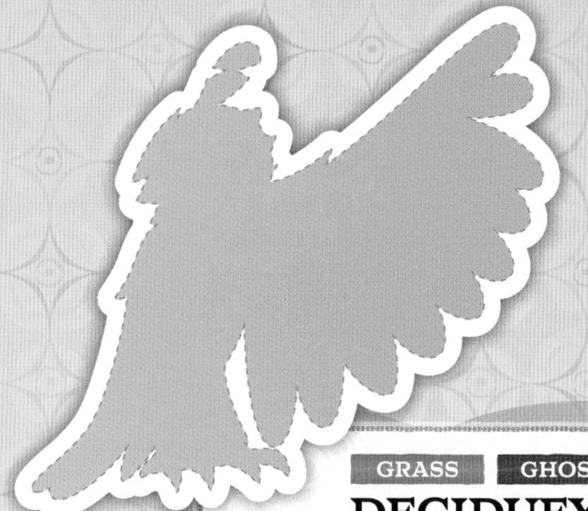

GRASS **GHOST**

DECIDUEYE

PRONUNCIATION: deh-SIH-joo-eye

HEIGHT:	WEIGHT:	CATEGORY:
1.6 m	36.6 kg	Arrow Quill
5'03"	80.7 lbs.	Pokémon

Melemele Island

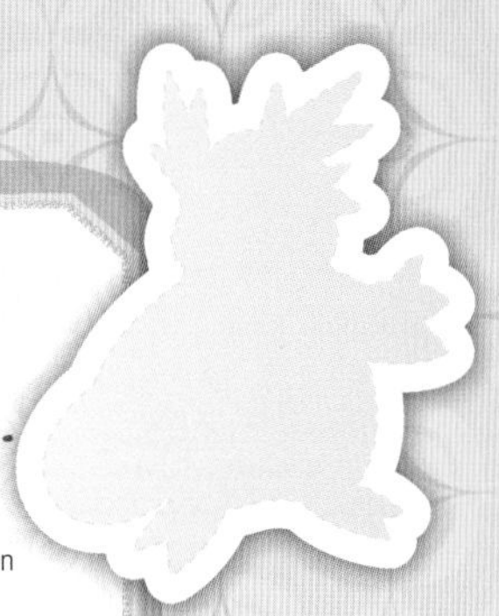

ICE **FLYING**

DELIBIRD

PRONUNCIATION: DELL-ee-bird

HEIGHT:	WEIGHT:	CATEGORY:
0.9 m	16.0 kg	Delivery Pokémon
2'11"	35.3 lbs.	

Melemele Island

GHOST **GRASS**

DHELMISE

PRONUNCIATION: dell-MIZE

HEIGHT:	WEIGHT:	CATEGORY:
3.9 m	210.0 kg	Sea Creeper
12'10"	463.0 lbs.	Pokémon

Poni Island

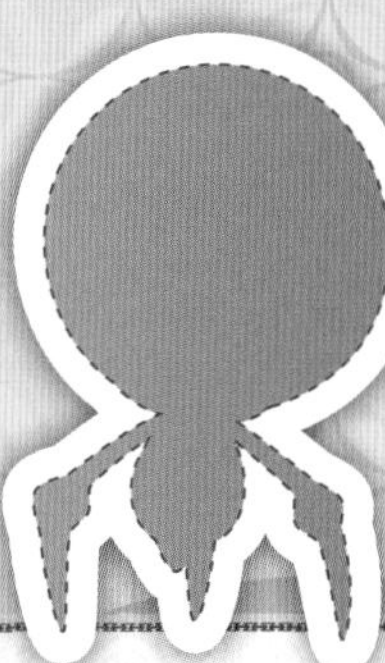

WATER **BUG**

DEWPIDER

PRONUNCIATION: DOO-pih-der

HEIGHT:	WEIGHT:	CATEGORY:
0.3 m	4.0 kg	Water Bubble
1'00"	8.8 lbs.	Pokémon

Akala Island

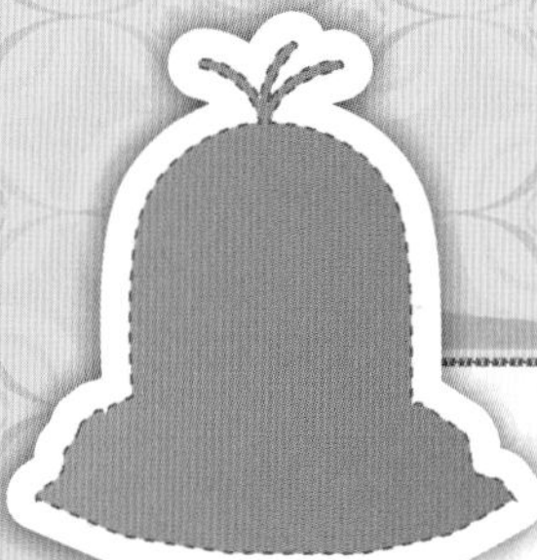

GROUND **STEEL**

DIGLETT
ALOLA FORM

PRONUNCIATION: DIG-let

HEIGHT:	WEIGHT:	CATEGORY:
0.2 m	1.0 kg	Mole Pokémon
0'08"	2.2 lbs.	

Melemele Island

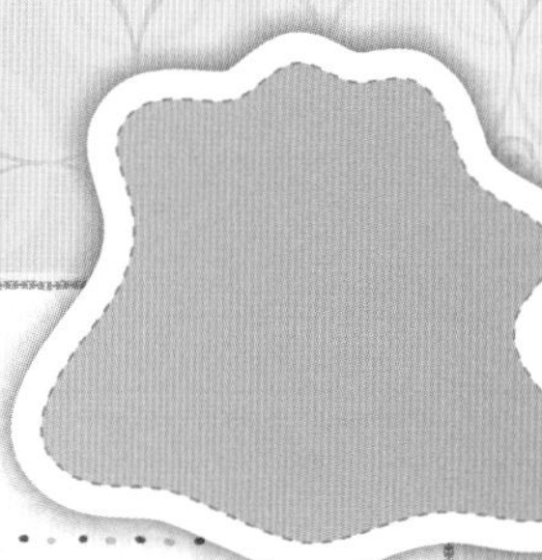

NORMAL

DITTO

PRONUNCIATION: DIT-toe

HEIGHT:	WEIGHT:	CATEGORY:
0.3 m	4.0 kg	Transform
1'00"	8.8 lbs.	Pokémon

Ula'ula Island

DRAGON
DRAGONAIR

PRONUNCIATION: DRAG-gon-AIR

HEIGHT:	WEIGHT:	CATEGORY:
4.0 m	16.5 kg	Dragon Pokémon
13'01"	36.4 lbs.	

◆ Poni Island

DRAGON FLYING
DRAGONITE

PRONUNCIATION: DRAG-gon-ite

HEIGHT:	WEIGHT:	CATEGORY:
2.2 m	210.0 kg	Dragon Pokémon
7'03"	463.0 lbs.	

◆ Poni Island

NORMAL DRAGON
DRAMPA

PRONUNCIATION: DRAM-puh

HEIGHT:	WEIGHT:	CATEGORY:
3.0 m	185.0 kg	Placid Pokémon
9'10"	407.9 lbs.	

◆ Ula'ula Island

DRAGON
DRATINI

PRONUNCIATION: dra-TEE-nee

HEIGHT:	WEIGHT:	CATEGORY:
1.8 m	3.3 kg	Dragon Pokémon
5'11"	7.3 lbs.	

◆ Poni Island

GHOST FLYING
DRIFBLIM

PRONUNCIATION: DRIFF-blim

HEIGHT:	WEIGHT:	CATEGORY:
1.2 m	15.0 kg	Blimp Pokémon
3'11"	33.1 lbs.	

◇ Melemele Island

GHOST FLYING
DRIFLOON

PRONUNCIATION: DRIFF-loon

HEIGHT:	WEIGHT:	CATEGORY:
0.4 m	1.2 kg	Balloon Pokémon
1'04"	2.6 lbs.	

◇ Melemele Island

D | ALOLA REGION STICKER BOOK

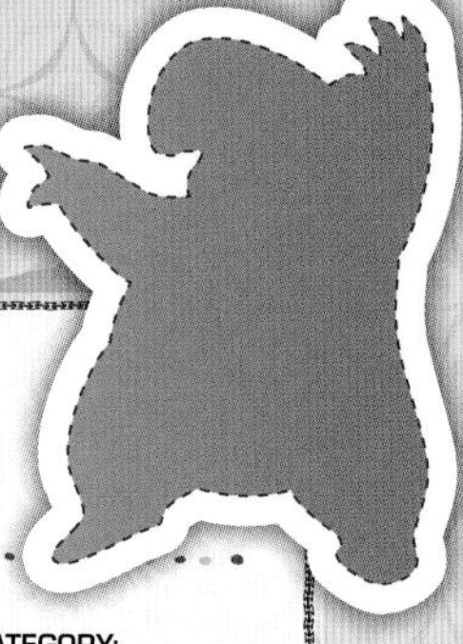

ALOLA REGION STICKER BOOK | **D–E**

PSYCHIC
DROWZEE

PRONUNCIATION: DROW-zee

HEIGHT:	WEIGHT:	CATEGORY:
1.0 m	32.4 kg	Hypnosis
3'03"	71.4 lbs.	Pokémon

Melemele Island

GROUND · STEEL
DUGTRIO
ALOLA FORM

PRONUNCIATION: DUG-TREE-oh

HEIGHT:	WEIGHT:	CATEGORY:
0.7 m	66.6 kg	Mole Pokémon
2'04"	146.8 lbs.	

Melemele Island

ELECTRIC
ELECTABUZZ

PRONUNCIATION: eh-LECK-ta-buzz

HEIGHT:	WEIGHT:	CATEGORY:
1.1 m	30.0 kg	Electric
3'07"	66.1 lbs.	Pokémon

Ula'ula Island

NORMAL
EEVEE

PRONUNCIATION: EE-vee

HEIGHT:	WEIGHT:	CATEGORY:
0.3 m	6.5 kg	Evolution
1'00"	14.3 lbs.	Pokémon

Akala Island

ELECTRIC
ELEKID

PRONUNCIATION: EL-eh-kid

HEIGHT:	WEIGHT:	CATEGORY:
0.6 m	23.5 kg	Electric
2'00"	51.8 lbs.	Pokémon

Ula'ula Island

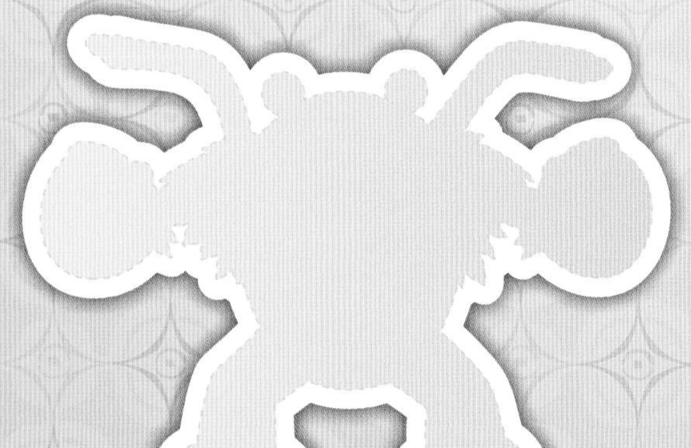

ELECTRIC
ELECTIVIRE

PRONUNCIATION: el-LECT-uh-vire

HEIGHT:	WEIGHT:	CATEGORY:
1.8 m	138.6 kg	Thunderbolt
5'11"	305.6 lbs.	Pokémon

Ula'ula Island

ELECTRIC · FLYING
EMOLGA

PRONUNCIATION: ee-MAHL-guh

HEIGHT:	WEIGHT:	CATEGORY:
0.4 m	5.0 kg	Sky Squirrel
1'04"	11.0 lbs.	Pokémon

Poni Island

PSYCHIC
ESPEON

PRONUNCIATION: ESS-pee-on

HEIGHT:	WEIGHT:	CATEGORY:
0.9 m	26.5 kg	Sun Pokémon
2'11"	58.4 lbs.	

Akala Island

GRASS **DRAGON**
EXEGGUTOR
ALOLA FORM

PRONUNCIATION: ecks-EGG-u-tore

HEIGHT:	WEIGHT:	CATEGORY:
10.9 m	415.6 kg	Coconut
35'09"	916.2 lbs.	Pokémon

Poni Island

GRASS **PSYCHIC**
EXEGGCUTE

PRONUNCIATION: ECKS-egg-cute

HEIGHT:	WEIGHT:	CATEGORY:
0.4 m	2.5 kg	Egg Pokémon
1'04"	5.5 lbs.	

Poni Island

WATER
FINNEON

PRONUNCIATION: FINN-ee-on

HEIGHT:	WEIGHT:	CATEGORY:
0.4 m	7.0 kg	Wing Fish
1'04"	15.4 lbs.	Pokémon

Melemele Island

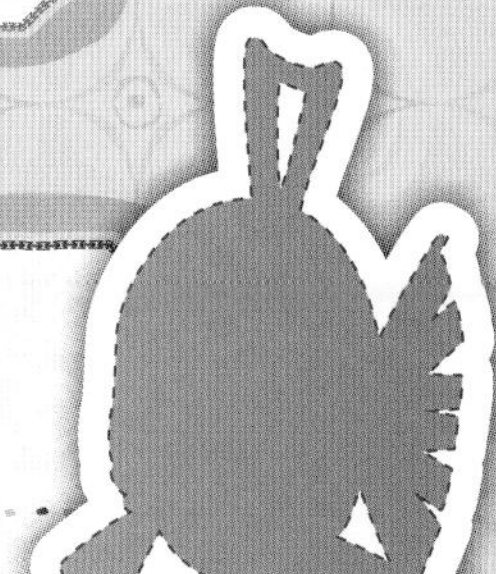

NORMAL **FLYING**
FEAROW

PRONUNCIATION: FEER-oh

HEIGHT:	WEIGHT:	CATEGORY:
1.2 m	38.0 kg	Beak Pokémon
3'11"	83.8 lbs.	

Melemele Island

WATER
FEEBAS

PRONUNCIATION: FEE-bass

HEIGHT:	WEIGHT:	CATEGORY:
0.6 m	7.4 kg	Fish Pokémon
2'00"	16.3 lbs.	

Akala Island

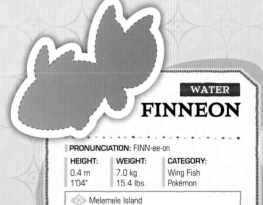

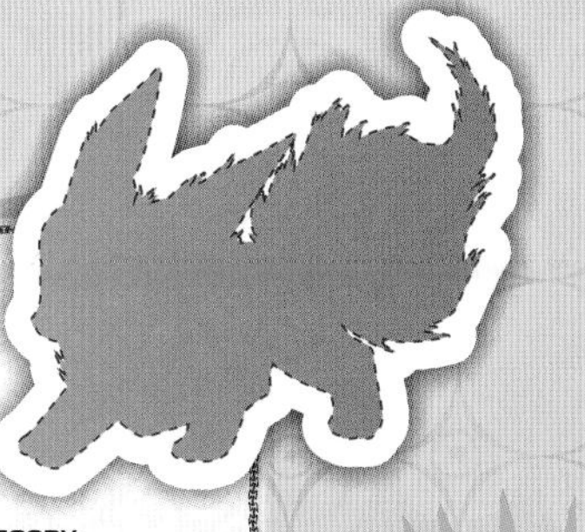

FIRE
FLAREON

PRONUNCIATION: FLAIR-ee-on

HEIGHT:	WEIGHT:	CATEGORY:
0.9 m	25.0 kg	Flame Pokémon
2'11"	55.1 lbs.	

Akala Island

E–F | ALOLA REGION STICKER BOOK

FIRE FLYING
FLETCHINDER

PRONUNCIATION: FLETCH-in-der

HEIGHT:	WEIGHT:	CATEGORY:
0.7 m	16.0 kg	Ember Pokémon
2'04"	35.3 lbs.	

◆ Akala Island

GROUND DRAGON
FLYGON

PRONUNCIATION: FLY-gon

HEIGHT:	WEIGHT:	CATEGORY:
2.0 m	82.0 kg	Mystic Pokémon
6'07"	180.8 lbs.	

◆ Ula'ula Island

NORMAL FLYING
FLETCHLING

PRONUNCIATION: FLETCH-ling

HEIGHT:	WEIGHT:	CATEGORY:
0.3 m	1.7 kg	Tiny Robin
1'00"	3.7 lbs.	Pokémon

◆ Akala Island

ICE GHOST
FROSLASS

PRONUNCIATION: FROS-lass

HEIGHT:	WEIGHT:	CATEGORY:
1.3 m	26.6 kg	Snow Land
4'03"	58.6 lbs.	Pokémon

◆ Ula'ula Island

GRASS
FOMANTIS

PRONUNCIATION: fo-MAN-tis

HEIGHT:	WEIGHT:	CATEGORY:
0.3 m	1.5 kg	Sickle Grass
1'00"	3.3 lbs.	Pokémon

◆ Akala Island

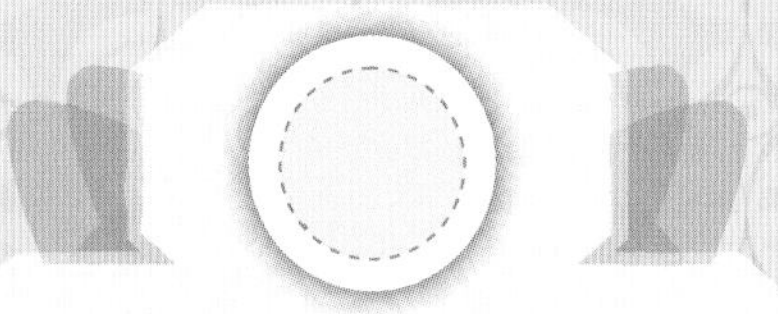

HEAL BALL

POISON
GARBODOR

PRONUNCIATION: gar-BOH-dur

HEIGHT:	WEIGHT:	CATEGORY:
1.9 m	107.3 kg	Trash Heap
6'03"	236.6 lbs.	Pokémon

◆ Ula'ula Island

GABITE

DRAGON **GROUND**

PRONUNCIATION: gab-BITE

HEIGHT:	WEIGHT:	CATEGORY:
1.4 m	56.0 kg	Cave Pokémon
4'07"	123.5 lbs.	

Ula'ula Island

GARCHOMPITE

GARCHOMP

DRAGON **GROUND**

PRONUNCIATION: GAR-chomp

HEIGHT:	WEIGHT:	CATEGORY:
1.9 m	95.0 kg	Mach Pokémon
6'03"	209.4 lbs.	

Ula'ula Island

MEGA GARCHOMP

DRAGON **GROUND**

PRONUNCIATION: Mega GAR-chomp

HEIGHT:	WEIGHT:	CATEGORY:
1.9 m	95.0 kg	Mach Pokémon
6'03"	209.4 lbs.	

Ula'ula Island

GASTLY

GHOST **POISON**

PRONUNCIATION: GAST-lee

HEIGHT:	WEIGHT:	CATEGORY:
1.3 m	0.1 kg	Gas Pokémon
4'03"	0.2 lbs.	

Melemele Island

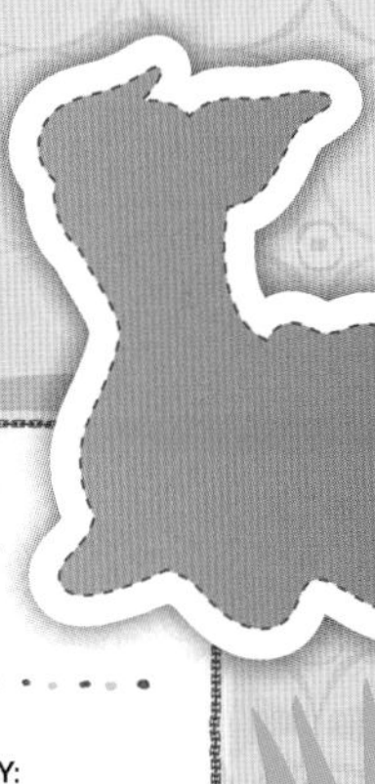

GASTRODON
EAST SEA

WATER **GROUND**

PRONUNCIATION: GAS-stroh-don

HEIGHT:	WEIGHT:	CATEGORY:
0.9 m	29.9 kg	Sea Slug
2'11"	65.9 lbs.	Pokémon

Poni Island

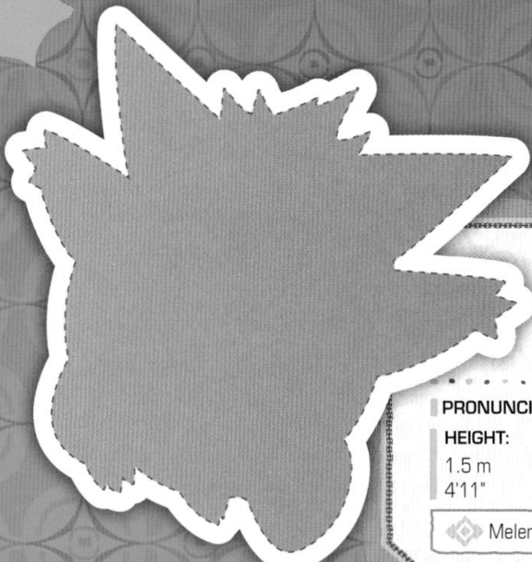

GHOST POISON

GENGAR

PRONUNCIATION: GHEN-gar

HEIGHT:	WEIGHT:	CATEGORY:
1.5 m 4'11"	40.5 kg 89.3 lbs.	Shadow Pokémon

Melemele Island

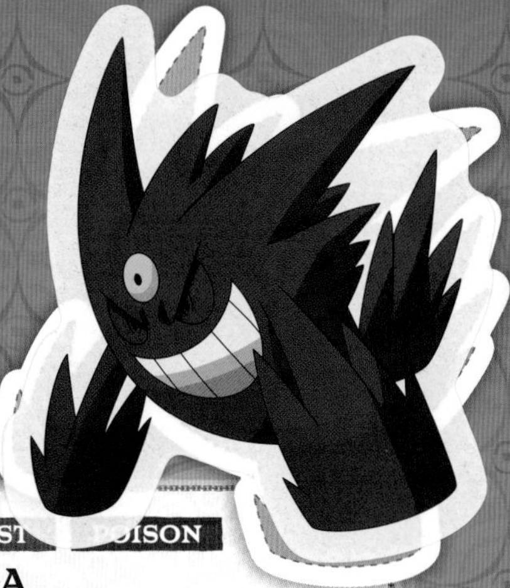

GHOST POISON

MEGA GENGAR

PRONUNCIATION: Mega GHEN-gar

HEIGHT:	WEIGHT:	CATEGORY:
1.4 m 4'07"	40.5 kg 89.3 lbs.	Shadow Pokémon

Melemele Island

ROCK ELECTRIC

GEODUDE

ALOLA FORM

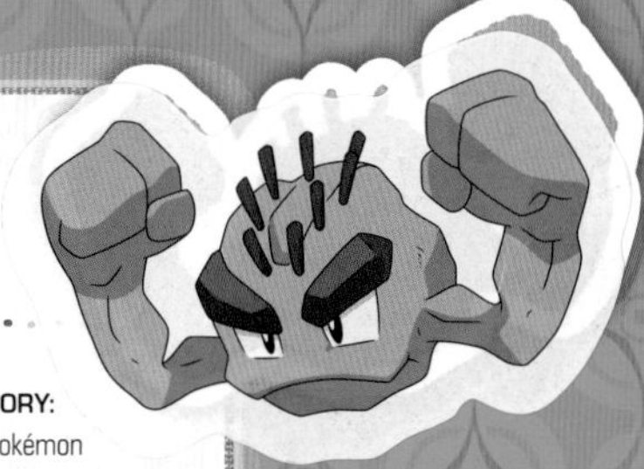

PRONUNCIATION: JEE-oh-dude

HEIGHT:	WEIGHT:	CATEGORY:
0.4 m 1'04"	20.3 kg 44.8 lbs.	Rock Pokémon

Ula'ula Island

GENGARITE

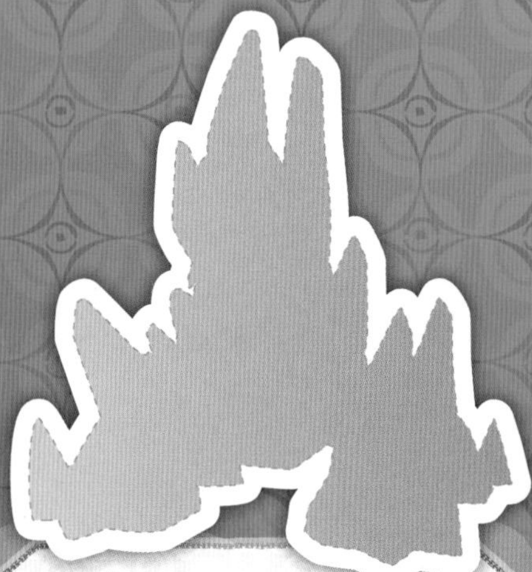

ROCK

GIGALITH

PRONUNCIATION: GIH-gah-lith

HEIGHT:	WEIGHT:	CATEGORY:
1.7 m 5'07"	260.0 kg 573.2 lbs.	Compressed Pokémon

Melemele Island

DRAGON GROUND

GIBLE

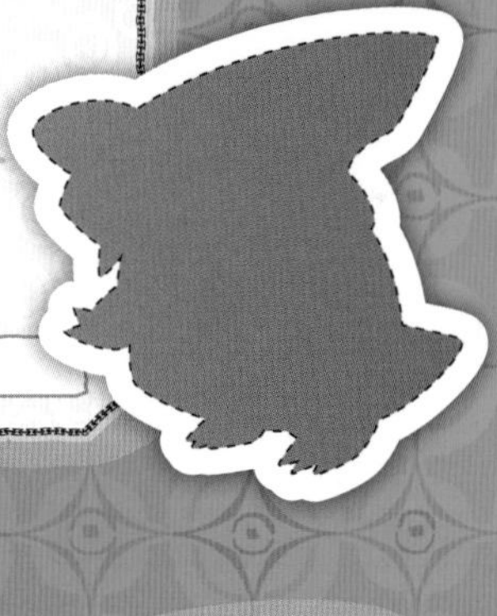

PRONUNCIATION: GIB-bull

HEIGHT:	WEIGHT:	CATEGORY:
0.7 m 2'04"	20.5 kg 45.2 lbs.	Land Shark Pokémon

Ula'ula Island

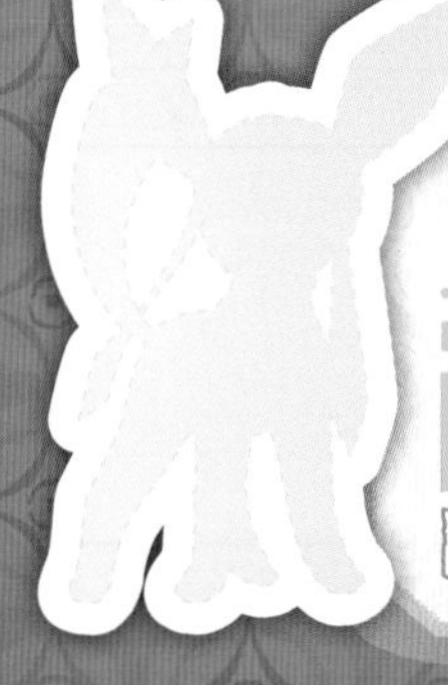

ICE

GLACEON

PRONUNCIATION: GLAY-cee-on

HEIGHT:	WEIGHT:	CATEGORY:
0.8 m 2'07"	25.9 kg 57.1 lbs.	Fresh Snow Pokémon

Akala Island

LUXURY BALL

ICE

MEGA GLALIE

PRONUNCIATION: Mega GLAY-lee

HEIGHT:	WEIGHT:	CATEGORY:
2.1 m 6'11"	350.2 kg 772.1 lbs.	Face Pokémon

Ula'ula Island

ICE

GLALIE

PRONUNCIATION: GLAY-lee

HEIGHT:	WEIGHT:	CATEGORY:
1.5 m 4'11"	256.5 kg 565.5 lbs.	Face Pokémon

Ula'ula Island

GLALITITE

WATER

GOLDEEN

PRONUNCIATION: GOL-deen

HEIGHT:	WEIGHT:	CATEGORY:
0.6 m 2'00"	15.0 kg 33.1 lbs.	Goldfish Pokémon

Akala Island

POISON FLYING

GOLBAT

PRONUNCIATION: GOHL-bat

HEIGHT:	WEIGHT:	CATEGORY:
1.6 m 5'03"	55.0 kg 121.3 lbs.	Bat Pokémon

Melemele Island

WATER

GOLDUCK

PRONUNCIATION: GOL-duck

HEIGHT:	WEIGHT:	CATEGORY:
1.7 m 5'07"	76.6 kg 168.9 lbs.	Duck Pokémon

Melemele Island

G | ALOLA REGION STICKER BOOK

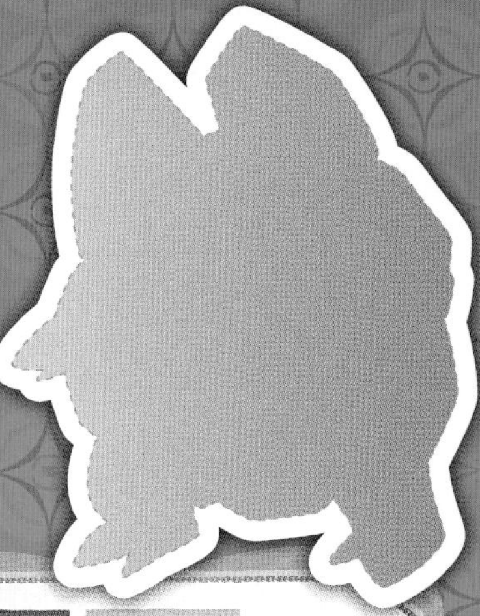

ROCK ELECTRIC

GOLEM

ALOLA FORM

PRONUNCIATION: GO-lum

HEIGHT:	WEIGHT:	CATEGORY:
1.7 m 5'07"	316.0 kg 696.7 lbs.	Megaton Pokémon

Ula'ula Island

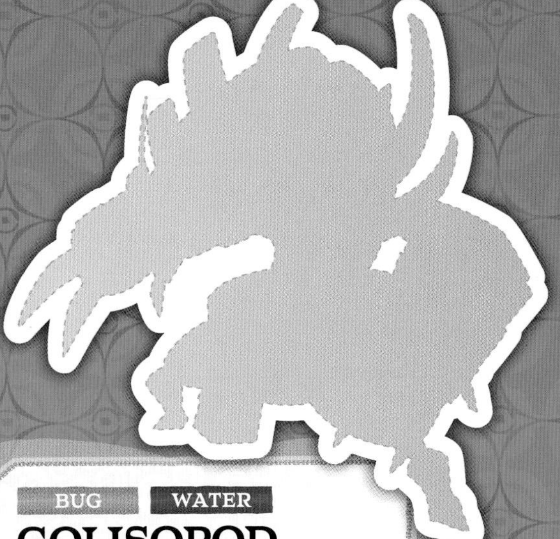

BUG WATER

GOLISOPOD

PRONUNCIATION: go-LIE-suh-pod

HEIGHT:	WEIGHT:	CATEGORY:
2.0 m 6'07"	108.0 kg 238.1 lbs.	Hard Scale Pokémon

Akala Island

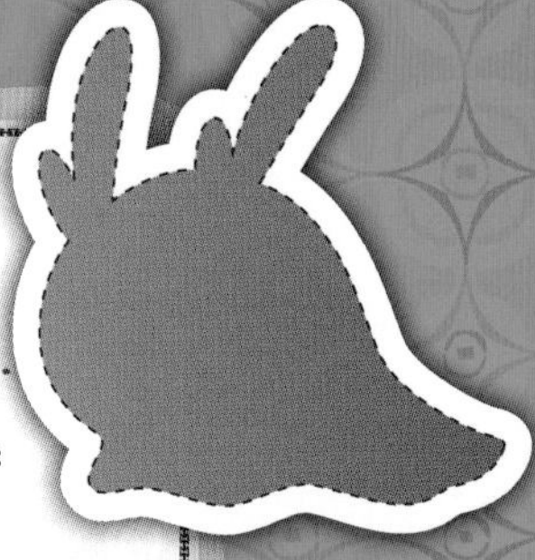

DRAGON

GOOMY

PRONUNCIATION: GOO-mee

HEIGHT:	WEIGHT:	CATEGORY:
0.3 m 1'00"	2.8 kg 6.2 lbs.	Soft Tissue Pokémon

Akala Island

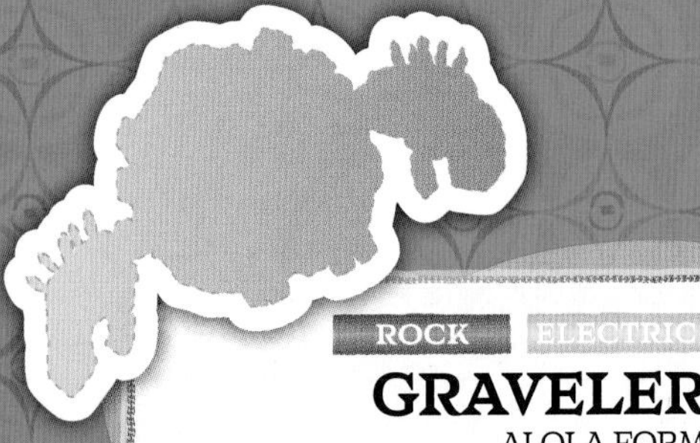

ROCK ELECTRIC

GRAVELER

ALOLA FORM

PRONUNCIATION: GRAV-el-ler

HEIGHT:	WEIGHT:	CATEGORY:
1.0 m 3'03"	110.0 kg 242.5 lbs.	Rock Pokémon

Ula'ula Island

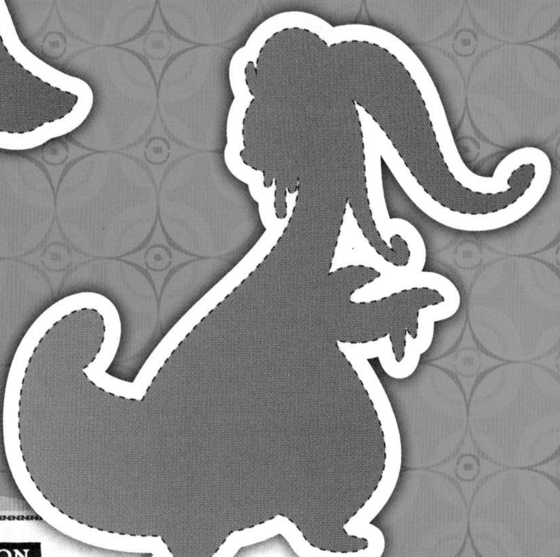

DRAGON

GOODRA

PRONUNCIATION: GOO-druh

HEIGHT:	WEIGHT:	CATEGORY:
2.0 m 6'07"	150.5 kg 331.8 lbs.	Dragon Pokémon

Akala Island

MASTER BALL

FAIRY
GRANBULL

PRONUNCIATION: GRAN-bull

HEIGHT:	WEIGHT:	CATEGORY:
1.4 m	48.7 kg	Fairy Pokémon
4'07"	107.4 lbs.	

◆ Poni Island

POISON | DARK
GRIMER
ALOLA FORM

PRONUNCIATION: GRY-mur

HEIGHT:	WEIGHT:	CATEGORY:
0.7 m	42.0 kg	Sludge Pokémon
2'04"	92.6 lbs.	

◆ Melemele Island

FIRE
GROWLITHE

PRONUNCIATION: GROWL-lith

HEIGHT:	WEIGHT:	CATEGORY:
0.7 m	19.0 kg	Puppy Pokémon
2'04"	41.9 lbs.	

◆ Melemele Island

BUG
GRUBBIN

PRONUNCIATION: GRUB-bin

HEIGHT:	WEIGHT:	CATEGORY:
0.4 m	4.4 kg	Larva Pokémon
1'04"	9.7 lbs.	

◆ Melemele Island

NORMAL
GUMSHOOS

PRONUNCIATION: GUM-shooss

HEIGHT:	WEIGHT:	CATEGORY:
0.7 m	14.2 kg	Stakeout
2'04"	31.3 lbs.	Pokémon

◆ Melemele Island

WATER | FLYING
GYARADOS

PRONUNCIATION: GARE-uh-dos

HEIGHT:	WEIGHT:	CATEGORY:
6.5 m	235.0 kg	Atrocious
21'04"	518.1 lbs.	Pokémon

◆ Melemele Island

GYARADOSITE

WATER   DARK
MEGA GYARADOS
PRONUNCIATION: Mega GARE-uh-dos

HEIGHT:	WEIGHT:	CATEGORY:
6.5 m	305.0 kg	Atrocious
21'04"	672.4 lbs.	Pokémon

Melemele Island

DRAGON   FIGHTING
HAKAMO-O
PRONUNCIATION: HAH-kah-MOH-oh

HEIGHT:	WEIGHT:	CATEGORY:
1.2 m	47.0 kg	Scaly Pokémon
3'11"	103.6 lbs.	

Poni Island

NORMAL
HAPPINY
PRONUNCIATION: hap-PEE-nee

HEIGHT:	WEIGHT:	CATEGORY:
0.6 m	24.4 kg	Playhouse
2'00"	53.8 lbs.	Pokémon

Melemele Island

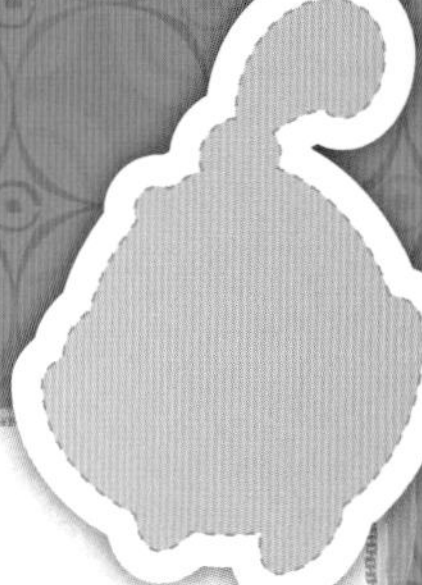

FIGHTING
HARIYAMA
PRONUNCIATION: HAR-ee-YAH-mah

HEIGHT:	WEIGHT:	CATEGORY:
2.3 m	253.8 kg	Arm Thrust
7'07"	559.5 lbs.	Pokémon

Melemele Island

GHOST   POISON
HAUNTER
PRONUNCIATION: HAUNT-ur

HEIGHT:	WEIGHT:	CATEGORY:
1.6 m	0.1 kg	Gas Pokémon
5'03"	0.2 lbs.	

Melemele Island

DARK · FLYING
HONCHKROW

PRONUNCIATION: HONCH-krow

HEIGHT:	WEIGHT:	CATEGORY:
0.9 m	27.3 kg	Big Boss
2'11"	60.2 lbs.	Pokémon

Poni Island

NORMAL
HERDIER

PRONUNCIATION: HERD-ee-er

HEIGHT:	WEIGHT:	CATEGORY:
0.9 m	14.7 kg	Loyal Dog
2'11"	32.4 lbs.	Pokémon

Akala Island

NEST BALL

NORMAL · FAIRY
IGGLYBUFF

PRONUNCIATION: IG-lee-buff

HEIGHT:	WEIGHT:	CATEGORY:
0.3 m	1.0 kg	Balloon Pokémon
1'00"	2.2 lbs.	

Akala Island

PSYCHIC
HYPNO

PRONUNCIATION: HIP-no

HEIGHT:	WEIGHT:	CATEGORY:
1.6 m	75.6 kg	Hypnosis
5'03"	166.7 lbs.	Pokémon

Melemele Island

DRAGON
JANGMO-O

PRONUNCIATION: JANG-MOH-oh

HEIGHT:	WEIGHT:	CATEGORY:
0.6 m	29.7 kg	Scaly Pokémon
2'00"	65.5 lbs.	

Poni Island

FIRE · DARK
INCINEROAR

PRONUNCIATION: in-SIN-uh-roar

HEIGHT:	WEIGHT:	CATEGORY:
1.8 m	83.0 kg	Heel Pokémon
5'11"	183.0 lbs.	

Melemele Island

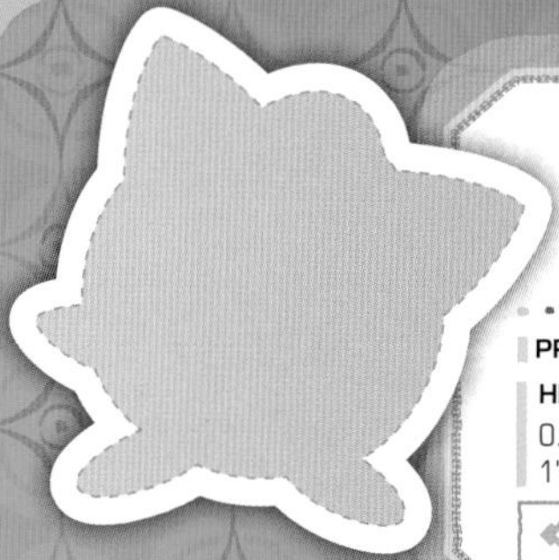

NORMAL FAIRY

JIGGLYPUFF

PRONUNCIATION: JIG-lee-puff

HEIGHT:	WEIGHT:	CATEGORY:
0.5 m 1'08"	5.5 kg 12.1 lbs.	Balloon Pokémon

Akala Island

ELECTRIC

JOLTEON

PRONUNCIATION: JOL-tee-on

HEIGHT:	WEIGHT:	CATEGORY:
0.8 m 2'07"	24.5 kg 54.0 lbs.	Lightning Pokémon

Akala Island

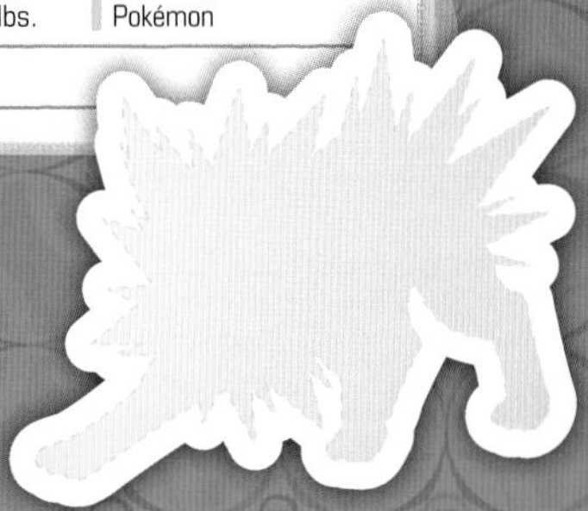

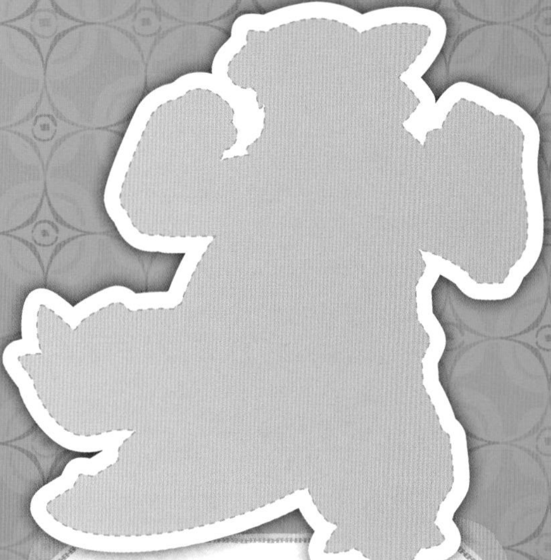

PSYCHIC

KADABRA

PRONUNCIATION: kuh-DAB-ra

HEIGHT:	WEIGHT:	CATEGORY:
1.3 m 4'03"	56.5 kg 124.6 lbs.	Psi Pokémon

Melemele Island

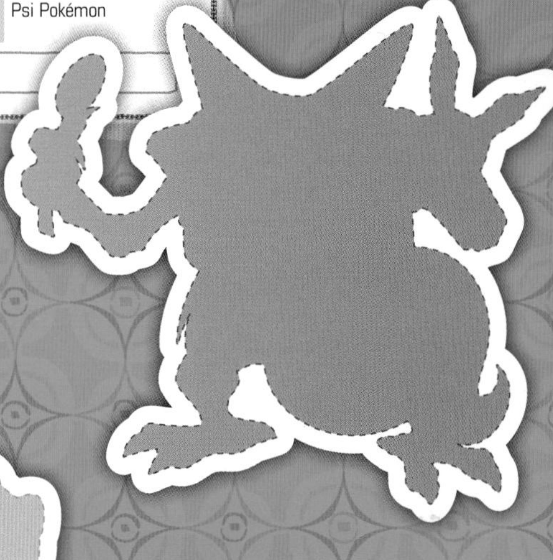

NORMAL

KANGASKHAN

PRONUNCIATION: KANG-gas-con

HEIGHT:	WEIGHT:	CATEGORY:
2.2 m 7'03"	80.0 kg 176.4 lbs.	Parent Pokémon

Akala Island

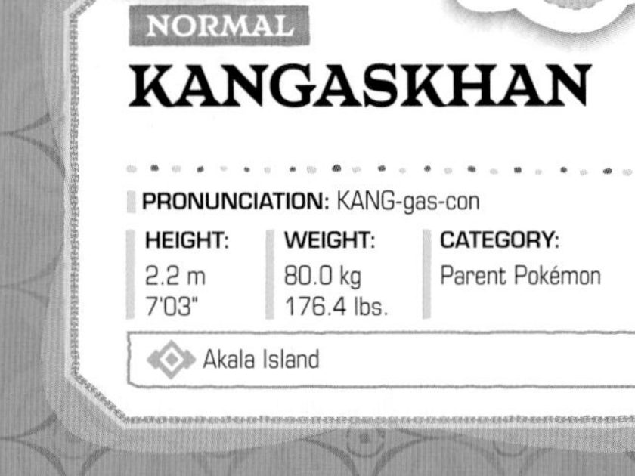

KANGASKHANITE

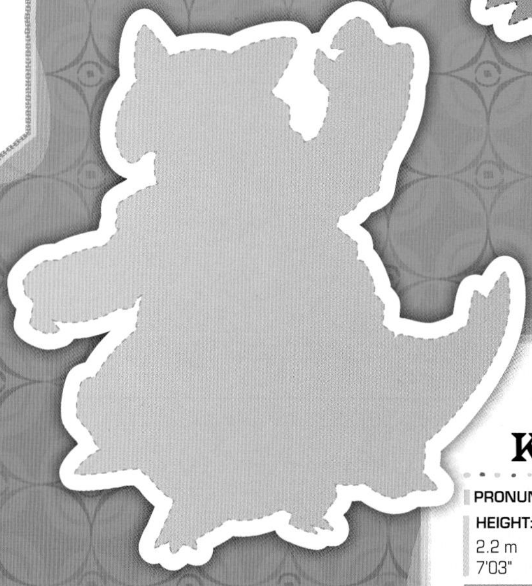

NORMAL

MEGA KANGASKHAN

PRONUNCIATION: Mega KANG-gas-con

HEIGHT:	WEIGHT:	CATEGORY:
2.2 m 7'03"	100.0 kg 220.5 lbs.	Parent Pokémon

Akala Island

NORMAL
KOMALA

PRONUNCIATION: koh-MAH-luh

HEIGHT:	WEIGHT:	CATEGORY:
0.4 m	19.9 kg	Drowsing
1'04"	43.9 lbs.	Pokémon

 Ula'ula Island

STEEL FAIRY
KLEFKI

PRONUNCIATION: KLEF-key

HEIGHT:	WEIGHT:	CATEGORY:
0.2 m	3.0 kg	Key Ring
0'08"	6.6 lbs.	Pokémon

Ula'ula Island

DRAGON FIGHTING
KOMMO-O

PRONUNCIATION: koh-MOH-oh

HEIGHT:	WEIGHT:	CATEGORY:
1.6 m	78.2 kg	Scaly Pokémon
5'03"	172.4 lbs.	

Poni Island

GROUND DARK
KROKOROK

PRONUNCIATION: KRAHK-oh-rahk

HEIGHT:	WEIGHT:	CATEGORY:
1.0 m	33.4 kg	Desert Croc
3'03"	73.6 lbs.	Pokémon

Ula'ula Island

GROUND DARK
KROOKODILE

PRONUNCIATION: KROOK-oh-dyle

HEIGHT:	WEIGHT:	CATEGORY:
1.5 m	96.3 kg	Intimidation
4'11"	212.3 lbs.	Pokémon

Ula'ula Island

WATER ELECTRIC
LANTURN

PRONUNCIATION: LAN-turn

HEIGHT:	WEIGHT:	CATEGORY:
1.2 m	22.5 kg	Light Pokémon
3'11"	49.6 lbs.	

Akala Island

K–L | ALOLA REGION STICKER BOOK

WATER ICE

LAPRAS

PRONUNCIATION: LAP-rus

HEIGHT:	WEIGHT:	CATEGORY:
2.5 m 8'02"	220.0 kg 485.0 lbs.	Transport Pokémon

Poni Island

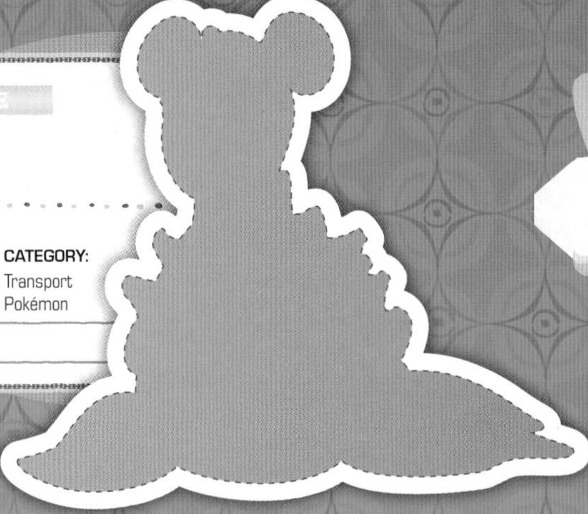

NET BALL

BUG FLYING

LEDIAN

PRONUNCIATION: LEH-dee-an

HEIGHT:	WEIGHT:	CATEGORY:
1.4 m 4'07"	35.6 kg 78.5 lbs.	Five Star Pokémon

Melemele Island

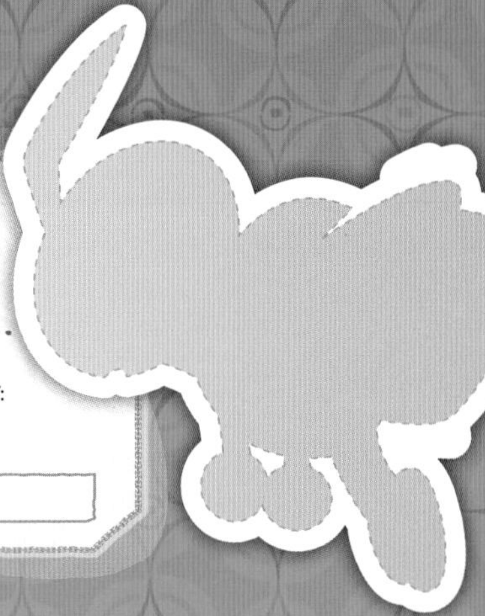

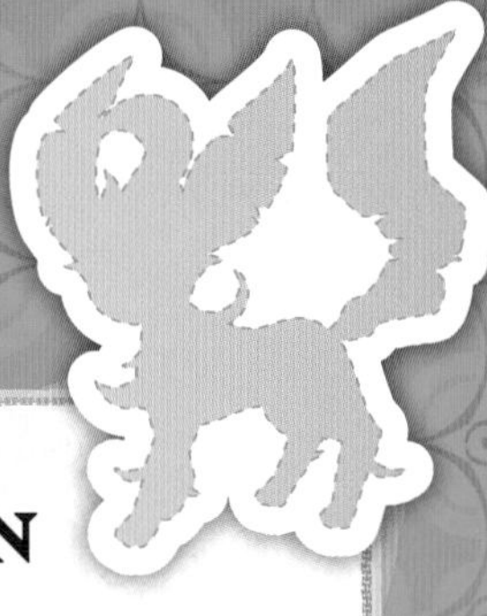

GRASS

LEAFEON

PRONUNCIATION: LEAF-ee-on

HEIGHT:	WEIGHT:	CATEGORY:
1.0 m 3'03"	25.5 kg 56.2 lbs.	Verdant Pokémon

Akala Island

BUG FLYING

LEDYBA

PRONUNCIATION: LEH-dee-bah

HEIGHT:	WEIGHT:	CATEGORY:
1.0 m 3'03"	10.8 kg 23.8 lbs.	Five Star Pokémon

Melemele Island

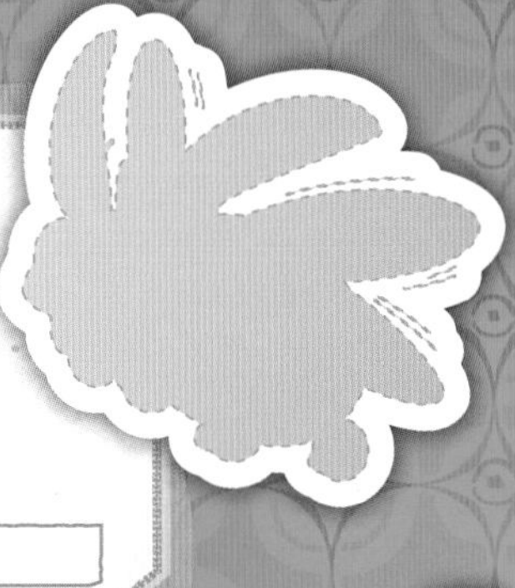

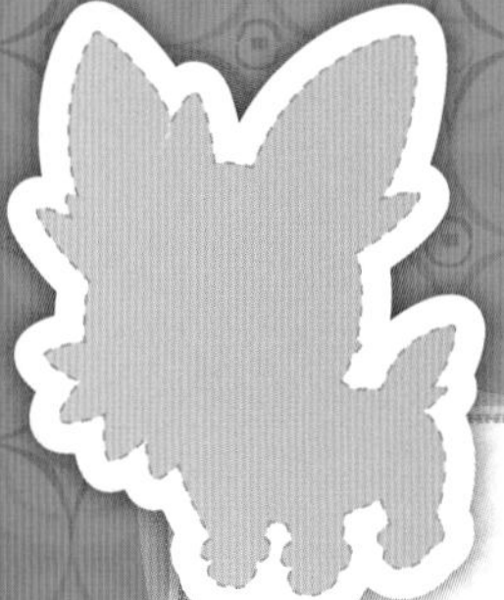

NORMAL

LILLIPUP

PRONUNCIATION: LIL-ee-pup

HEIGHT:	WEIGHT:	CATEGORY:
0.4 m 1'04"	4.1 kg 9.0 lbs.	Puppy Pokémon

Akala Island

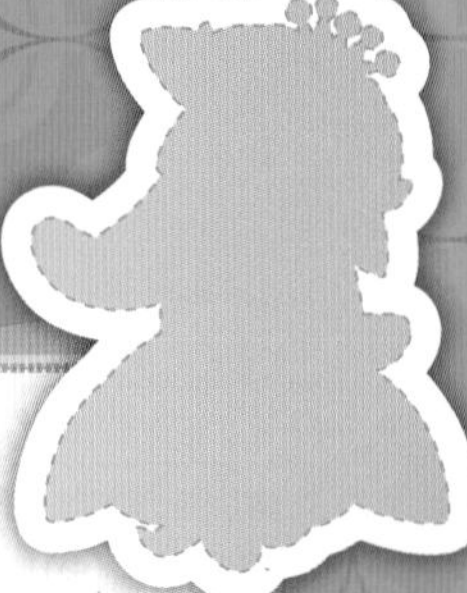

GRASS

LILLIGANT

PRONUNCIATION: LIL-lih-gunt

HEIGHT:	WEIGHT:	CATEGORY:
1.1 m 3'07"	16.3 kg 35.9 lbs.	Flowering Pokémon

Melemele Island

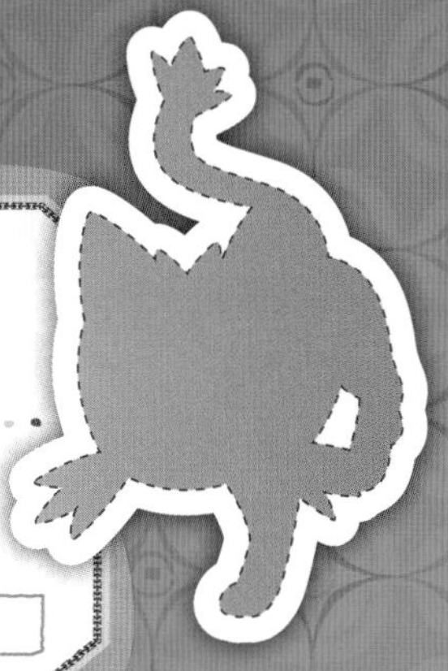

FIRE

LITTEN

PRONUNCIATION: LIT-n

HEIGHT:	WEIGHT:	CATEGORY:
0.4 m 1'04"	4.3 kg 9.5 lbs.	Fire Cat Pokémon

Melemele Island

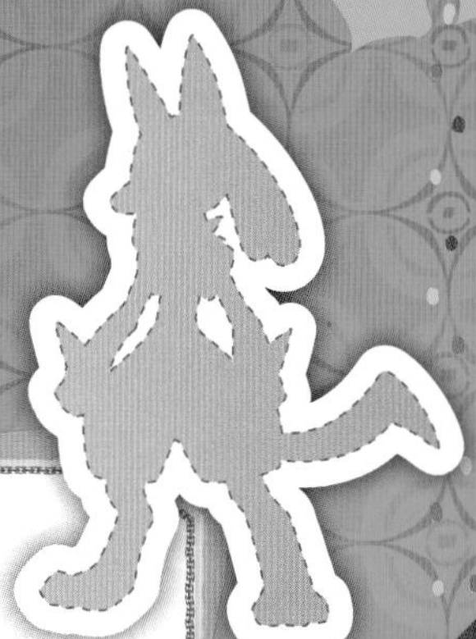

FIGHTING STEEL

LUCARIO

PRONUNCIATION: loo-CAR-ee-oh

HEIGHT:	WEIGHT:	CATEGORY:
1.2 m 3'11"	54.0 kg 119.0 lbs.	Aura Pokémon

Poni Island

LUCARIONITE

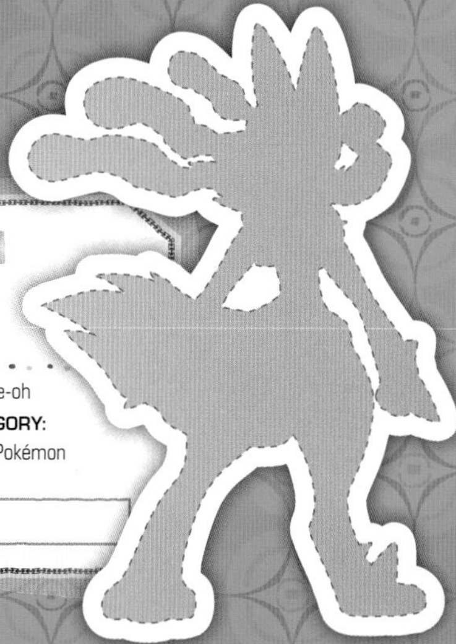

FIGHTING STEEL

MEGA LUCARIO

PRONUNCIATION: Mega loo-CAR-ee-oh

HEIGHT:	WEIGHT:	CATEGORY:
1.3 m 4'03"	57.5 kg 126.8 lbs.	Aura Pokémon

Poni Island

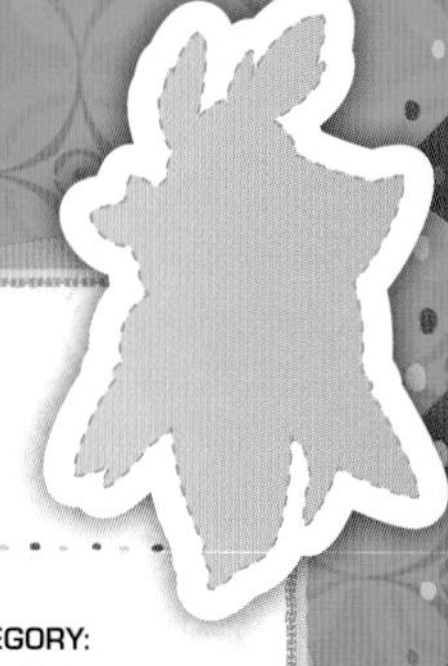

GRASS

LURANTIS

PRONUNCIATION: loor-RAN-tis

HEIGHT:	WEIGHT:	CATEGORY:
0.9 m 2'11"	18.5 kg 40.8 lbs.	Bloom Sickle Pokémon

Akala Island

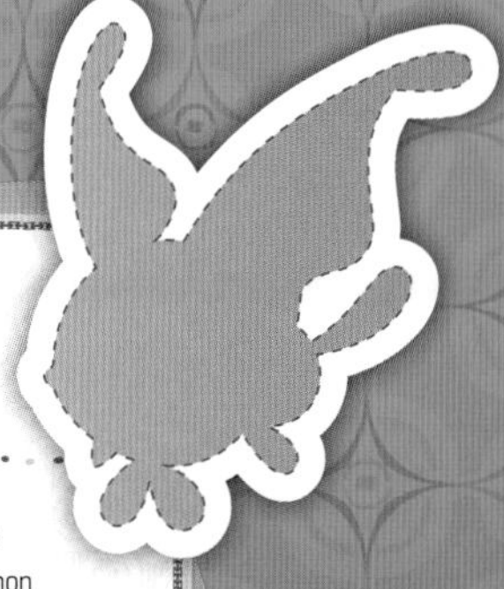

WATER

LUMINEON

PRONUNCIATION: loo-MIN-ee-on

HEIGHT:	WEIGHT:	CATEGORY:
1.2 m 3'11"	24.0 kg 52.9 lbs.	Neon Pokémon

Melemele Island

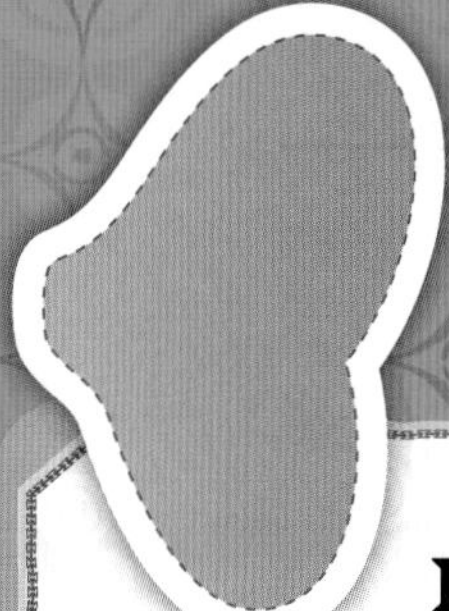

WATER

LUVDISC

PRONUNCIATION: LOVE-disk

HEIGHT:	WEIGHT:	CATEGORY:
0.6 m 2'00"	8.7 kg 19.2 lbs.	Rendezvous Pokémon

Melemele Island

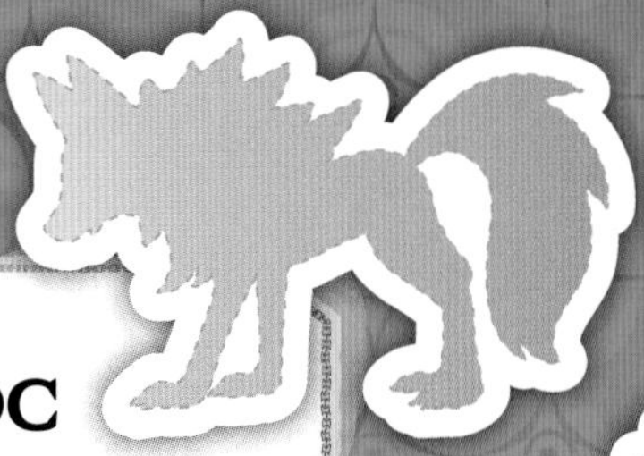

ROCK

LYCANROC

MIDDAY FORM

PRONUNCIATION: LIE-can-rock

HEIGHT:	WEIGHT:	CATEGORY:
0.8 m 2'07"	25.0 kg 55.1 lbs.	Wolf Pokémon

Melemele Island

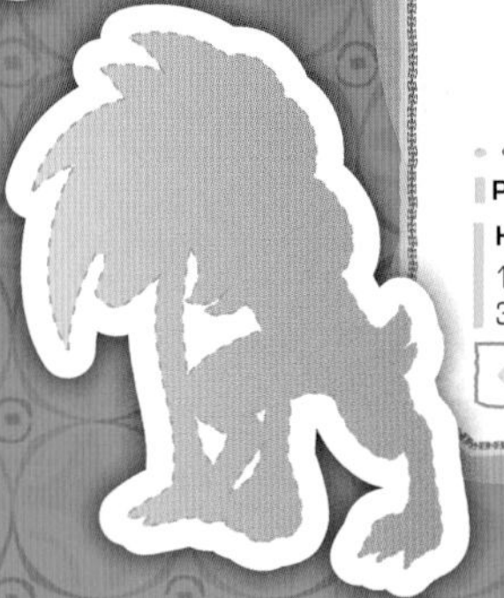

ROCK

LYCANROC

MIDNIGHT FORM

PRONUNCIATION: LIE-can-rock

HEIGHT:	WEIGHT:	CATEGORY:
1.1 m 3'07"	25.0 kg 55.1 lbs.	Wolf Pokémon

Melemele Island

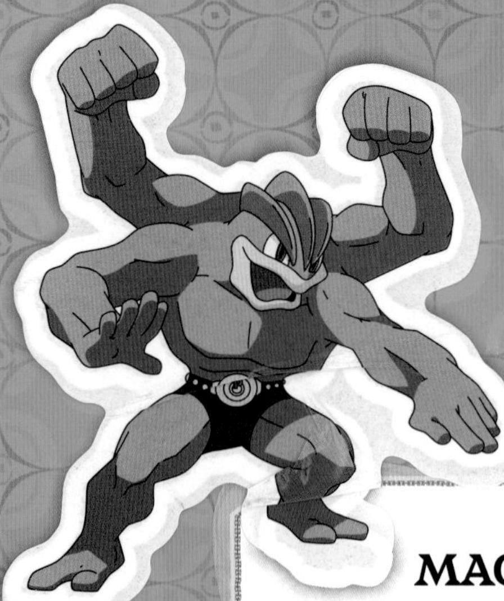

FIGHTING

MACHOKE

PRONUNCIATION: muh-CHOKE

HEIGHT:	WEIGHT:	CATEGORY:
1.5 m 4'11"	70.5 kg 155.4 lbs.	Superpower Pokémon

Melemele Island

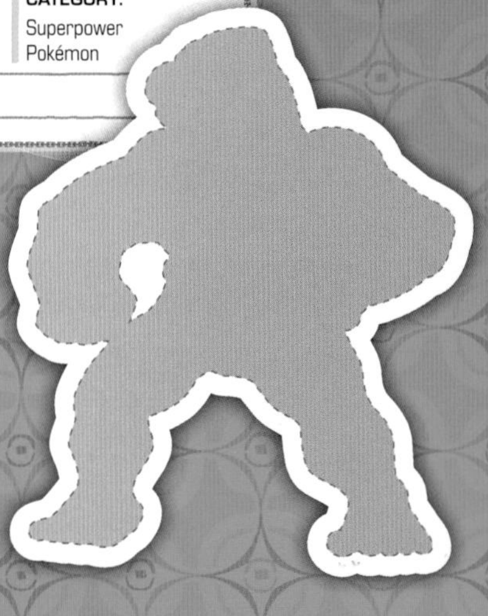

FIGHTING

MACHAMP

PRONUNCIATION: muh-CHAMP

HEIGHT:	WEIGHT:	CATEGORY:
1.6 m 5'03"	130.0 kg 286.6 lbs.	Superpower Pokémon

Melemele Island

WATER

MAGIKARP

PRONUNCIATION: MADGE-eh-karp

HEIGHT:	WEIGHT:	CATEGORY:
0.9 m 2'11"	10.0 kg 22.0 lbs.	Fish Pokémon

Melemele Island

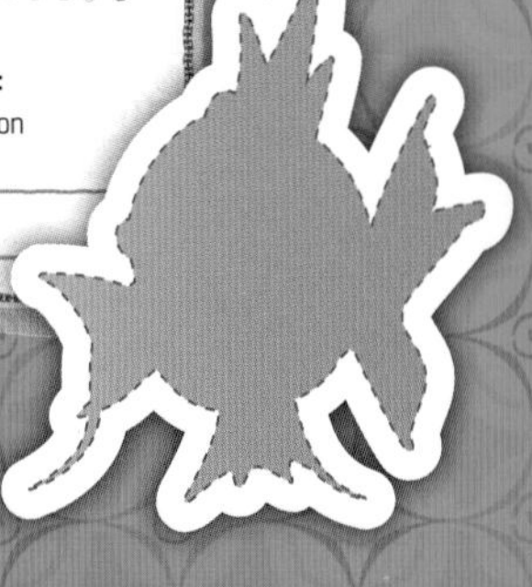

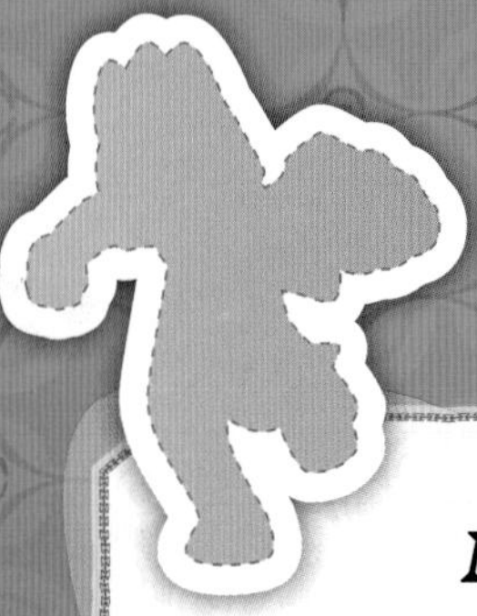

FIGHTING

MACHOP

PRONUNCIATION: muh-CHOP

HEIGHT:	WEIGHT:	CATEGORY:
0.8 m 2'07"	19.5 kg 43.0 lbs.	Superpower Pokémon

Melemele Island

FIRE

MAGBY

PRONUNCIATION: MAG-bee

HEIGHT:	WEIGHT:	CATEGORY:
0.7 m 2'04"	21.4 kg 47.2 lbs.	Live Coal Pokémon

Akala Island

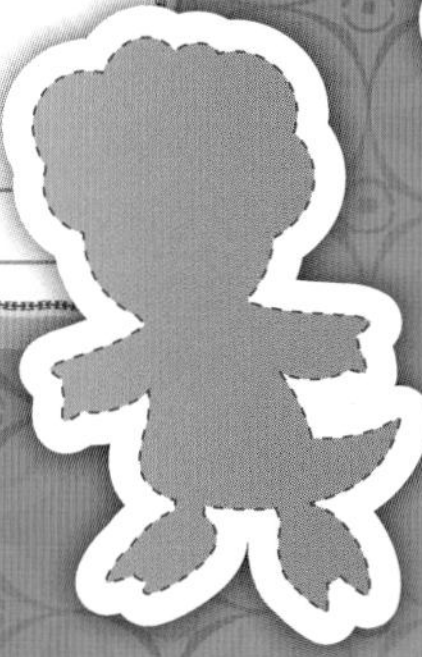

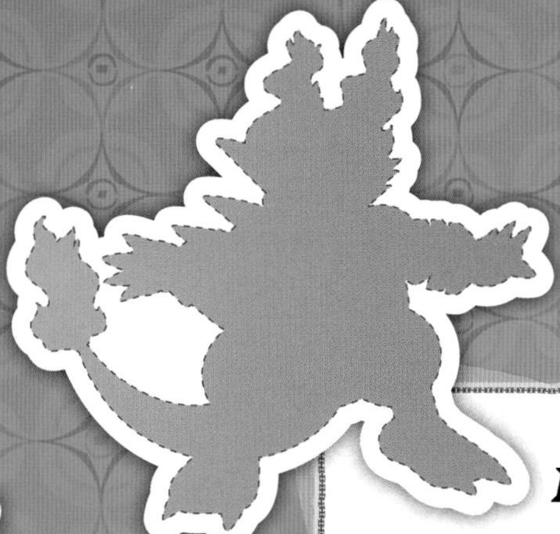

FIRE

MAGMAR

PRONUNCIATION: MAG-marr

HEIGHT:	WEIGHT:	CATEGORY:
1.3 m 4'03"	44.5 kg 98.1 lbs.	Spitfire Pokémon

Akala Island

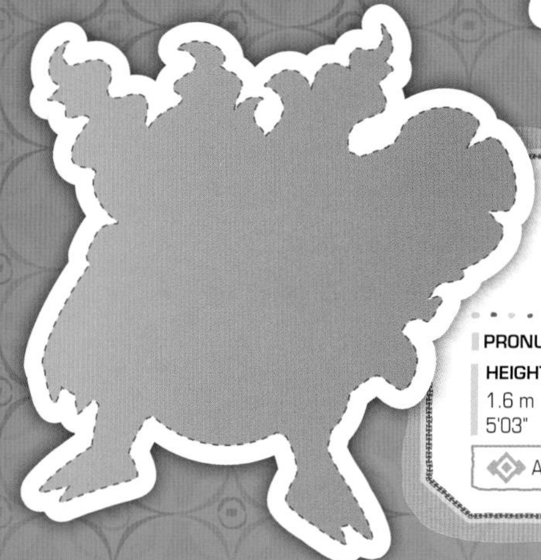

FIRE

MAGMORTAR

PRONUNCIATION: mag-MORT-ur

HEIGHT:	WEIGHT:	CATEGORY:
1.6 m 5'03"	68.0 kg 149.9 lbs.	Blast Pokémon

Akala Island

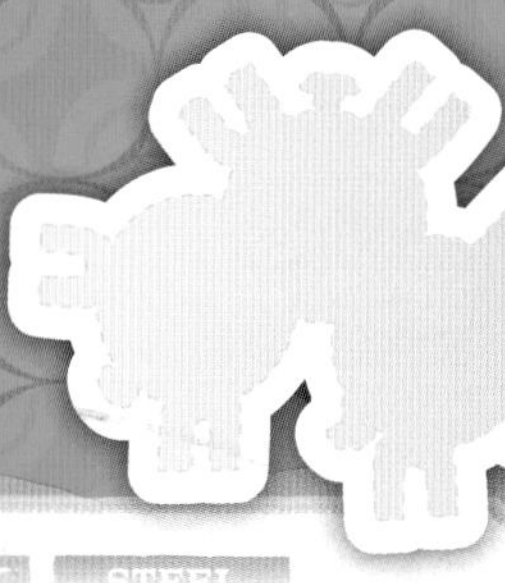

ELECTRIC STEEL

MAGNETON

PRONUNCIATION: MAG-ne-ton

HEIGHT:	WEIGHT:	CATEGORY:
1.0 m 3'03"	60.0 kg 132.3 lbs.	Magnet Pokémon

Melemele Island

ELECTRIC STEEL

MAGNEMITE

PRONUNCIATION: MAG-ne-mite

HEIGHT:	WEIGHT:	CATEGORY:
0.3 m 1'00"	6.0 kg 13.2 lbs.	Magnet Pokémon

Melemele Island

FIGHTING

MAKUHITA

PRONUNCIATION: MAK-oo-HEE-ta

HEIGHT:	WEIGHT:	CATEGORY:
1.0 m 3'03"	86.4 kg 190.5 lbs.	Guts Pokémon

Melemele Island

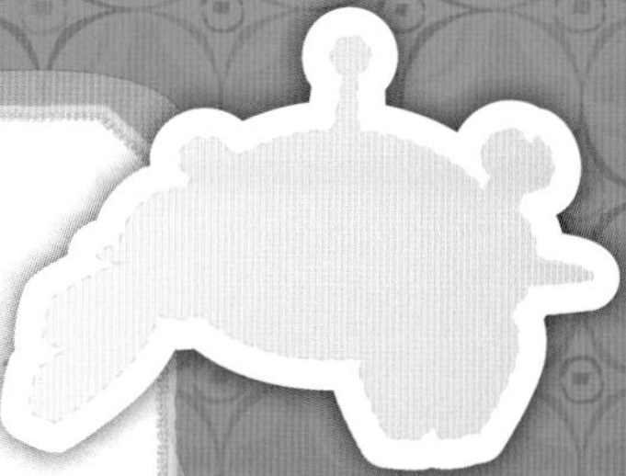

ELECTRIC STEEL

MAGNEZONE

PRONUNCIATION: MAG-nuh-zone

HEIGHT:	WEIGHT:	CATEGORY:
1.2 m 3'11"	180.0 kg 396.8 lbs.	Magnet Area Pokémon

Melemele Island

DARK · FLYING
MANDIBUZZ

PRONUNCIATION: MAN-dih-buz

HEIGHT:	WEIGHT:	CATEGORY:
1.2 m	39.5 kg	Bone Vulture
3'11"	87.1 lbs.	Pokémon

Melemele Island

FIGHTING
MANKEY

PRONUNCIATION: MANG-key

HEIGHT:	WEIGHT:	CATEGORY:
0.5 m	28.0 kg	Pig Monkey
1'08"	61.7 lbs.	Pokémon

Melemele Island

BUG · FLYING
MASQUERAIN

PRONUNCIATION: mas-ker-RAIN

HEIGHT:	WEIGHT:	CATEGORY:
0.8 m	3.6 kg	Eyeball Pokémon
2'07"	7.9 lbs.	

Akala Island

ORAN BERRY

POISON · WATER
MAREANIE

PRONUNCIATION: muh-REE-nee

HEIGHT:	WEIGHT:	CATEGORY:
0.4 m	8.0 kg	Brutal Star
1'04"	17.6 lbs.	Pokémon

Melemele Island

FIRE · GHOST
MAROWAK
ALOLA FORM

PRONUNCIATION: MARE-oh-wack

HEIGHT:	WEIGHT:	CATEGORY:
1.0 m	34.0 kg	Bone Keeper
3'03"	75.0 lbs.	Pokémon

Akala Island

DARK
MEOWTH
ALOLA FORM

PRONUNCIATION: mee-OWTH

HEIGHT:	WEIGHT:	CATEGORY:
0.4 m	4.2 kg	Scratch Cat
1'04"	9.3 lbs.	Pokémon

Melemele Island

METAGROSS

STEEL **PSYCHIC**

PRONUNCIATION: MET-uh-gross

HEIGHT:	WEIGHT:	CATEGORY:
1.6 m	550.0 kg	Iron Leg
5'03"	1212.5 lbs.	Pokémon

 Ula'ula Island

MEGA METAGROSS

STEEL **PSYCHIC**

PRONUNCIATION: Mega MET-uh-gross

HEIGHT:	WEIGHT:	CATEGORY:
2.5 m	942.9 kg	Iron Leg
8'02"	2078.7 lbs.	Pokémon

Ula'ula Island

METANG

STEEL **PSYCHIC**

PRONUNCIATION: met-TANG

HEIGHT:	WEIGHT:	CATEGORY:
1.2 m	202.5 kg	Iron Claw
3'11"	446.4 lbs.	Pokémon

Ula'ula Island

METAGROSSITE

METAPOD

BUG

PRONUNCIATION: MET-uh-pod

HEIGHT:	WEIGHT:	CATEGORY:
0.7 m	9.9 kg	Cocoon Pokémon
2'04"	21.8 lbs.	

Melemele Island

MILOTIC

WATER

PRONUNCIATION: MY-low-tic

HEIGHT:	WEIGHT:	CATEGORY:
6.2 m	162.0 kg	Tender Pokémon
20'04"	357.1 lbs.	

Akala Island

M | ALOLA REGION STICKER BOOK

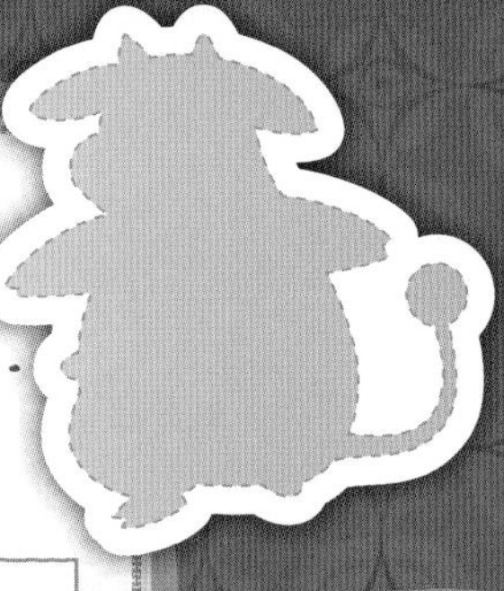

NORMAL

MILTANK

PRONUNCIATION: MILL-tank

HEIGHT:	WEIGHT:	CATEGORY:
1.2 m 3'11"	75.5 kg 166.4 lbs.	Milk Cow Pokémon

Akala Island

GHOST FAIRY

MIMIKYU

PRONUNCIATION: MEE-mee-kyoo

HEIGHT:	WEIGHT:	CATEGORY:
0.2 m 0'08"	0.7 kg 1.5 lbs.	Disguise Pokémon

Ula'ula Island

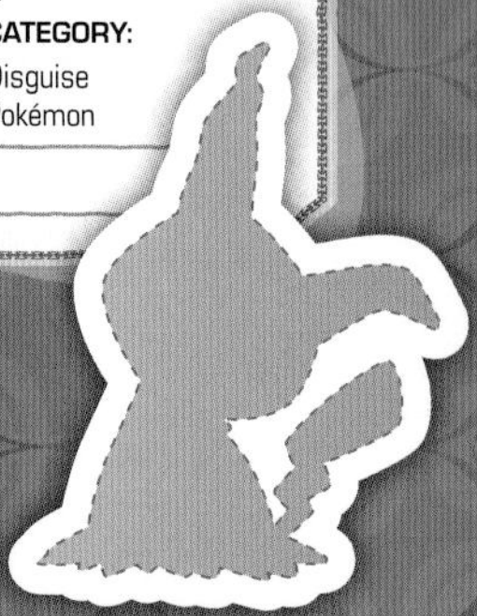

ROCK FLYING

MINIOR

METEOR FORM

PRONUNCIATION: MIN-ee-or

HEIGHT:	WEIGHT:	CATEGORY:
0.3 m 1'00"	40.0 kg 88.2 lbs.	Meteor Pokémon

Ula'ula Island

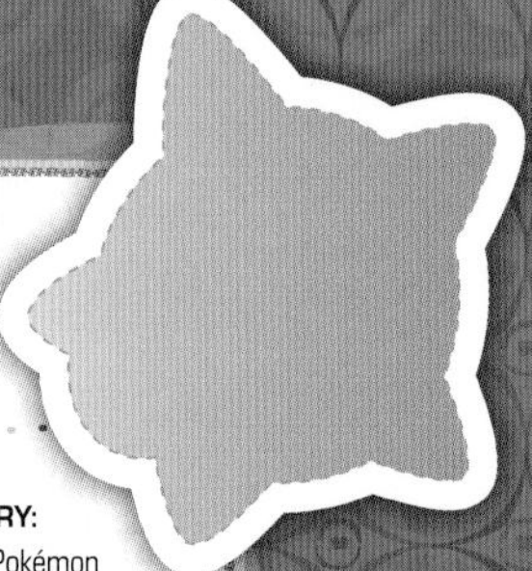

ROCK FLYING

MINIOR

RED CORE

PRONUNCIATION: MIN-ee-or

HEIGHT:	WEIGHT:	CATEGORY:
0.3 m 1'00"	0.3 kg 0.7 lbs.	Meteor Pokémon

Ula'ula Island

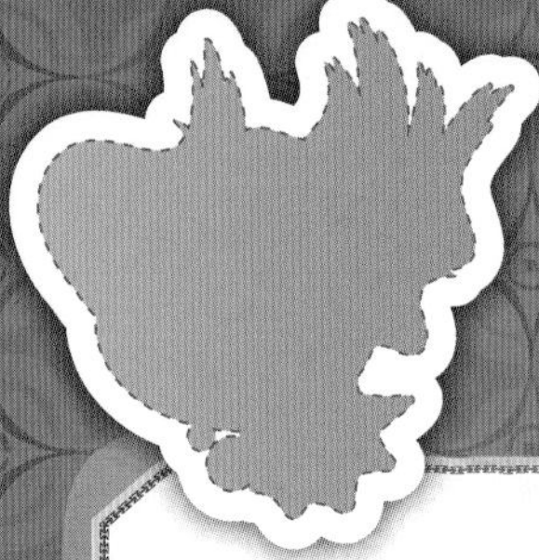

GHOST

MISDREAVUS

PRONUNCIATION: mis-DREE-vuss

HEIGHT:	WEIGHT:	CATEGORY:
0.7 m 2'04"	1.0 kg 2.2 lbs.	Screech Pokémon

Melemele Island

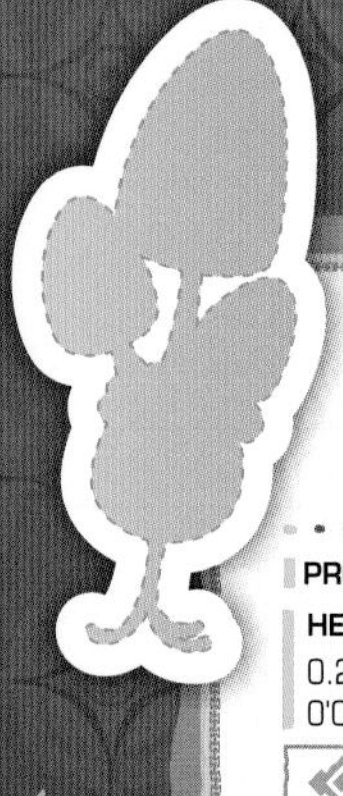

GRASS FAIRY

MORELULL

PRONUNCIATION: MORE-eh-lull

HEIGHT:	WEIGHT:	CATEGORY:
0.2 m 0'08"	1.5 kg 3.3 lbs.	Illuminating Pokémon

Akala Island

GHOST

MISMAGIUS

PRONUNCIATION: miss-MAG-ee-us

HEIGHT:	WEIGHT:	CATEGORY:
0.9 m 2'11"	4.4 kg 9.7 lbs.	Magical Pokémon

Melemele Island

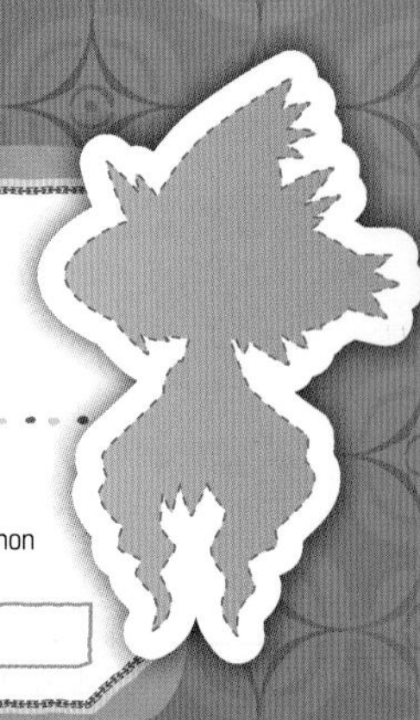

GROUND
MUDBRAY

PRONUNCIATION: MUD-bray

HEIGHT:	WEIGHT:	CATEGORY:
1.0 m	110.0 kg	Donkey Pokémon
3'03"	242.5 lbs.	

 Akala Island

GROUND
MUDSDALE

PRONUNCIATION: MUDZ-dale

HEIGHT:	WEIGHT:	CATEGORY:
2.5 m	920.0 kg	Draft Horse
8'02"	2028.3 lbs.	Pokémon

Akala Island

POISON   DARK
MUK
ALOLA FORM

PRONUNCIATION: MUCK

HEIGHT:	WEIGHT:	CATEGORY:
1.0 m	52.0 kg	Sludge Pokémon
3'03"	114.6 lbs.	

Melemele Island

NORMAL
MUNCHLAX

PRONUNCIATION: MUNCH-lax

HEIGHT:	WEIGHT:	CATEGORY:
0.6 m	105.0 kg	Big Eater
2'00"	231.5 lbs.	Pokémon

Melemele Island

DARK   FLYING
MURKROW

PRONUNCIATION: MUR-crow

HEIGHT:	WEIGHT:	CATEGORY:
0.5 m	2.1 kg	Darkness
1'08"	4.6 lbs.	Pokémon

Poni Island

ICE   FAIRY
NINETALES
ALOLA FORM

PRONUNCIATION: NINE-tails

HEIGHT:	WEIGHT:	CATEGORY:
1.1 m	19.9 kg	Fox Pokémon
3'07"	43.9 lbs.	

Ula'ula Island

ROCK
NOSEPASS

PRONUNCIATION: NOSE-pass

HEIGHT:	WEIGHT:	CATEGORY:
1.0 m	97.0 kg	Compass
3'03"	213.8 lbs.	Pokémon

Akala Island

NORMAL PSYCHIC

ORANGURU

PRONUNCIATION: or-RANG-goo-roo

HEIGHT:	WEIGHT:	CATEGORY:
1.5 m 4'11"	76.0 kg 167.6 lbs.	Sage Pokémon

Akala Island

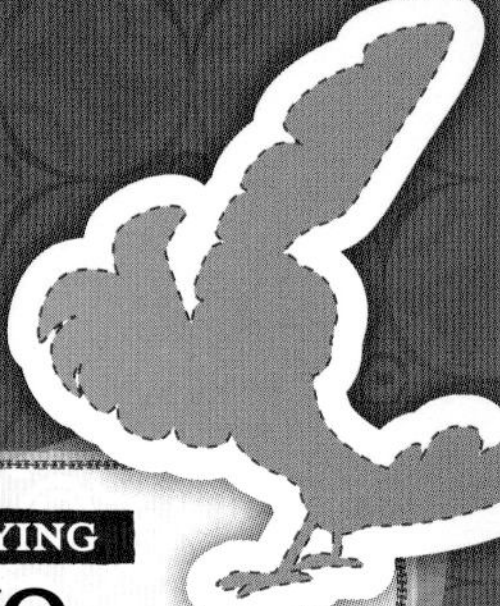

FIRE FLYING

ORICORIO

BAILE STYLE

PRONUNCIATION: or-ih-KOR-ee-oh

HEIGHT:	WEIGHT:	CATEGORY:
0.6 m 2'00"	3.4 kg 7.5 lbs.	Dancing Pokémon

Melemele Island

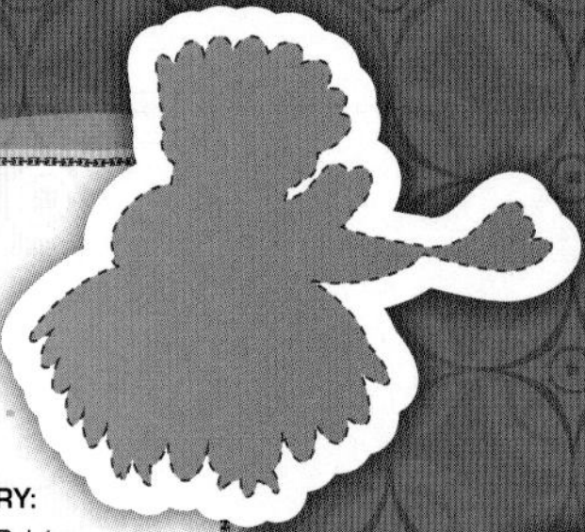

PSYCHIC FLYING

ORICORIO

PA'U STYLE

PRONUNCIATION: or-ih-KOR-ee-oh

HEIGHT:	WEIGHT:	CATEGORY:
0.6 m 2'00"	3.4 kg 7.5 lbs.	Dancing Pokémon

Melemele Island

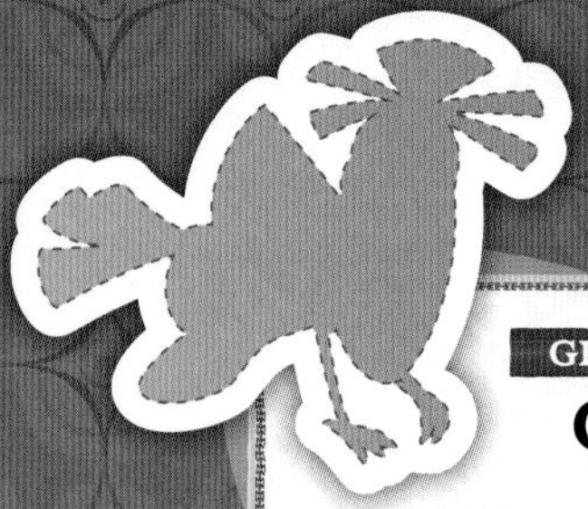

GHOST FLYING

ORICORIO

SENSU STYLE

PRONUNCIATION: or-ih-KOR-ee-oh

HEIGHT:	WEIGHT:	CATEGORY:
0.6 m 2'00"	3.4 kg 7.5 lbs.	Dancing Pokémon

Melemele Island

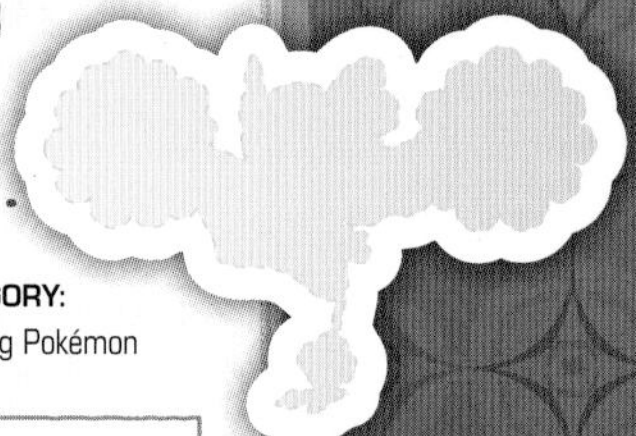

ELECTRIC FLYING

ORICORIO

POM-POM STYLE

PRONUNCIATION: or-ih-KOR-ee-oh

HEIGHT:	WEIGHT:	CATEGORY:
0.6 m 2'00"	3.4 kg 7.5 lbs.	Dancing Pokémon

Melemele Island

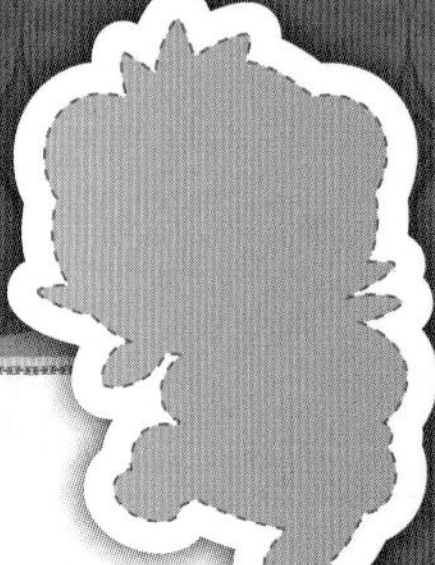

FIGHTING

PANCHAM

PRONUNCIATION: PAN-chum

HEIGHT:	WEIGHT:	CATEGORY:
0.6 m 2'00"	8.0 kg 17.6 lbs.	Playful Pokémon

Ula'ula Island

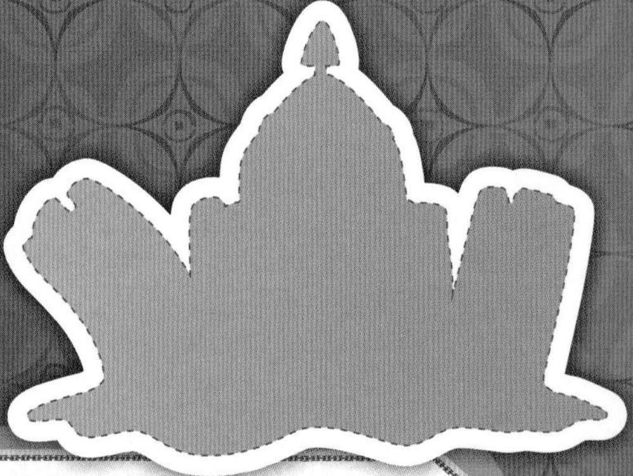

GHOST GROUND

PALOSSAND

PRONUNCIATION: PAL-uh-sand

HEIGHT:	WEIGHT:	CATEGORY:
1.3 m 4'03"	250.0 kg 551.2 lbs.	Sand Castle Pokémon

Akala Island

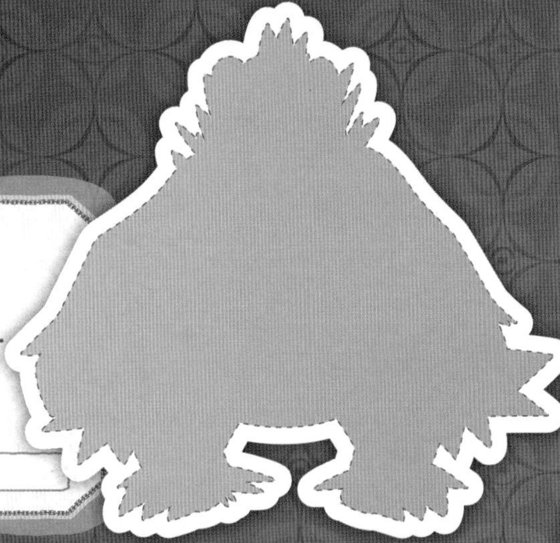

FIGHTING   DARK
PANGORO

PRONUNCIATION: PAN-go-roh

HEIGHT:	WEIGHT:	CATEGORY:
2.1 m	136.0 kg	Daunting
6'11"	299.8 lbs.	Pokémon

 Ula'ula Island

BUG   GRASS
PARASECT

PRONUNCIATION: PARA-sekt

HEIGHT:	WEIGHT:	CATEGORY:
1.0 m	29.5 kg	Mushroom
3'03"	65.0 lbs.	Pokémon

 Akala Island

BUG   GRASS
PARAS

PRONUNCIATION: PAIR-us

HEIGHT:	WEIGHT:	CATEGORY:
0.3 m	5.4 kg	Mushroom
1'00"	11.9 lbs.	Pokémon

Akala Island

WATER   FLYING
PELIPPER

PRONUNCIATION: PEL-ip-purr

HEIGHT:	WEIGHT:	CATEGORY:
1.2 m	28.0 kg	Water Bird
3'11"	61.7 lbs.	Pokémon

Melemele Island

DARK
PERSIAN
ALOLA FORM

PRONUNCIATION: PER-zhun

HEIGHT:	WEIGHT:	CATEGORY:
1.1 m	33.0 kg	Classy Cat
3'07"	72.8 lbs.	Pokémon

Melemele Island

FIGHTING
PASSIMIAN

PRONUNCIATION: pass-SIM-ee-uhn

HEIGHT:	WEIGHT:	CATEGORY:
2.0 m	82.8 kg	Teamwork
6'07"	182.5 lbs.	Pokémon

Akala Island

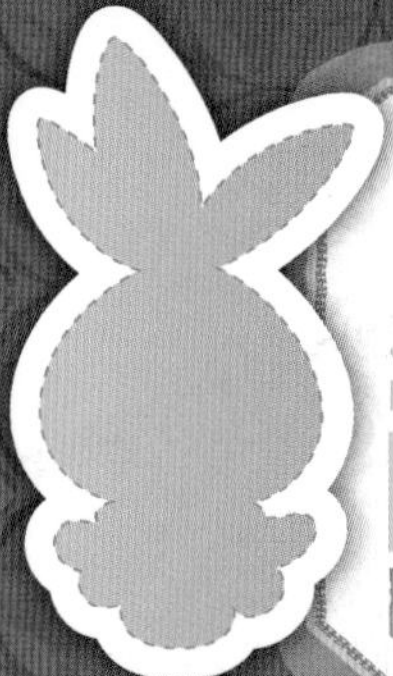

GRASS

PETILIL

PRONUNCIATION: PEH-tuh-LIL

HEIGHT:	WEIGHT:	CATEGORY:
0.5 m 1'08"	6.6 kg 14.6 lbs.	Bulb Pokémon

Melemele Island

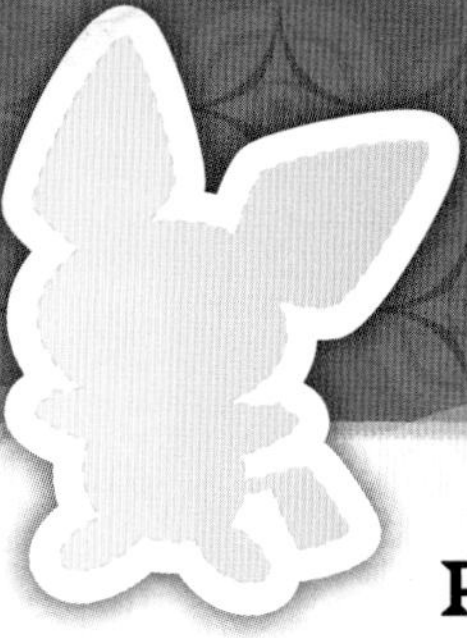

ELECTRIC

PICHU

PRONUNCIATION: PEE-choo

HEIGHT:	WEIGHT:	CATEGORY:
0.3 m 1'00"	2.0 kg 4.4 lbs.	Tiny Mouse Pokémon

Melemele Island

GHOST GRASS

PHANTUMP

PRONUNCIATION: FAN-tump

HEIGHT:	WEIGHT:	CATEGORY:
0.4 m 1'04"	7.0 kg 15.4 lbs.	Stump Pokémon

Akala Island

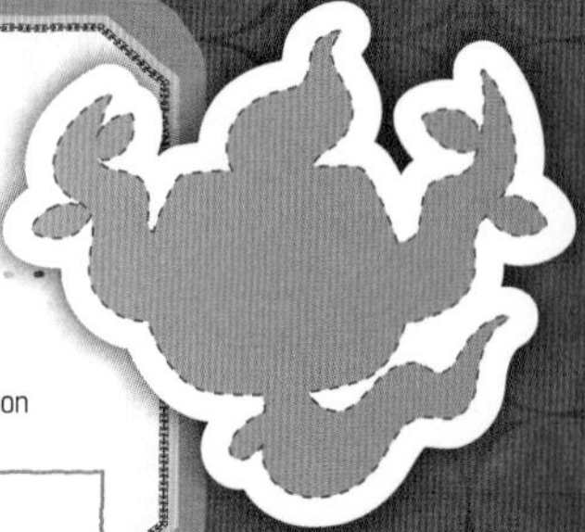

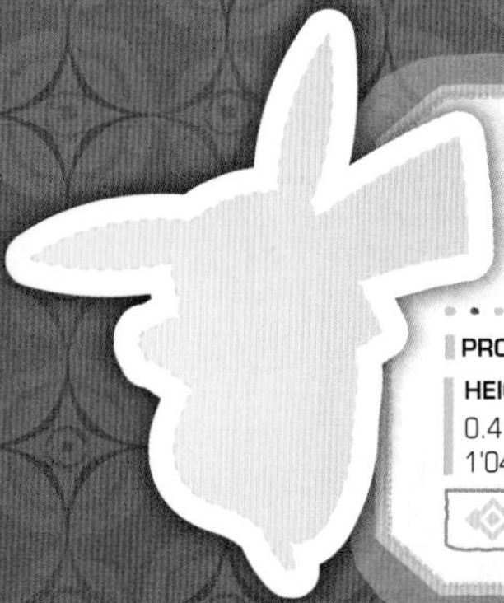

ELECTRIC

PIKACHU

PRONUNCIATION: PEE-ka-choo

HEIGHT:	WEIGHT:	CATEGORY:
0.4 m 1'04"	6.0 kg 13.2 lbs.	Mouse Pokémon

Melemele Island

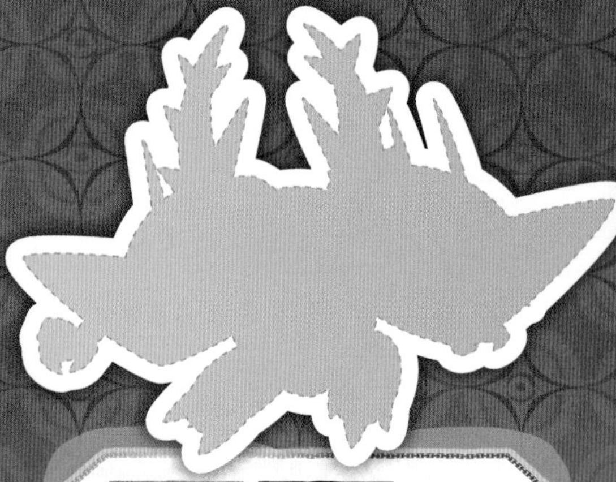

BUG FLYING

MEGA PINSIR

PRONUNCIATION: Mega PIN-sir

HEIGHT:	WEIGHT:	CATEGORY:
1.7 m 5'07"	59.0 kg 130.1 lbs.	Stag Beetle Pokémon

Akala Island

BUG

PINSIR

PRONUNCIATION: PIN-sir

HEIGHT:	WEIGHT:	CATEGORY:
1.5 m 4'11"	55.0 kg 121.3 lbs.	Stag Beetle Pokémon

Akala Island

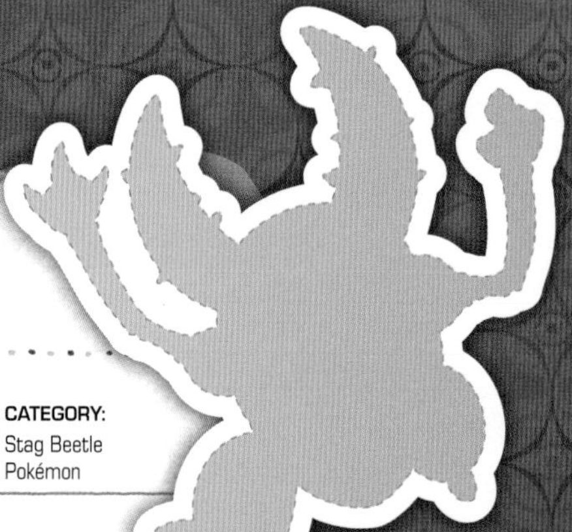

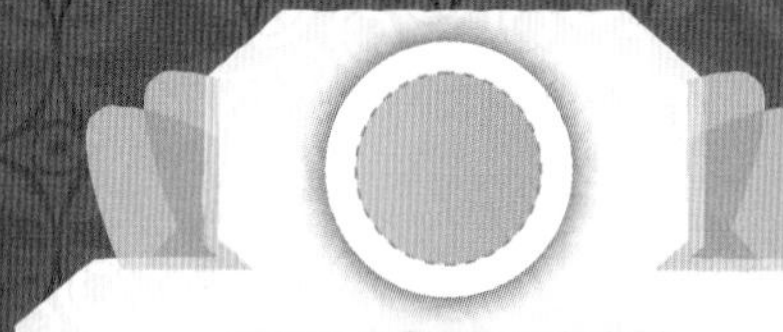

PINSIRITE

NORMAL **FLYING**
PIKIPEK

PRONUNCIATION: PICK-kee-peck

HEIGHT:	WEIGHT:	CATEGORY:
0.3 m	1.2 kg	Woodpecker
1'00"	2.6 lbs.	Pokémon

Melemele Island

WATER
POLIWAG

PRONUNCIATION: PAUL-lee-wag

HEIGHT:	WEIGHT:	CATEGORY:
0.6 m	12.4 kg	Tadpole Pokémon
2'00"	27.3 lbs.	

Akala Island

WATER
POLITOED

PRONUNCIATION: PAUL-lee-TOED

HEIGHT:	WEIGHT:	CATEGORY:
1.1 m	33.9 kg	Frog Pokémon
3'07"	74.7 lbs.	

Akala Island

WATER
POLIWHIRL

PRONUNCIATION: PAUL-lee-wirl

HEIGHT:	WEIGHT:	CATEGORY:
1.0 m	20.0 kg	Tadpole Pokémon
3'03"	44.1 lbs.	

Akala Island

WATER **FIGHTING**
POLIWRATH

PRONUNCIATION: PAUL-lee-rath

HEIGHT:	WEIGHT:	CATEGORY:
1.3 m	54.0 kg	Tadpole Pokémon
4'03"	119.0 lbs.	

Akala Island

WATER
POPPLIO

PRONUNCIATION: POP-lee-oh

HEIGHT:	WEIGHT:	CATEGORY:
0.4 m	7.5 kg	Sea Lion
1'04"	16.5 lbs.	Pokémon

Melemele Island

NORMAL
PORYGON2

PRONUNCIATION: PORE-ee-gon TWO

HEIGHT:	WEIGHT:	CATEGORY:
0.6 m	32.5 kg	Virtual Pokémon
2'00"	71.6 lbs.	

Ula'ula Island

P | ALOLA REGION STICKER BOOK

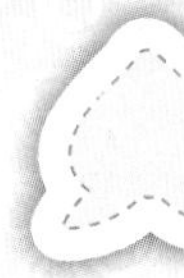

PECHA BERRY

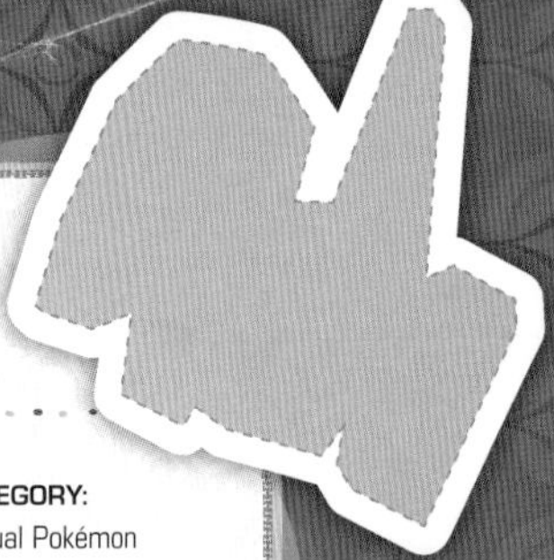

NORMAL

PORYGON

PRONUNCIATION: PORE-ee-gon

HEIGHT:	WEIGHT:	CATEGORY:
0.8 m 2'07"	36.5 kg 80.5 lbs.	Virtual Pokémon

Ula'ula Island

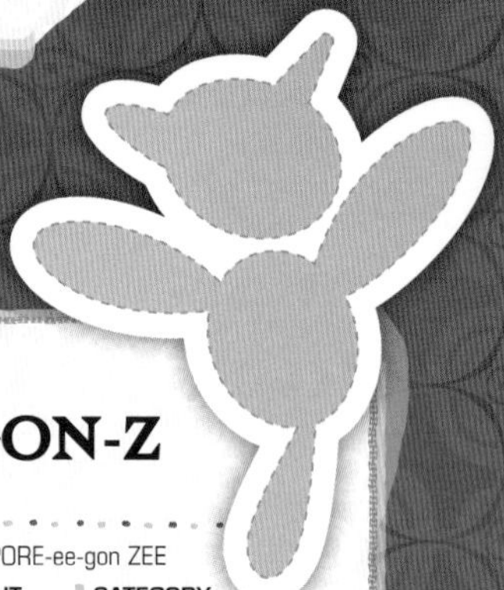

NORMAL

PORYGON-Z

PRONUNCIATION: PORE-ee-gon ZEE

HEIGHT:	WEIGHT:	CATEGORY:
0.9 m 2'11"	34.0 kg 75.0 lbs.	Virtual Pokémon

Ula'ula Island

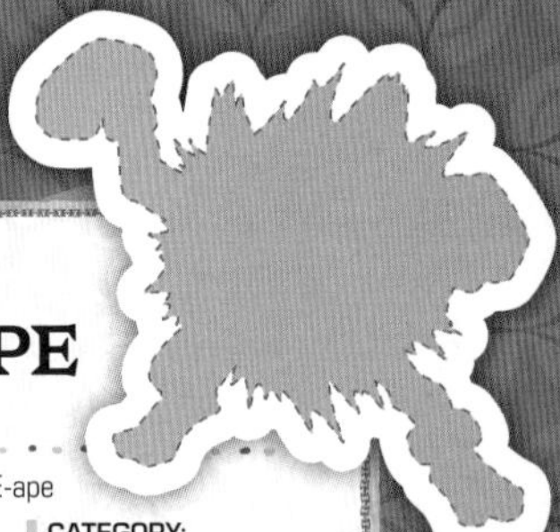

FIGHTING

PRIMEAPE

PRONUNCIATION: PRIME-ape

HEIGHT:	WEIGHT:	CATEGORY:
1.0 m 3'03"	32.0 kg 70.5 lbs.	Pig Monkey Pokémon

Melemele Island

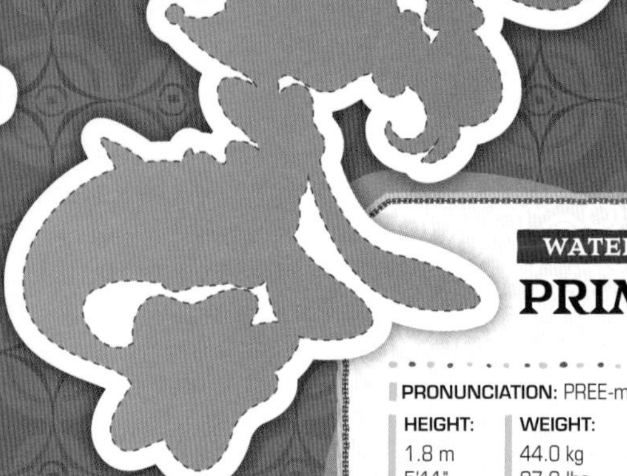

WATER FAIRY

PRIMARINA

PRONUNCIATION: PREE-muh-REE-nuh

HEIGHT:	WEIGHT:	CATEGORY:
1.8 m 5'11"	44.0 kg 97.0 lbs.	Soloist Pokémon

Melemele Island

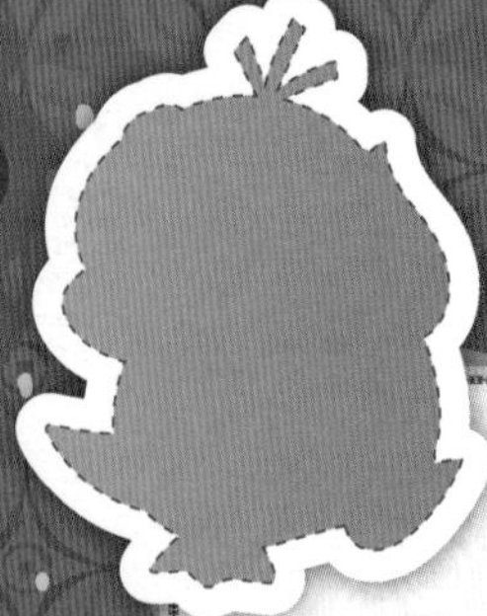

WATER

PSYDUCK

PRONUNCIATION: SY-duck

HEIGHT:	WEIGHT:	CATEGORY:
0.8 m 2'07"	19.6 kg 43.2 lbs.	Duck Pokémon

Melemele Island

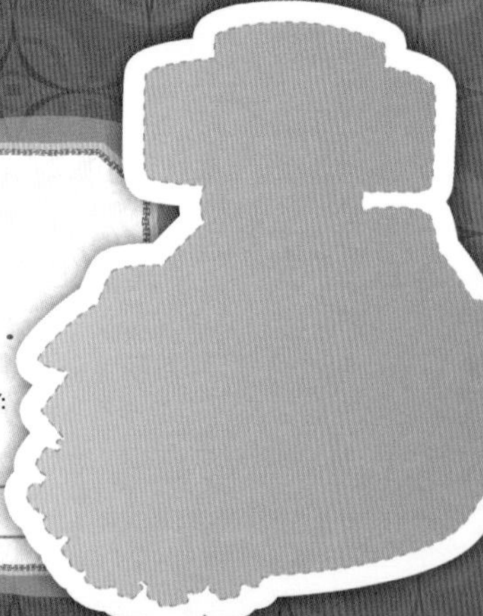

ROCK STEEL

PROBOPASS

PRONUNCIATION: PRO-bow-pass

HEIGHT:	WEIGHT:	CATEGORY:
1.4 m 4'07"	340.0 kg 749.6 lbs.	Compass Pokémon

Akala Island

WATER

PYUKUMUKU

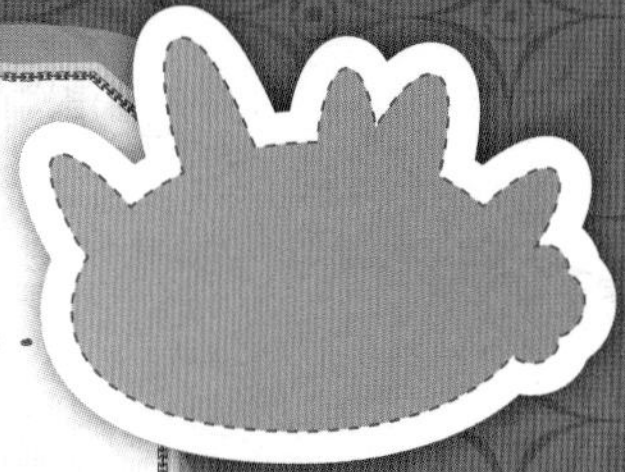

PRONUNCIATION: PYOO-koo-MOO-koo

HEIGHT:	WEIGHT:	CATEGORY:
0.3 m 1'00"	1.2 kg 2.6 lbs.	Sea Cucumber Pokémon

Akala Island

ELECTRIC PSYCHIC

RAICHU

ALOLA FORM

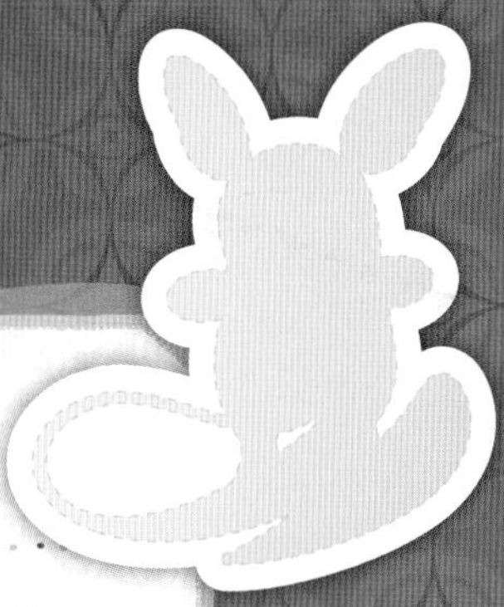

PRONUNCIATION: RYE-choo

HEIGHT:	WEIGHT:	CATEGORY:
0.7 m 2'04"	21.0 kg 46.3 lbs.	Mouse Pokémon

Melemele Island

ROCK

RAMPARDOS

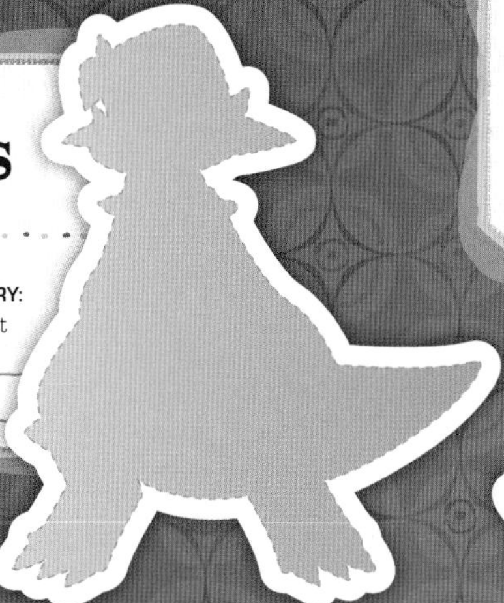

PRONUNCIATION: ram-PAR-dose

HEIGHT:	WEIGHT:	CATEGORY:
1.6 m 5'03"	102.5 kg 226.0 lbs.	Head Butt Pokémon

Akala Island

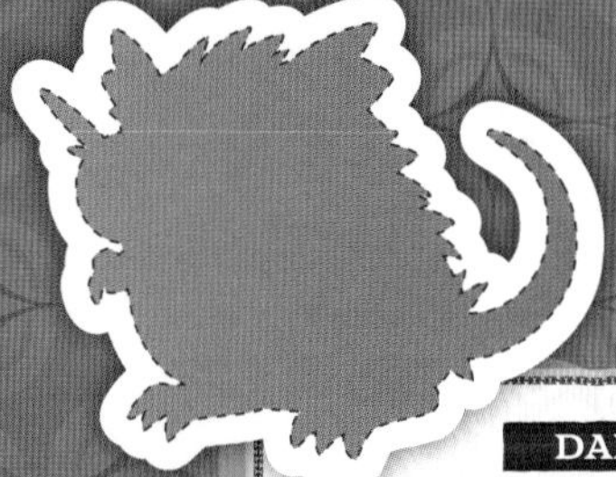

DARK NORMAL

RATICATE

ALOLA FORM

PRONUNCIATION: RAT-ih-kate

HEIGHT:	WEIGHT:	CATEGORY:
0.7 m 2'04"	25.5 kg 56.2 lbs.	Mouse Pokémon

Melemele Island

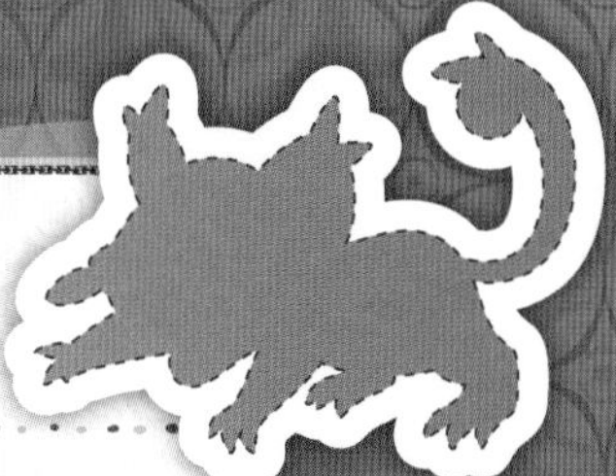

DARK NORMAL

RATTATA

ALOLA FORM

PRONUNCIATION: RA-TAT-ta

HEIGHT:	WEIGHT:	CATEGORY:
0.3 m 1'00"	3.8 kg 8.4 lbs.	Mouse Pokémon

Melemele Island

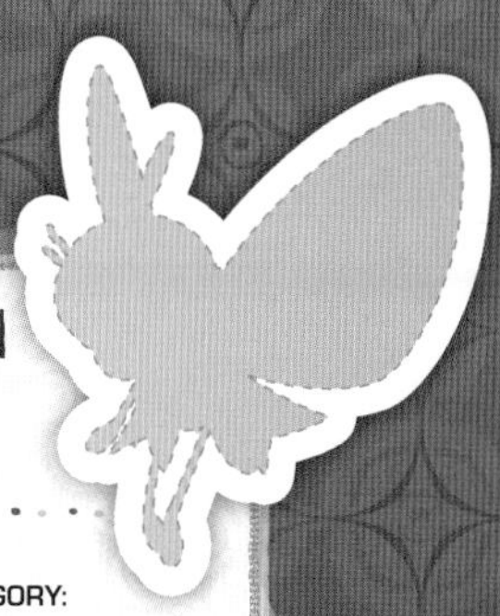

BUG FAIRY

RIBOMBEE

PRONUNCIATION: rih-BOMB-bee

HEIGHT:	WEIGHT:	CATEGORY:
0.2 m 0'08"	0.5 kg 1.1 lbs.	Bee Fly Pokémon

Melemele Island

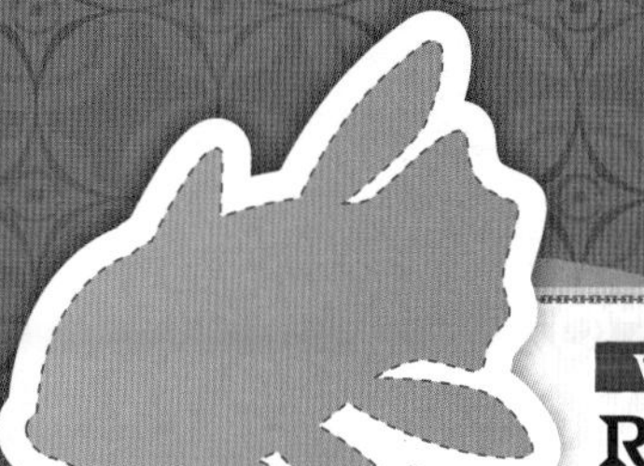

WATER ROCK

RELICANTH

PRONUNCIATION: REL-uh-canth

HEIGHT:	WEIGHT:	CATEGORY:
1.0 m 3'03"	23.4 kg 51.6 lbs.	Longevity Pokémon

Poni Island

FIGHTING
RIOLU

PRONUNCIATION: ree-OH-loo

HEIGHT:	WEIGHT:	CATEGORY:
0.7 m	20.2 kg	Emanation
2'04"	44.5 lbs.	Pokémon

Poni Island

POKÉ BALL

ROCK
ROCKRUFF

PRONUNCIATION: Rock-ruff

HEIGHT:	WEIGHT:	CATEGORY:
0.5 m	9.2 kg	Puppy Pokémon
1'08"	20.3 lbs.	

Melemele Island

ROCK
ROGGENROLA

PRONUNCIATION: rah-gen-ROH-lah

HEIGHT:	WEIGHT:	CATEGORY:
0.4 m	18.0 kg	Mantle Pokémon
1'04"	39.7 lbs.	

Melemele Island

NORMAL   FLYING
RUFFLET

PRONUNCIATION: RUF-lit

HEIGHT:	WEIGHT:	CATEGORY:
0.5 m	10.5 kg	Eaglet Pokémon
1'08"	23.1 lbs.	

Melemele Island

GRASS   FLYING
ROWLET

PRONUNCIATION: ROW-let

HEIGHT:	WEIGHT:	CATEGORY:
0.3 m	1.5 kg	Grass Quill
1'00"	3.3 lbs.	Pokémon

Melemele Island

DARK   GHOST
SABLEYE

PRONUNCIATION: SAY-bull-eye

HEIGHT:	WEIGHT:	CATEGORY:
0.5 m	11.0 kg	Darkness
1'08"	24.3 lbs.	Pokémon

Melemele Island

SABLENITE

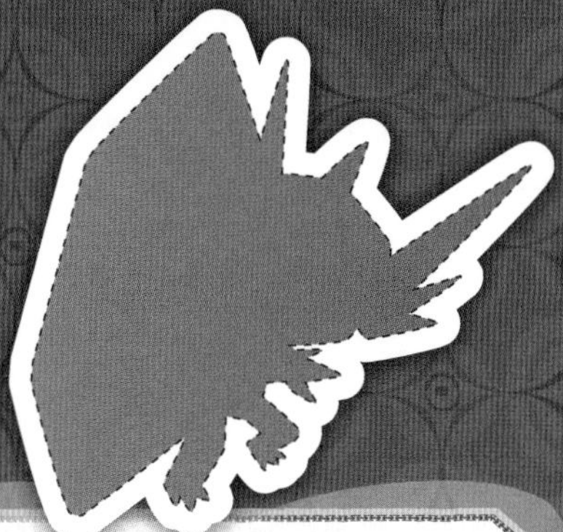

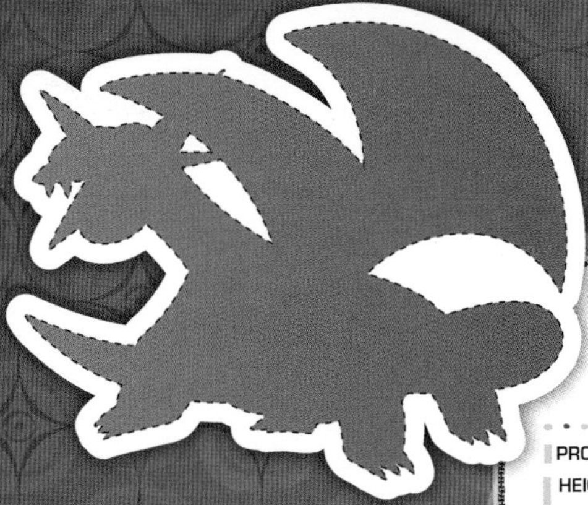

DRAGON FLYING

SALAMENCE

PRONUNCIATION: SAL-uh-mence

HEIGHT:	WEIGHT:	CATEGORY:
1.5 m 4'11"	102.6 kg 226.2 lbs.	Dragon Pokémon

Melemele Island

DARK GHOST

MEGA SABLEYE

PRONUNCIATION: Mega SAY-bull-eye

HEIGHT:	WEIGHT:	CATEGORY:
0.5 m 1'08"	11.0 kg 24.3 lbs.	Darkness Pokémon

Melemele Island

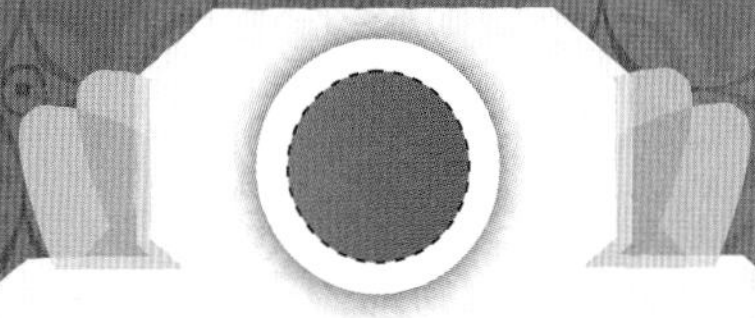

SALAMENCITE

DRAGON FLYING

MEGA SALAMENCE

PRONUNCIATION: Mega SAL-uh-mence

HEIGHT:	WEIGHT:	CATEGORY:
1.8 m 5'11"	112.6 kg 248.2 lbs.	Dragon Pokémon

Melemele Island

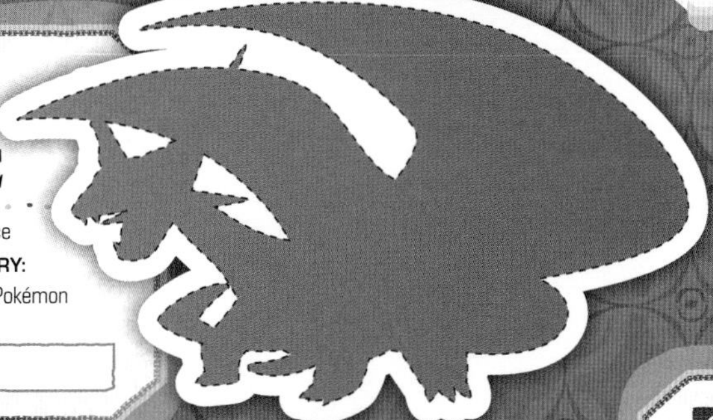

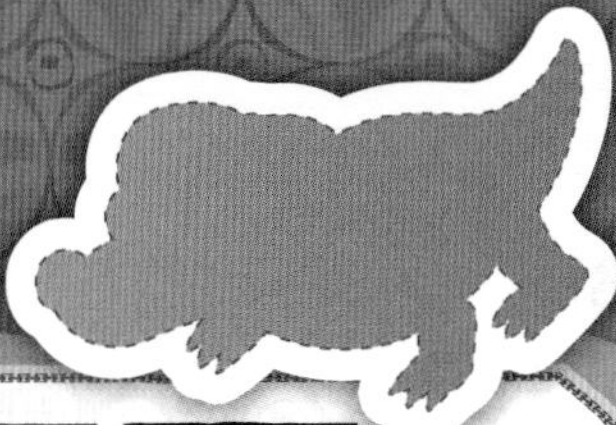

GROUND DARK

SANDILE

PRONUNCIATION: SAN-dyle

HEIGHT:	WEIGHT:	CATEGORY:
0.7 m 2'04"	15.2 kg 33.5 lbs.	Desert Croc Pokémon

Ula'ula Island

POISON FIRE

SALANDIT

PRONUNCIATION: suh-LAN-dit

HEIGHT:	WEIGHT:	CATEGORY:
0.6 m 2'00"	4.8 kg 10.6 lbs.	Toxic Lizard Pokémon

Akala Island

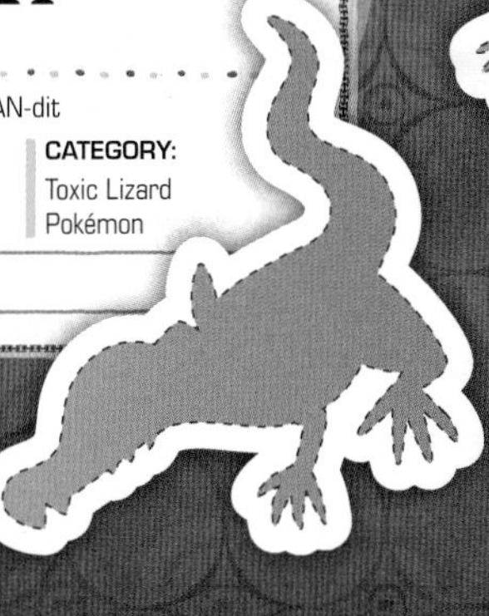

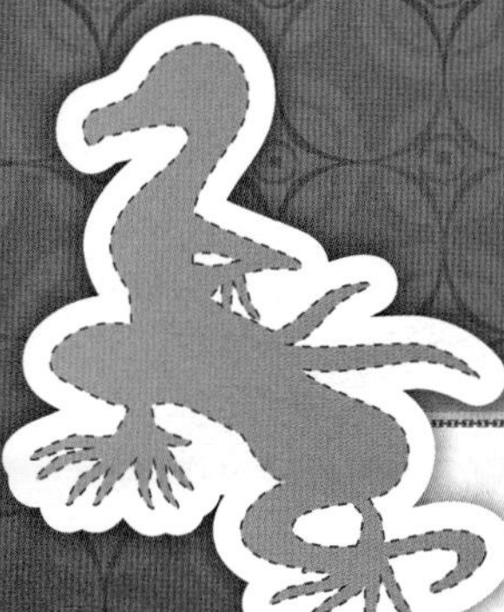

POISON FIRE

SALAZZLE

PRONUNCIATION: suh-LAZ-zuhl

HEIGHT:	WEIGHT:	CATEGORY:
1.2 m 3'11"	22.2 kg 48.9 lbs.	Toxic Lizard Pokémon

Akala Island

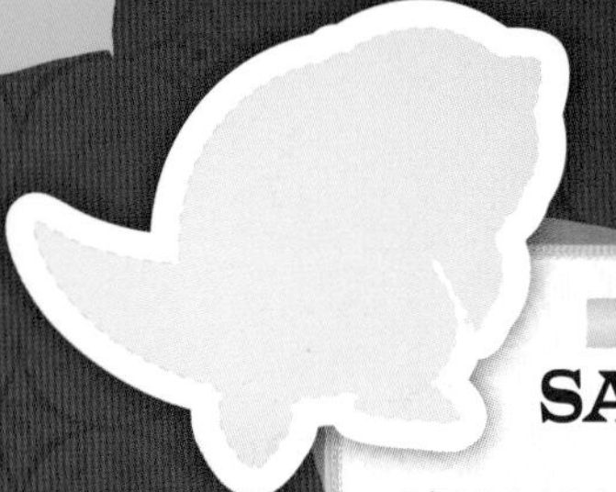

ICE STEEL

SANDSHREW

ALOLA FORM

PRONUNCIATION: SAND-shroo

HEIGHT:	WEIGHT:	CATEGORY:
0.7 m 2'04"	40.0 kg 88.2 lbs.	Mouse Pokémon

Ula'ula Island

PREMIER BALL

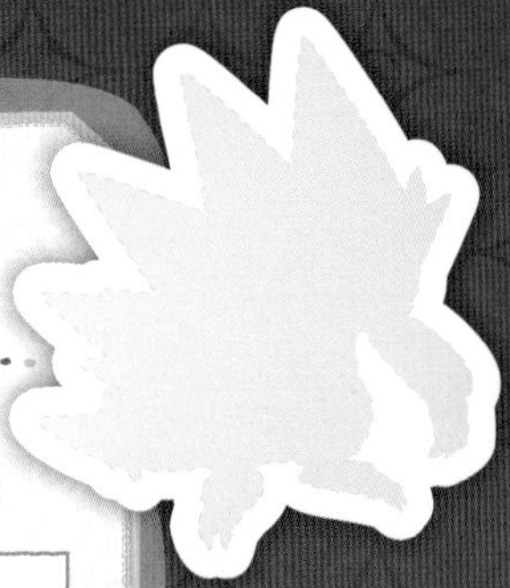

ICE STEEL

SANDSLASH

ALOLA FORM

PRONUNCIATION: SAND-slash

HEIGHT:	WEIGHT:	CATEGORY:
1.2 m 3'11"	55.0 kg 121.3 lbs.	Mouse Pokémon

Ula'ula Island

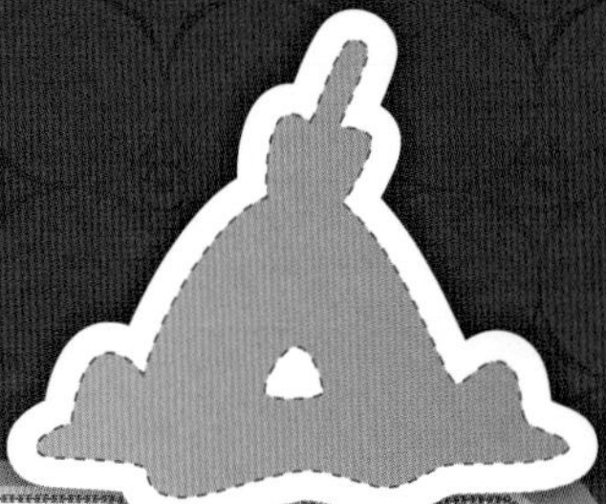

GHOST GROUND

SANDYGAST

PRONUNCIATION: SAN-dee-GAST

HEIGHT:	WEIGHT:	CATEGORY:
0.5 m 1'08"	70.0 kg 154.3 lbs.	Sand Heap Pokémon

Akala Island

BUG STEEL

SCIZOR

PRONUNCIATION: SIH-zor

HEIGHT:	WEIGHT:	CATEGORY:
1.8 m 5'11"	118.0 kg 260.1 lbs.	Pincer Pokémon

Poni Island

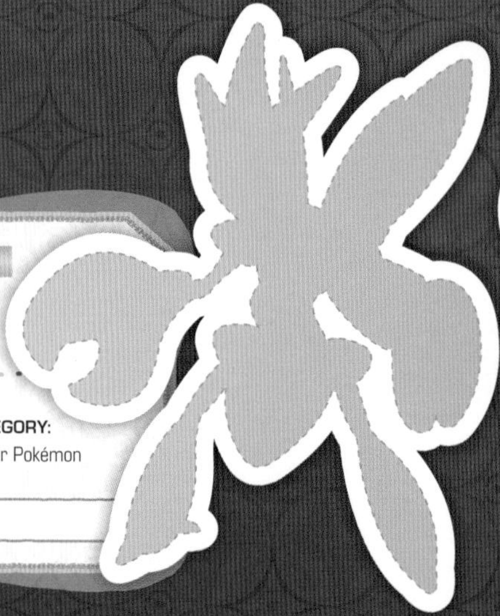

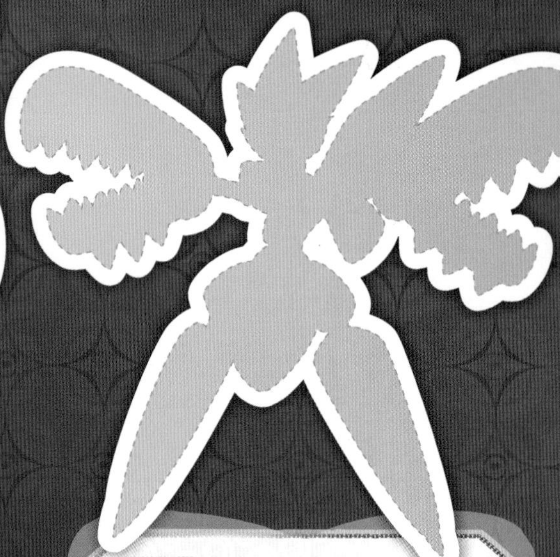

SCIZORITE

BUG STEEL

MEGA SCIZOR

PRONUNCIATION: Mega SIH-zor

HEIGHT:	WEIGHT:	CATEGORY:
2.0 m 6'07"	125.0 kg 275.6 lbs.	Pincer Pokémon

Poni Island

QUICK BALL

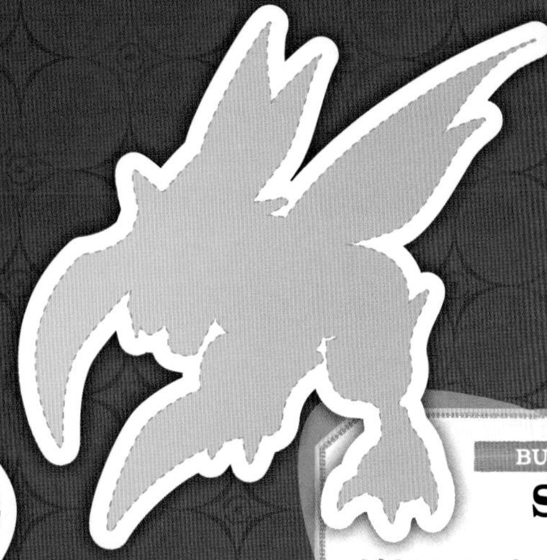

BUG | FLYING

SCYTHER

PRONUNCIATION: SY-thur

HEIGHT:	WEIGHT:	CATEGORY:
1.5 m 4'11"	56.0 kg 123.5 lbs.	Mantis Pokémon

Poni Island

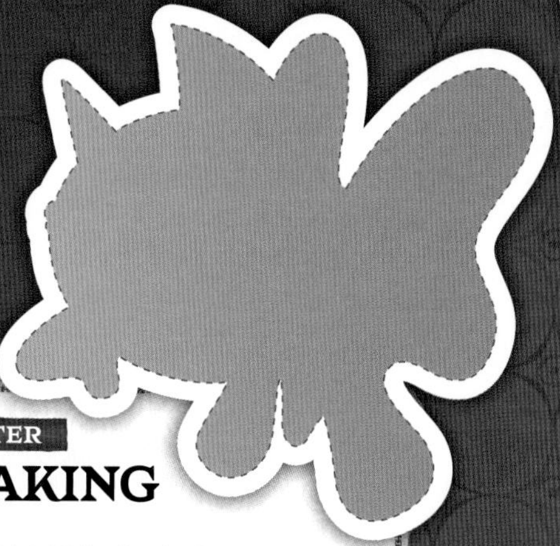

WATER

SEAKING

PRONUNCIATION: SEE-king

HEIGHT:	WEIGHT:	CATEGORY:
1.3 m 4'03"	39.0 kg 86.0 lbs.	Goldfish Pokémon

Akala Island

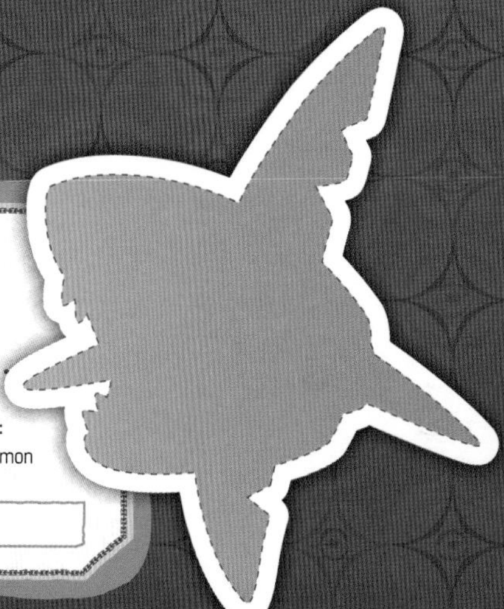

WATER | DARK

SHARPEDO

PRONUNCIATION: shar-PEE-do

HEIGHT:	WEIGHT:	CATEGORY:
1.8 m 5'11"	88.8 kg 195.8 lbs.	Brutal Pokémon

Poni Island

SHARPEDONITE

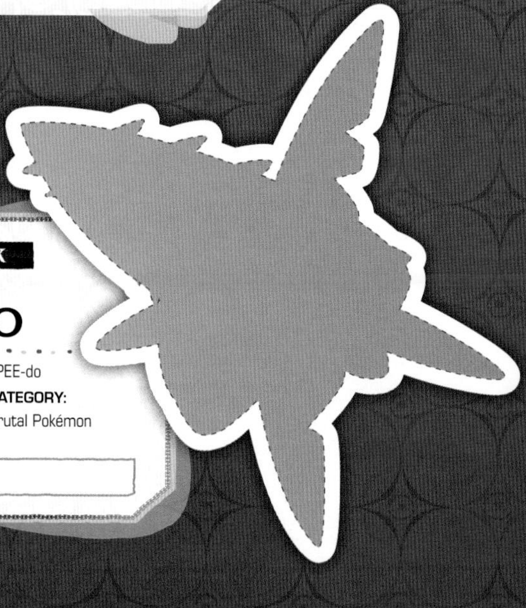

WATER | DARK

MEGA SHARPEDO

PRONUNCIATION: Mega shar-PEE-do

HEIGHT:	WEIGHT:	CATEGORY:
2.5 m 8'02"	130.3 kg 287.3 lbs.	Brutal Pokémon

Poni Island

DRAGON

SHELGON

PRONUNCIATION: SHELL-gon

HEIGHT:	WEIGHT:	CATEGORY:
1.1 m 3'07"	110.5 kg 243.6 lbs.	Endurance Pokémon

Melemele Island

WATER
SHELLDER

PRONUNCIATION: SHELL-der

HEIGHT:	WEIGHT:	CATEGORY:
0.3 m	4.0 kg	Bivalve Pokémon
1'00"	8.8 lbs.	

 Melemele Island

WATER
SHELLOS
EAST SEA

PRONUNCIATION: SHELL-loss

HEIGHT:	WEIGHT:	CATEGORY:
0.3 m	6.3 kg	Sea Slug
1'00"	13.9 lbs.	Pokémon

 Poni Island

ROCK   STEEL
SHIELDON

PRONUNCIATION: SHEEL-don

HEIGHT:	WEIGHT:	CATEGORY:
0.5 m	57.0 kg	Shield Pokémon
1'08"	125.7 lbs.	

Akala Island

GRASS   FAIRY
SHIINOTIC

PRONUNCIATION: shee-NAH-tick

HEIGHT:	WEIGHT:	CATEGORY:
1.0 m	11.5 kg	Illuminating
3'03"	25.4 lbs.	Pokémon

Akala Island

REPEAT BALL

STEEL   FLYING
SKARMORY

PRONUNCIATION: SKAR-more-ree

HEIGHT:	WEIGHT:	CATEGORY:
1.7 m	50.5 kg	Armor Bird
5'07"	111.3 lbs.	Pokémon

 Ula'ula Island

DRAGON
SLIGGOO

PRONUNCIATION: SLIH-goo

HEIGHT:	WEIGHT:	CATEGORY:
0.8 m	17.5 kg	Soft Tissue
2'07"	38.6 lbs.	Pokémon

Akala Island

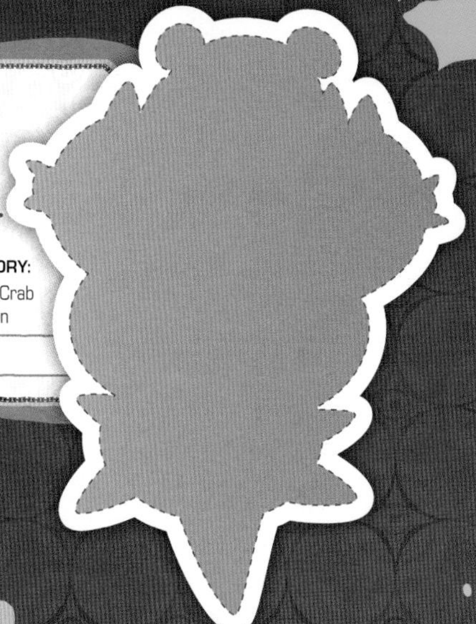

WATER PSYCHIC

MEGA SLOWBRO

PRONUNCIATION: Mega SLOW-bro

HEIGHT:	WEIGHT:	CATEGORY:
2.0 m 6'07"	120.0 kg 264.6 lbs.	Hermit Crab Pokémon

Melemele Island

WATER PSYCHIC

SLOWBRO

PRONUNCIATION: SLOW-bro

HEIGHT:	WEIGHT:	CATEGORY:
1.6 m 5'03"	78.5 kg 173.1 lbs.	Hermit Crab Pokémon

Melemele Island

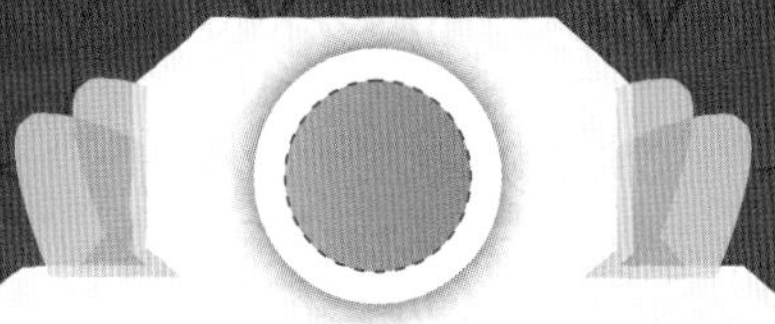

SLOWBRONITE

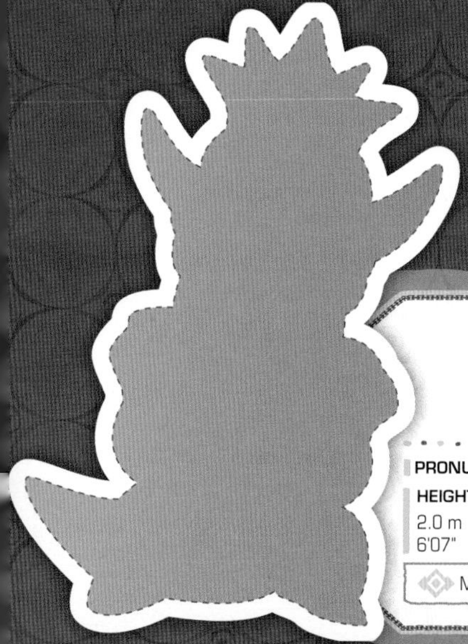

WATER PSYCHIC

SLOWKING

PRONUNCIATION: SLOW-king

HEIGHT:	WEIGHT:	CATEGORY:
2.0 m 6'07"	79.5 kg 175.3 lbs.	Royal Pokémon

Melemele Island

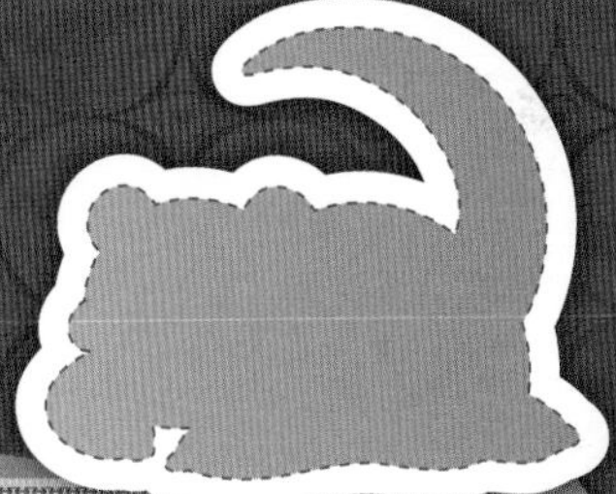

WATER PSYCHIC

SLOWPOKE

PRONUNCIATION: SLOW-poke

HEIGHT:	WEIGHT:	CATEGORY:
1.2 m 3'11"	36.0 kg 79.4 lbs.	Dopey Pokémon

Melemele Island

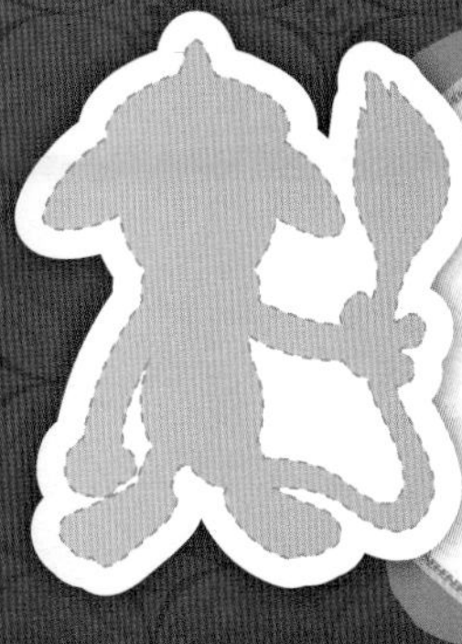

NORMAL

SMEARGLE

PRONUNCIATION: SMEAR-gull

HEIGHT:	WEIGHT:	CATEGORY:
1.2 m 3'11"	58.0 kg 127.9 lbs.	Painter Pokémon

Melemele Island

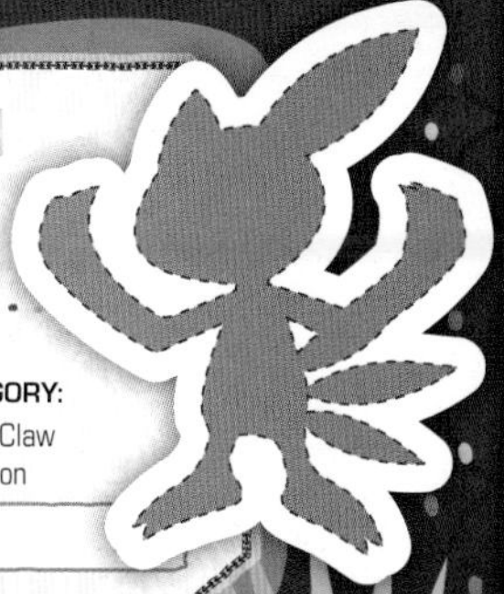

DARK ICE

SNEASEL

PRONUNCIATION: SNEE-zul

HEIGHT:	WEIGHT:	CATEGORY:
0.9 m 2'11"	28.0 kg 61.7 lbs.	Sharp Claw Pokémon

Ula'ula Island

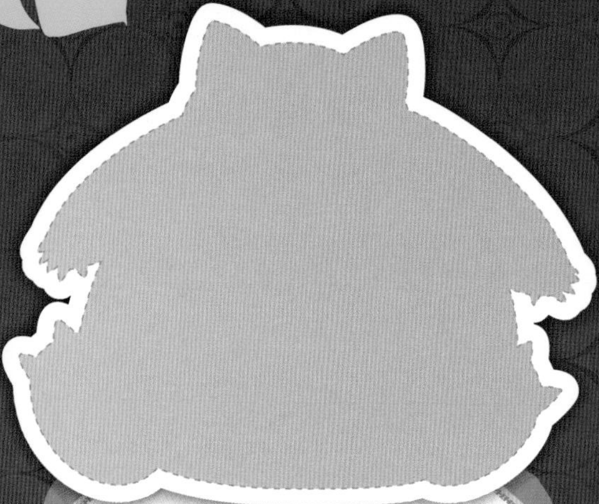

NORMAL

SNORLAX

PRONUNCIATION: SNOR-lacks

HEIGHT:	WEIGHT:	CATEGORY:
2.1 m 6'11"	460.0 kg 1014.1 lbs.	Sleeping Pokémon

Melemele Island

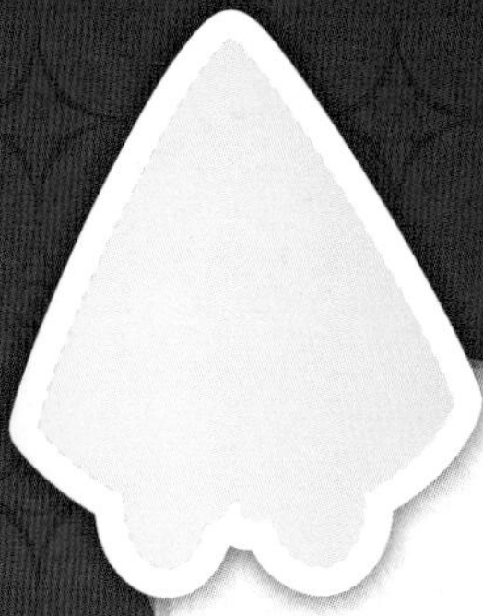

ICE

SNORUNT

PRONUNCIATION: SNOW-runt

HEIGHT:	WEIGHT:	CATEGORY:
0.7 m 2'04"	16.8 kg 37.0 lbs.	Snow Hat Pokémon

Ula'ula Island

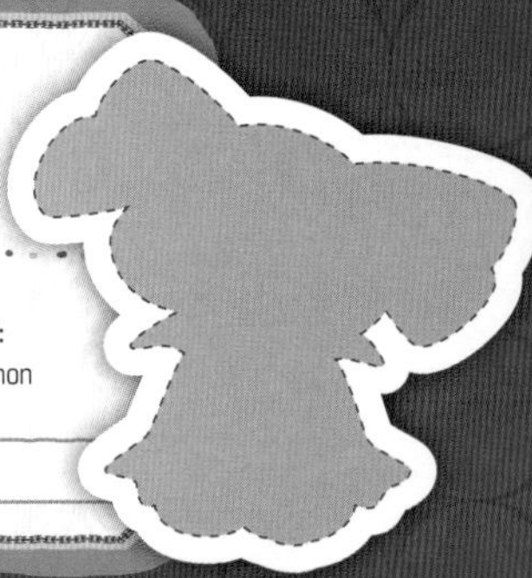

FAIRY

SNUBBULL

PRONUNCIATION: SNUB-bull

HEIGHT:	WEIGHT:	CATEGORY:
0.6 m 2'00"	7.8 kg 17.2 lbs.	Fairy Pokémon

Poni Island

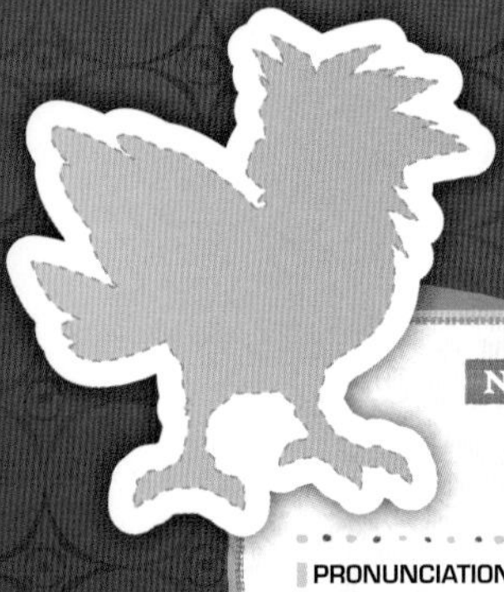

NORMAL FLYING

SPEAROW

PRONUNCIATION: SPEER-oh

HEIGHT:	WEIGHT:	CATEGORY:
0.3 m 1'00"	2.0 kg 4.4 lbs.	Tiny Bird Pokémon

Melemele Island

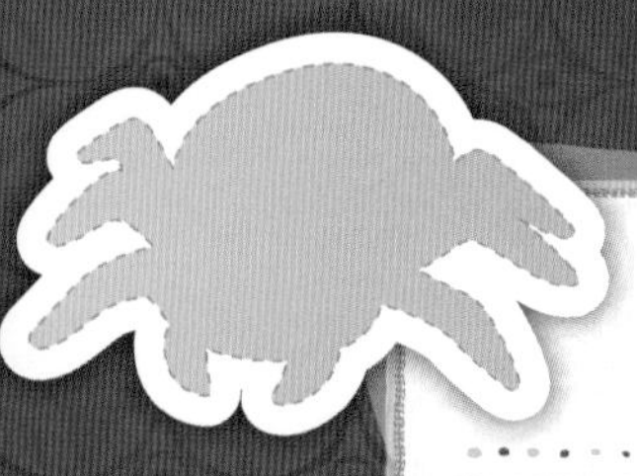

BUG POISON

SPINARAK

PRONUNCIATION: SPIN-uh-rack

HEIGHT:	WEIGHT:	CATEGORY:
0.5 m 1'08"	8.5 kg 18.7 lbs.	String Spit Pokémon

Melemele Island

NORMAL

SPINDA

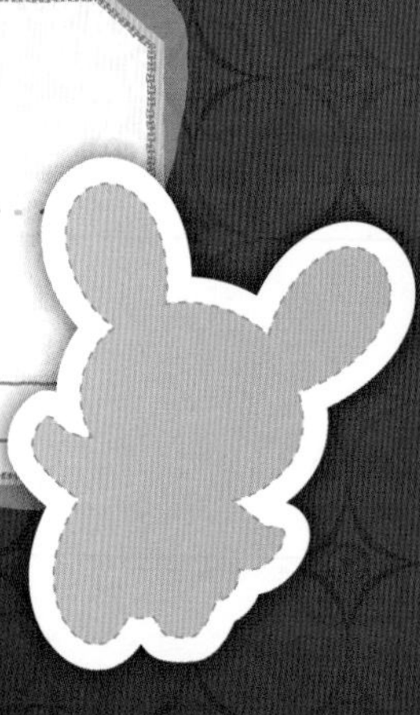

PRONUNCIATION: SPIN-dah

HEIGHT:	WEIGHT:	CATEGORY:
1.1 m 3'07"	5.0 kg 11.0 lbs.	Spot Panda Pokémon

Melemele Island

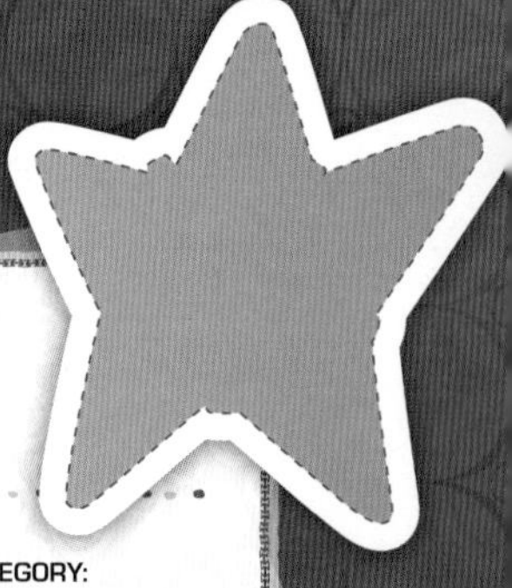

WATER

STARYU

PRONUNCIATION: STAR-you

HEIGHT:	WEIGHT:	CATEGORY:
0.8 m 2'07"	34.5 kg 76.1 lbs.	Star Shape Pokémon

Akala Island

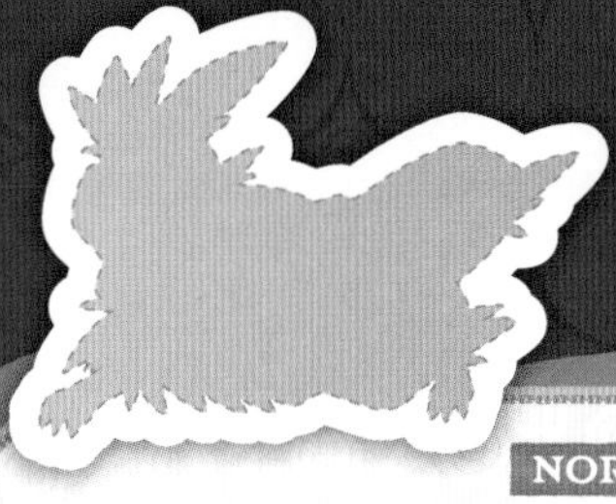

NORMAL

STOUTLAND

PRONUNCIATION: STOWT-lund

HEIGHT:	WEIGHT:	CATEGORY:
1.2 m 3'11"	61.0 kg 134.5 lbs.	Big-Hearted Pokémon

Akala Island

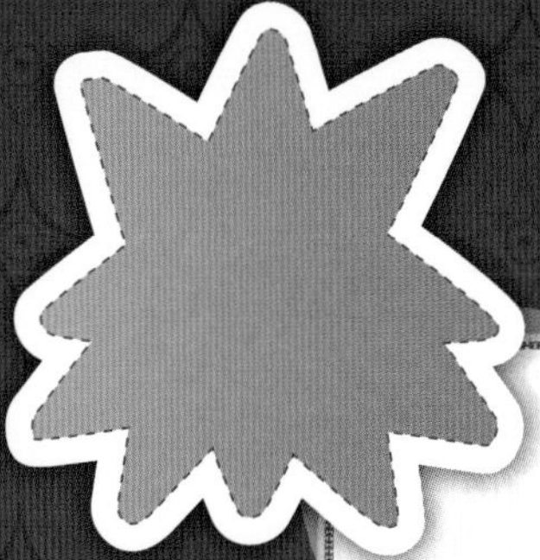

WATER PSYCHIC

STARMIE

PRONUNCIATION: STAR-mee

HEIGHT:	WEIGHT:	CATEGORY:
1.1 m 3'07"	80.0 kg 176.4 lbs.	Mysterious Pokémon

Akala Island

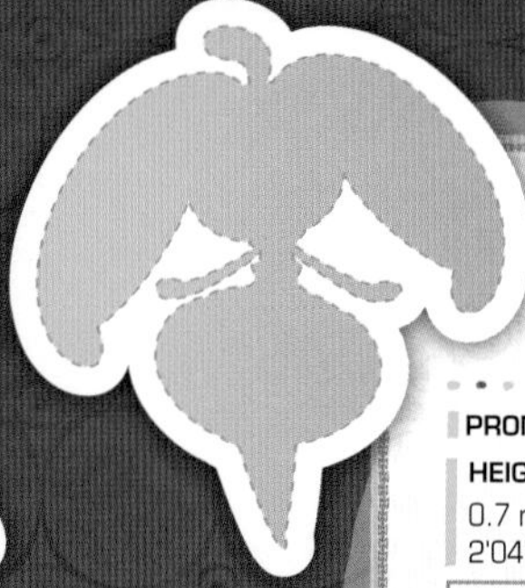

GRASS

STEENEE

PRONUNCIATION: STEE-nee

HEIGHT:	WEIGHT:	CATEGORY:
0.7 m 2'04"	8.2 kg 18.1 lbs.	Fruit Pokémon

Akala Island

ROCK

SUDOWOODO

PRONUNCIATION: SOO-doe-WOO-doe

HEIGHT:	WEIGHT:	CATEGORY:
1.2 m 3'11"	38.0 kg 83.8 lbs.	Imitation Pokémon

Melemele Island

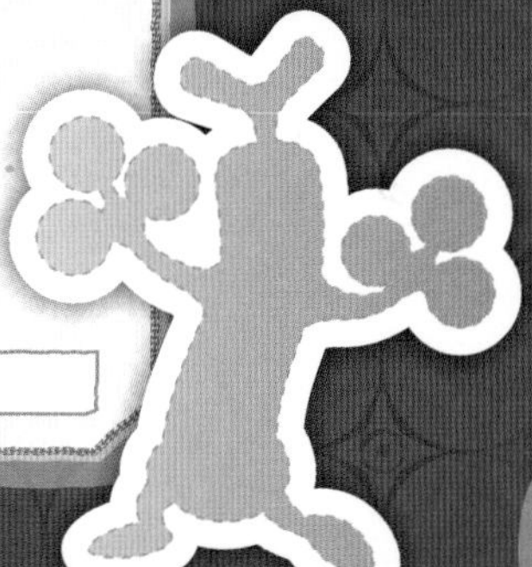

NORMAL FIGHTING

STUFFUL

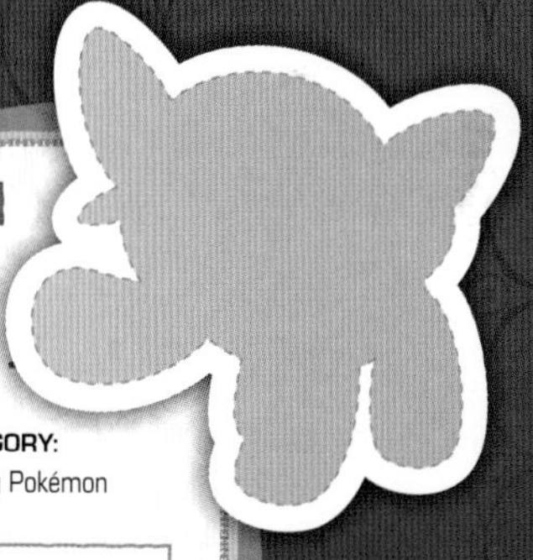

PRONUNCIATION: STUFF-fuhl

HEIGHT:	WEIGHT:	CATEGORY:
0.5 m 1'08"	6.8 kg 15.0 lbs.	Flailing Pokémon

Akala Island

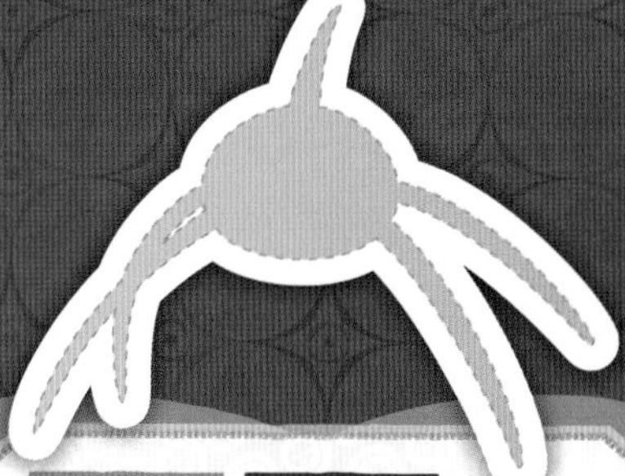

BUG WATER

SURSKIT

PRONUNCIATION: SUR-skit

HEIGHT:	WEIGHT:	CATEGORY:
0.5 m 1'08"	1.7 kg 3.7 lbs.	Pond Skater Pokémon

Akala Island

FAIRY

SYLVEON

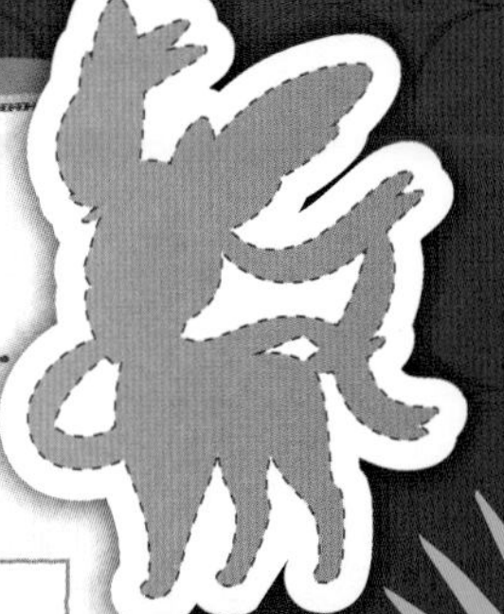

PRONUNCIATION: SIL-vee-on

HEIGHT:	WEIGHT:	CATEGORY:
1.0 m 3'03"	23.5 kg 51.8 lbs.	Intertwining Pokémon

Akala Island

FIRE **FLYING**

TALONFLAME

PRONUNCIATION: TAL-un-flame

HEIGHT:	WEIGHT:	CATEGORY:
1.2 m	24.5 kg	Scorching
3'11"	54.0 lbs.	Pokémon

 Akala Island

NORMAL

TAUROS

PRONUNCIATION: TORE-ros

HEIGHT:	WEIGHT:	CATEGORY:
1.4 m	88.4 kg	Wild Bull
4'07"	194.9 lbs.	Pokémon

 Akala Island

ROTOM POKÉDEX

WATER **POISON**

TENTACRUEL

PRONUNCIATION: TEN-ta-crool

HEIGHT:	WEIGHT:	CATEGORY:
1.6 m	55.0 kg	Jellyfish Pokémon
5'03"	121.3 lbs.	

 Melemele Island

WATER **POISON**

TENTACOOL

PRONUNCIATION: TEN-ta-cool

HEIGHT:	WEIGHT:	CATEGORY:
0.9 m	45.5 kg	Jellyfish Pokémon
2'11"	100.3 lbs.	

Melemele Island

WATER **ROCK**

TIRTOUGA

PRONUNCIATION: teer-TOO-gah

HEIGHT:	WEIGHT:	CATEGORY:
0.7 m	16.5 kg	Prototurtle
2'04"	36.4 lbs.	Pokémon

 Akala Island

ELECTRIC **STEEL**

TOGEDEMARU

PRONUNCIATION: TOH-geh-deh-MAH-roo

HEIGHT:	WEIGHT:	CATEGORY:
0.3 m	3.3 kg	Roly-Poly
1'00"	7.3 lbs.	Pokémon

  Ula'ula Island

FIRE
TORKOAL

PRONUNCIATION: TOR-coal

HEIGHT:	WEIGHT:	CATEGORY:
0.5 m	80.4 kg	Coal Pokémon
1'08"	177.2 lbs.	

◆ Ula'ula Island

FIRE
TORRACAT

PRONUNCIATION: TOR-ruh-cat

HEIGHT:	WEIGHT:	CATEGORY:
0.7 m	25.0 kg	Fire Cat Pokémon
2'04"	55.1 lbs.	

◆ Melemele Island

NORMAL FLYING
TOUCANNON

PRONUNCIATION: too-CAN-nun

HEIGHT:	WEIGHT:	CATEGORY:
1.1 m	26.0 kg	Cannon Pokémon
3'07"	57.3 lbs.	

◆ Melemele Island

GROUND
TRAPINCH

PRONUNCIATION: TRAP-inch

HEIGHT:	WEIGHT:	CATEGORY:
0.7 m	15.0 kg	Ant Pit Pokémon
2'04"	33.1 lbs.	

◆ Ula'ula Island

POISON WATER
TOXAPEX

PRONUNCIATION: TOX-uh-pex

HEIGHT:	WEIGHT:	CATEGORY:
0.7 m	14.5 kg	Brutal Star
2'04"	32.0 lbs.	Pokémon

◆ Melemele Island

POISON
TRUBBISH

PRONUNCIATION: TRUB-bish

HEIGHT:	WEIGHT:	CATEGORY:
0.6 m	31.0 kg	Trash Bag
2'00"	68.3 lbs.	Pokémon

◆ Ula'ula Island

GHOST GRASS
TREVENANT

PRONUNCIATION: TREV-uh-nunt

HEIGHT:	WEIGHT:	CATEGORY:
1.5 m	71.0 kg	Elder Tree
4'11"	156.5 lbs.	Pokémon

◆ Akala Island

NORMAL   FLYING
TRUMBEAK

PRONUNCIATION: TRUM-beak

HEIGHT:	WEIGHT:	CATEGORY:
0.6 m	14.8 kg	Bugle Beak
2'00"	32.6 lbs.	Pokémon

Melemele Island

SITRUS BERRY

GRASS
TSAREENA

PRONUNCIATION: zar-EE-nuh

HEIGHT:	WEIGHT:	CATEGORY:
1.2 m	21.4 kg	Fruit Pokémon
3'11"	47.2 lbs.	

Akala Island

FIRE   DRAGON
TURTONATOR

PRONUNCIATION: TURT-nay-ter

HEIGHT:	WEIGHT:	CATEGORY:
2.0 m	212.0 kg	Blast Turtle
6'07"	467.4 lbs.	Pokémon

Ula'ula Island

DARK
UMBREON

PRONUNCIATION: UM-bree-on

HEIGHT:	WEIGHT:	CATEGORY:
1.0 m	27.0 kg	Moonlight
3'03"	59.5 lbs.	Pokémon

Akala Island

ICE
VANILLISH

PRONUNCIATION: vuh-NIHL-lish

HEIGHT:	WEIGHT:	CATEGORY:
1.1 m	41.0 kg	Icy Snow
3'07"	90.4 lbs.	Pokémon

Ula'ula Island

ICE
VANILLITE

PRONUNCIATION: vuh-NIHL-lyte

HEIGHT:	WEIGHT:	CATEGORY:
0.4 m	5.7 kg	Fresh Snow
1'04"	12.6 lbs.	Pokémon

Ula'ula Island

WATER
VAPOREON

PRONUNCIATION: vay-POUR-ree-on

HEIGHT:	WEIGHT:	CATEGORY:
1.0 m	29.0 kg	Bubble Jet
3'03"	63.9 lbs.	Pokémon

Akala Island

ICE
VANILLUXE

PRONUNCIATION: vuh-NIHL-lux

HEIGHT:	WEIGHT:	CATEGORY:
1.3 m	57.5 kg	Snowstorm
4'03"	126.8 lbs.	Pokémon

Ula'ula Island

TAMATO BERRY

GROUND DRAGON
VIBRAVA

PRONUNCIATION: VY-BRAH-va

HEIGHT:	WEIGHT:	CATEGORY:
1.1 m	15.3 kg	Vibration
3'07"	33.7 lbs.	Pokémon

Ula'ula Island

BUG ELECTRIC
VIKAVOLT

PRONUNCIATION: VIE-kuh-volt

HEIGHT:	WEIGHT:	CATEGORY:
1.5 m	45.0 kg	Levitate Pokémon
4'11"	99.2 lbs.	

Melemele Island

DARK FLYING
VULLABY

PRONUNCIATION: VUL-luh-bye

HEIGHT:	WEIGHT:	CATEGORY:
0.5 m	9.0 kg	Diapered
1'08"	19.8 lbs.	Pokémon

Melemele Island

TIMER BALL

ICE
VULPIX
ALOLA FORM

PRONUNCIATION: VULL-picks

HEIGHT:	WEIGHT:	CATEGORY:
0.6 m	9.9 kg	Fox Pokémon
2'00"	21.8 lbs.	

Ula'ula Island

V | ALOLA REGION STICKER BOOK

49

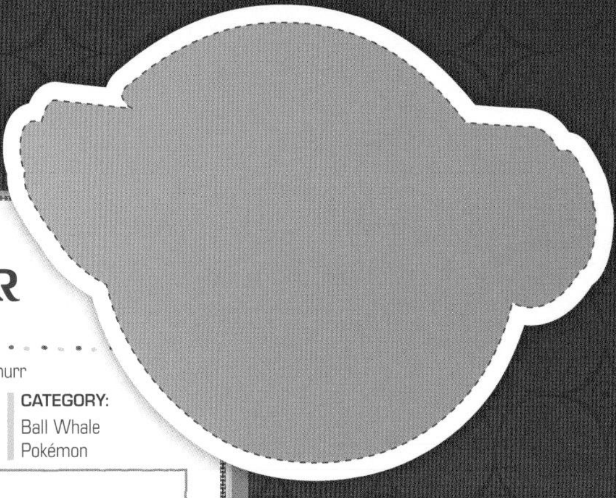

ULTRA BALL

WATER

WAILMER

PRONUNCIATION: WAIL-murr

HEIGHT:	WEIGHT:	CATEGORY:
2.0 m 6'07"	130.0 kg 286.6 lbs.	Ball Whale Pokémon

Poni Island

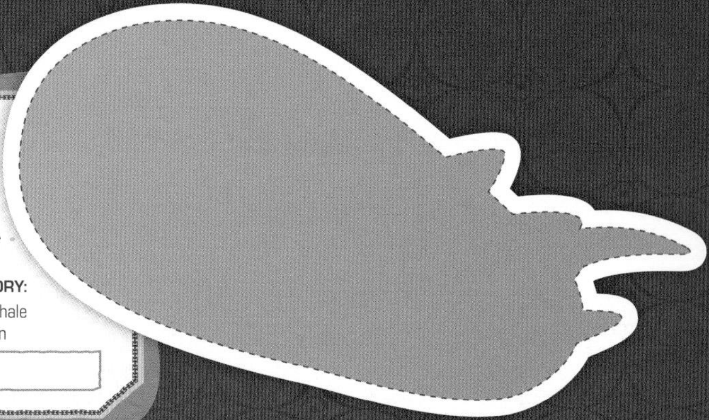

WATER

WAILORD

PRONUNCIATION: WAIL-ord

HEIGHT:	WEIGHT:	CATEGORY:
14.5 m 47'07"	398.0 kg 877.4 lbs.	Float Whale Pokémon

Poni Island

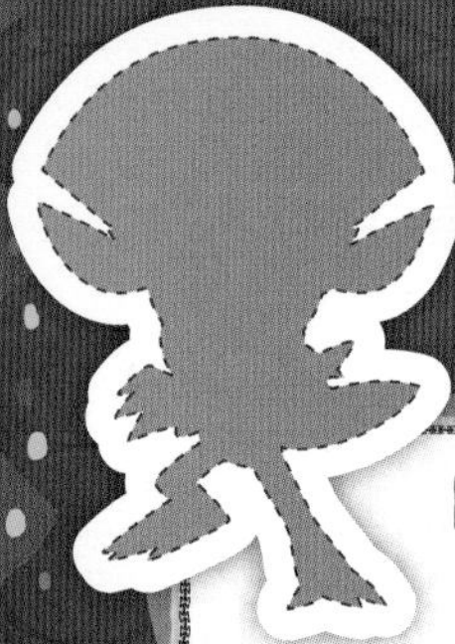

DARK ICE

WEAVILE

PRONUNCIATION: WEE-vile

HEIGHT:	WEIGHT:	CATEGORY:
1.1 m 3'07"	34.0 kg 75.0 lbs.	Sharp Claw Pokémon

Ula'ula Island

GRASS FAIRY

WHIMSICOTT

PRONUNCIATION: WHIM-sih-kot

HEIGHT:	WEIGHT:	CATEGORY:
0.7 m 2'04"	6.6 kg 14.6 lbs.	Windveiled Pokémon

Melemele Island

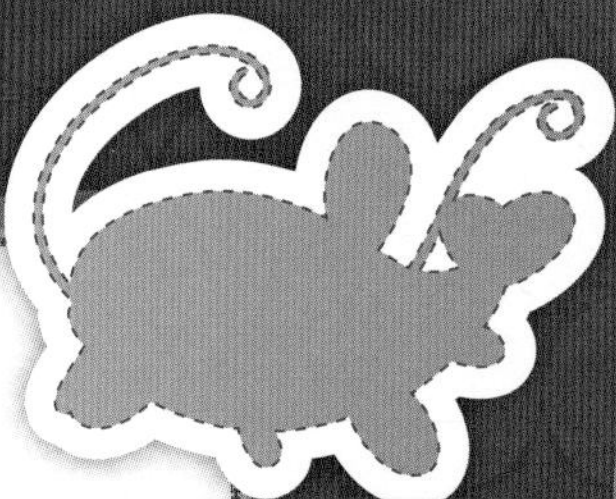

WATER GROUND

WHISCASH

PRONUNCIATION: WISS-cash

HEIGHT:	WEIGHT:	CATEGORY:
0.9 m 2'11"	23.6 kg 52.0 lbs.	Whiskers Pokémon

Melemele Island

NORMAL FAIRY

WIGGLYTUFF

PRONUNCIATION: WIG-lee-tuff

HEIGHT:	WEIGHT:	CATEGORY:
1.0 m 3'03"	12.0 kg 26.5 lbs.	Balloon Pokémon

Akala Island

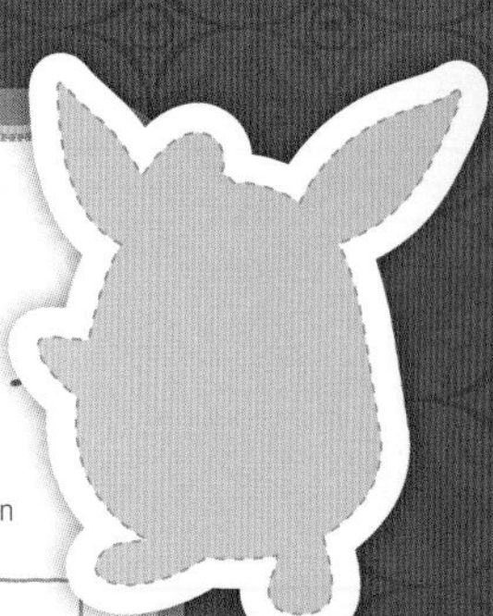

WATER **FLYING**

WINGULL

PRONUNCIATION: WING-gull

HEIGHT:	WEIGHT:	CATEGORY:
0.6 m	9.5 kg	Seagull Pokémon
2'00"	20.9 lbs.	

Melemele Island

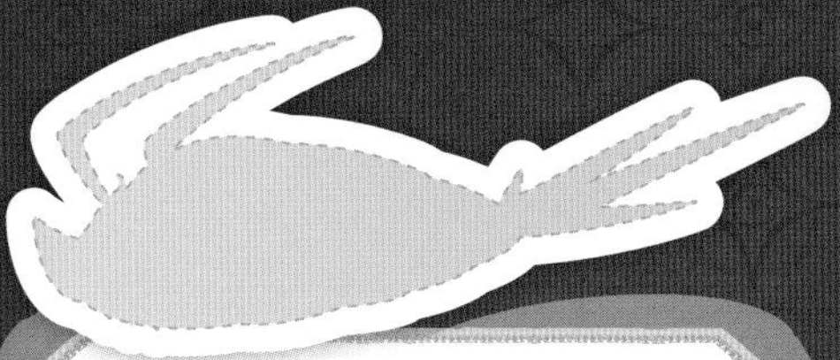

BUG **WATER**

WIMPOD

PRONUNCIATION: WIM-pod

HEIGHT:	WEIGHT:	CATEGORY:
0.5 m	12.0 kg	Turn Tail
1'08"	26.5 lbs.	Pokémon

Akala Island

Z-RING

WATER

WISHIWASHI
SOLO FORM

PRONUNCIATION: WISH-ee-WASH-ee

HEIGHT:	WEIGHT:	CATEGORY:
0.2 m	0.3 kg	Small Fry
0'08"	0.7 lbs.	Pokémon

Melemele Island

WATER

WISHIWASHI
SCHOOL FORM

PRONUNCIATION: WISH-ee-WASH-ee

HEIGHT:	WEIGHT:	CATEGORY:
8.2 m	78.6 kg	Small Fry
26'11"	173.3 lbs.	Pokémon

Melemele Island

NORMAL

YUNGOOS

PRONUNCIATION: YUNG-goose

HEIGHT:	WEIGHT:	CATEGORY:
0.4 m	6.0 kg	Loitering
1'04"	13.2 lbs.	Pokémon

Melemele Island

POISON **FLYING**

ZUBAT

PRONUNCIATION: ZOO-bat

HEIGHT:	WEIGHT:	CATEGORY:
0.8 m	7.5 kg	Bat Pokémon
2'07"	16.5 lbs.	

Melemele Island

SAY HELLO TO LEGENDARY POKÉMON— INCLUDING THE ISLAND GUARDIANS!

Four Legendary Pokémon are the guardians of the various islands of the Alola region. Tapu Koko, the guardian of Melemele Island, is quick to anger and quick to forget. Tapu Lele loves the sweet-smelling flowers of Akala Island. Tapu Bulu, who can control vines and plants, guards Ula'ula Island. Finally, Tapu Fini purifies water and can call up a thick fog when needed to guard Poni Island. Alola's magnificent Legendary Pokémon include the dusty little Cosmog and the incredibly heavy Cosmoem—who evolves into the Legendary Solgaleo and Lunala. Strangest of all, perhaps, are the Legendary Zygarde, who has many impressive forms, and the Mythical Magearna, the Pokémon with the Soul-Heart at its core.

GRASS   FAIRY
TAPU BULU

PRONUNCIATION: TAH-poo BOO-loo

HEIGHT:	WEIGHT:	CATEGORY:
1.9 m	45.5 kg	Land Spirit
6'03"	100.3 lbs.	Pokémon

Ula'ula Island Guardian

WATER   FAIRY
TAPU FINI

PRONUNCIATION: TAH-poo FEE-nee

HEIGHT:	WEIGHT:	CATEGORY:
1.3 m	21.2 kg	Land Spirit
4'03"	46.7 lbs.	Pokémon

Poni Island Guardian

ELECTRIC   FAIRY
TAPU KOKO

PRONUNCIATION: TAH-poo KO-ko

HEIGHT:	WEIGHT:	CATEGORY:
1.8 m	20.5 kg	Land Spirit
5'11"	45.2 lbs.	Pokémon

Melemele Island Guardian

PSYCHIC   FAIRY
TAPU LELE

PRONUNCIATION: TAH-poo LEH-leh

HEIGHT:	WEIGHT:	CATEGORY:
1.2 m	18.6 kg	Land Spirit
3'11"	41.0 lbs.	Pokémon

Akala Island Guardian

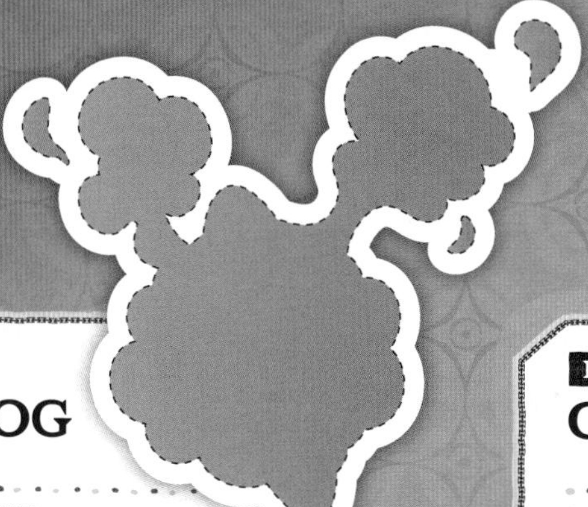

PSYCHIC

COSMOG

PRONUNCIATION: KOZ-mog

HEIGHT:	WEIGHT:	CATEGORY:
0.2 m 0'08"	0.1 kg 0.2 lbs.	Nebula Pokémon

Legendary Pokémon

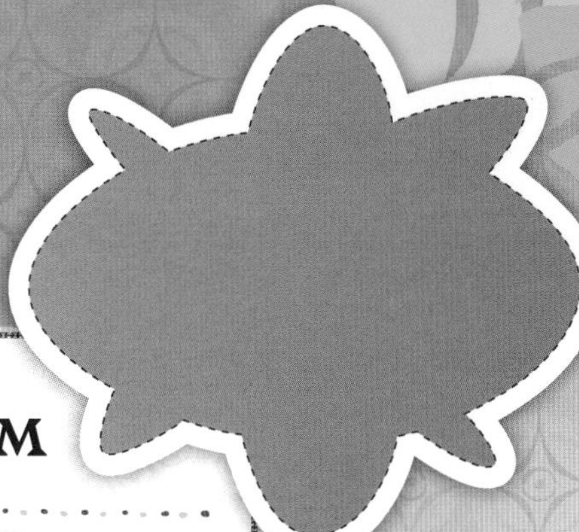

PSYCHIC

COSMOEM

PRONUNCIATION: KOZ-mo-em

HEIGHT:	WEIGHT:	CATEGORY:
0.1 m 0'04"	999.9 kg 2204.4 lbs.	Protostar Pokémon

Legendary Pokémon

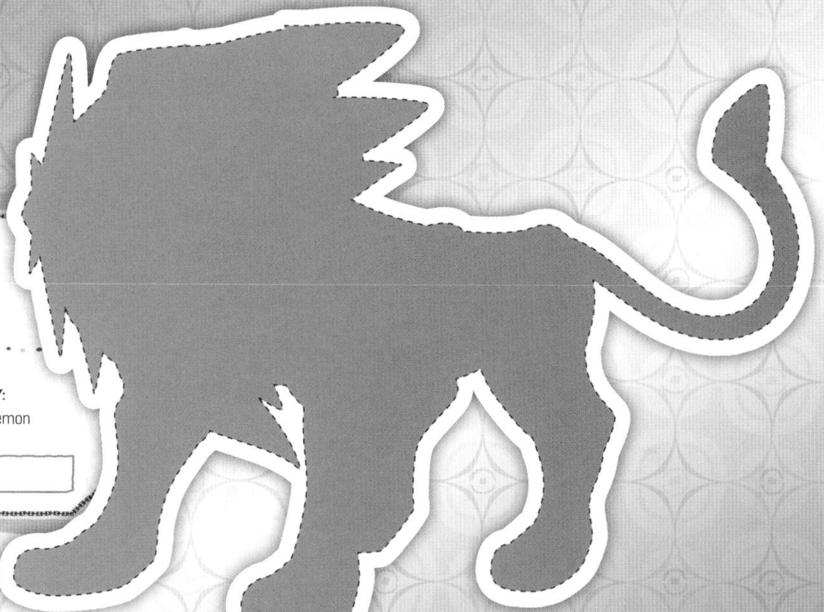

PSYCHIC STEEL

SOLGALEO

PRONUNCIATION: SOUL-gah-LAY-oh

HEIGHT:	WEIGHT:	CATEGORY:
3.4 m 11'02"	230.0 kg 507.1 lbs.	Sunne Pokémon

Legendary Pokémon

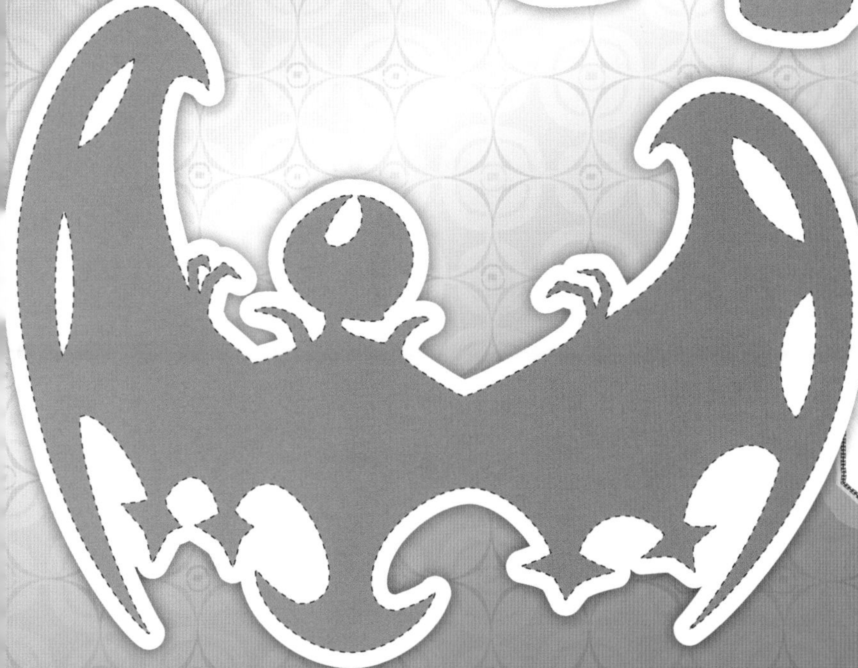

PSYCHIC GHOST

LUNALA

PRONUNCIATION: loo-NAH-luh

HEIGHT:	WEIGHT:	CATEGORY:
4.0 m 13'01"	120.0 kg 264.6 lbs.	Moone Pokémon

Legendary Pokémon

DRAGON	GROUND

ZYGARDE
10% FORME

PRONUNCIATION: ZY-gard

HEIGHT:	WEIGHT:	CATEGORY:
1.2 m	33.5 kg	Order Pokémon
3'11"	73.9 lbs.	

Legendary Pokémon

DRAGON	GROUND

ZYGARDE
50% FORME

PRONUNCIATION: ZY-gard

HEIGHT:	WEIGHT:	CATEGORY:
5.0 m	305.0 kg	Order Pokémon
16'05"	672.4 lbs.	

Legendary Pokémon

ZYGARDE CORE

DRAGON	GROUND

ZYGARDE
COMPLETE FORME

PRONUNCIATION: ZY-gard

HEIGHT:	WEIGHT:	CATEGORY:
4.5 m	610.0 kg	Order Pokémon
14'09"	1344.8 lbs.	

Legendary Pokémon

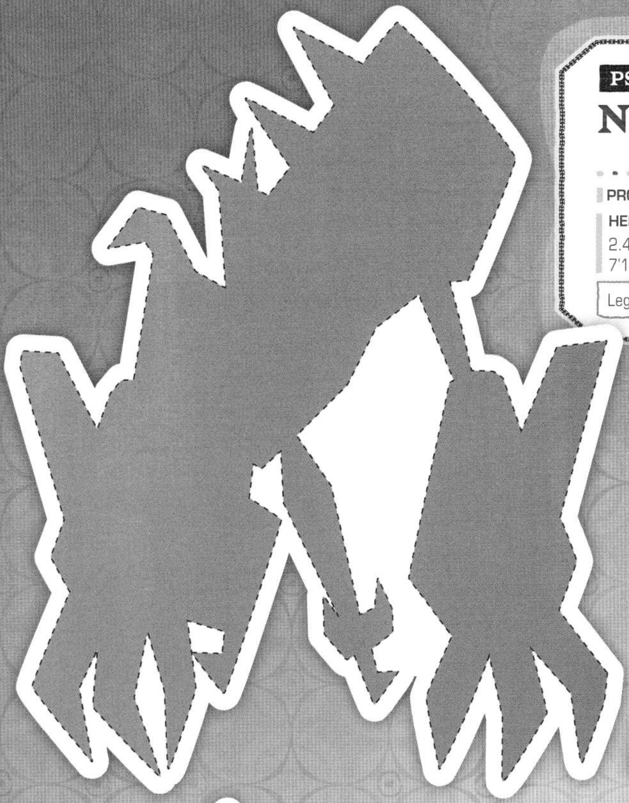

PSYCHIC

NECROZMA

PRONUNCIATION: neh-KROHZ-muh

HEIGHT:	WEIGHT:	CATEGORY:
2.4 m 7'10"	230.0 kg 507.1 lbs.	Prism Pokémon

Legendary Pokémon

NORMAL

TYPE: NULL

PRONUNCIATION: TYPE NULL

HEIGHT:	WEIGHT:	CATEGORY:
1.9 m 6'03"	120.5 kg 265.7 lbs.	Synthetic Pokémon

Legendary Pokémon

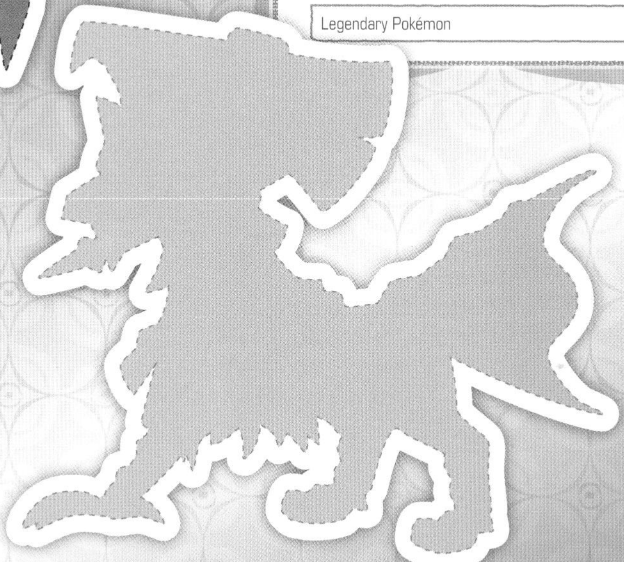

NORMAL

SILVALLY

PRONUNCIATION: sill-VAL-lie

HEIGHT:	WEIGHT:	CATEGORY:
2.3 m 7'07"	100.5 kg 221.6 lbs.	Synthetic Pokémon

Legendary Pokémon

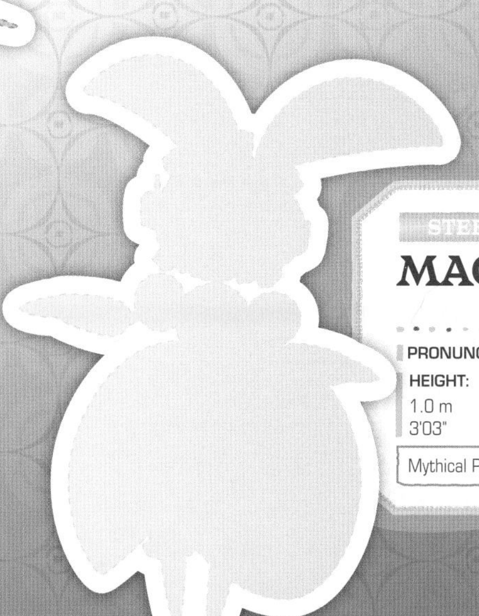

STEEL FAIRY

MAGEARNA

PRONUNCIATION: muh-GEER-nuh

HEIGHT:	WEIGHT:	CATEGORY:
1.0 m 3'03"	80.5 kg 177.5 lbs.	Artificial Pokémon

Mythical Pokémon

THE ULTRA BEASTS APPEAR!

Ultra Beasts are ultra rare, but sometimes they appear from an Ultra Wormhole—or in an ultra-cool sticker collection! This book includes the parasitic Nihilego, mighty Buzzwole, speedy Pheromosa, electrical Xurkitree, explosive Celesteela, sharp-edged Kartana, and the gluttonous Guzzlord, which eats just about everything, including whole buildings!

Ultra Beasts are strange, powerful, and mysterious, and they're included here as oversize stickers. It's a rare opportunity to see all these Pokémon from another dimension at once!

DARK	DRAGON

GUZZLORD

PRONUNCIATION: GUZZ-lord

HEIGHT:	WEIGHT:	CATEGORY:
5.5 m	888.0 kg	Junkivore
18'01"	1957.7 lbs.	Pokémon

Ultra Beast

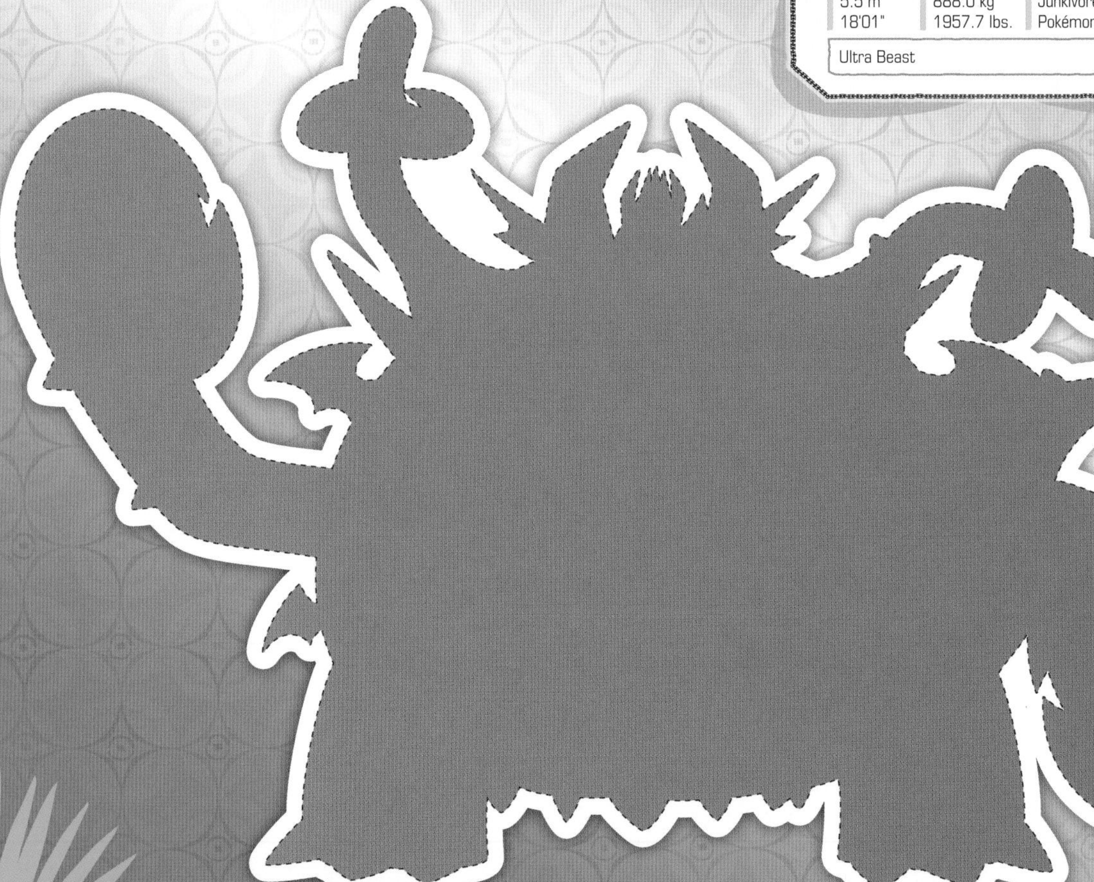

BUG FIGHTING

BUZZWOLE

PRONUNCIATION: BUZZ-wole

HEIGHT:	WEIGHT:	CATEGORY:
2.4 m 7'10"	333.6 kg 735.5 lbs.	Swollen Pokémon

Ultra Beast

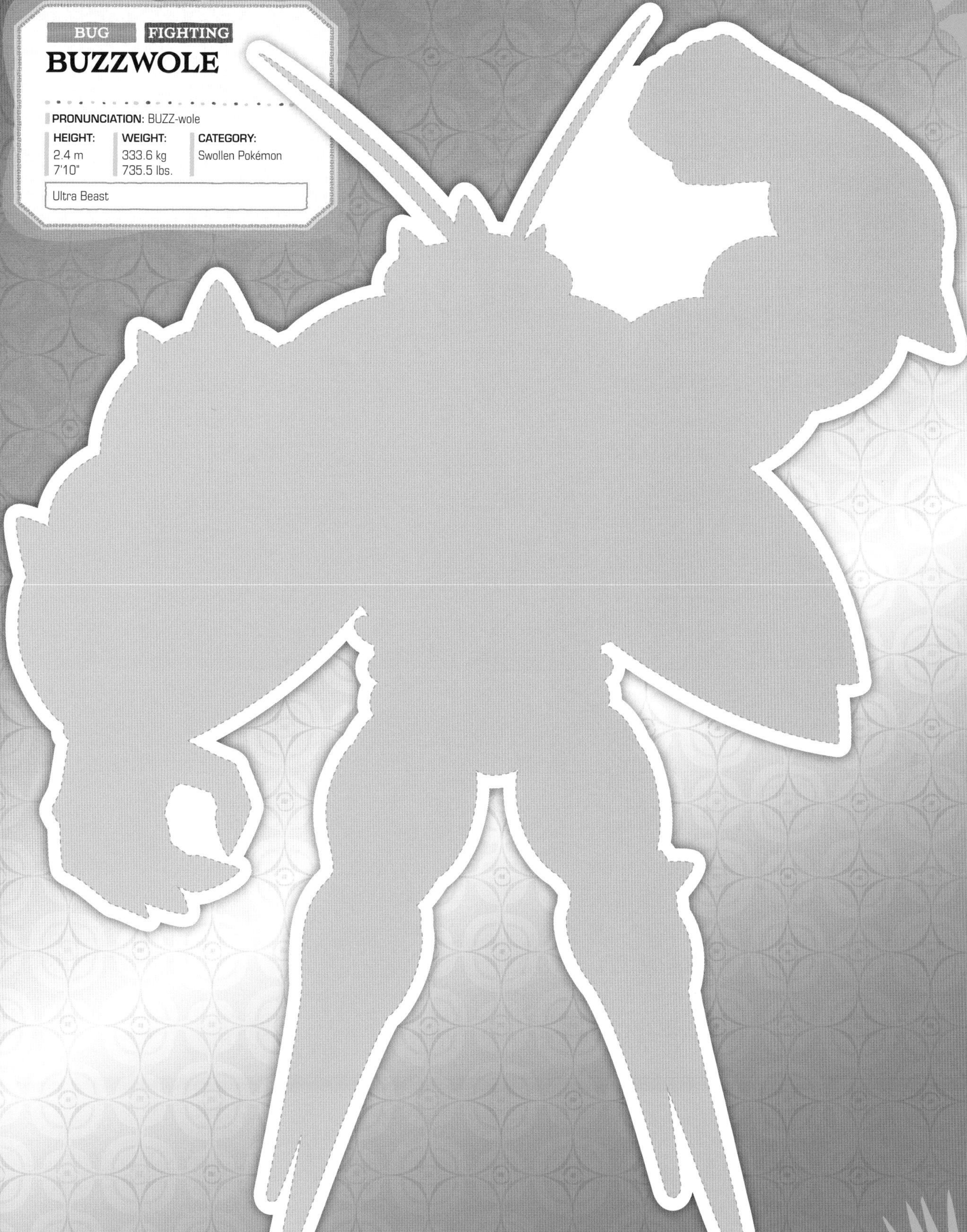

GRASS STEEL

KARTANA

PRONUNCIATION: kar-TAH-nuh

HEIGHT:	WEIGHT:	CATEGORY:
0.3 m 1'00"	0.1 kg 0.2 lbs.	Drawn Sword Pokémon

Ultra Beast

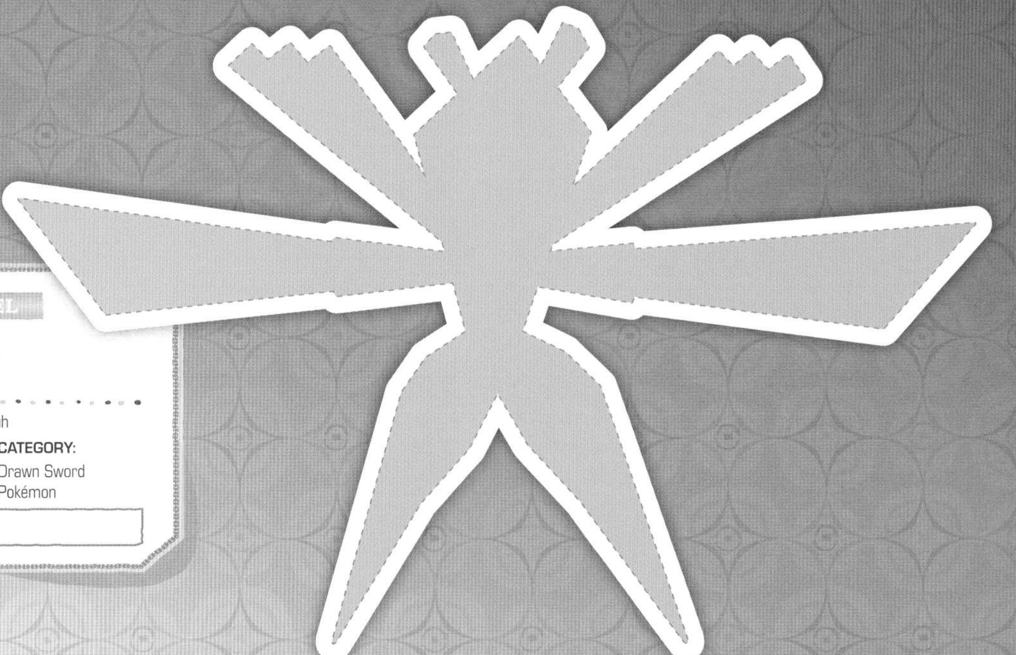

STEEL FLYING

CELESTEELA

PRONUNCIATION: sell-uh-STEEL-uh

HEIGHT:	WEIGHT:	CATEGORY:
9.2 m 30'02"	999.9 kg 2204.4 lbs.	Launch Pokémon

Ultra Beast

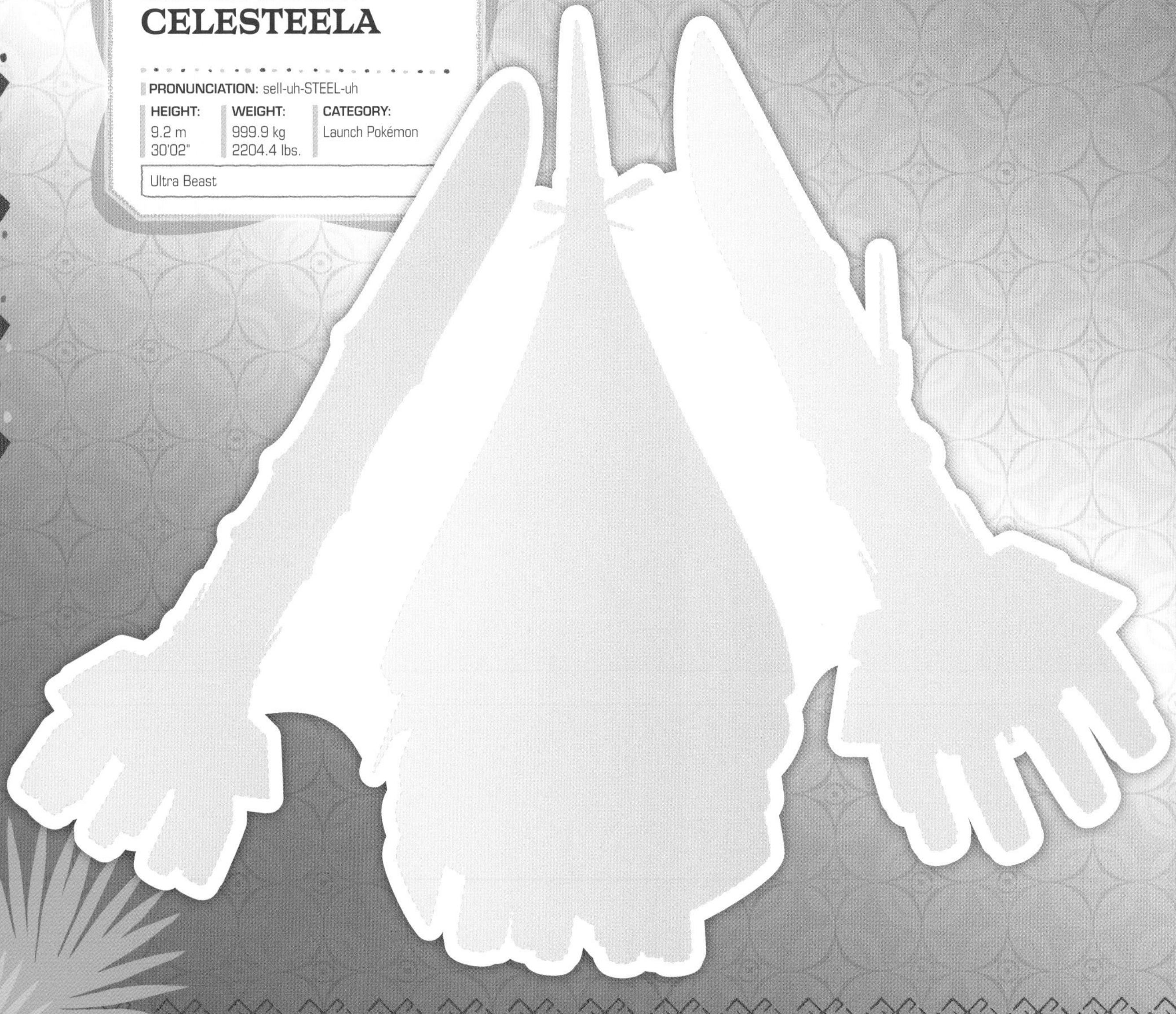

ROCK **POISON**

NIHILEGO

PRONUNCIATION: NIE-uh-LEE-go

HEIGHT:	WEIGHT:	CATEGORY:
1.2 m	55.5 kg	Parasite
3'11"	122.4 lbs.	Pokémon

Ultra Beast

BUG **FIGHTING**

PHEROMOSA

PRONUNCIATION: fair-uh-MO-suh

HEIGHT:	WEIGHT:	CATEGORY:
1.8 m	25.0 kg	Lissome
5'11"	55.1 lbs.	Pokémon

Ultra Beast

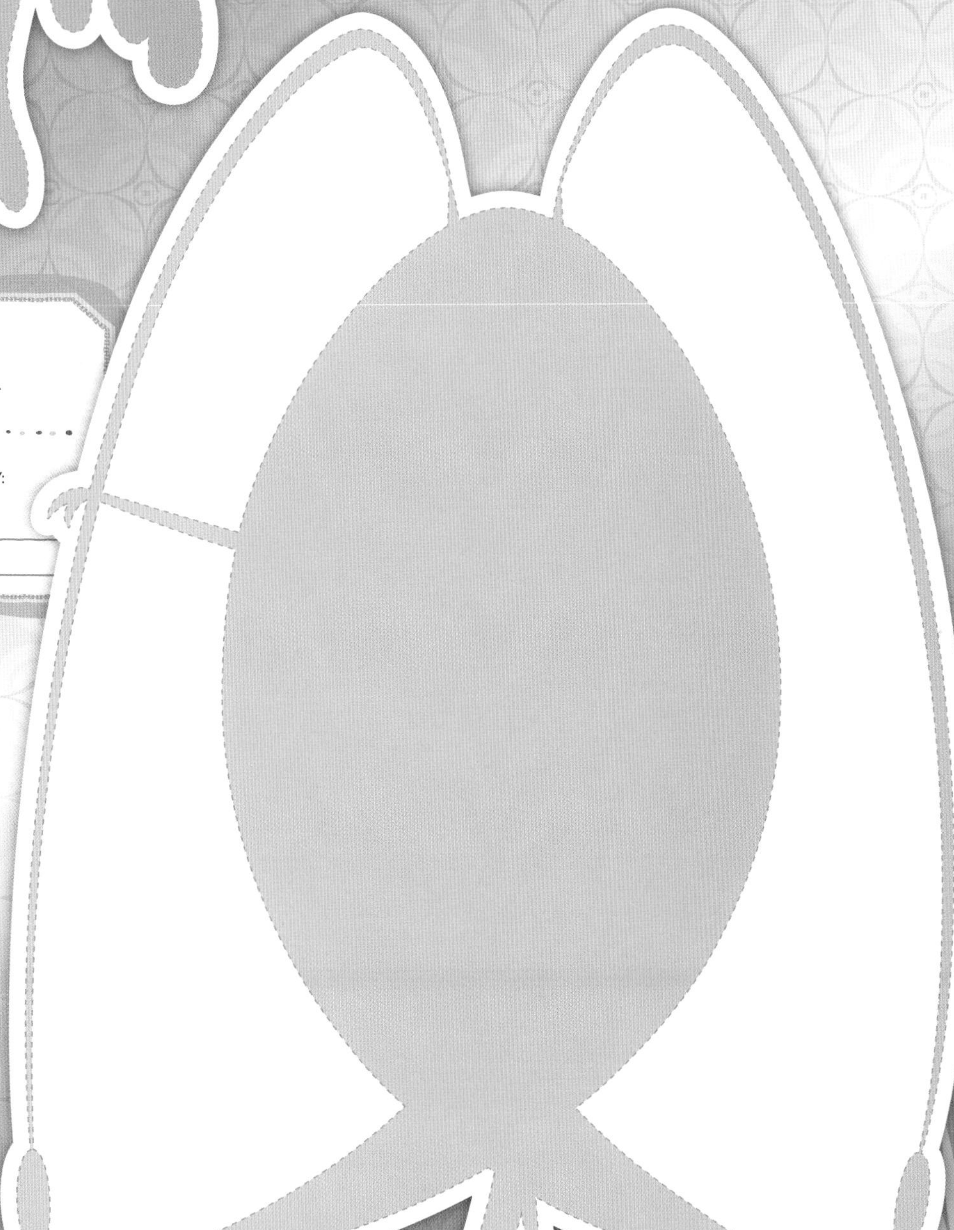

ELECTRIC

XURKITREE

PRONUNCIATION: ZURK-ih-tree

HEIGHT:	**WEIGHT:**	**CATEGORY:**
3.8 m 12'06"	100.0 kg 220.5 lbs.	Glowing Pokémon

Ultra Beast

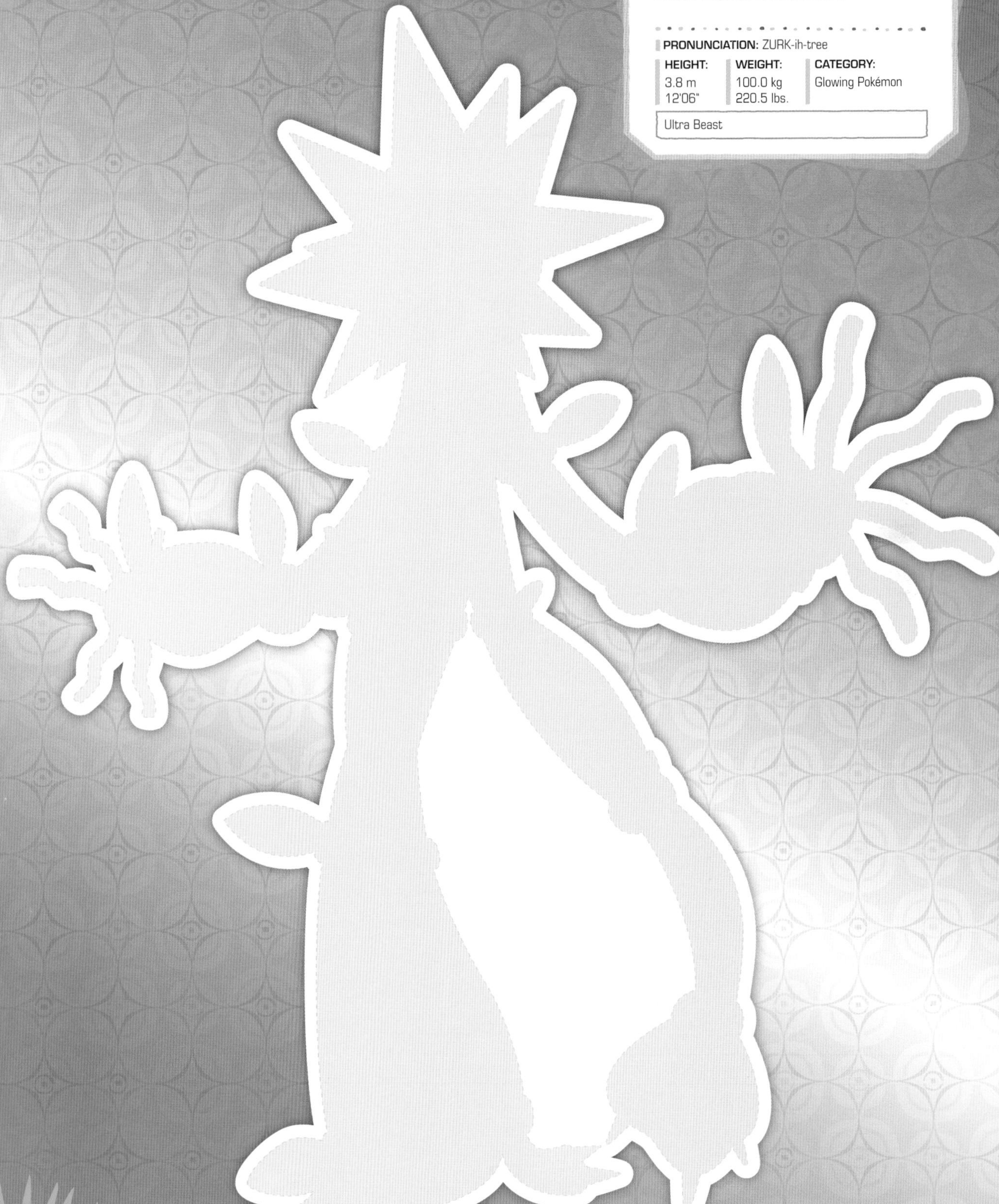

POKÉMON STICKERS

⬆ ABSOL

⬆ ABRA

⬆ MEGA ALAKAZAM

⬆ MEGA ABSOL

⬆ ALAKAZAM

⬆ ARCHEN

ARCHEOPS ⬆

⬆ AERODACTYL

⬆ ALOMOMOLA

MEGA AERODACTYL ➡

ARCANINE ➡

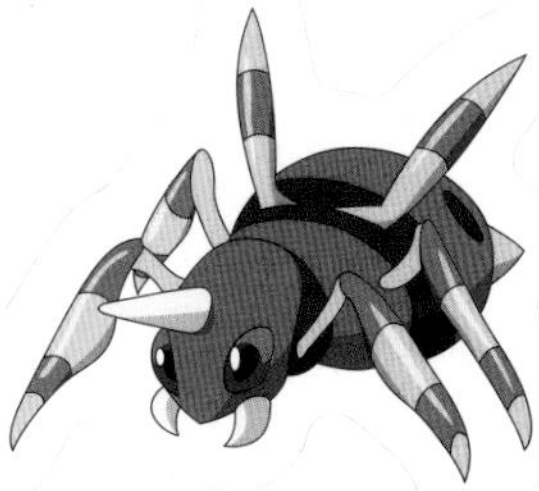

↑ ARIADOS

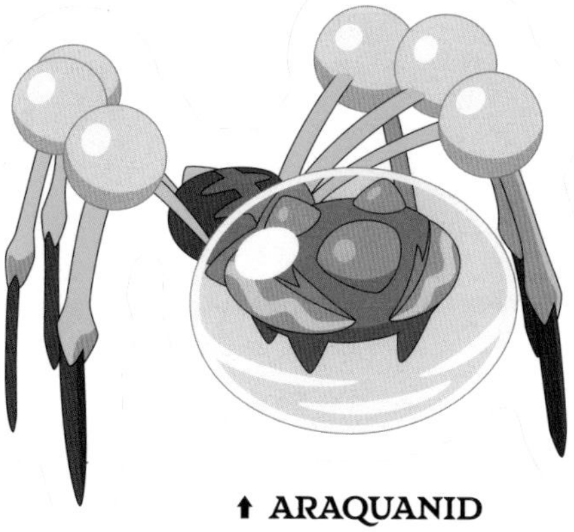

↑ ARAQUANID

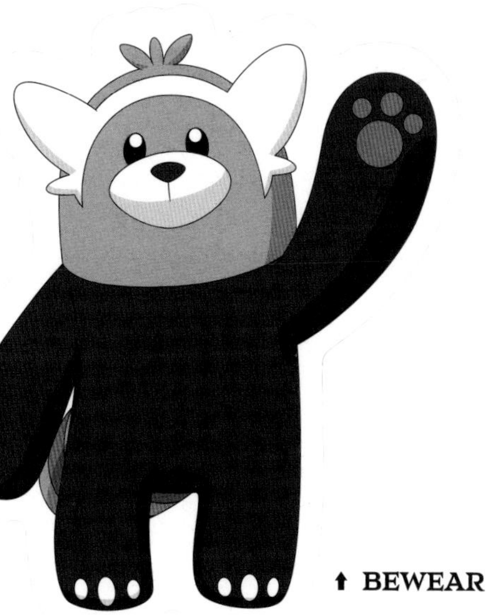

↑ BEWEAR

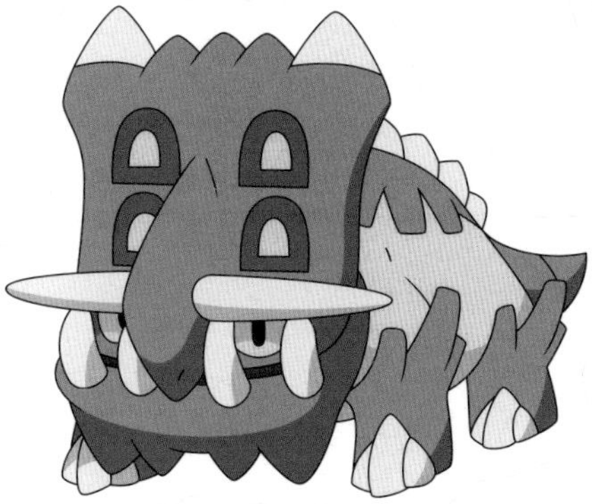

↑ BASTIODON

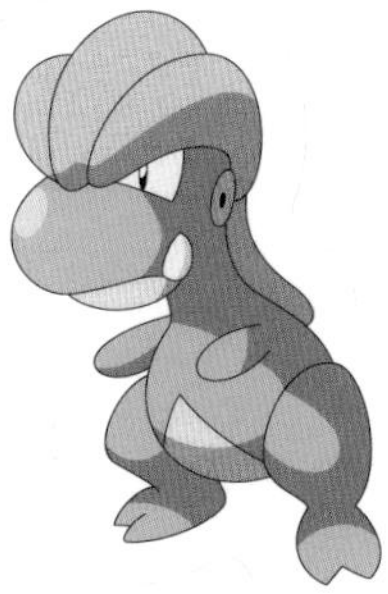

↑ BAGON

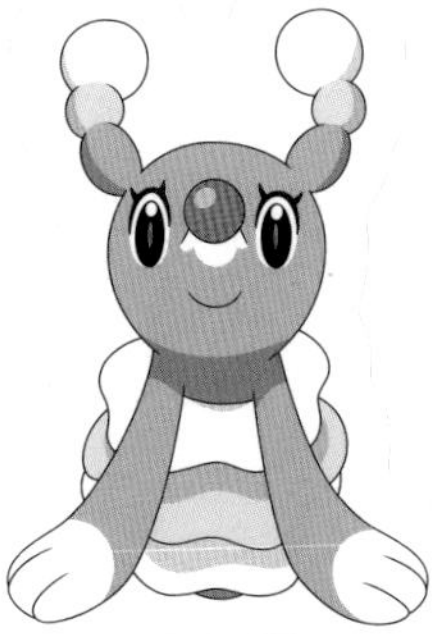

↑ BRIONNE

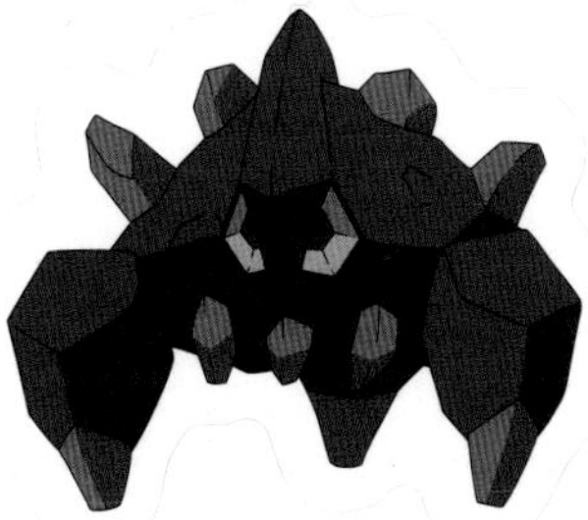

↑ BOLDORE

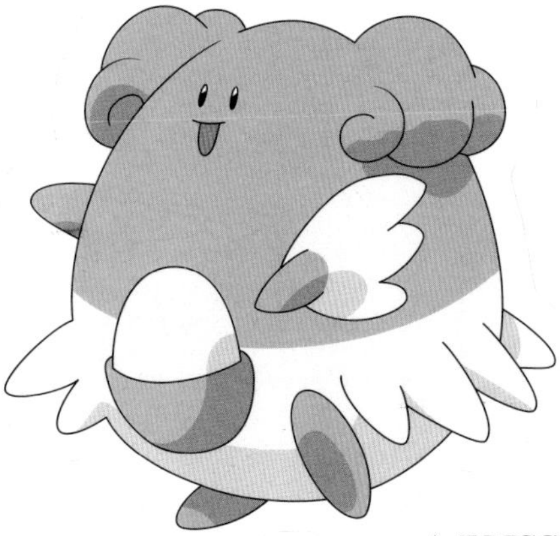

↑ BLISSEY

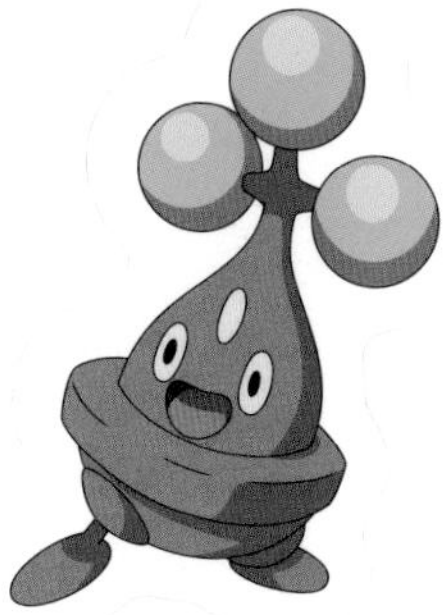

↑ BONSLY

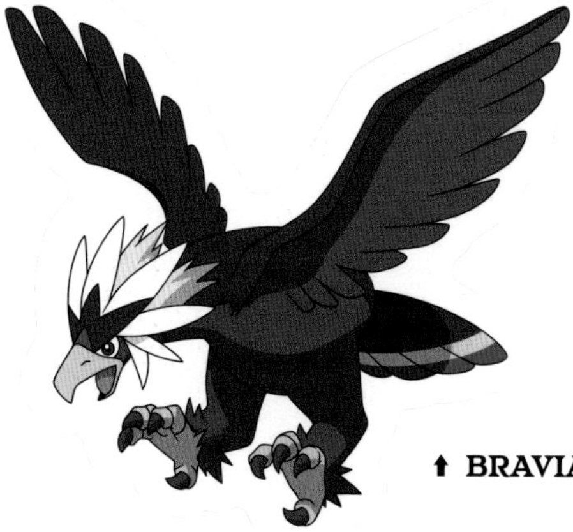

↑ BRAVIARY

← BELDUM

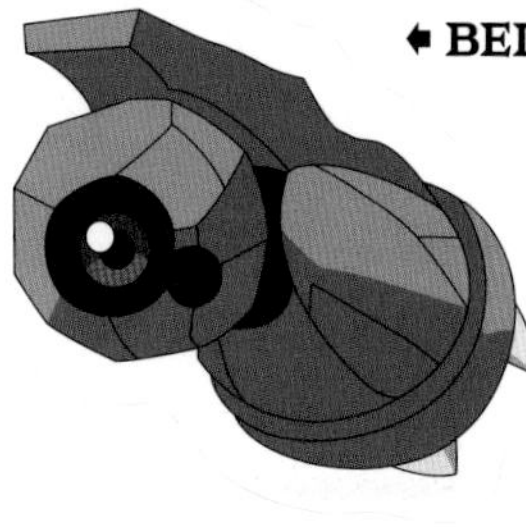

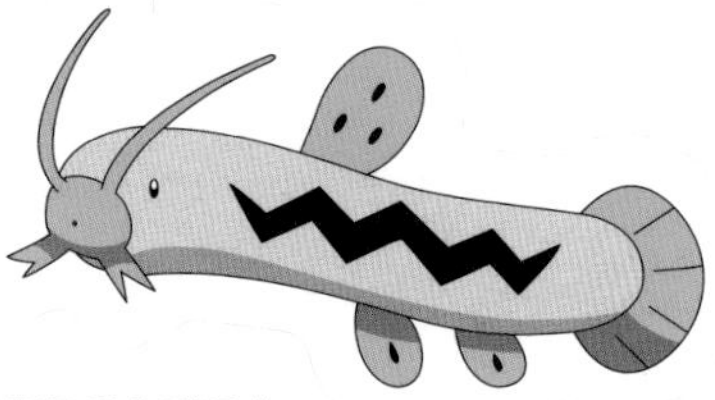

BARBOACH ↑

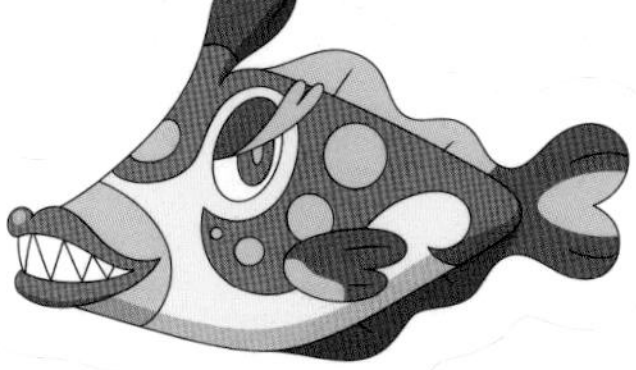

↑ BRUXISH

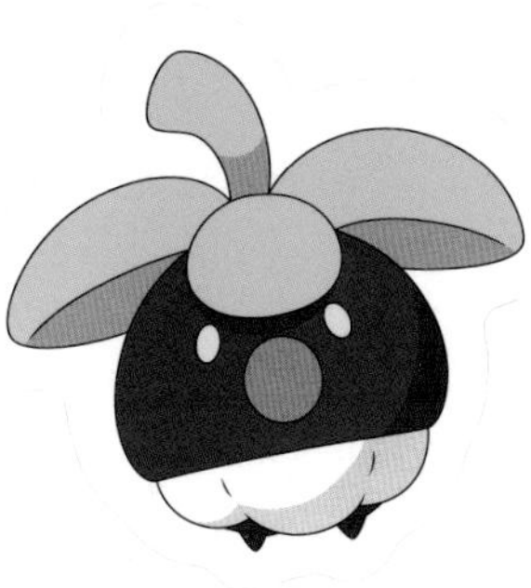

← BOUNSWEET

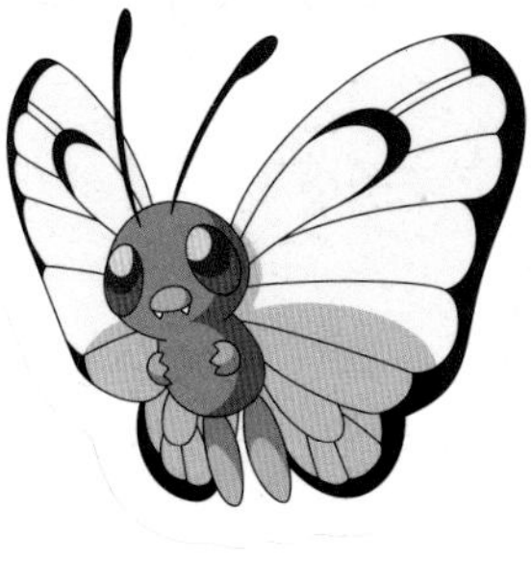

↑ BUTTERFREE

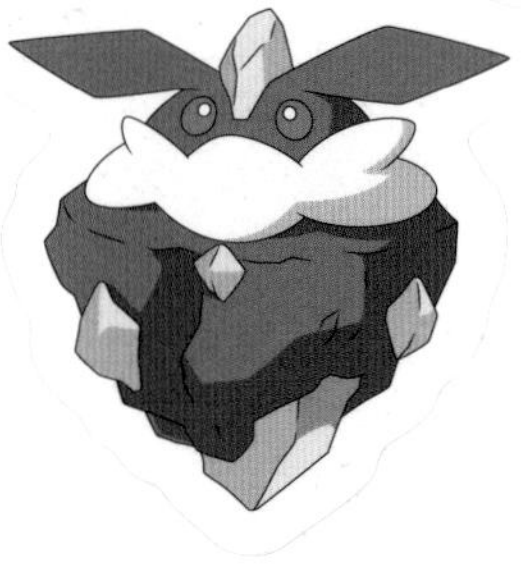

↑ CARBINK

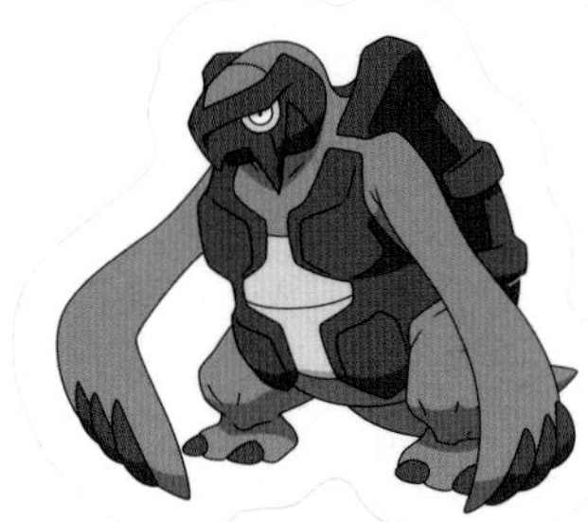

↑ CARRACOSTA

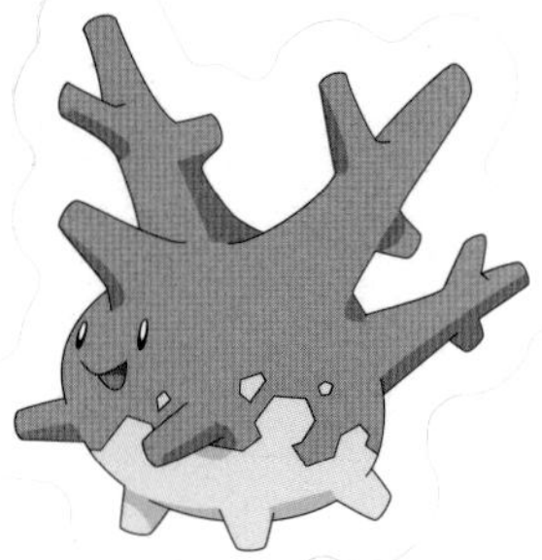

↑ CORSOLA

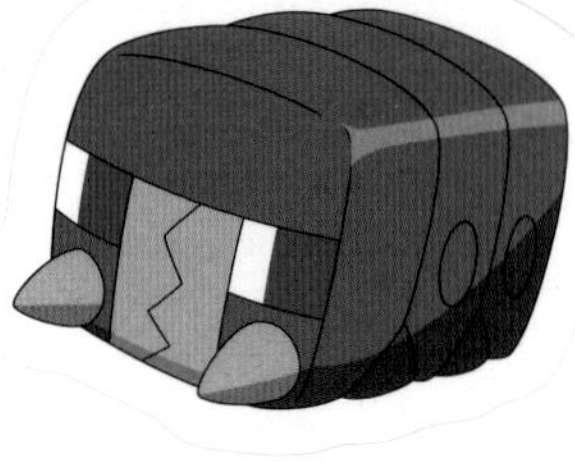

↑ CHARJABUG

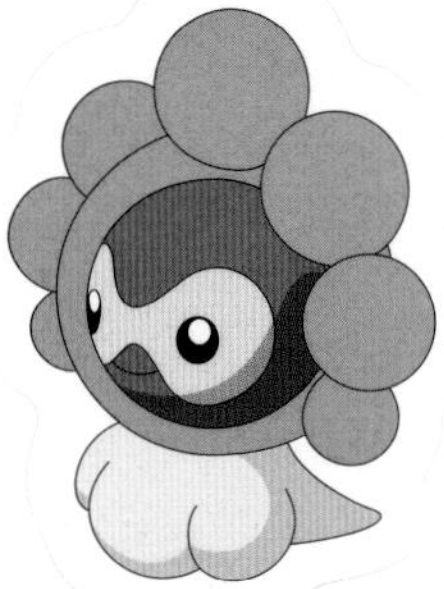

↑ CASTFORM (SUNNY FORM)

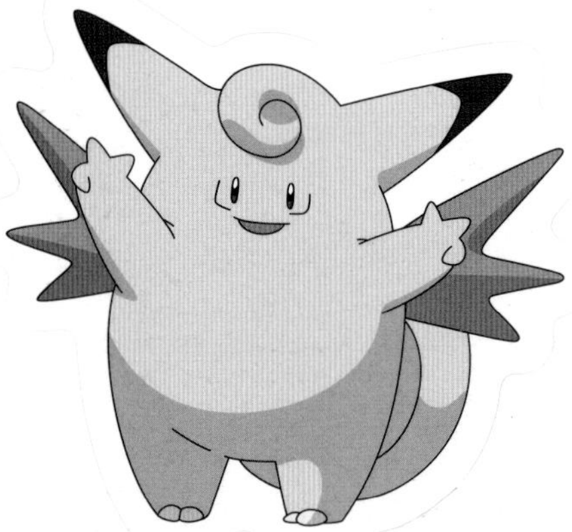

↑ CLEFABLE

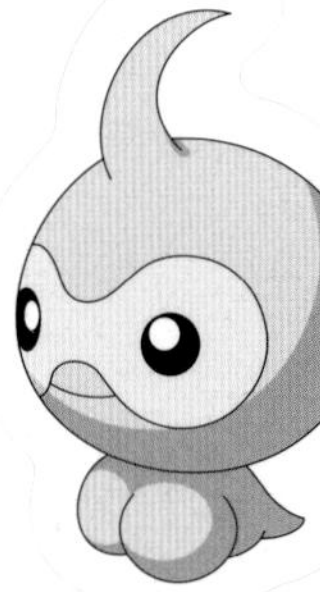

↑ CASTFORM (NORMAL FORM)

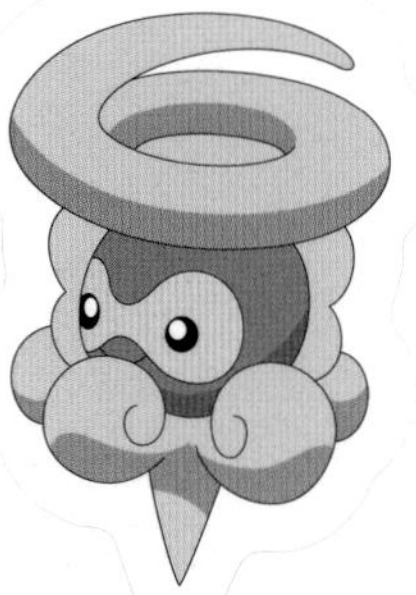

↑ CASTFORM (SNOWY FORM)

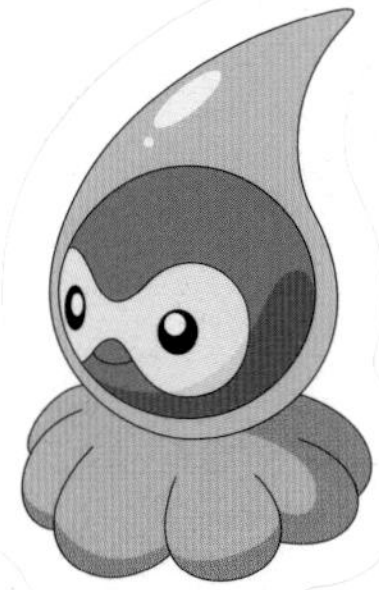

↑ CASTFORM (RAINY FORM)

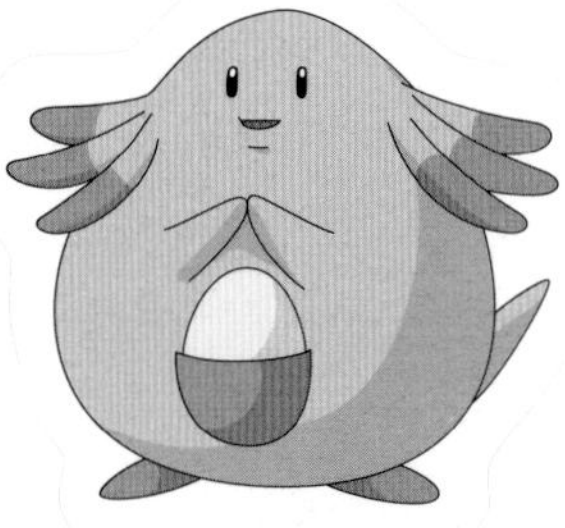

↑ CHANSEY

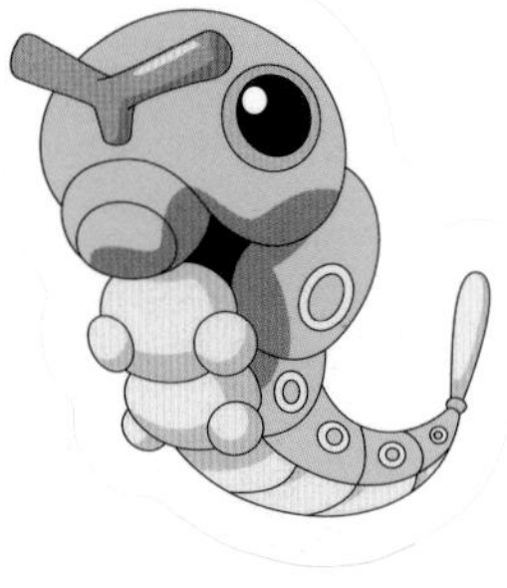

↑ CATERPIE

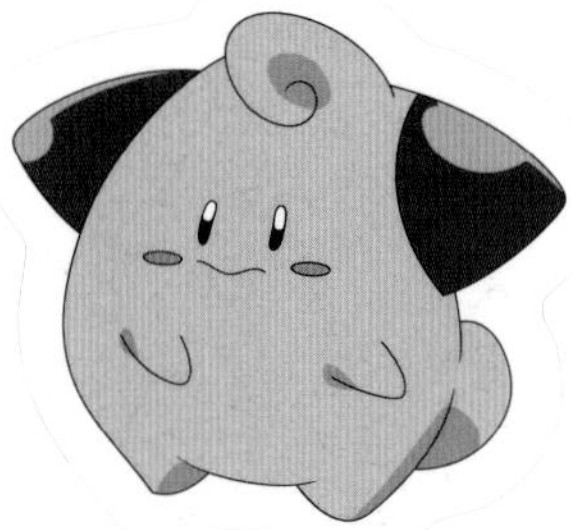

↑ CLEFFA

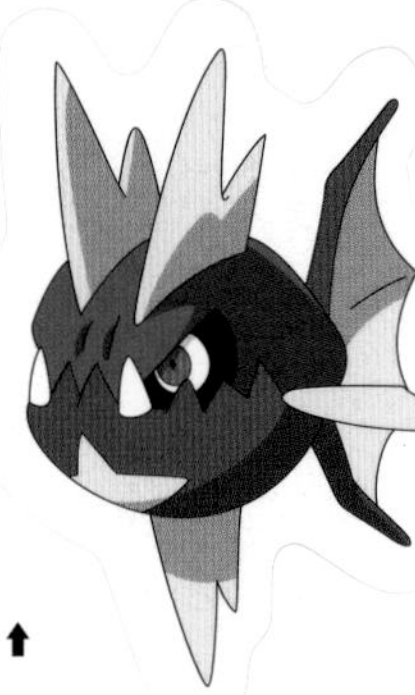

CARVANHA ↑

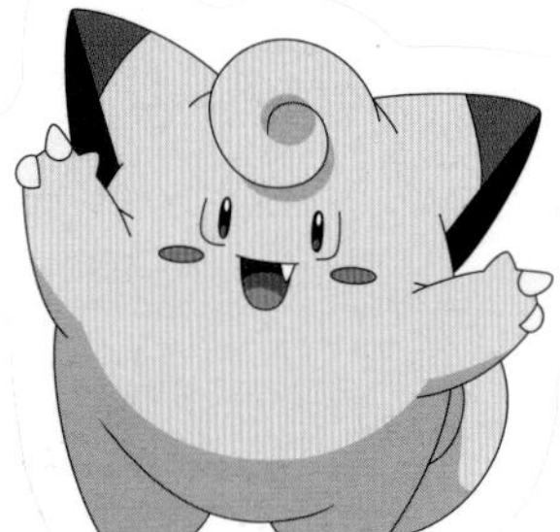

↑ CLEFAIRY

↓ CRABOMINABLE

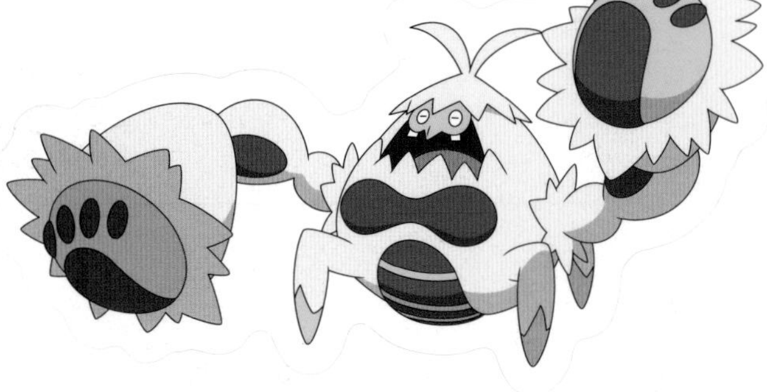

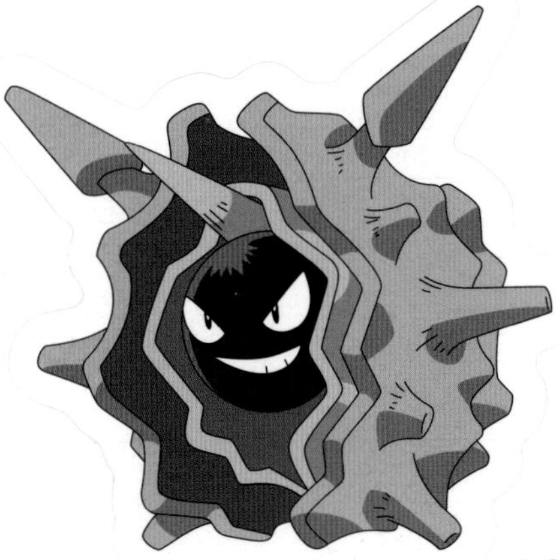

← CLOYSTER

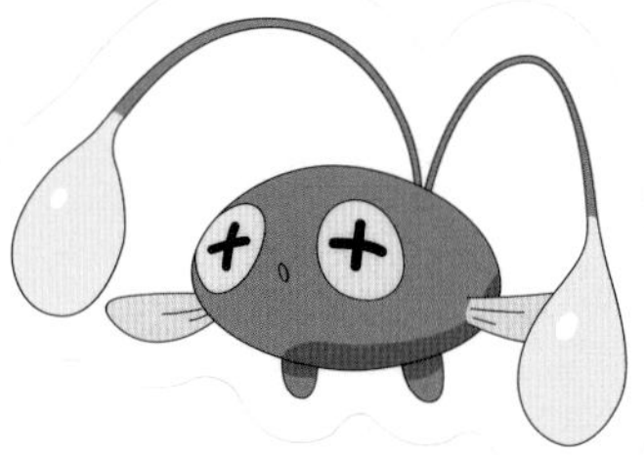

↑ CHINCHOU

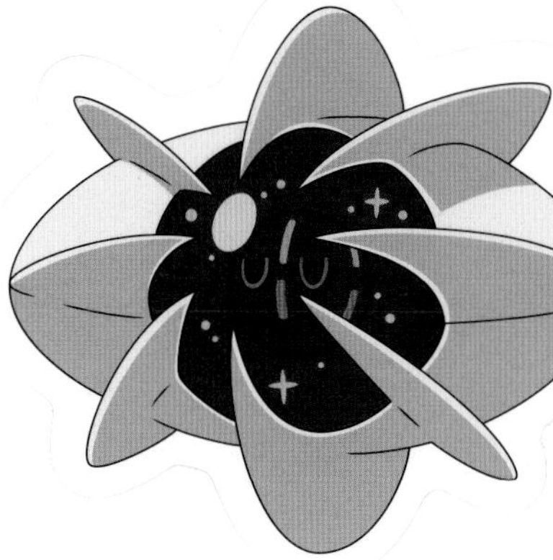

↑ COSMOEM

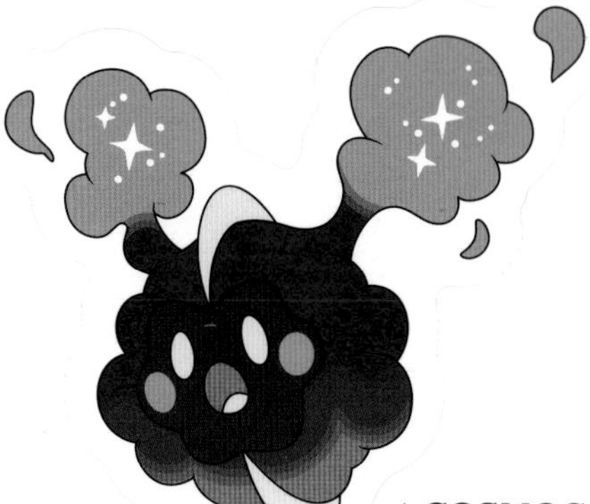

← COSMOG

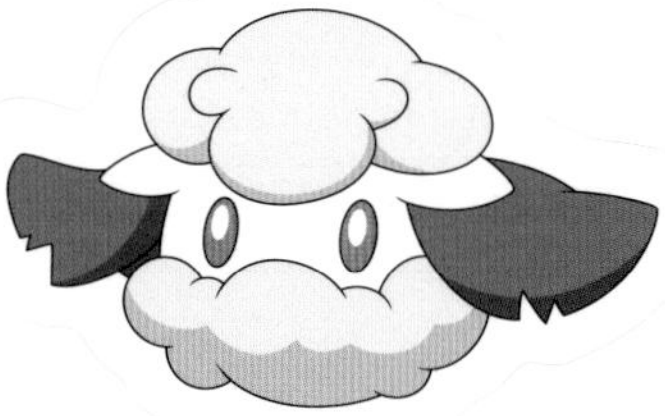

↑ COTTONEE

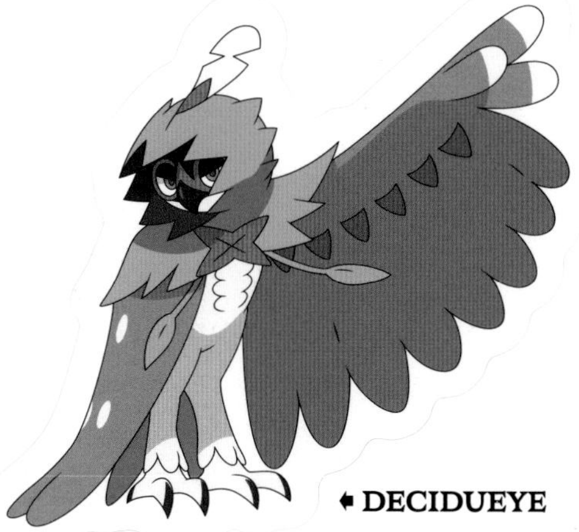

← DECIDUEYE

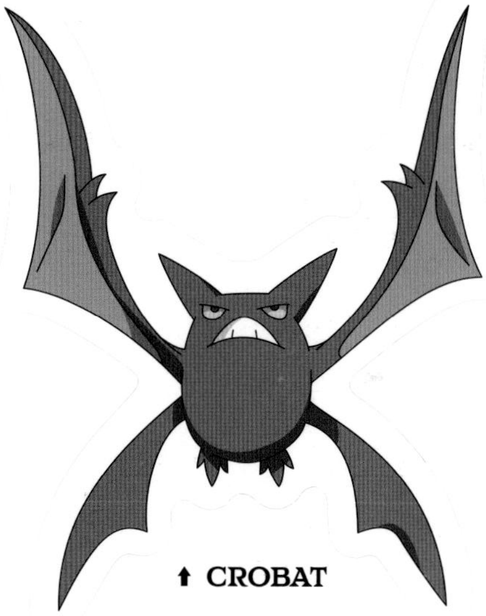

↑ CROBAT

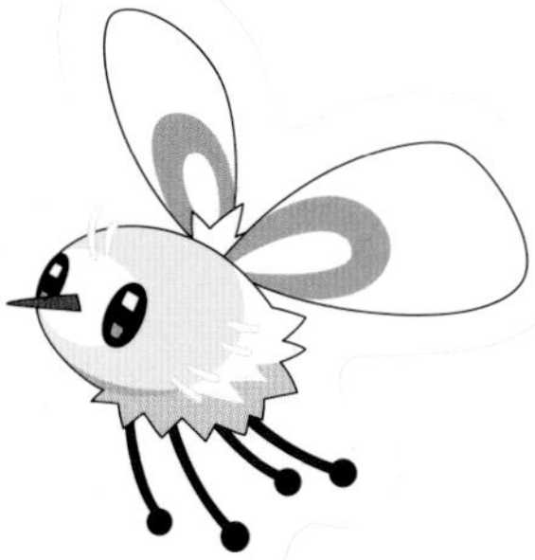

↑ CUTIEFLY

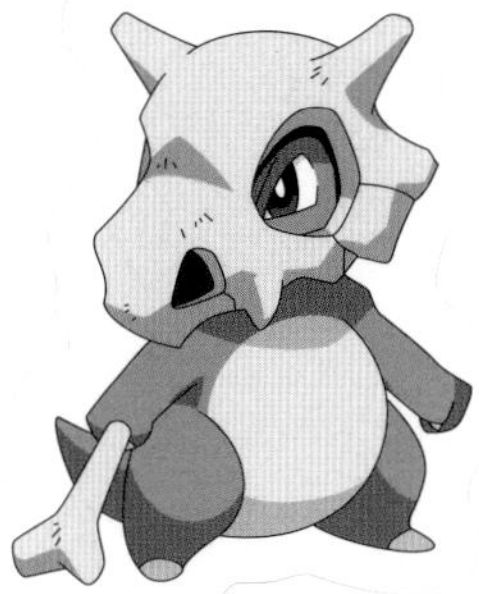

↑ CUBONE

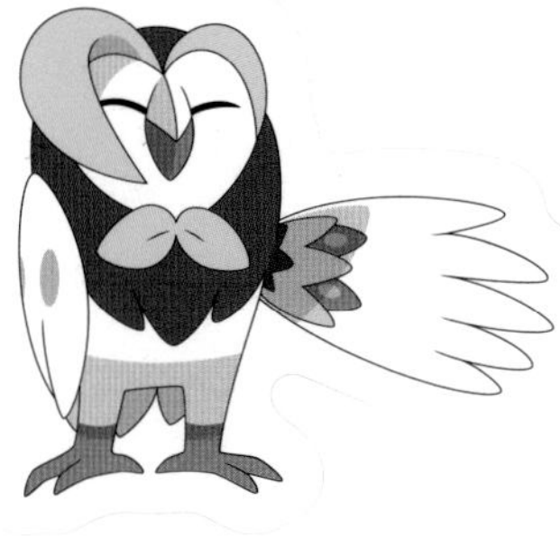

↑ DARTRIX

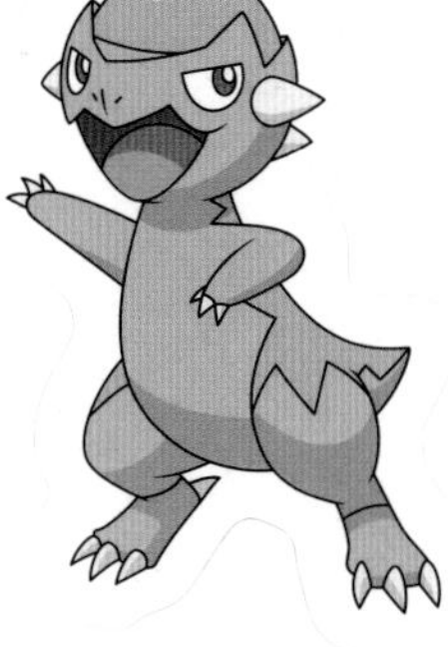

↑ CRANIDOS

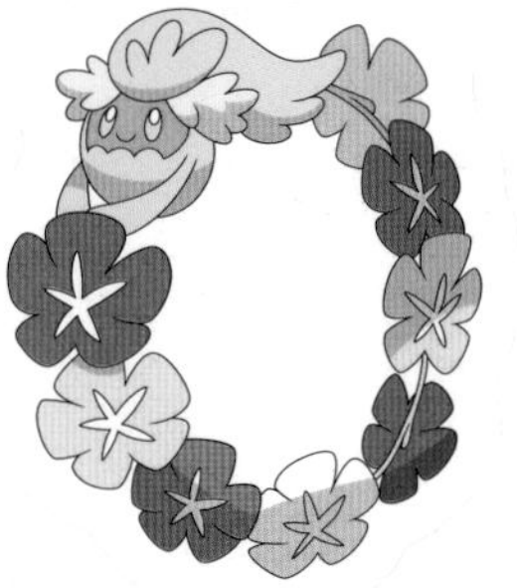

↑ COMFEY

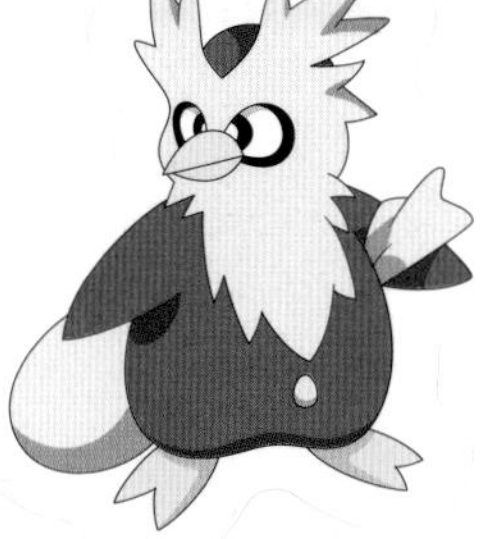

↑ DELIBIRD

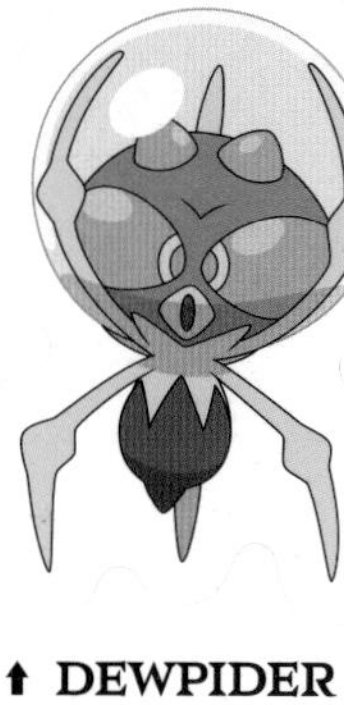

↑ DEWPIDER

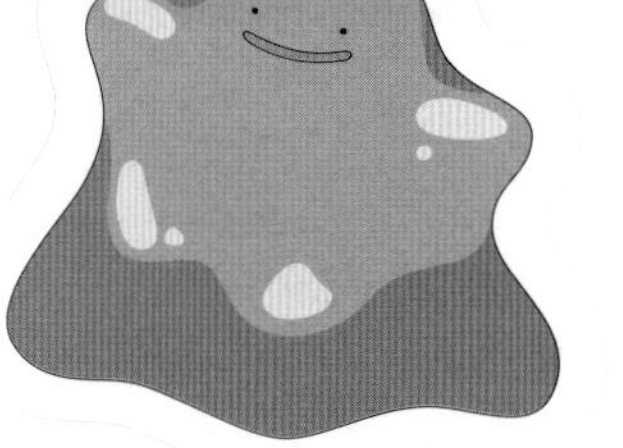

↑ DITTO

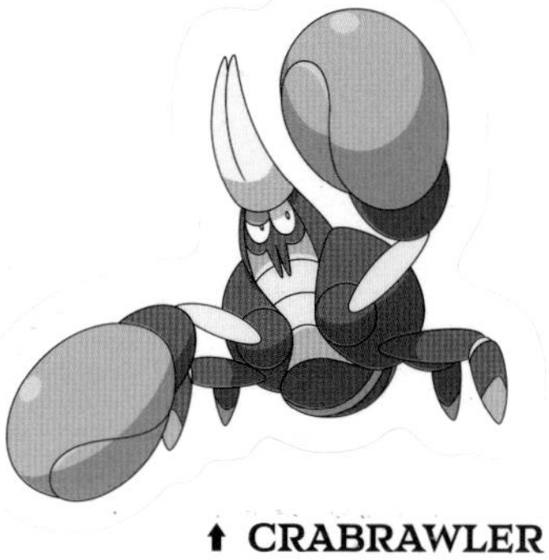

↑ CRABRAWLER

↑ DRIFBLIM

↑ DRIFLOON

↑ DUGTRIO (ALOLA FORM)

↑ DROWZEE

↑ ELECTIVIRE

↑ DRAMPA

← ELECTABUZZ

← DRAGONAIR

↑ ESPEON

← DHELMISE

↑ DRATINI

↑ DRAGONITE

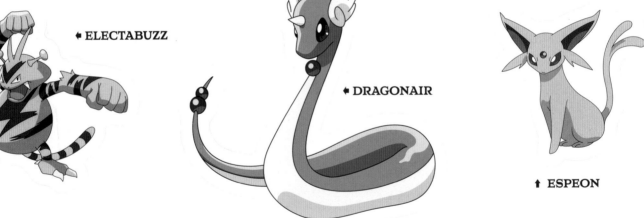

★ EXEGGCUTE

★ FEAROW

★ EEVEE

★ DIGLETT (ALOLA FORM)

★ EMOLGA

★ FROSLASS

★ FLYGON

★ FLETCHINDER

★ FINNEON

★ FOMANTIS

★ ELEKID

★ FLETCHLING

★ FLAREON

★ GASTLY   ★ EXEGGUTOR (ALOLA FORM)

↑ FEEBAS

↑ MEGA GENGAR

↑ GOLDEEN

↑ MEGA GARCHOMP

← GABITE

↑ GASTRODON (EAST SEA)

↑ MEGA GLALIE

↑ GENGAR

GARBODOR ↓   ↑ GIBLE

↑ GLALIE

↑ GLACEON

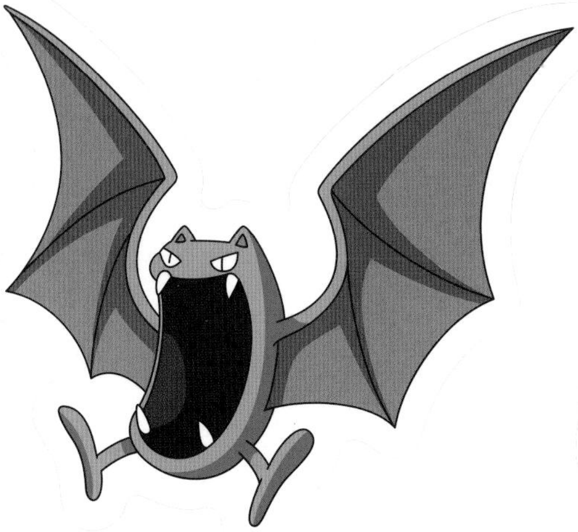

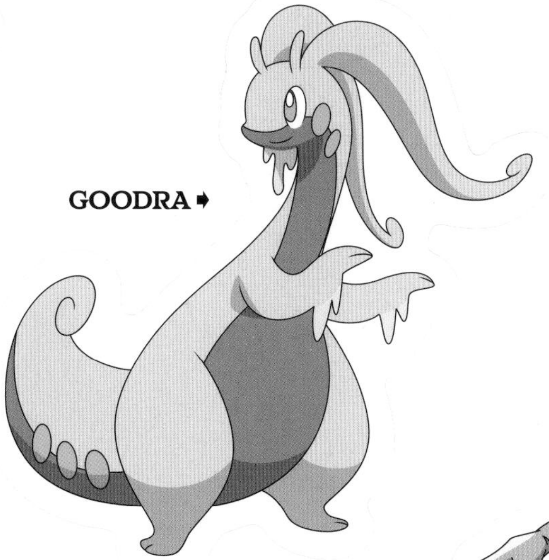

GOODRA →

GROWLITHE →

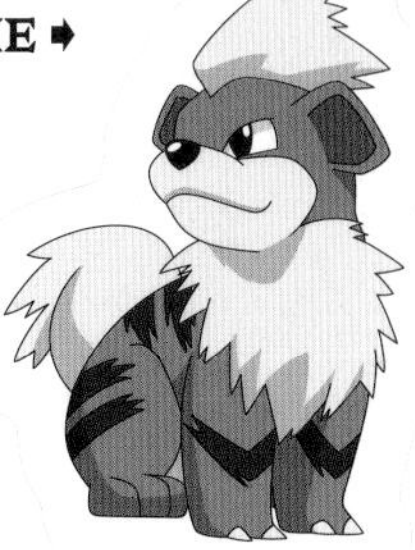

↑ GOLBAT

↓ GOLDUCK

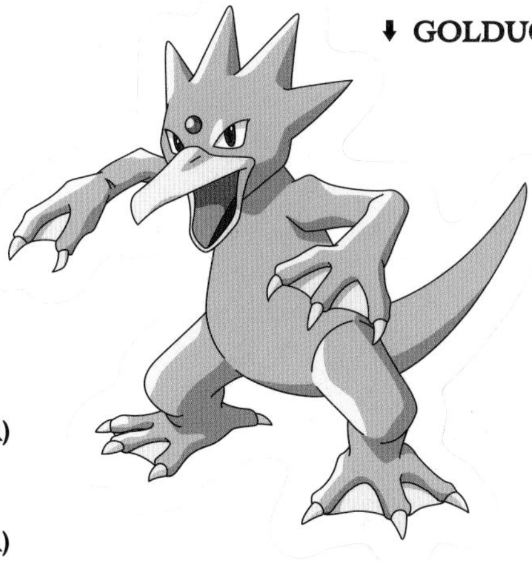

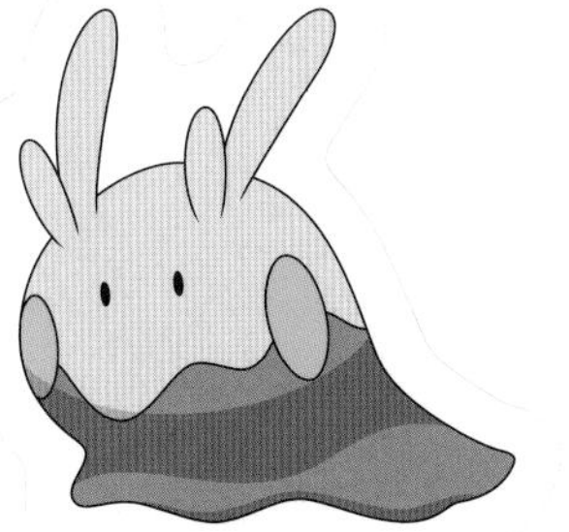

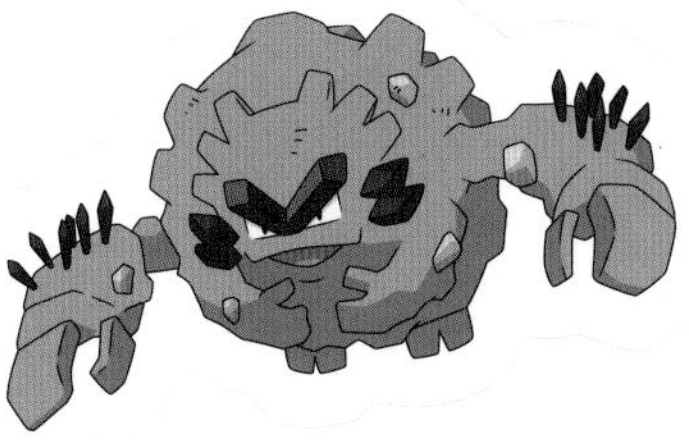

← GRAVELER (ALOLA FORM)

↓ GEODUDE (ALOLA FORM)

↑ GOOMY

↓ GOLEM (ALOLA FORM)

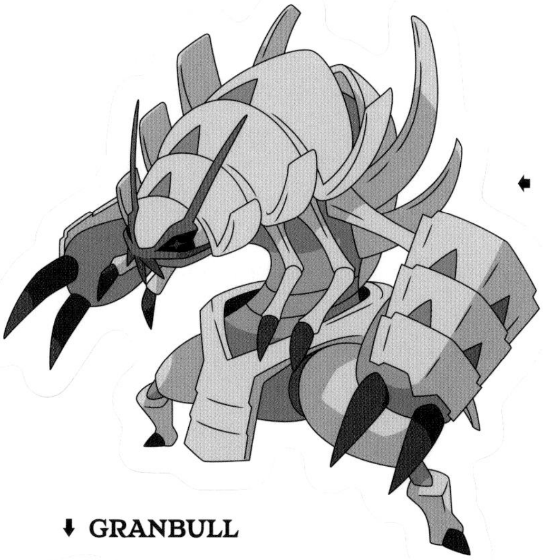

← GOLISOPOD

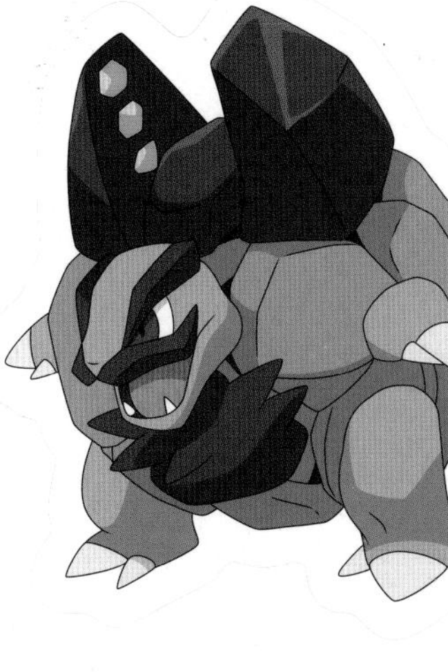

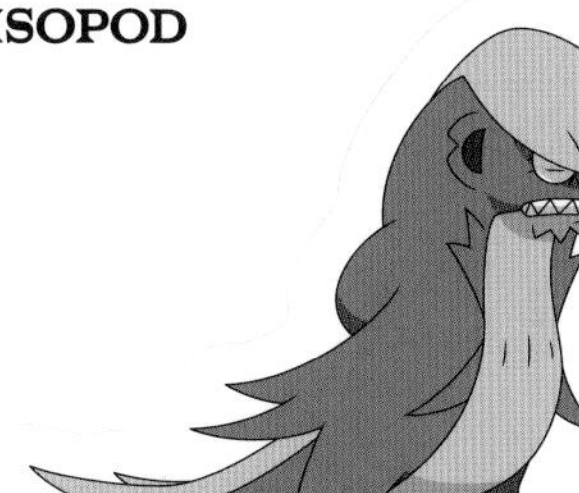

↓ GRANBULL

↑ GUMSHOOS

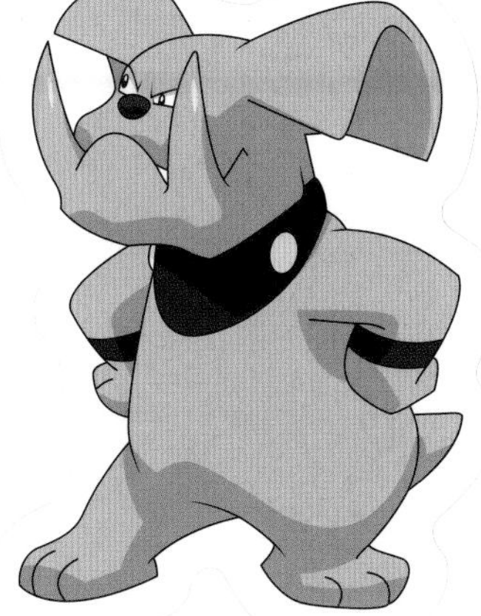

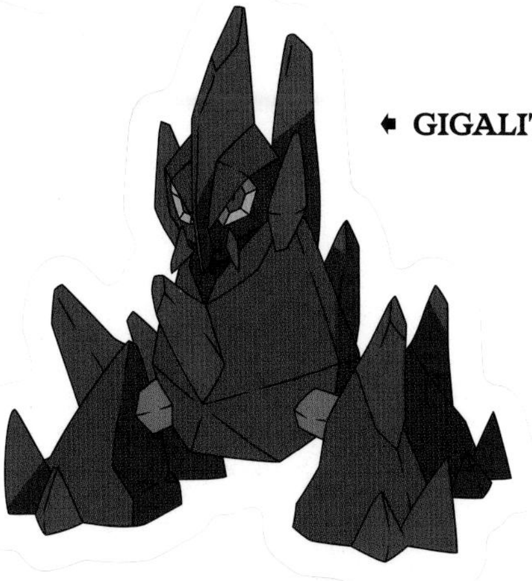

← GIGALITH

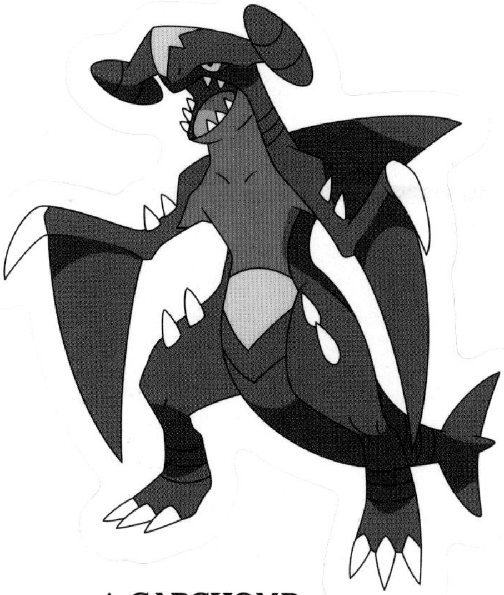

↑ GARCHOMP

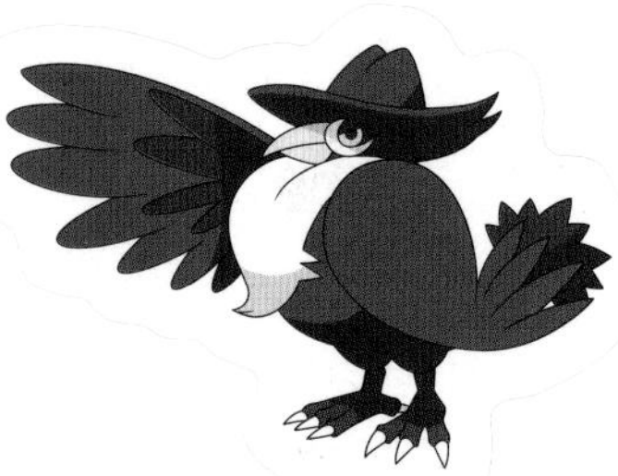

↑ HONCHKROW

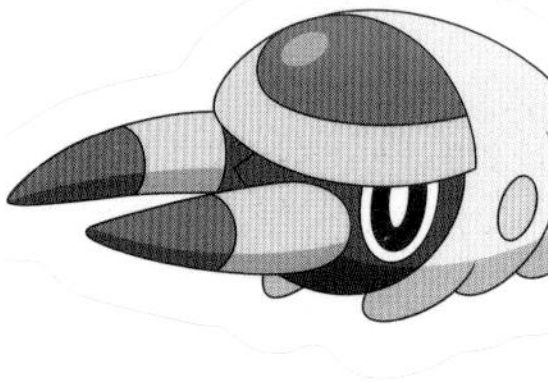

↑ GRUBBIN

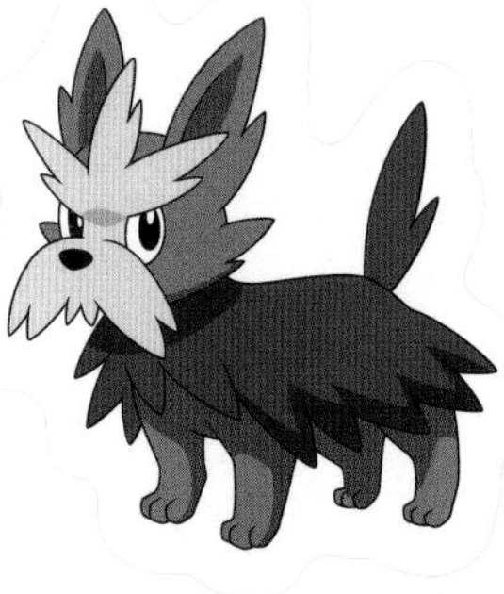

↑ HERDIER

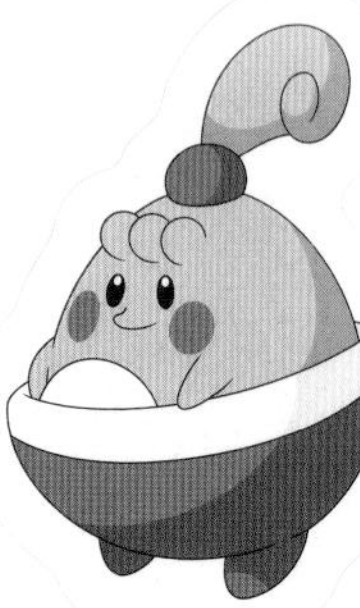

↑ HAPPINY

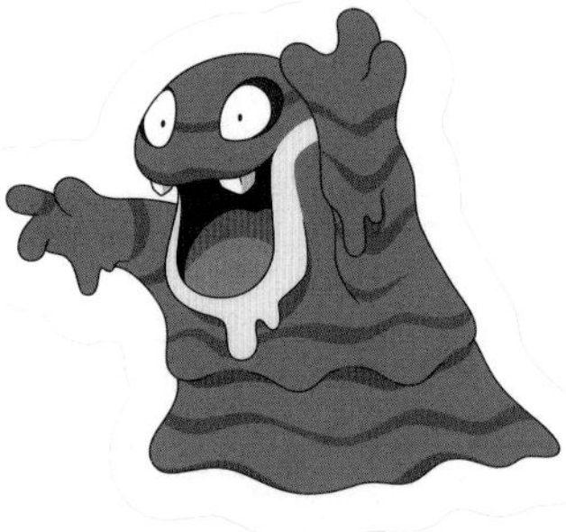

↑ GRIMER (ALOLA FORM)

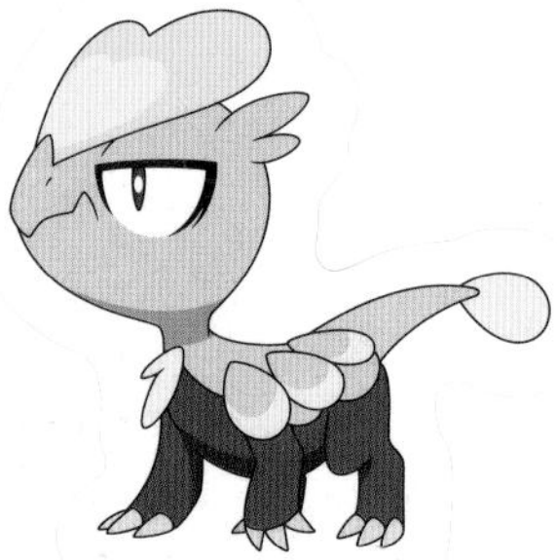

↑ JANGMO-O

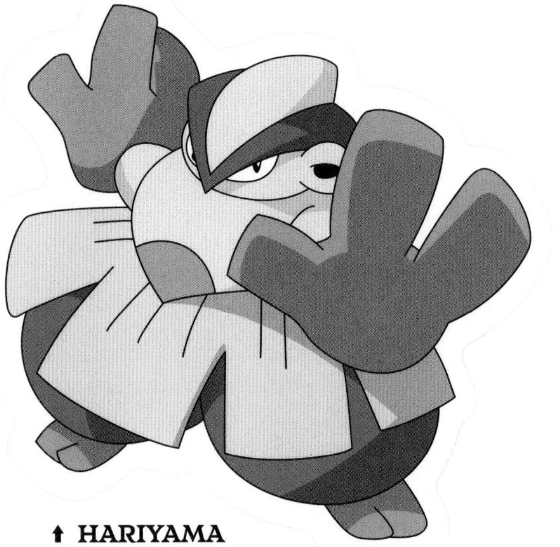

↑ HARIYAMA

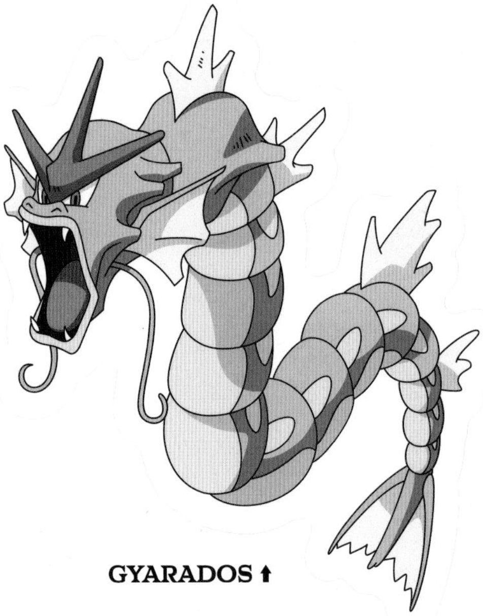

GYARADOS ↑

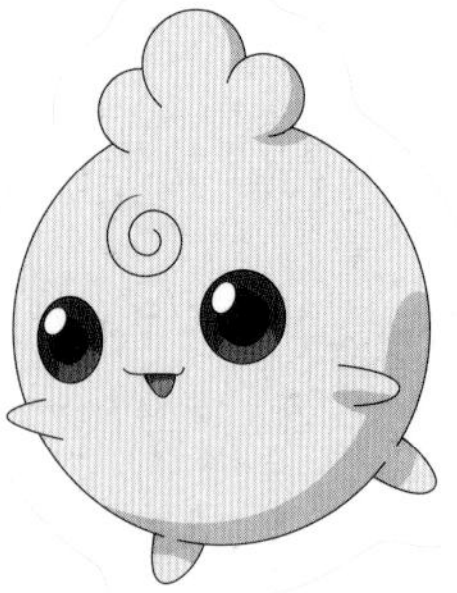

↑ IGGLYBUFF

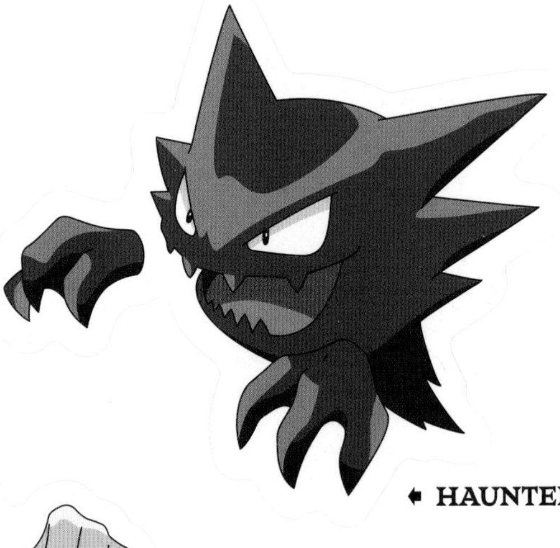

← HAUNTER

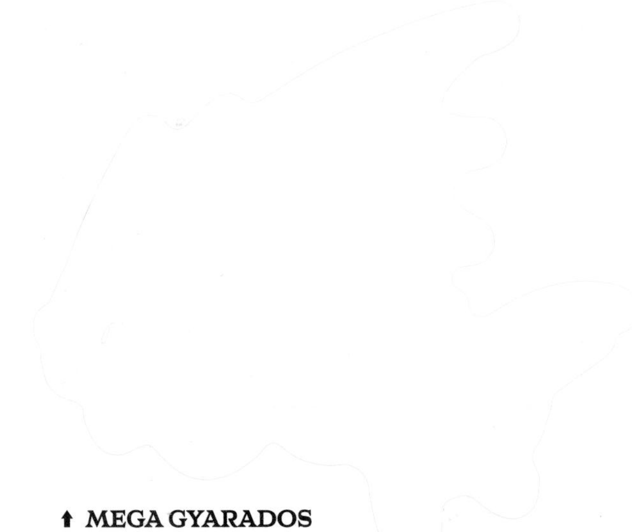

↑ MEGA GYARADOS

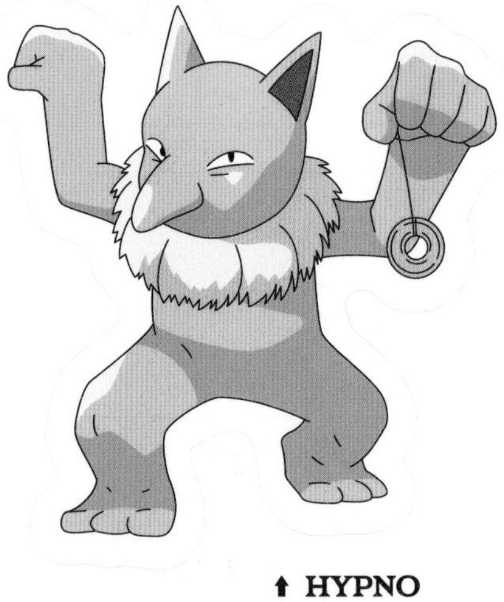

↑ HYPNO

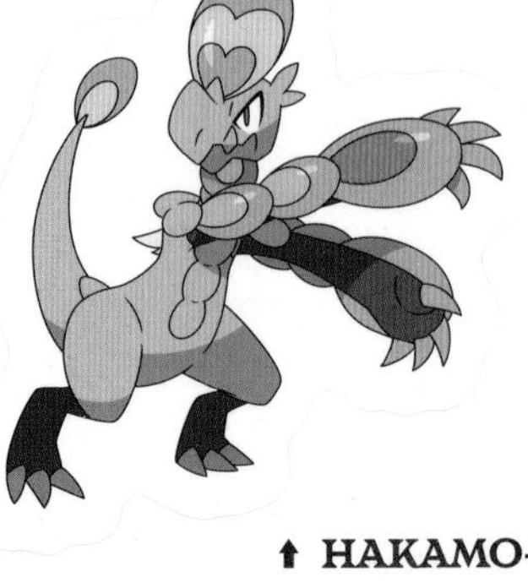

↑ HAKAMO-O

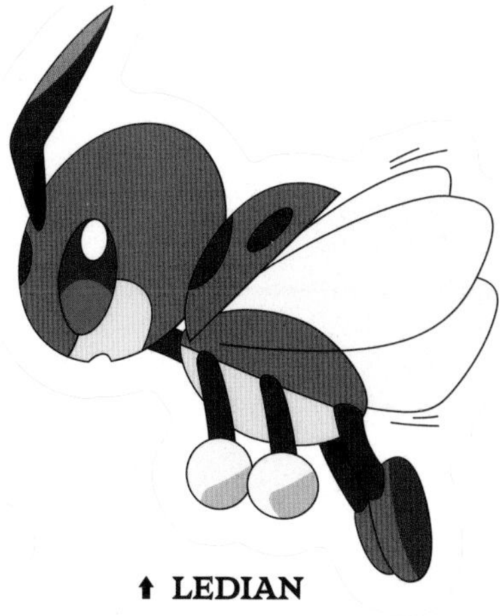

↑ INCINEROAR

↑ LAPRAS

↑ LEDIAN

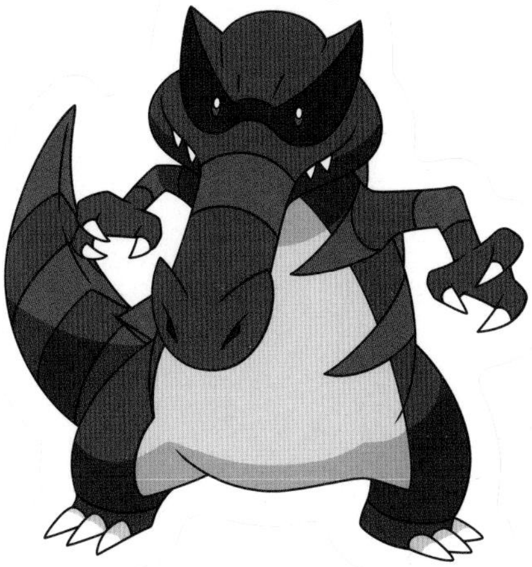

↑ KROOKODILE

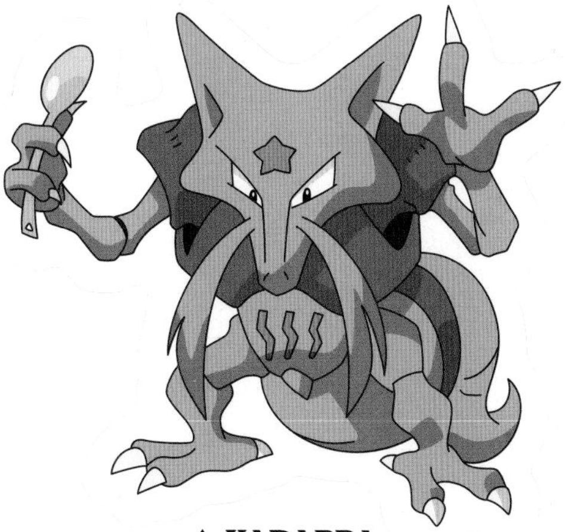

↑ KADABRA

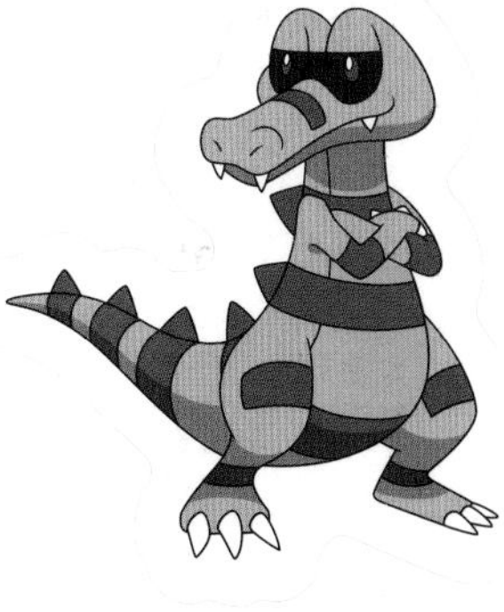

↑ KROKOROK

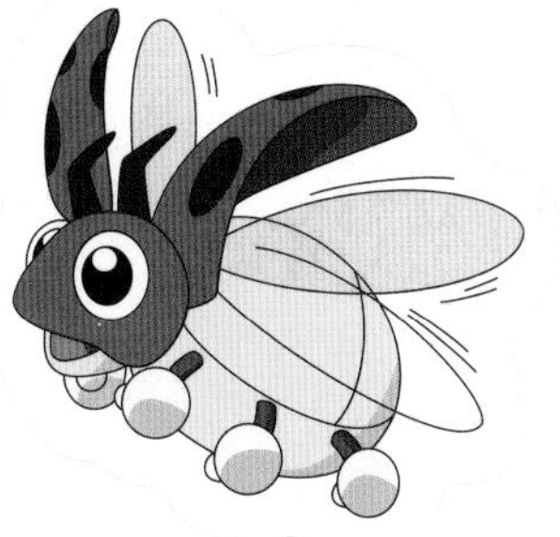

↑ LEDYBA

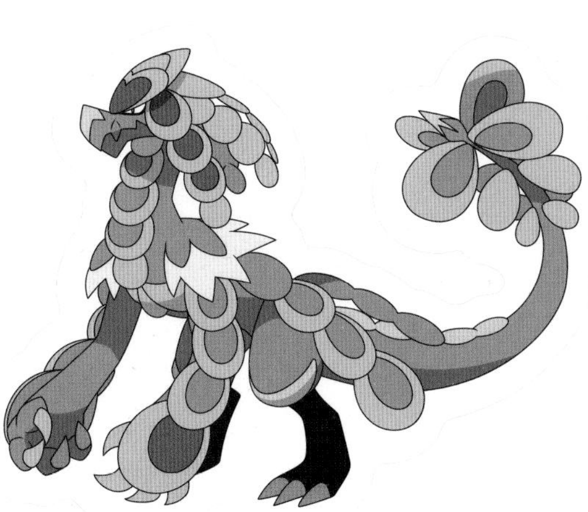

↑ KOMMO-O

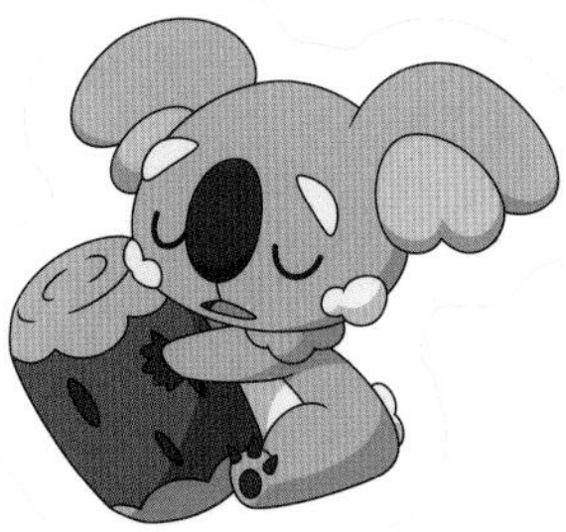

↑ KOMALA

KLEFKI ➡

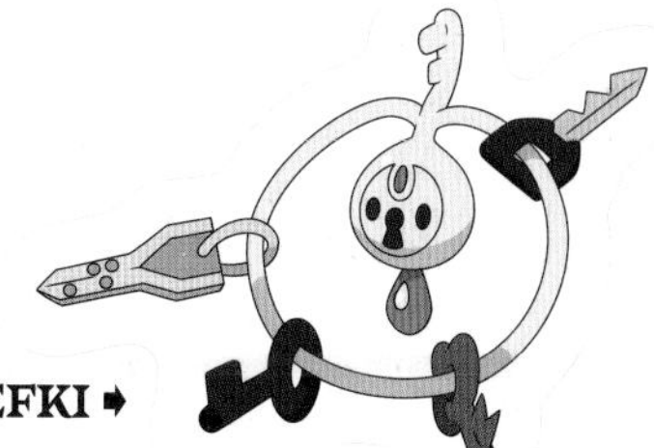

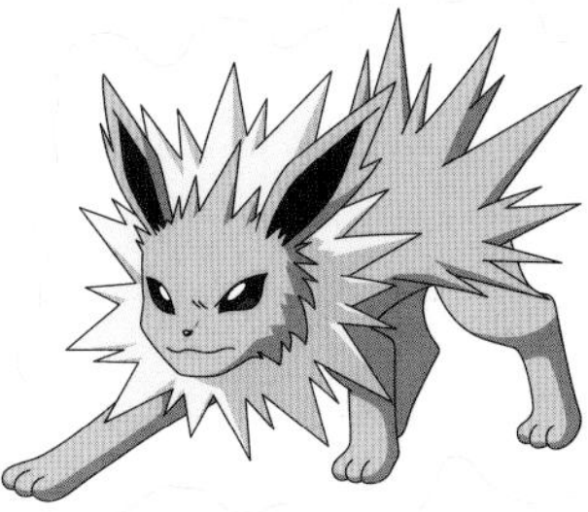

↑ JOLTEON

↑ JIGGLYPUFF

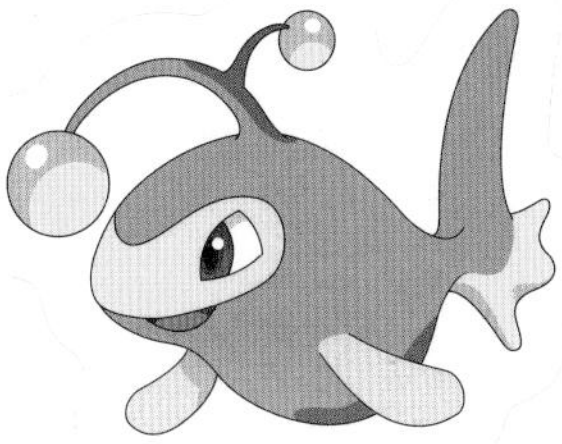

⬅ LANTURN

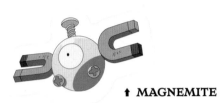

⬆ LILLIGANT

⬆ LITTEN

MAGNETON ⬆

⬆ LYCANROC
(MIDNIGHT FORM)

⬆ MAGNEMITE

⬆ MAGNEZONE

⬆ LUCARIO

⬆ MACHAMP

⬆ MEGA LUCARIO

⬆ MACHOKE

⬆ MEGA KANGASKHAN

⬆ KANGASKHAN

LILLIPUP ➡

↑ MAGMORTAR

↑ MAGBY

↑ LYCANROC
(MIDDAY FORM)

↑ LUVDISC

↑ MAGMAR

↑ LEAFEON

← LURANTIS

↑ LUMINEON

↑ MAROWAK (ALOLA FORM)

↑ MACHOP

↑ LUNALA

↑ MAKUHITA

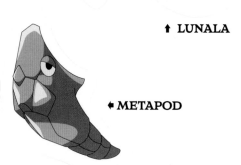

← METAPOD

↑ MAGIKARP

⬆ **MANDIBUZZ**

⬆ **MUNCHLAX**

⬆ **NOSEPASS**

MAGEARNA ⬆

⬆ **MINIOR
(METEOR FORM)**

⬆ **MAREANIE**

⬆ **MANKEY**

⬆ **MILTANK**

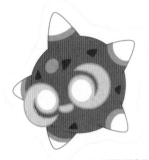

⬆ **MINIOR
(RED CORE)**

⬆ **MIMIKYU**

⬆ **MASQUERAIN**

MISMAGIUS ➡

⬆ **MISDREAVUS**

⬅ **MEOWTH
(ALOLA FORM)**

⬆ **MURKROW**

MORELULL ➡

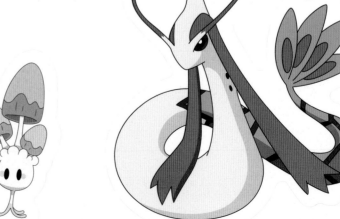

⬆ **MILOTIC**

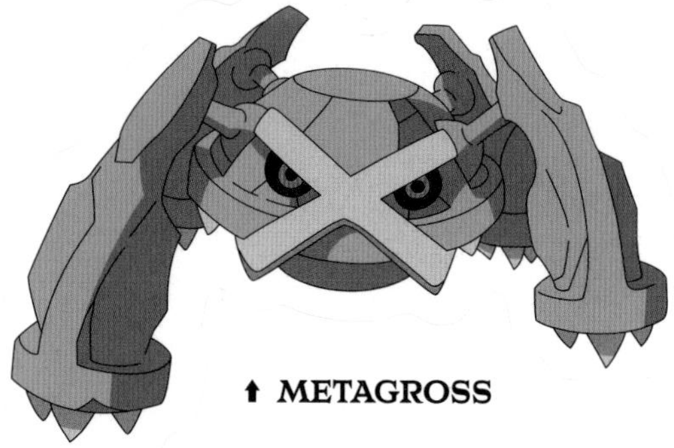

↑ METAGROSS

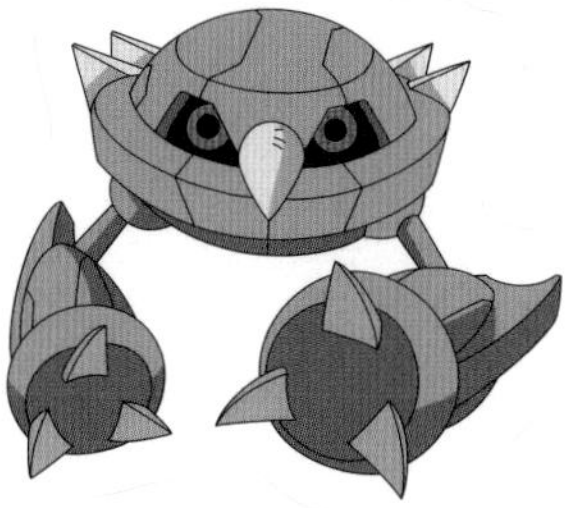

↑ METANG

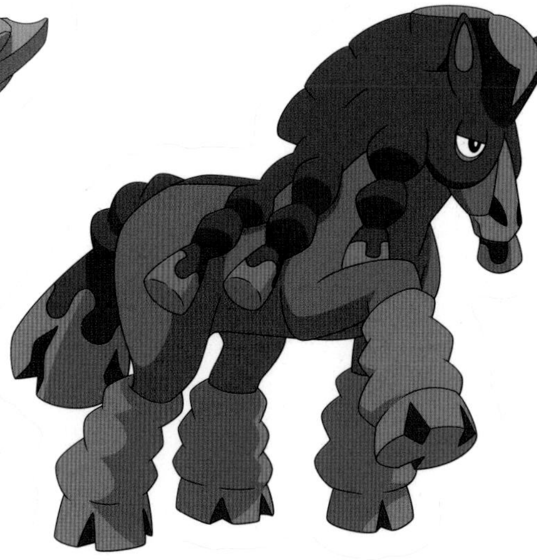

↑ MUDSDALE

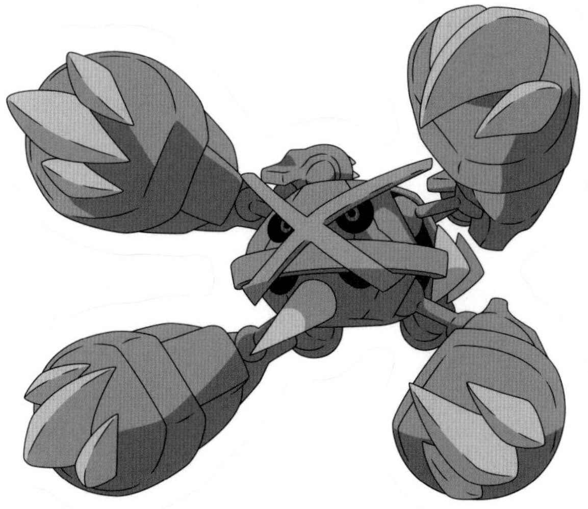

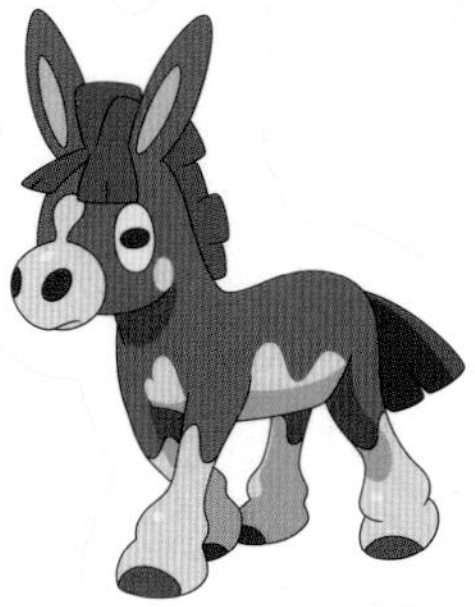

← MUDBRAY

↑ MEGA METAGROSS

PETILIL →

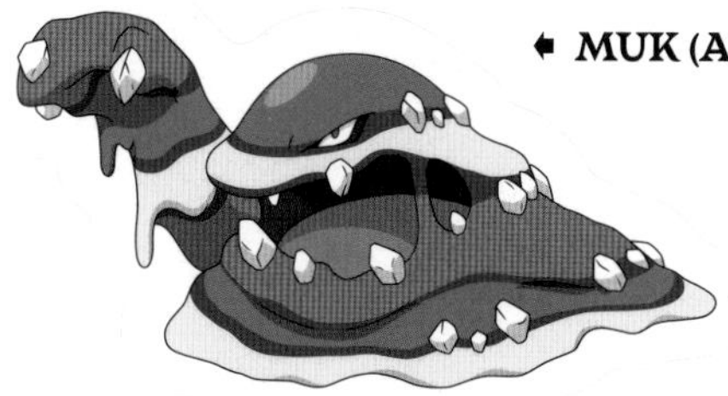

← MUK (ALOLA FORM)

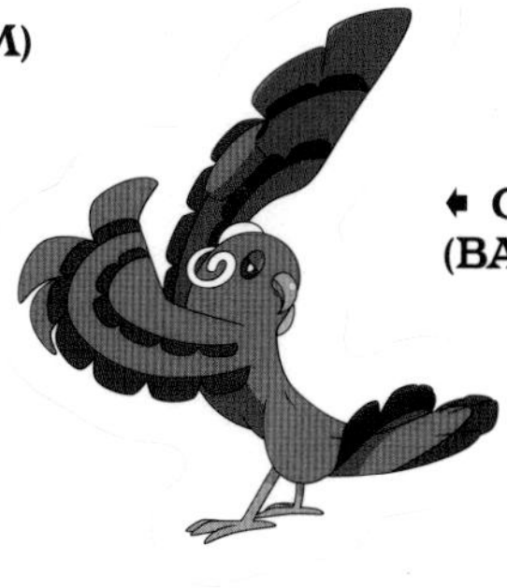

← ORICORIO (BAILE STYLE)

ORICORIO → (SENSU STYLE)

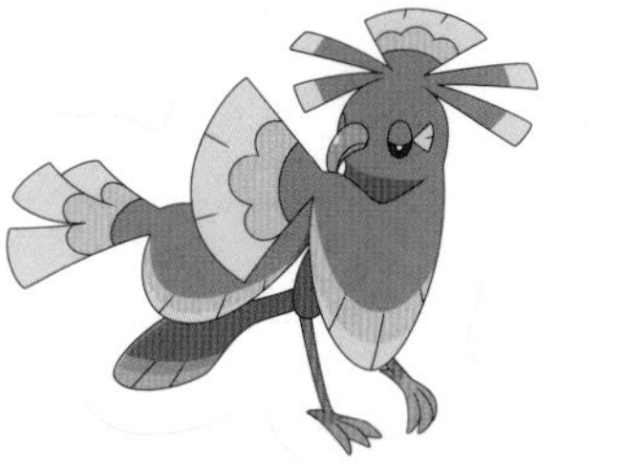

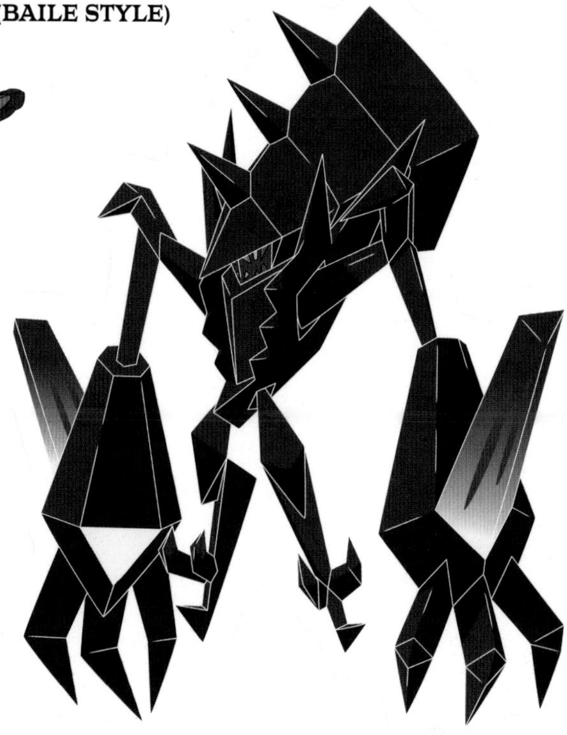

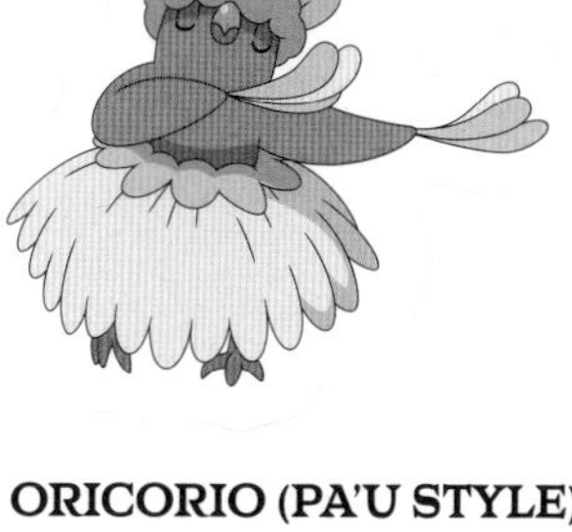

↓ ORICORIO (POM-POM STYLE)

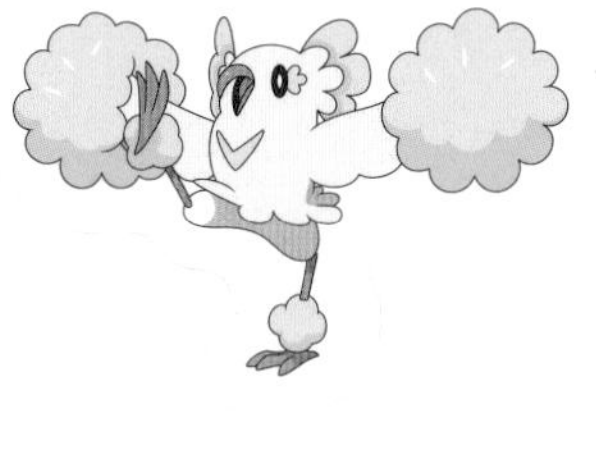

↑ ORICORIO (PA'U STYLE)

↑ NECROZMA

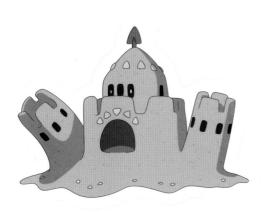

↓ NINETALES (ALOLA FORM)

↑ ORANGURU

↑ PALOSSAND

↓ PIKIPEK

↑ PERSIAN
(ALOLA FORM)

↑ PINSIR

↑ PARASECT

◄ PANGORO

↑ PASSIMIAN

↑ PICHU

PANCHAM ↓

↓ PARAS

PIKACHU ►

↑ POPPLIO

MEGA PINSIR

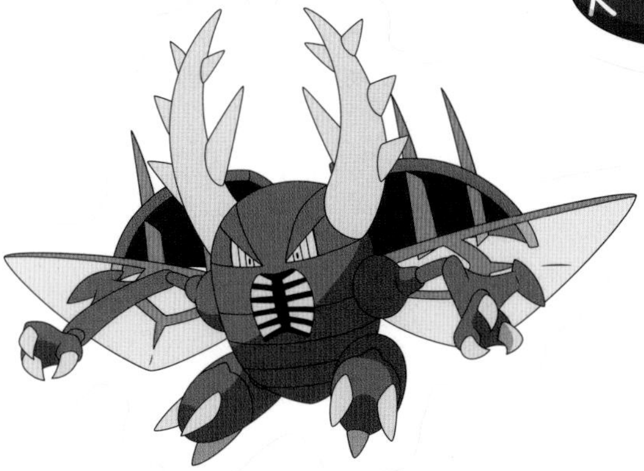

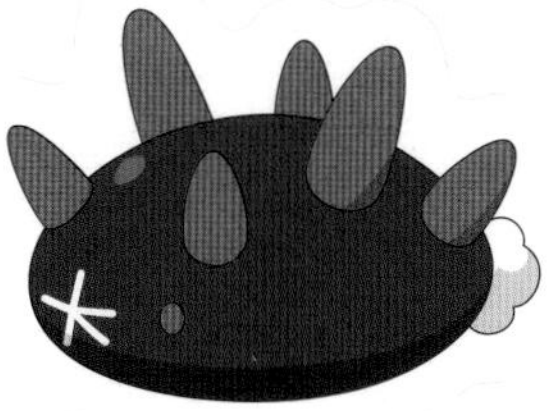

PYUKUMUKU

POLIWHIRL

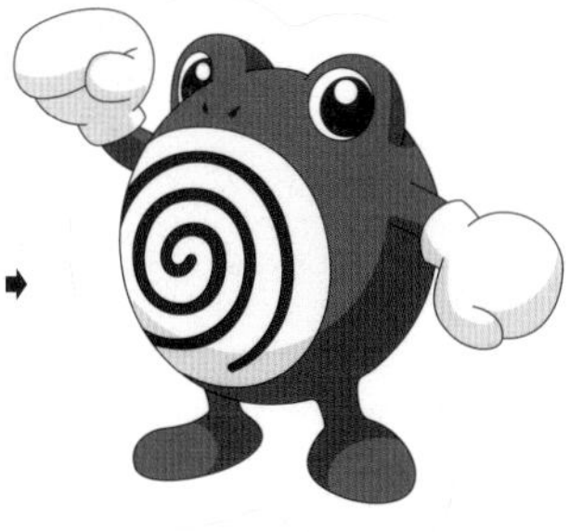

POLIWRATH

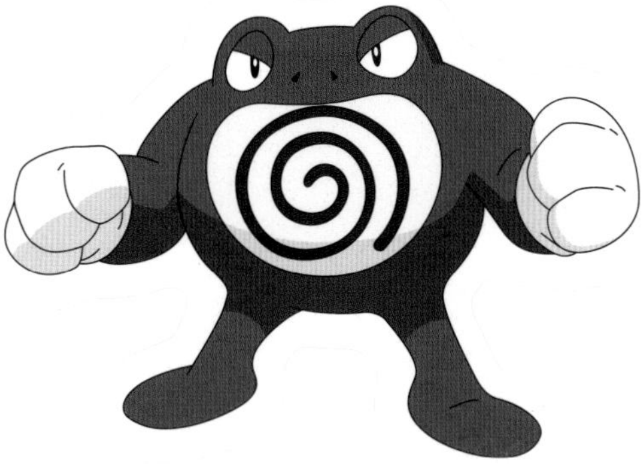

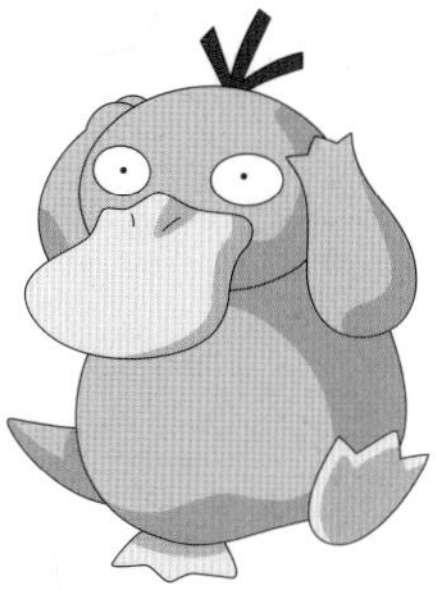

PSYDUCK

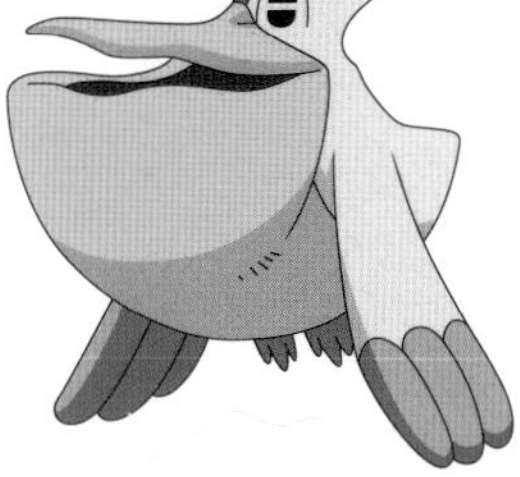

PELIPPER

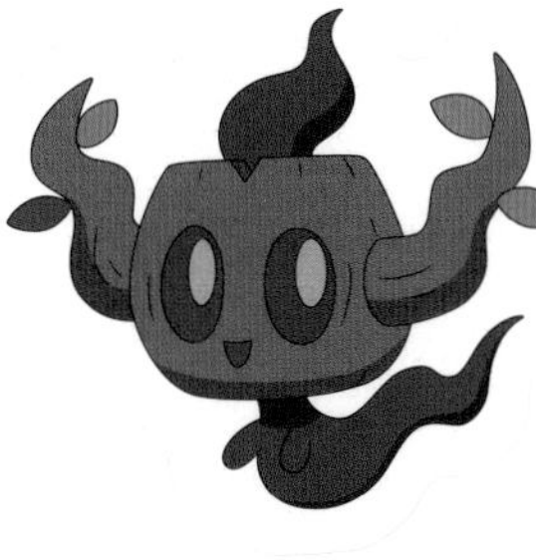

PHANTUMP

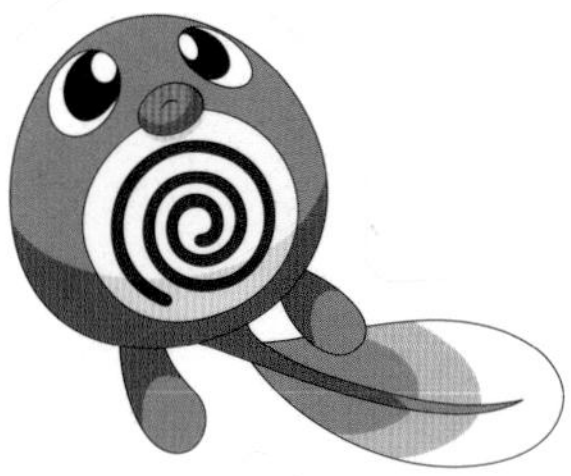

POLIWAG

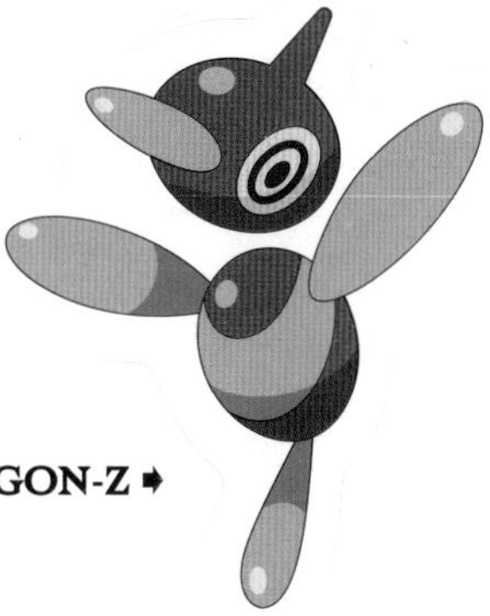

PORYGON-Z

PRIMARINA

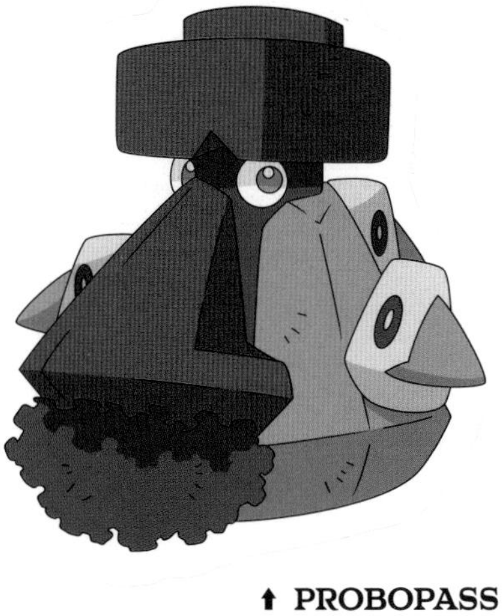

PROBOPASS

PORYGON2

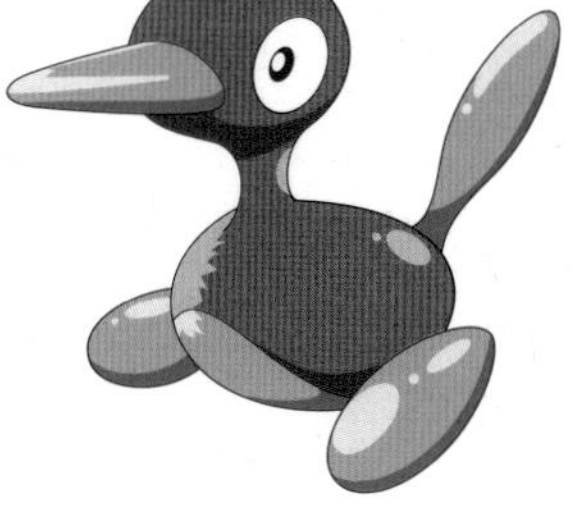

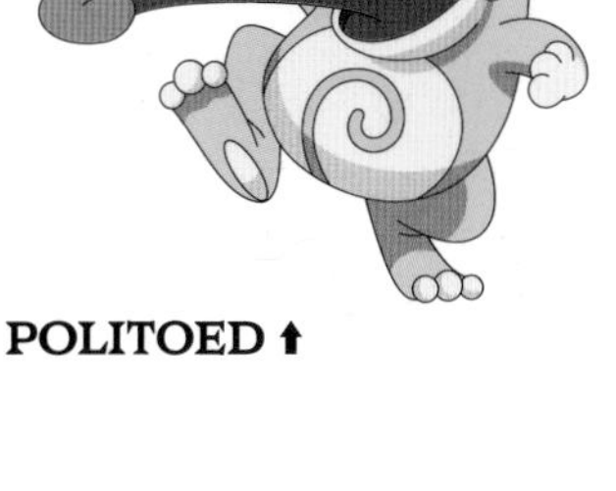

POLITOED

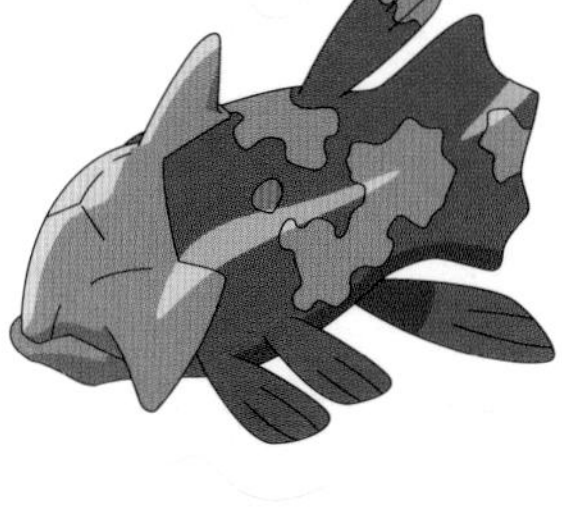

RELICANTH

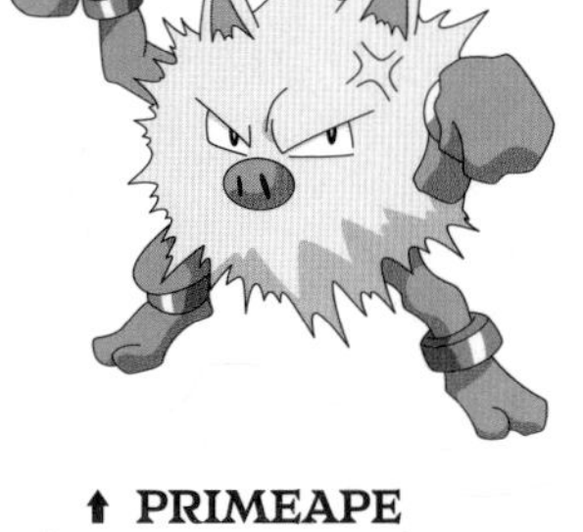

PRIMEAPE

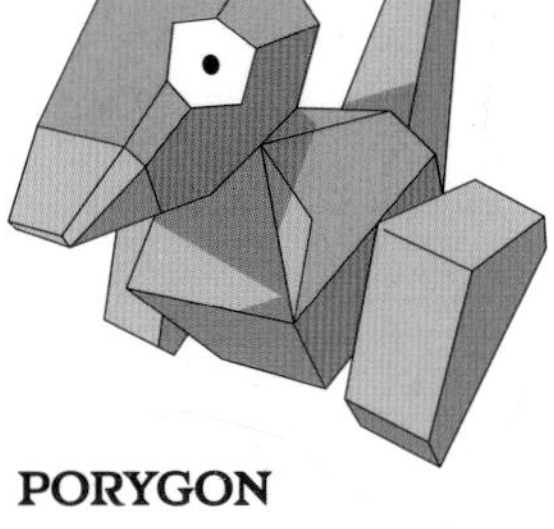

PORYGON

↓ SALAMENCE

↑ RIOLU

↑ MEGA SALAMENCE

↑ ROGGENROLA

RUFFLET →

↑ RAICHU
(ALOLA FORM)

↑ MEGA SABLEYE

SABLEYE →

↑ RAMPARDOS

↓ MEGA SCIZOR

↑ SCYTHER

↑ ROWLET

↑ SCIZOR

↑ SANDILE

↑ ROCKRUFF

↑ RATICATE (ALOLA FORM)

RATTATA
(ALOLA FORM) ↓

↑ SNORUNT

SHELGON ↑

SANDSHREW
(ALOLA FORM) ↓

SALAZZLE ↑

↑ RIBOMBEE

SEAKING →

↑ SALANDIT

SANDSLASH (ALOLA FORM)

MEGA
SHARPEDO ↑

↑ SANDYGAST

↑ SHELLDER

SHARPEDO

↑ SHELLOS (EAST SEA)

↑ SHIINOTIC

SHIELDON →

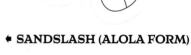
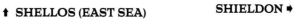

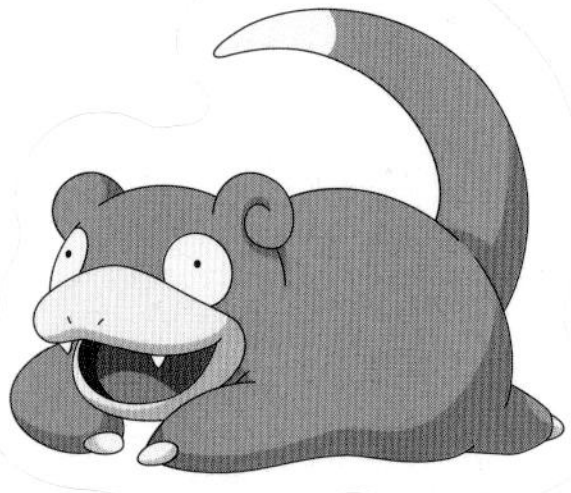

↑ SLOWPOKE

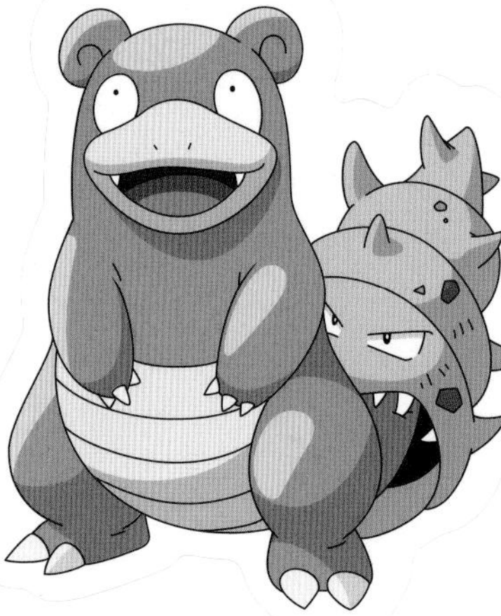

↑ SLOWBRO

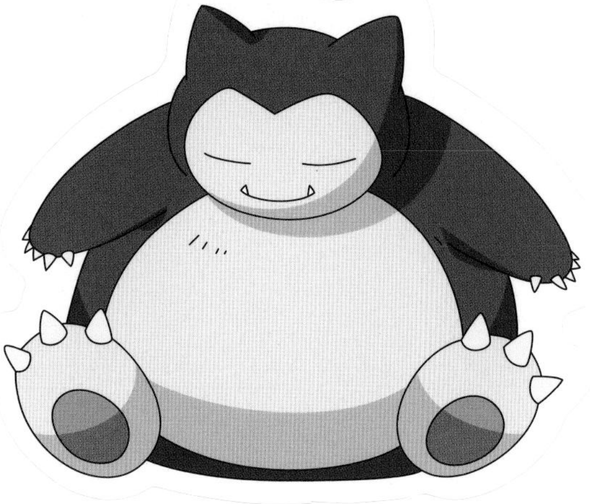

↑ SNORLAX

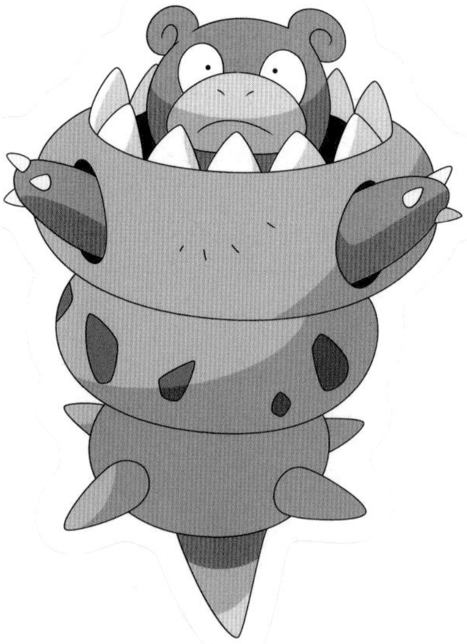

↑ MEGA SLOWBRO

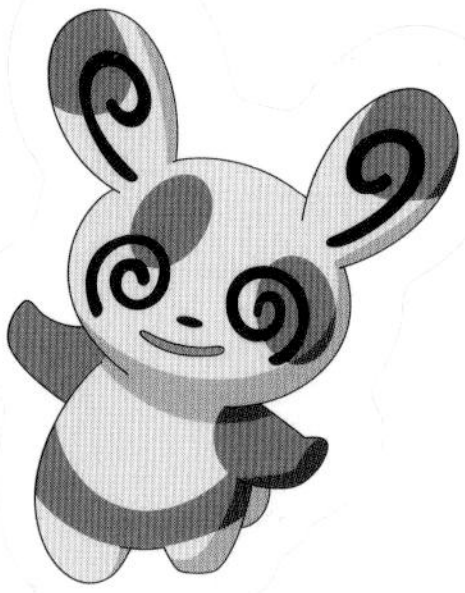

← SPINDA

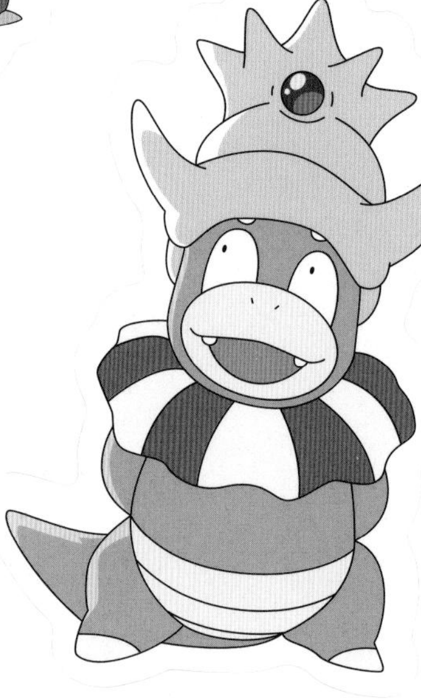

↑ SLOWKING

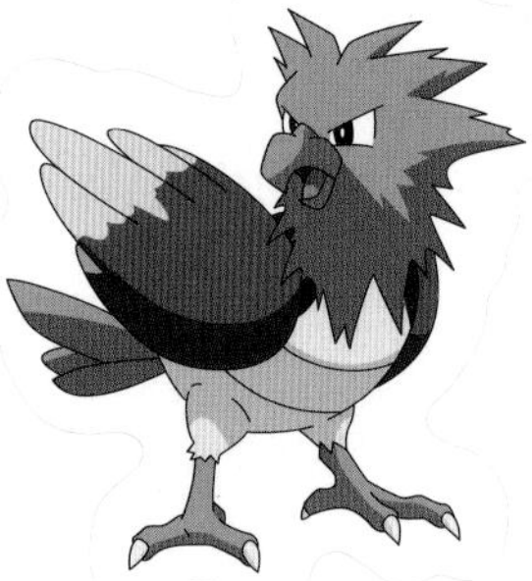

↑ SPEAROW

SLIGGOO →

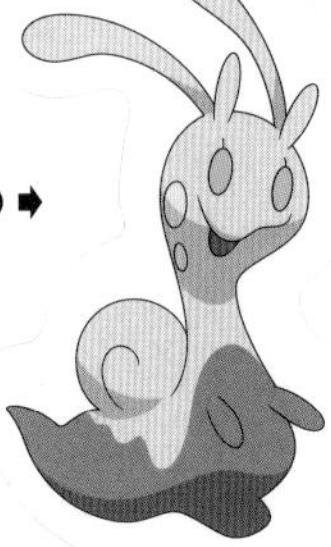

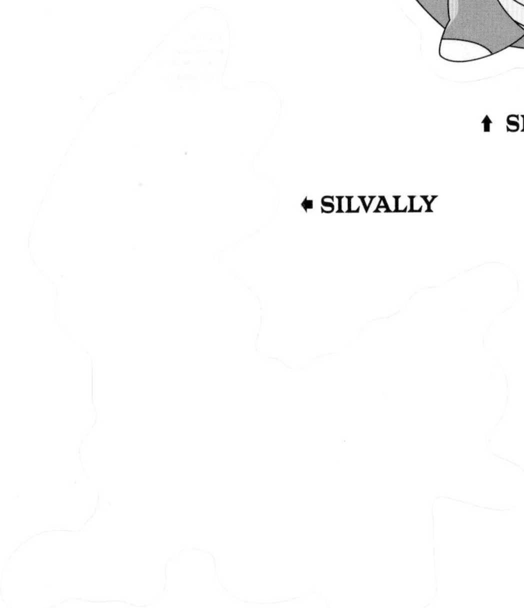

← SILVALLY

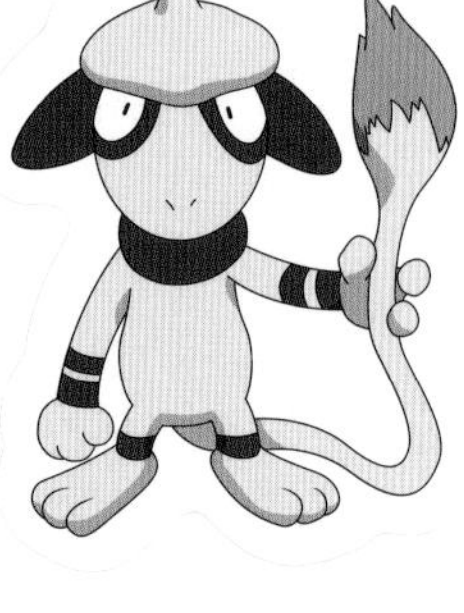

↑ SMEARGLE

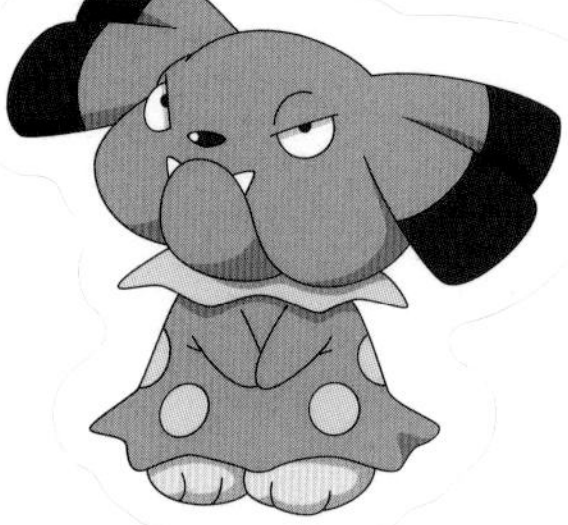

← SNUBBULL

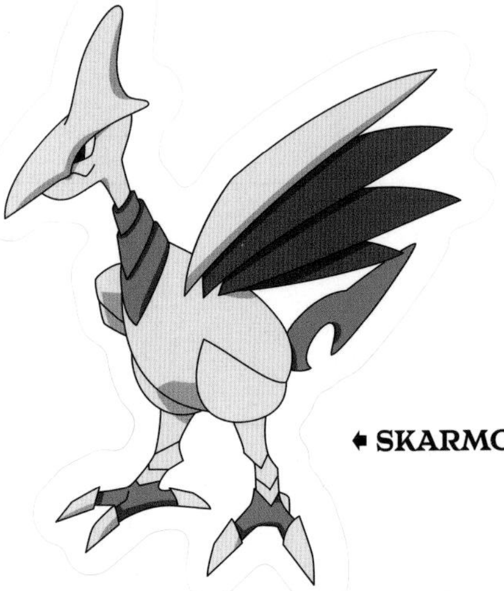

← SKARMORY

STEENEE →

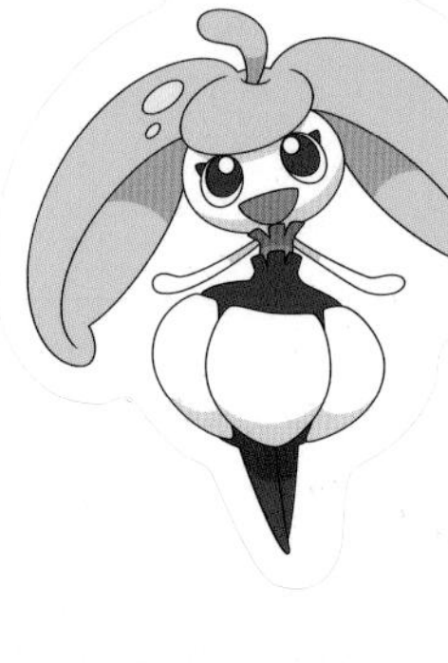

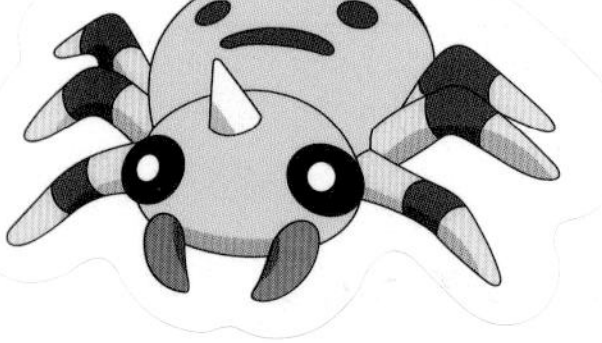

← SPINARAK

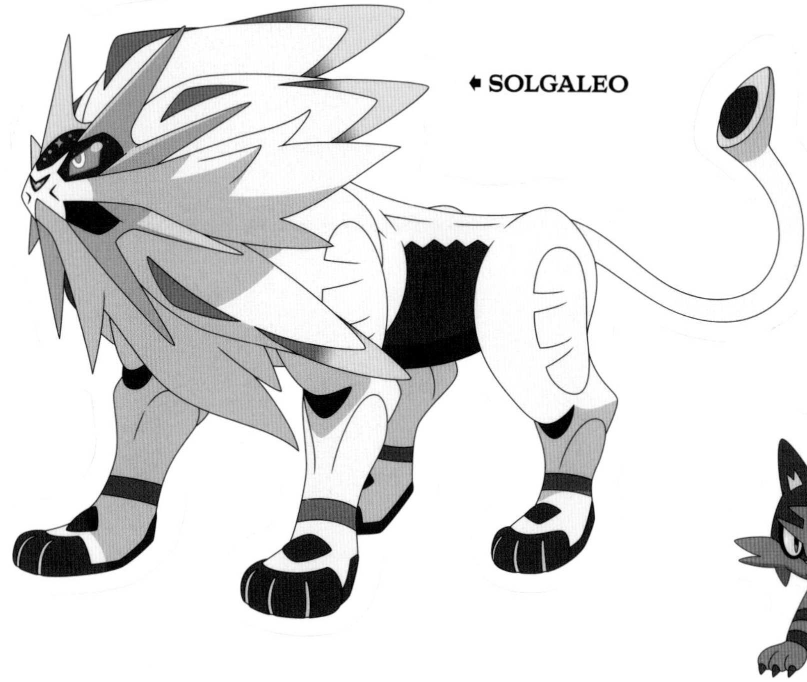

← SOLGALEO

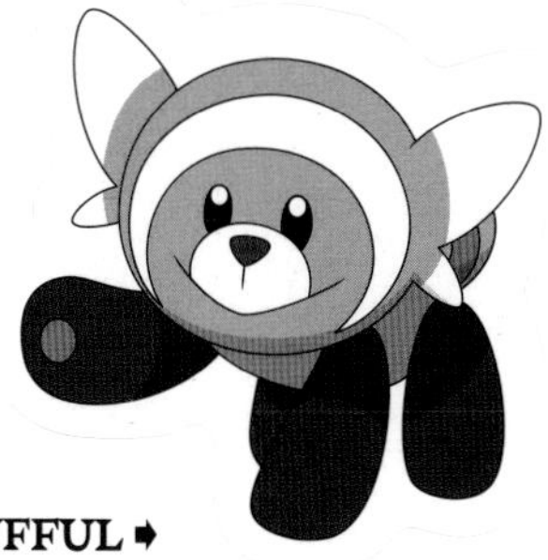

STUFFUL →

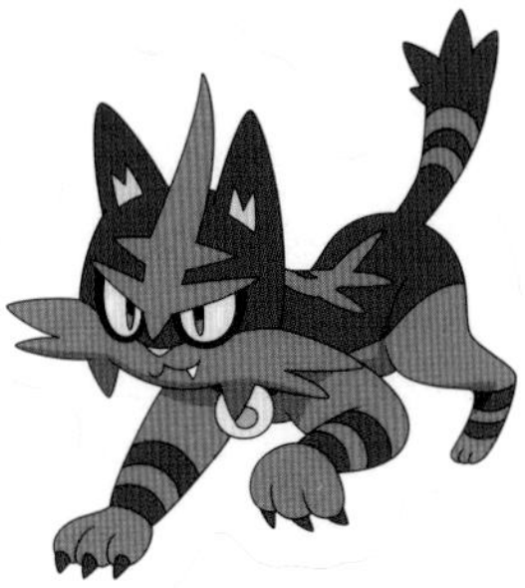

↑ TORRACAT

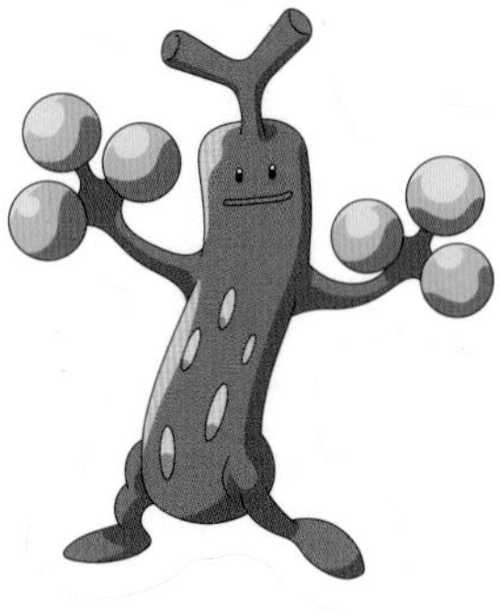

↑ SUDOWOODO

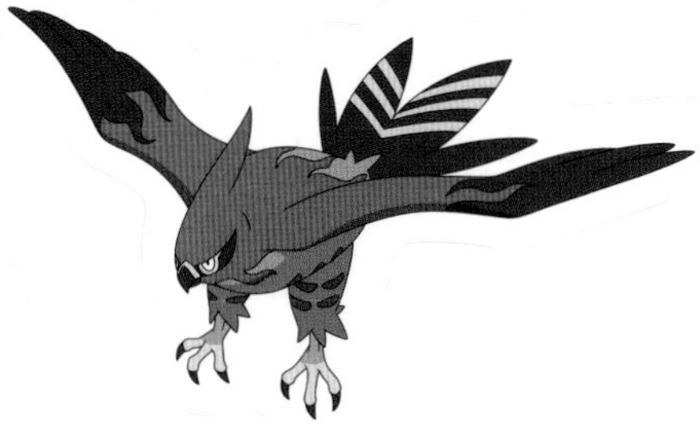

↑ TALONFLAME

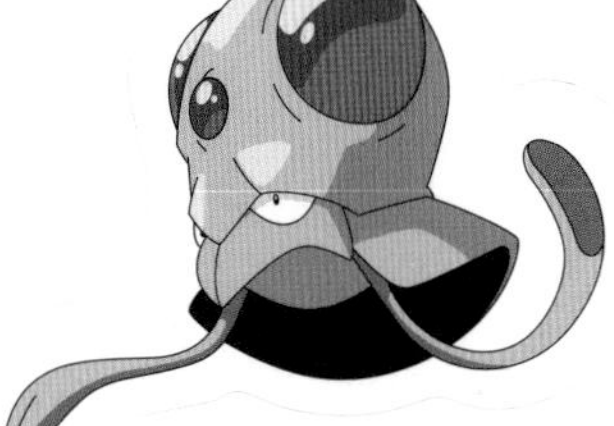

↑ TENTACOOL

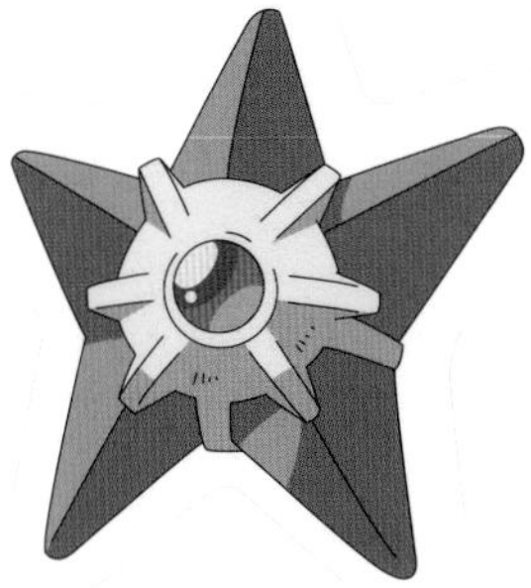

↑ STARYU

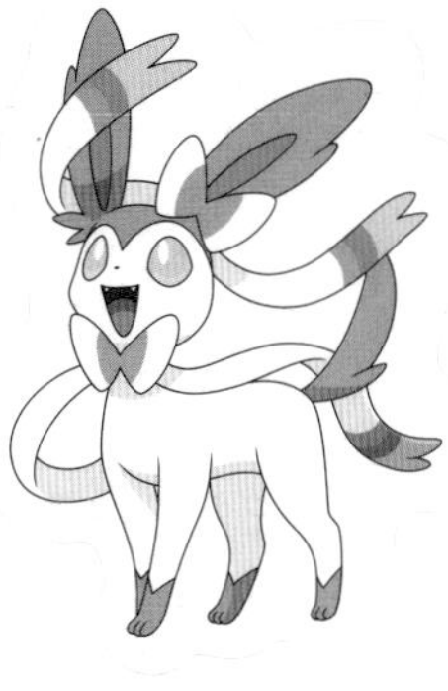

↑ SYLVEON

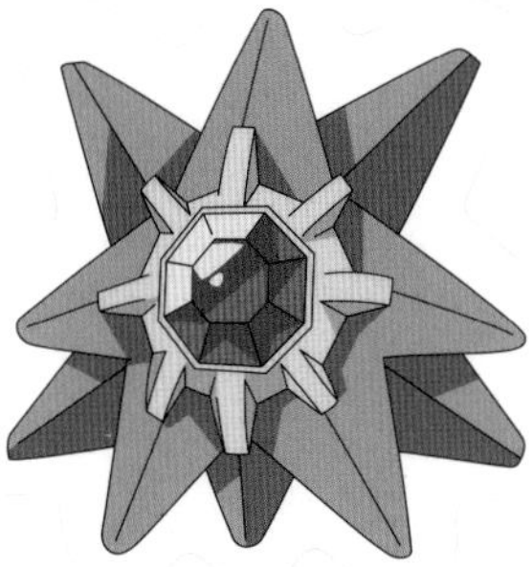

↑ STARMIE

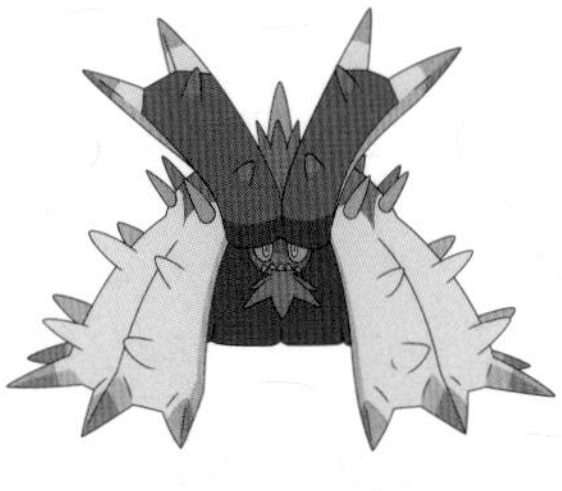

↑ TOXAPEX

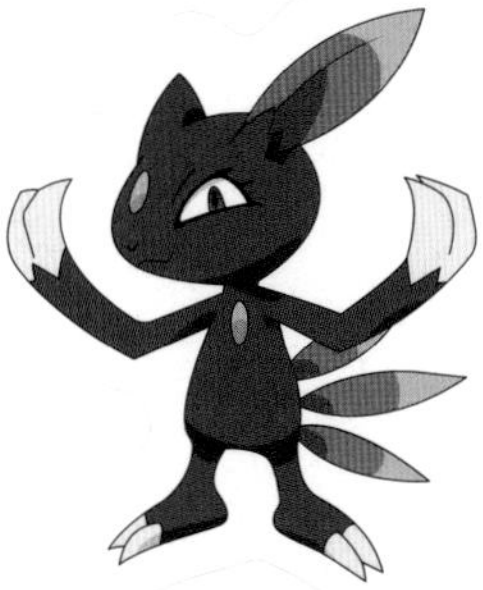

↑ SNEASEL

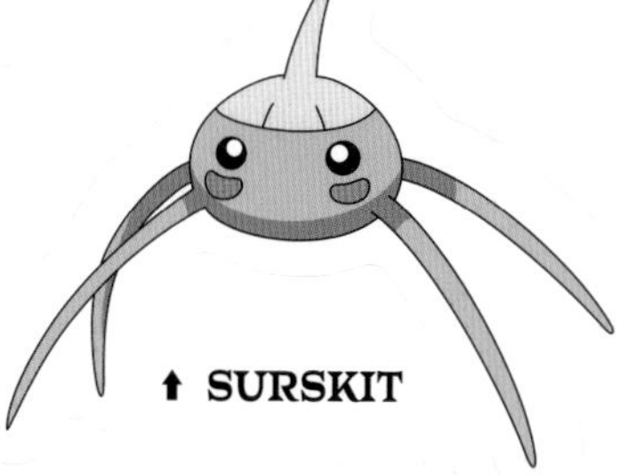

↑ SURSKIT

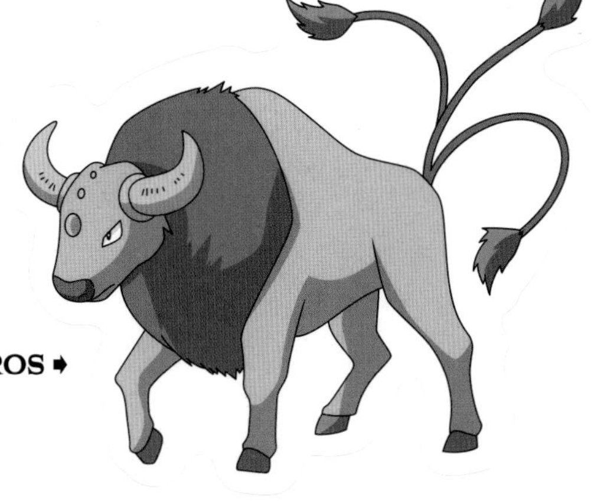

TAUROS →

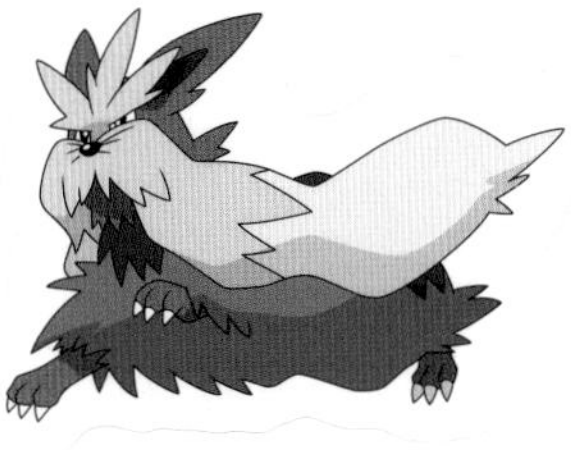

↑ STOUTLAND

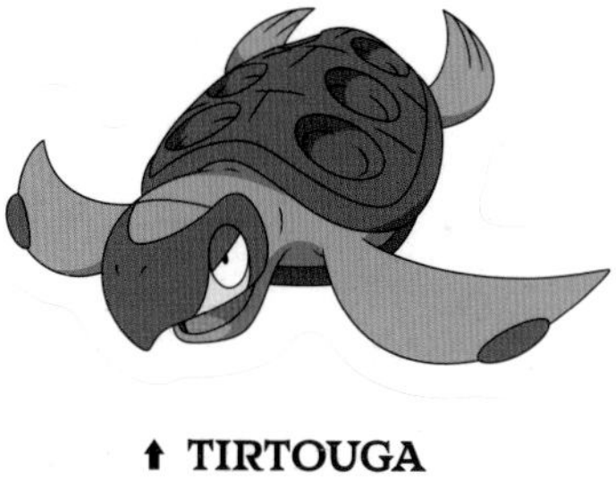

↑ TIRTOUGA

TAPU KOKO ⬇

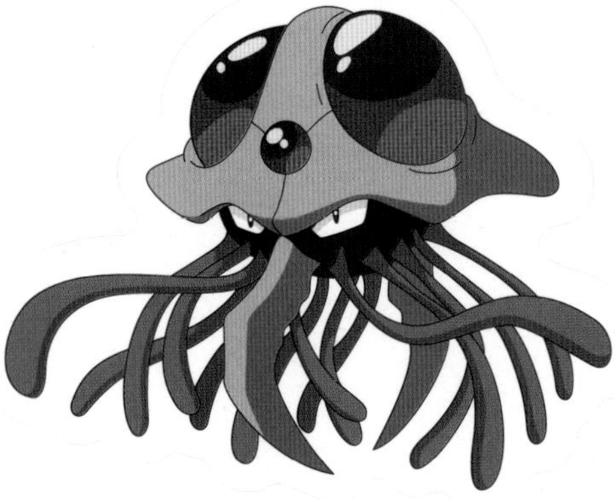

⬆ TENTACRUEL

TAPU BULU ⬆

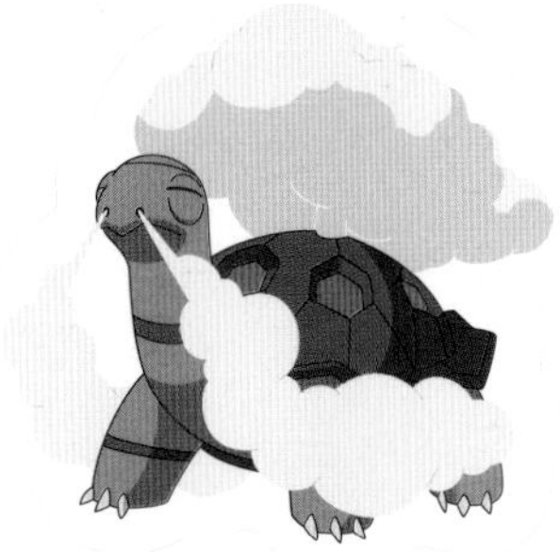

⬆ TORKOAL

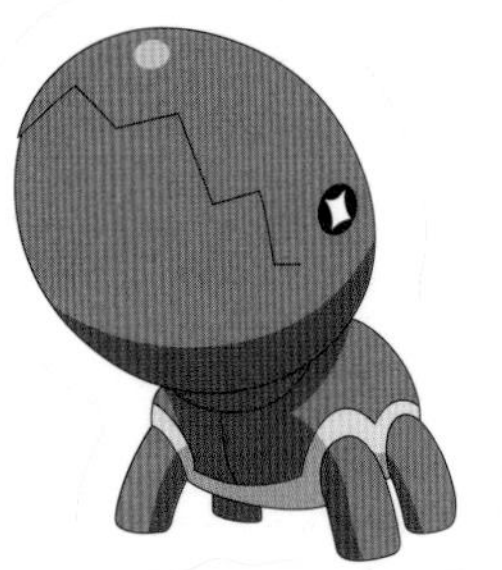

⬆ TRAPINCH

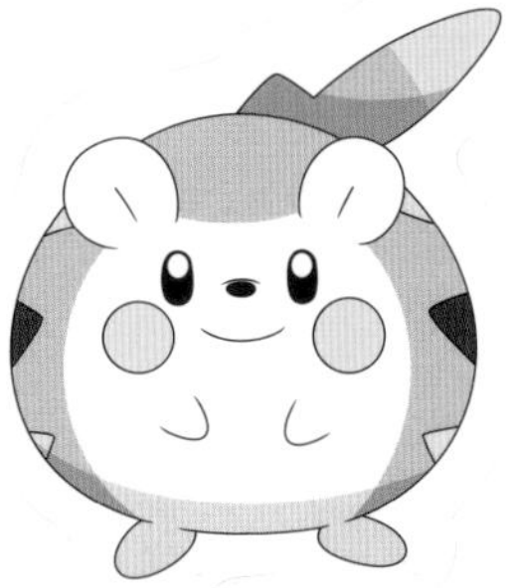

⬆ TOGEDEMARU

⬇ TAPU FINI

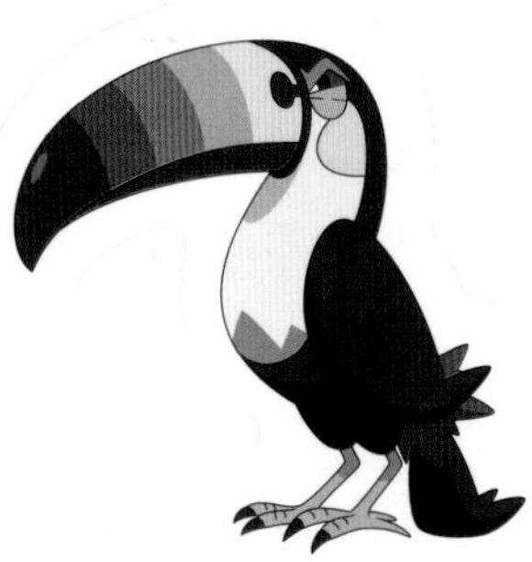

⬆ TOUCANNON

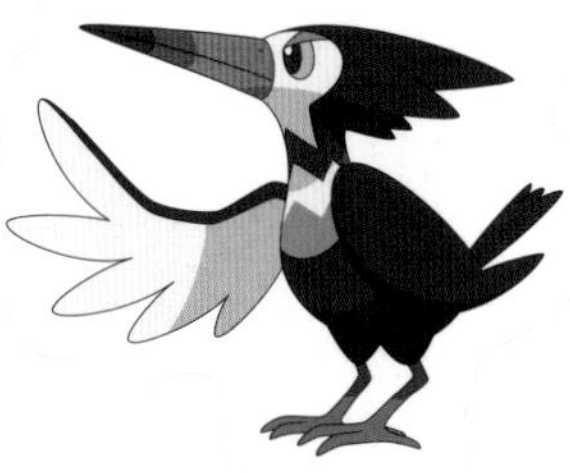

⬆ TRUMBEAK

⬆ TAPU LELE

TRUBBISH ➡

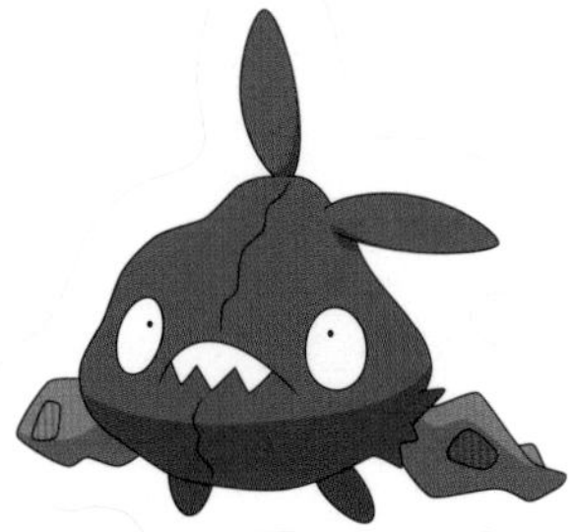

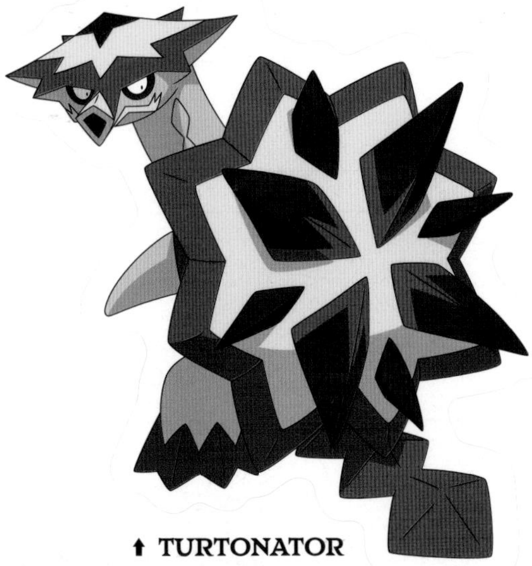

⬆ TURTONATOR

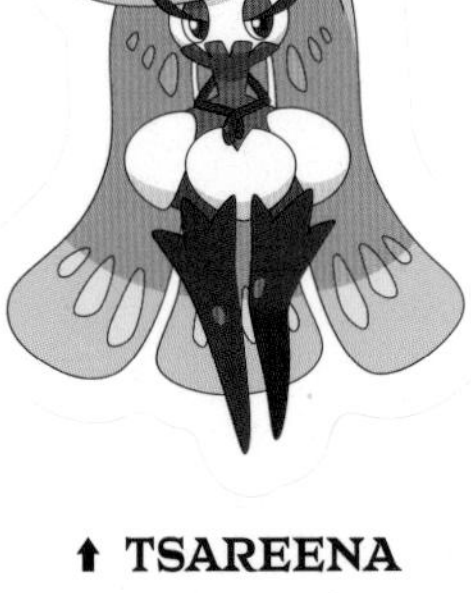

⬆ TSAREENA

TREVENANT ➡

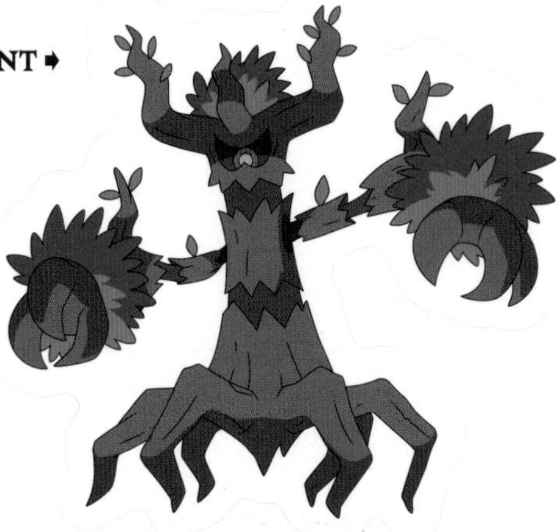

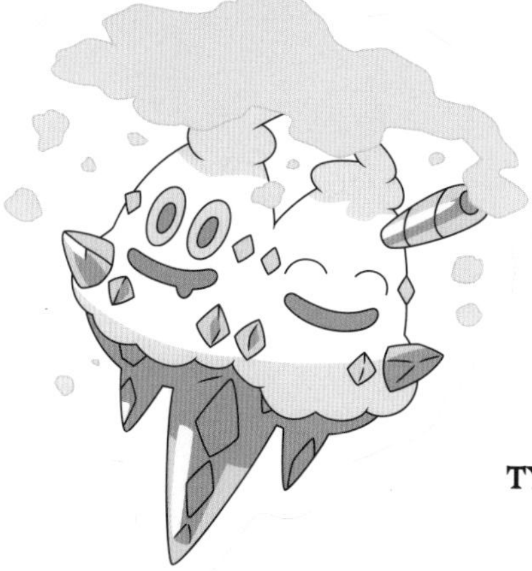

↑ VANILLUXE

TYPE: NULL →

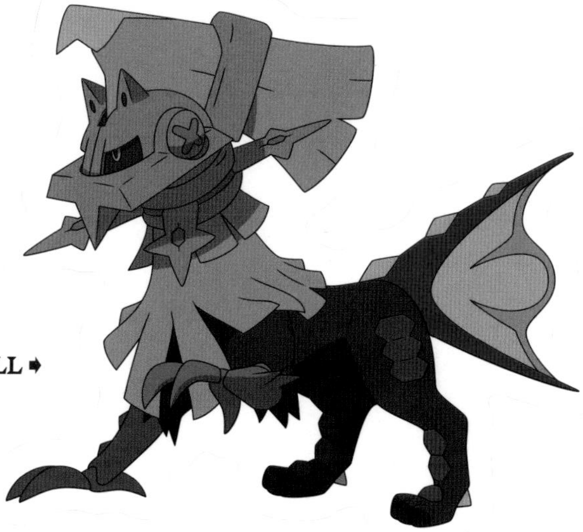

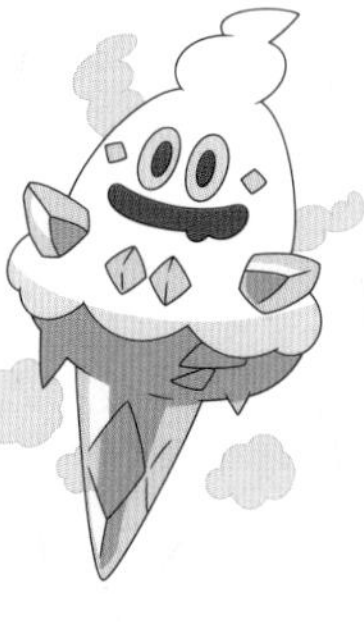

↑ VANILLISH

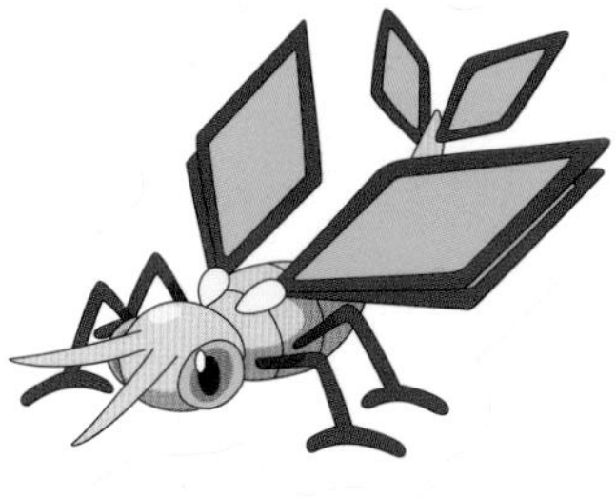

↑ VIBRAVA

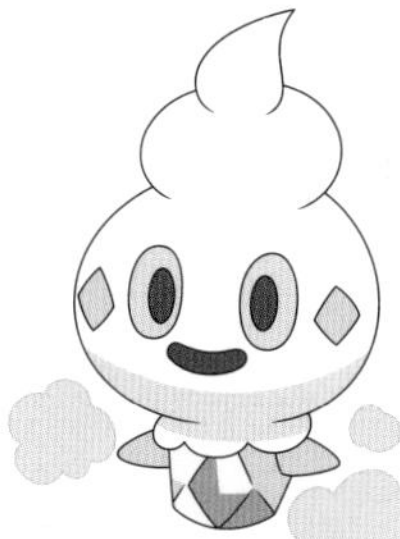

↑ VANILLITE

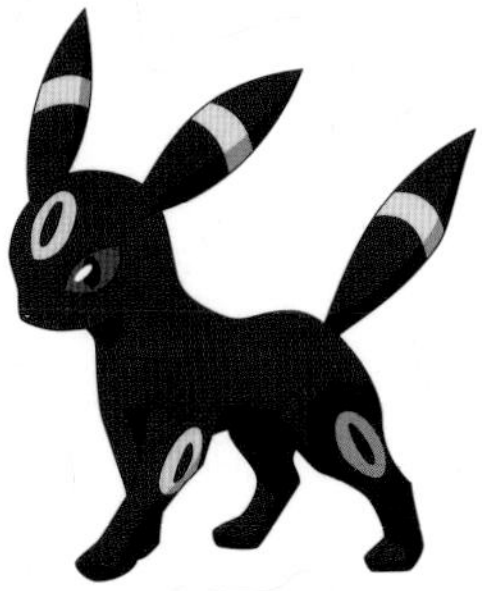

↑ UMBREON

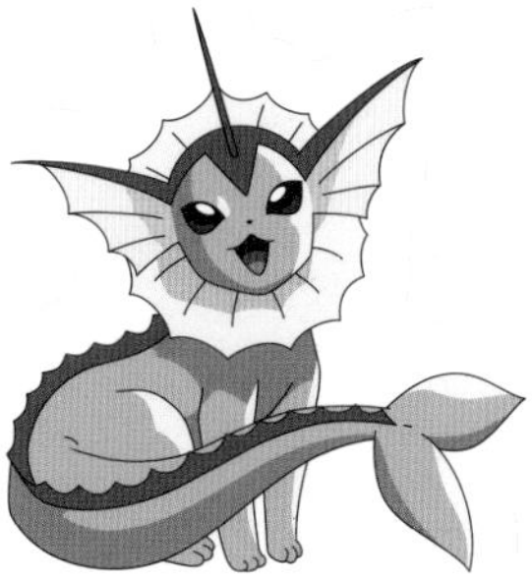

↑ VAPOREON

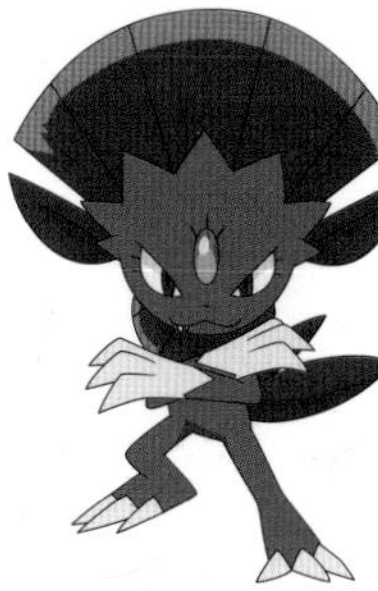

↑ WEAVILE

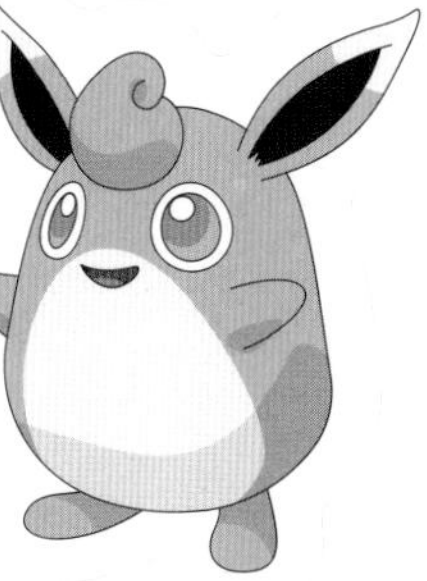

↑ WIGGLYTUFF

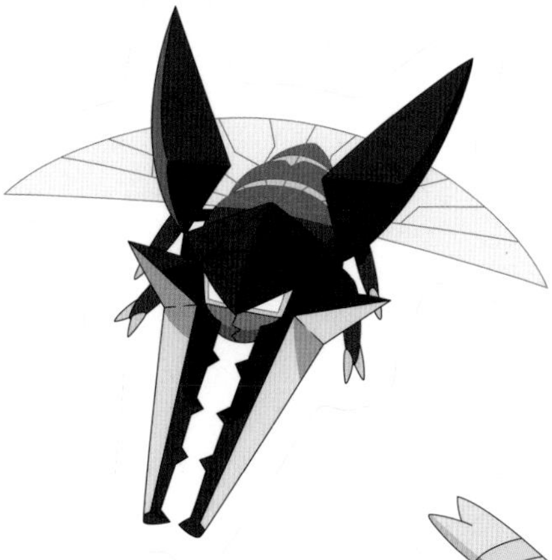

VIKAVOLT ↑

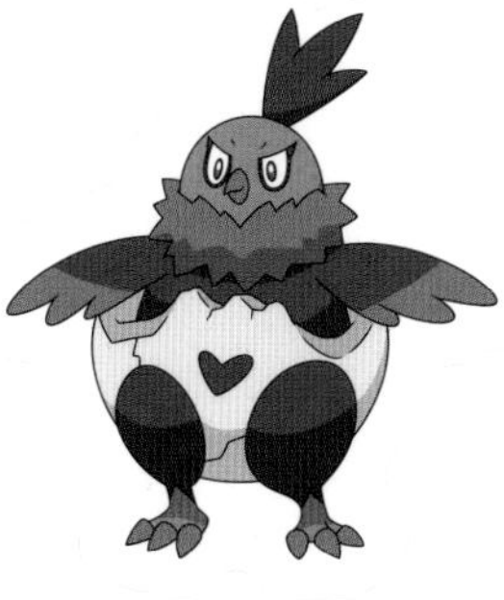

↑ VULLABY

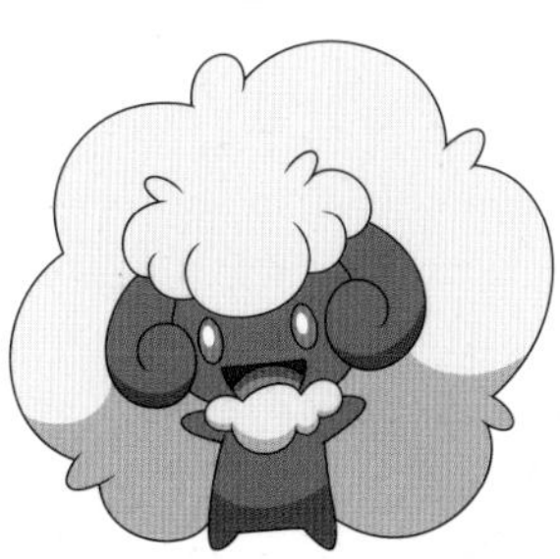

↑ WHIMSICOTT

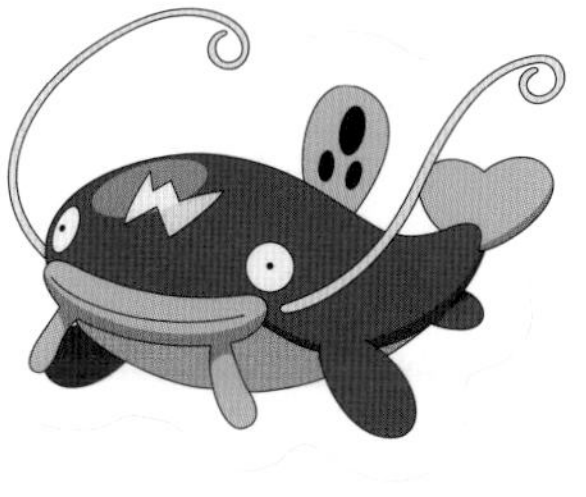

↑ WHISCASH

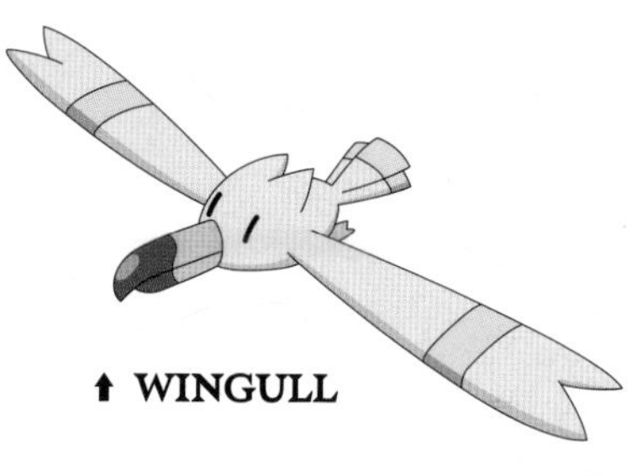

↑ WINGULL

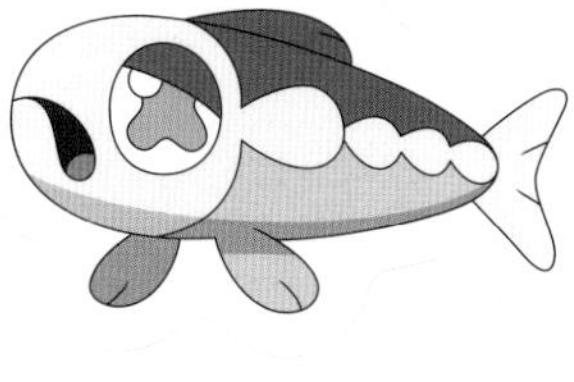

↑ WISHIWASHI (SOLO FORM)

↑ WIMPOD

↑ VULPIX (ALOLA FORM)

↑ WAILORD

↑ WAILMER

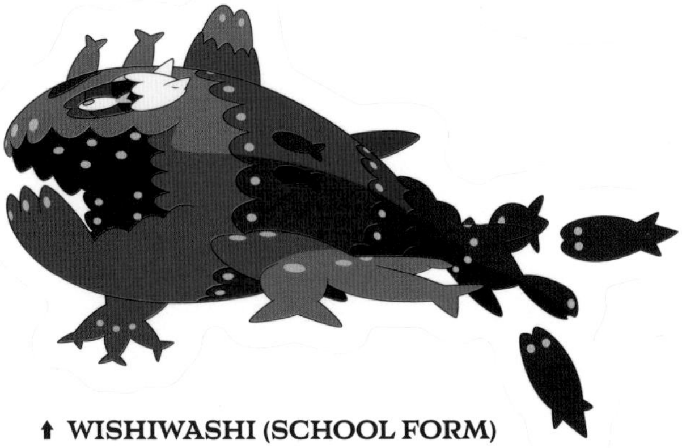

↑ WISHIWASHI (SCHOOL FORM)

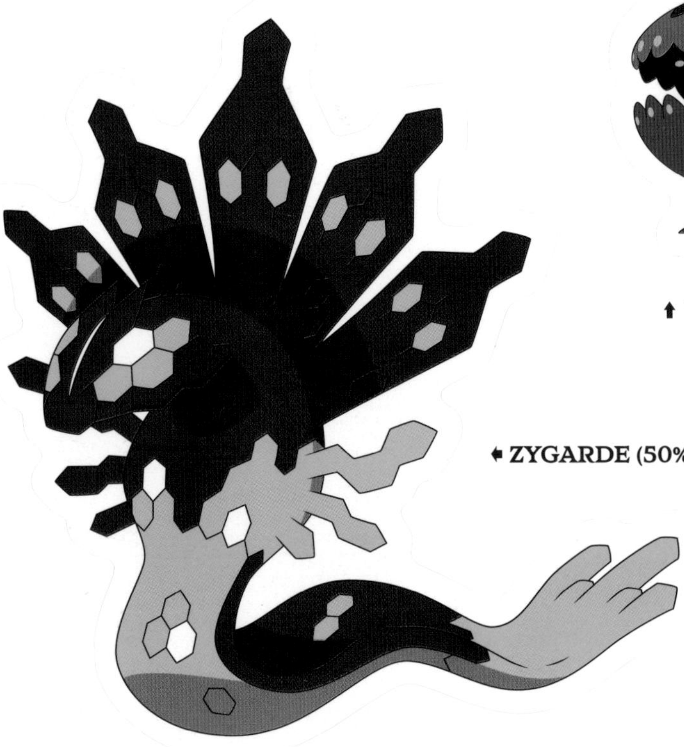

← ZYGARDE (50% FORME)

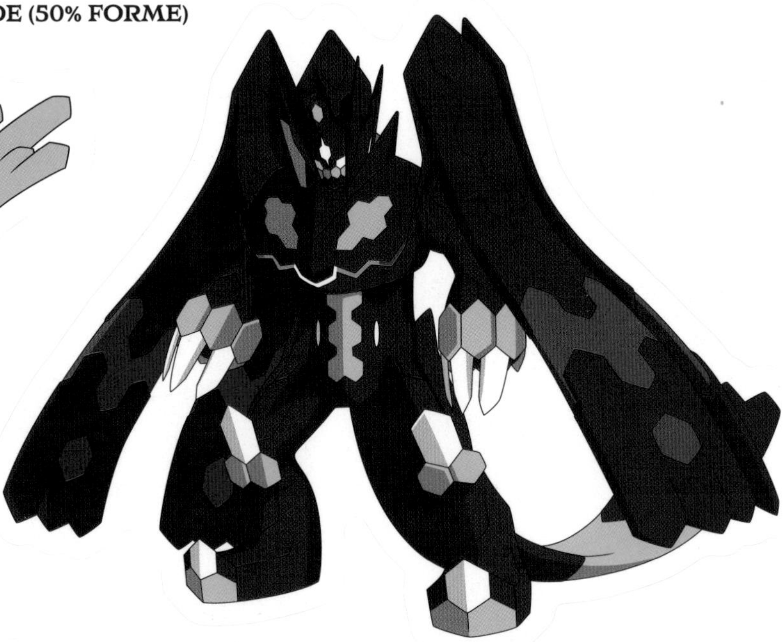

↑ ZYGARDE (COMPLETE FORME)

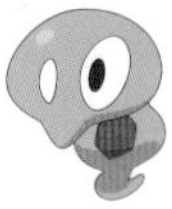

← ZYGARDE CORE

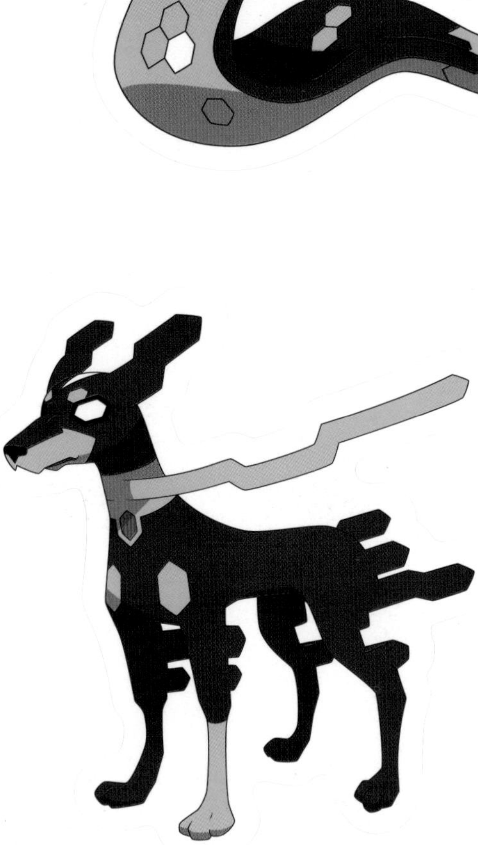

↑ ZYGARDE (10% FORME)

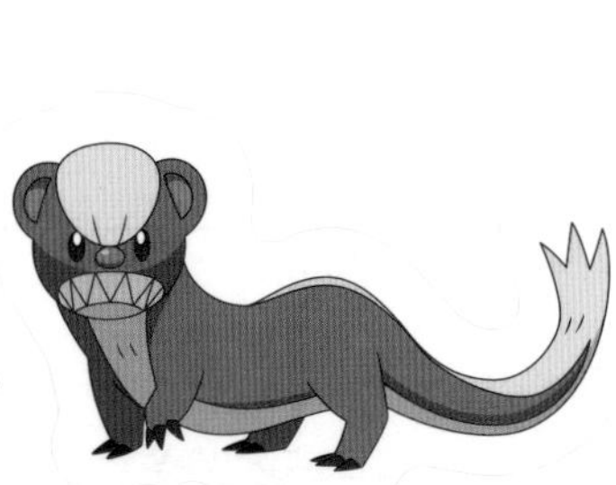

YUNGOOS →

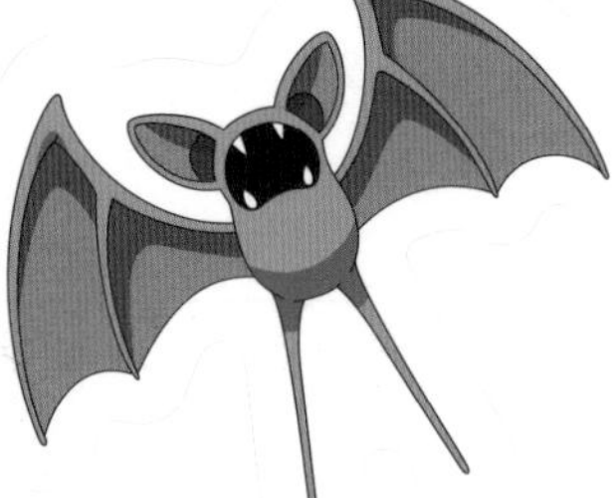

↑ ZUBAT

ITEM STICKERS

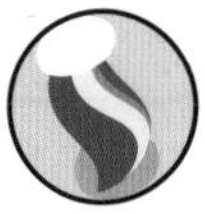
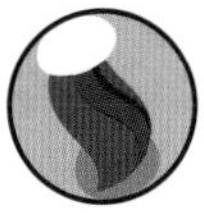
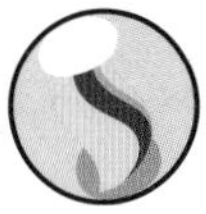
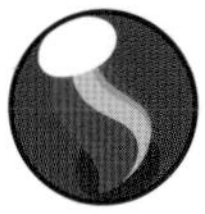

↑ ABSOLITE ↑ AERODACTYLITE ↑ ALAKAZITE ↑ DIVE BALL ↑ DUSK BALL ↑ GARCHOMPITE

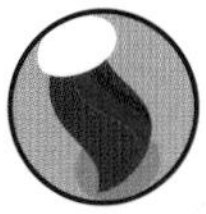
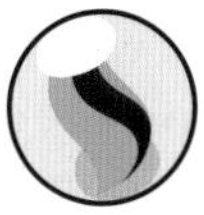
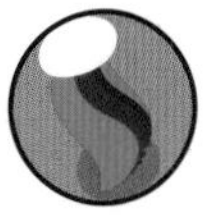
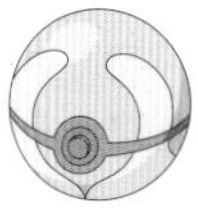
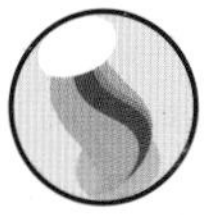

↑ GENGARITE ↑ GLALITITE ↑ GREAT BALL ↑ GYARADOSITE ↑ HEAL BALL ↑ KANGASKHANITE

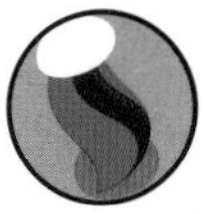
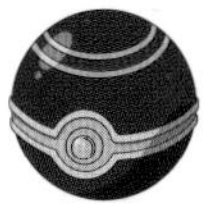
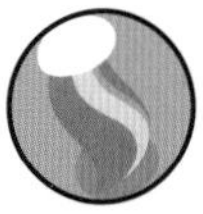

↑ LUCARIONITE ↑ LUXURY BALL ↑ MASTER BALL ↑ METAGROSSITE ↑ NEST BALL ↑ NET BALL

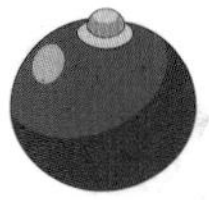
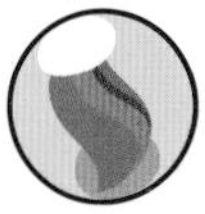

↑ ORAN BERRY ↑ PECHA BERRY ↑ PINSIRITE ↑ POKÉ BALL ↑ PREMIER BALL ↑ QUICK BALL

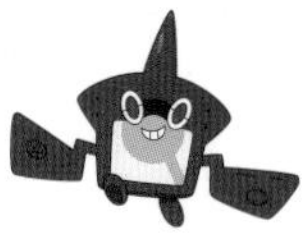
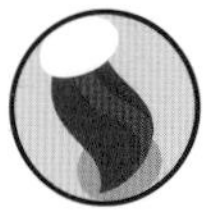
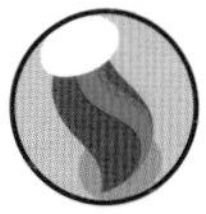
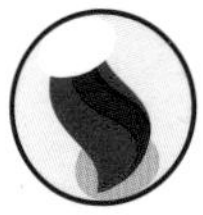
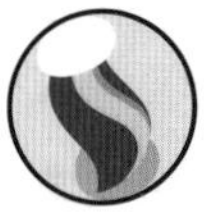

↑ REPEAT BALL ↑ ROTOM POKÉDEX ↑ SABLENITE ↑ SALAMENCITE ↑ SCIZORITE ↑ SHARPEDONITE

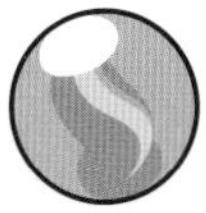
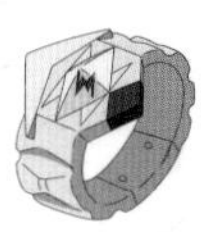

↑ SITRUS BERRY ↑ SLOWBRONITE ↑ TAMATO BERRY ↑ TIMER BALL ↑ ULTRA BALL ↑ Z-RING

ULTRA BEAST STICKERS

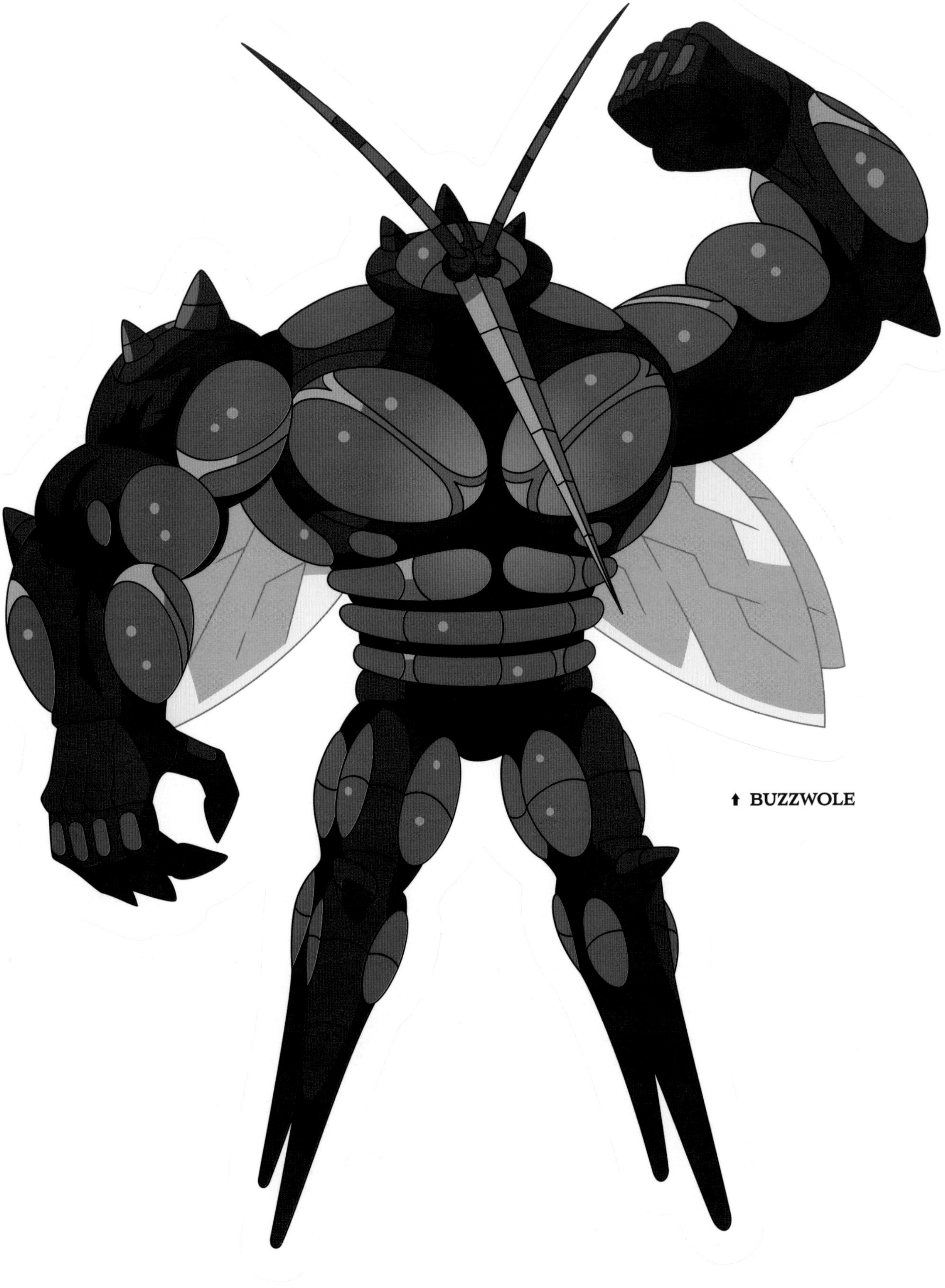

↑ BUZZWOLE

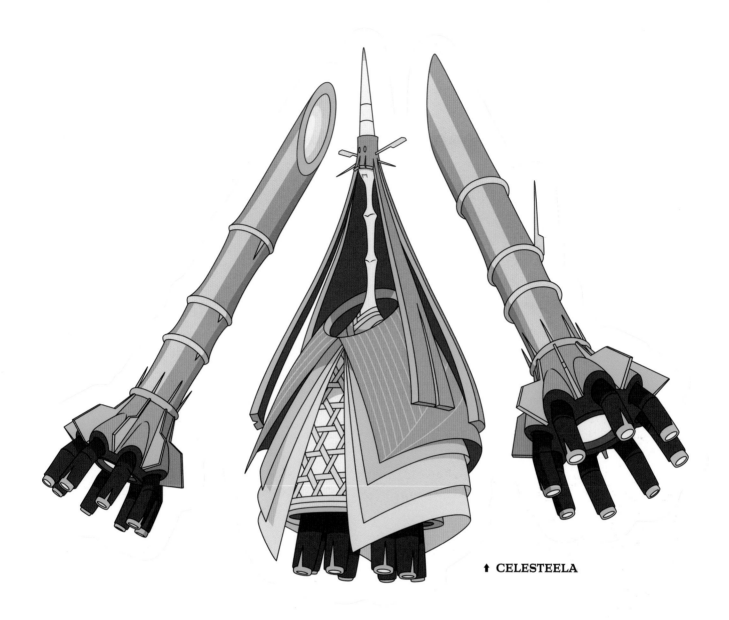

↑ CELESTEELA

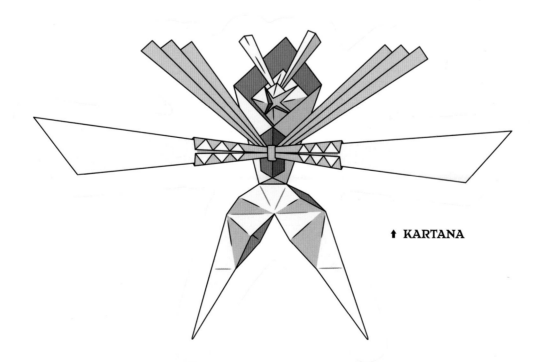

↑ KARTANA

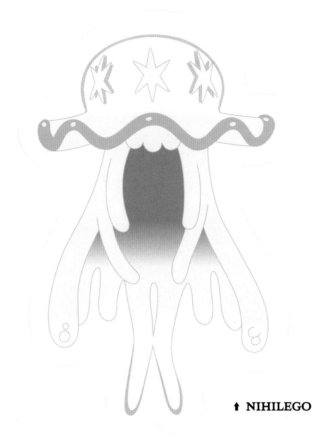

⬆ NIHILEGO

⬆ GUZZLORD

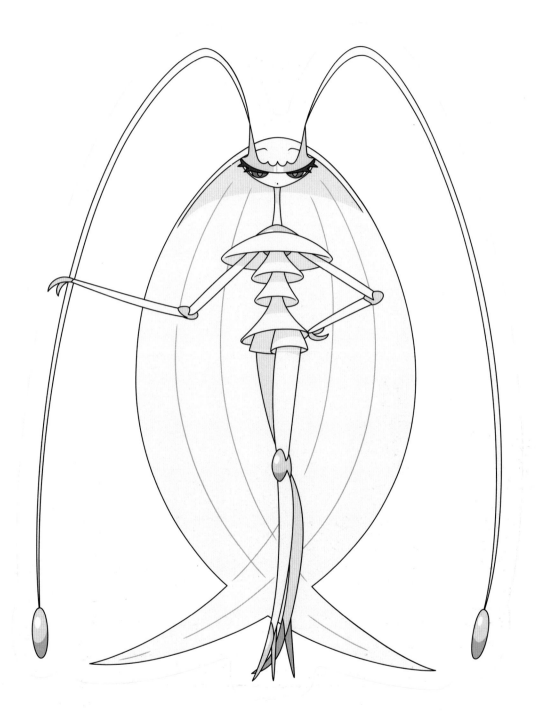

↑ PHEROMOSA

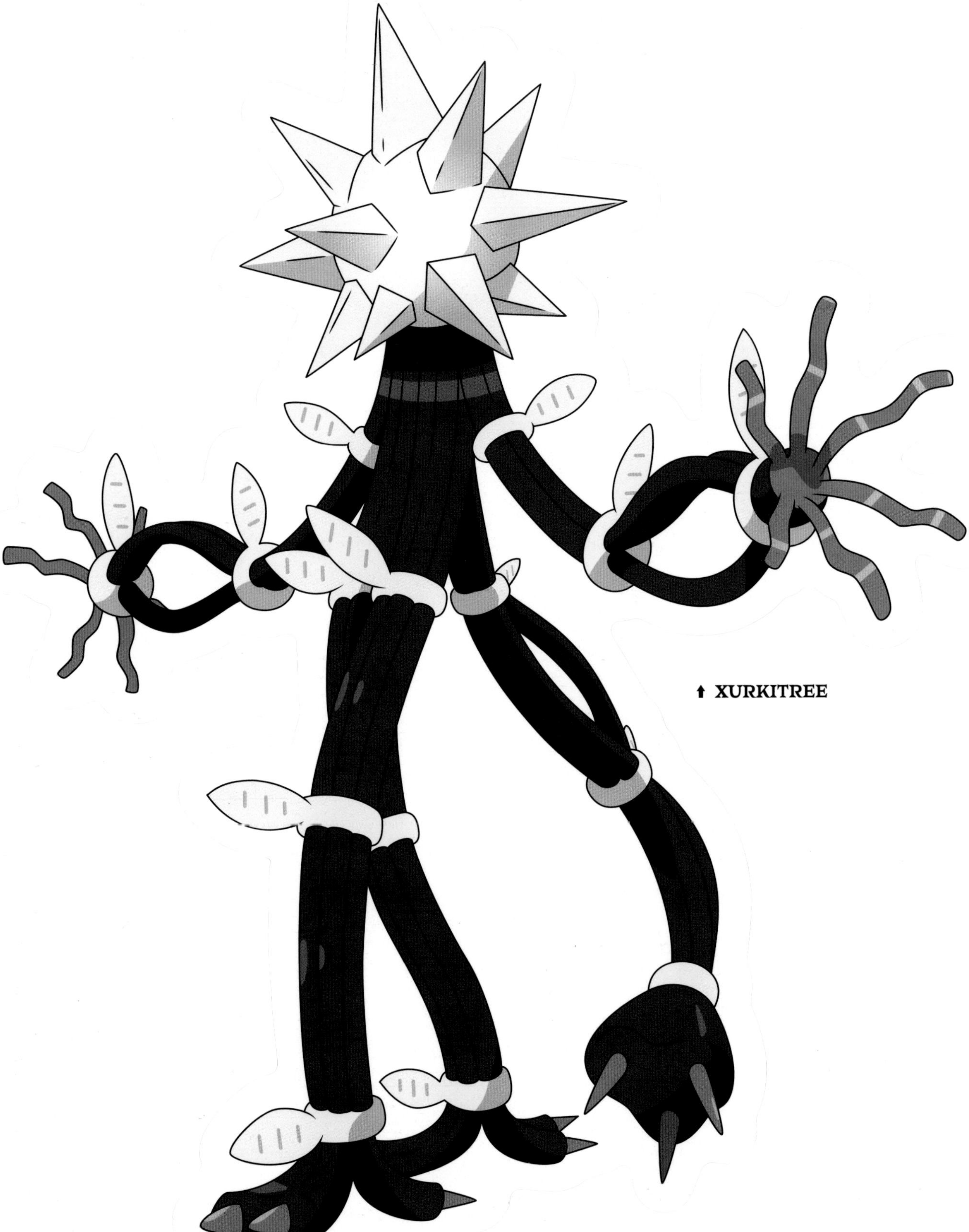

↑ XURKITREE

SCENE STICKERS

Time to get your sticker Pokémon together! You can combine them with the sticker scene pages to put stickers into action. The four scenes from Alola feature a beach, a cave and grassy field, a tropical jungle, and a snowy mountain. Mix up your terrain and Pokémon, or arrange them just so—it's up to you!

BEACH SCENE STICKERS

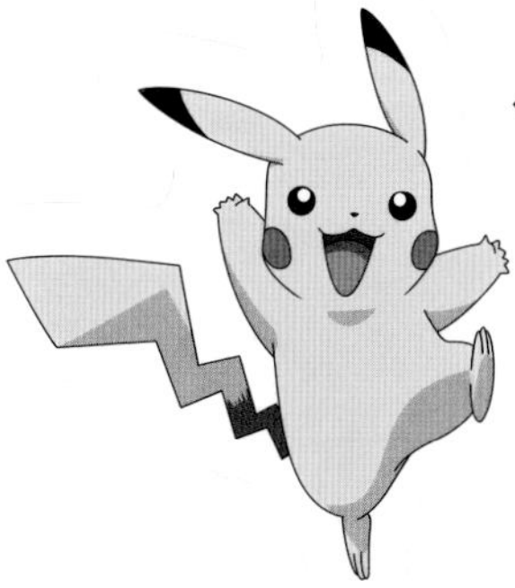

← PIKACHU

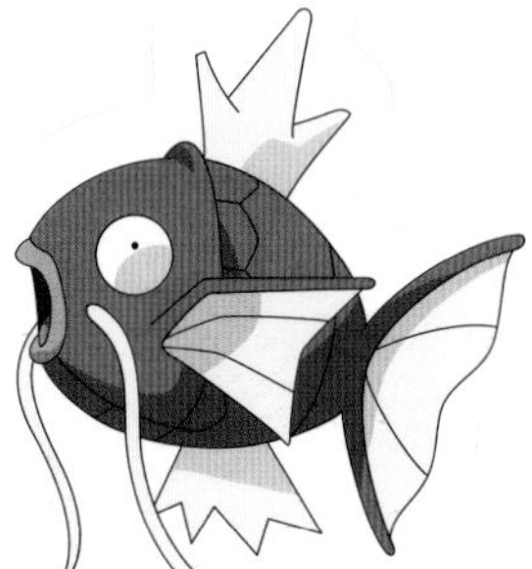

↑ MAGIKARP

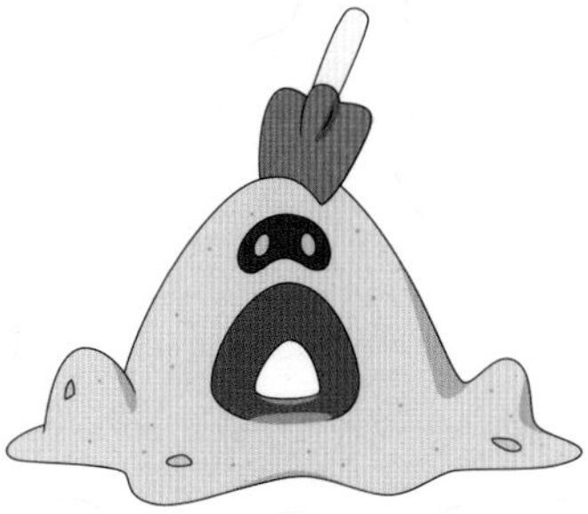

↑ SANDYGAST

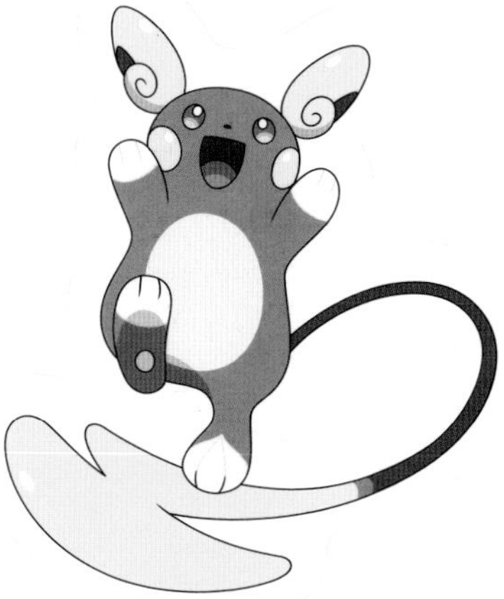

↑ RAICHU (ALOLA FORM)

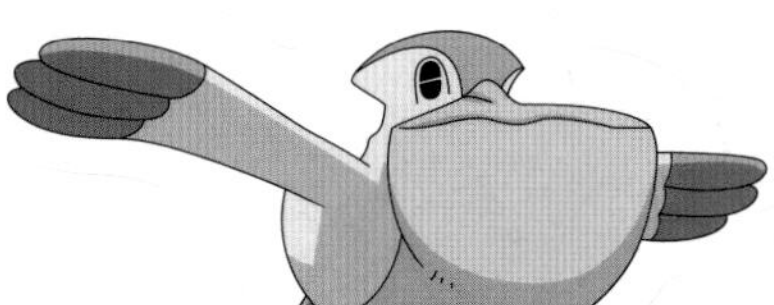

↑ PELIPPER

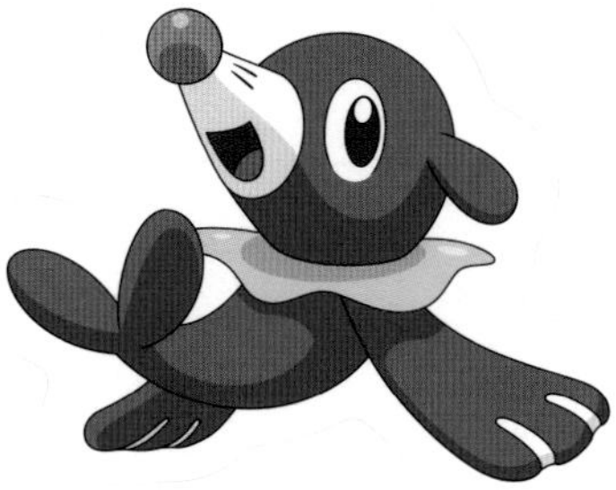

↑ POPPLIO

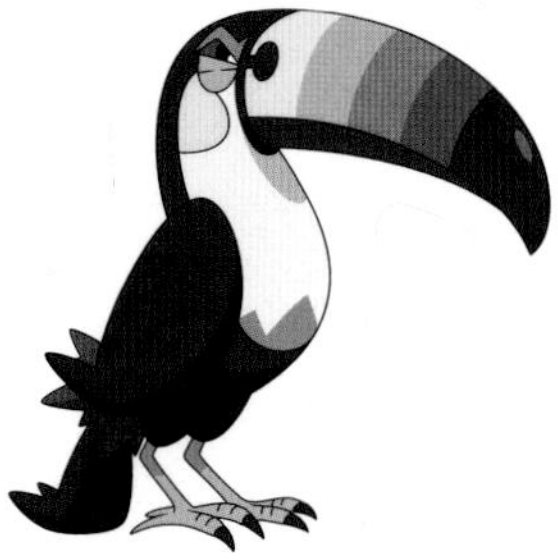

↑ TOUCANNON

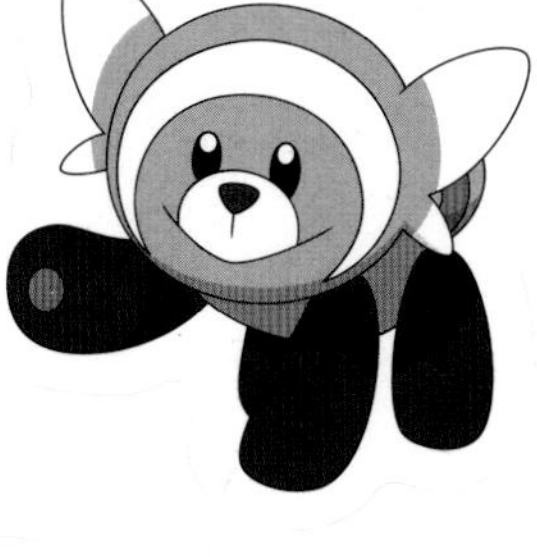

↑ STUFFUL

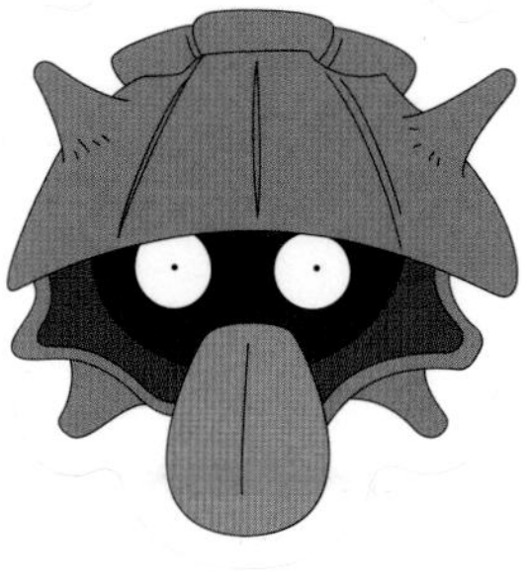

↑ SHELLDER

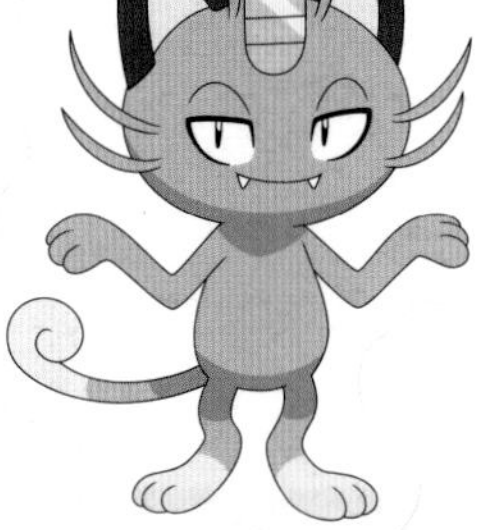

↑ MEOWTH (ALOLA FORM)

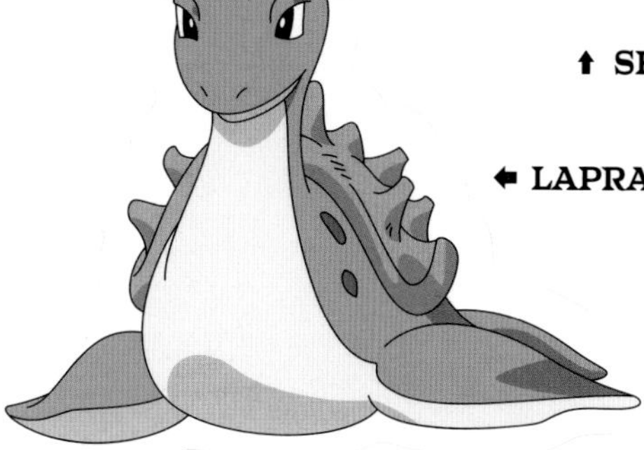

← LAPRAS

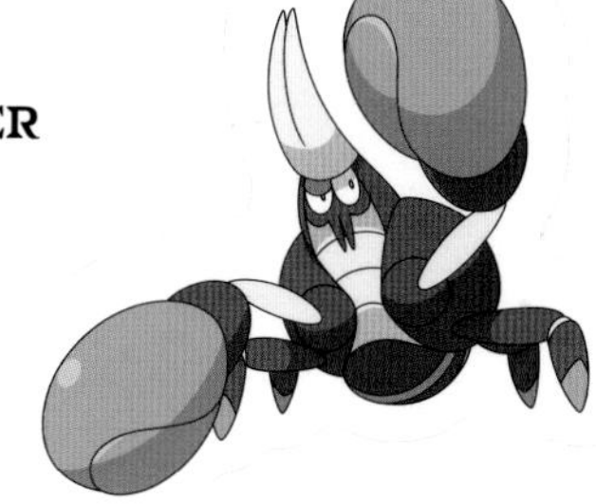

↑ CRABRAWLER

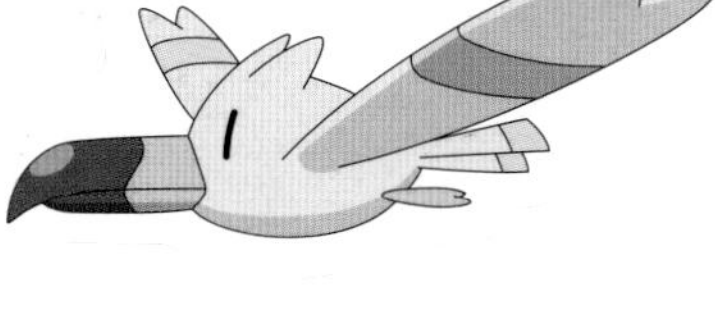

↑ WINGULL

↑ CUTIEFLY

↑ WIMPOD

↑ BUTTERFREE

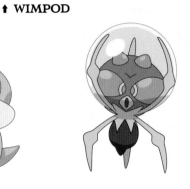

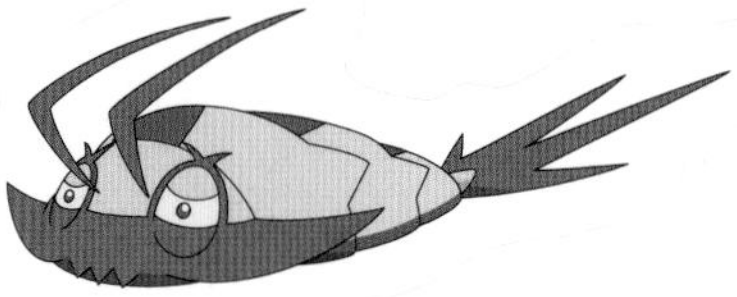

↑ PYUKUMUKU

↑ PSYDUCK

↑ DEWPIDER

↑ MAREANIE

CAVE AND GRASSY FIELD SCENE STICKERS

← GEODUDE (ALOLA FORM)

↑ LITTEN

↑ ZUBAT

↑ ROCKRUFF

↑ KOMALA

↑ RATTATA (ALOLA FORM)

↑ DUGTRIO (ALOLA FORM)

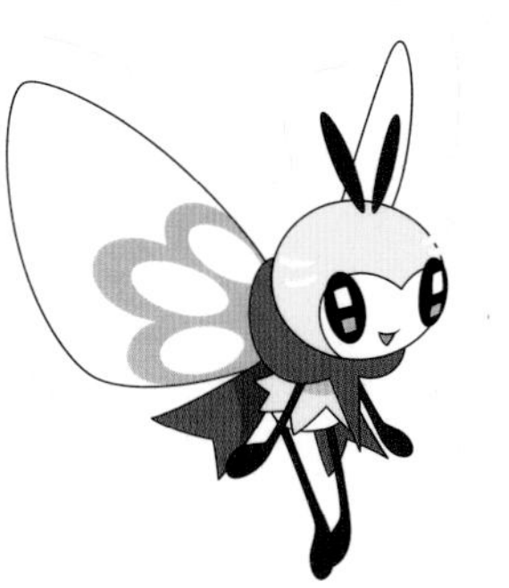

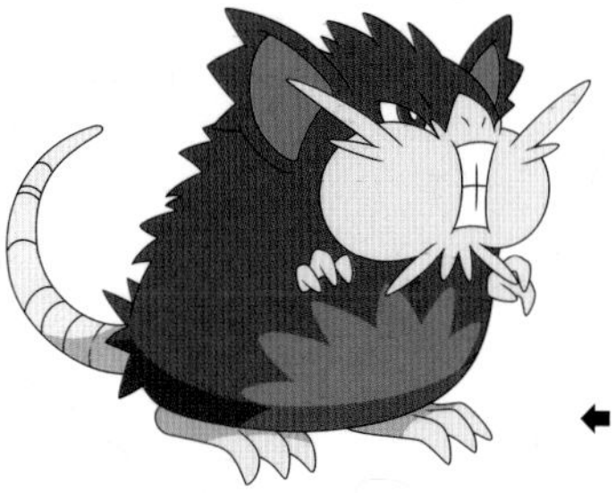

⬅ RATICATE (ALOLA FORM)

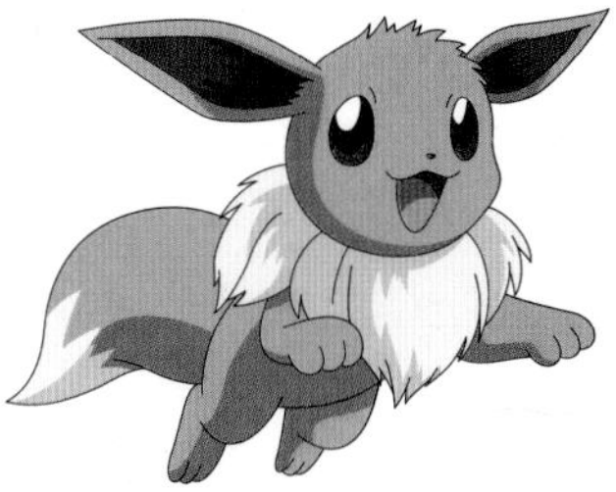

⬆ RIBOMBEE

⬆ EEVEE

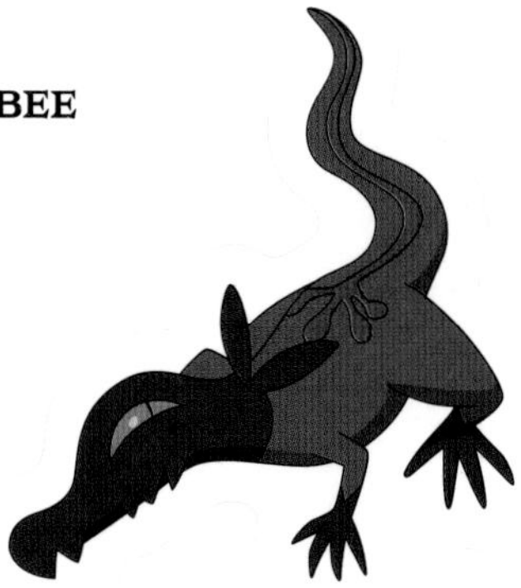

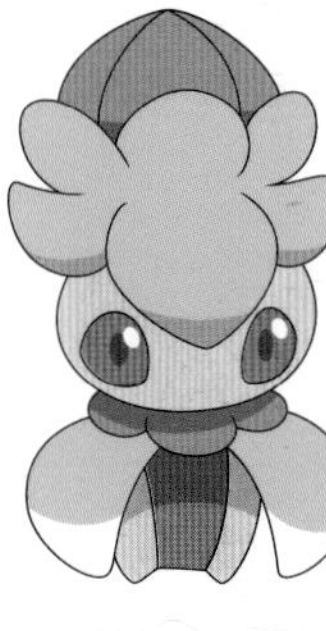

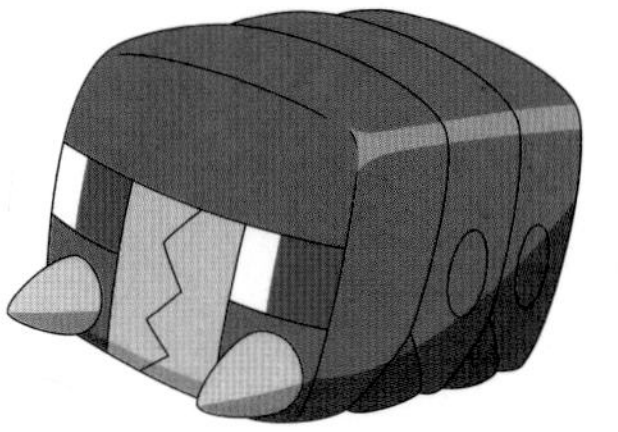

⬆ FOMANTIS

⬆ SALANDIT

⬆ CHARJABUG

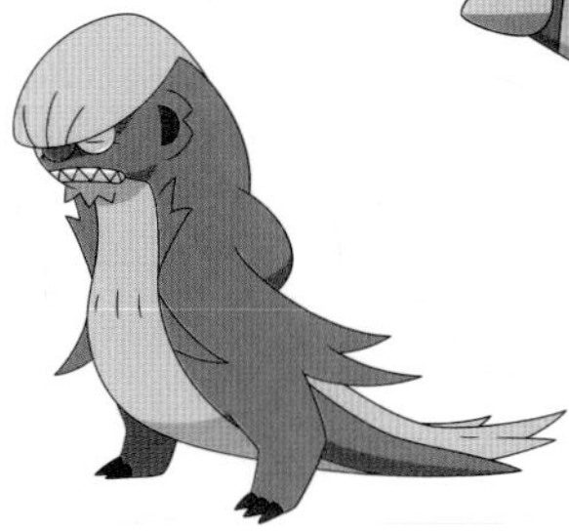

⬆ GUMSHOOS

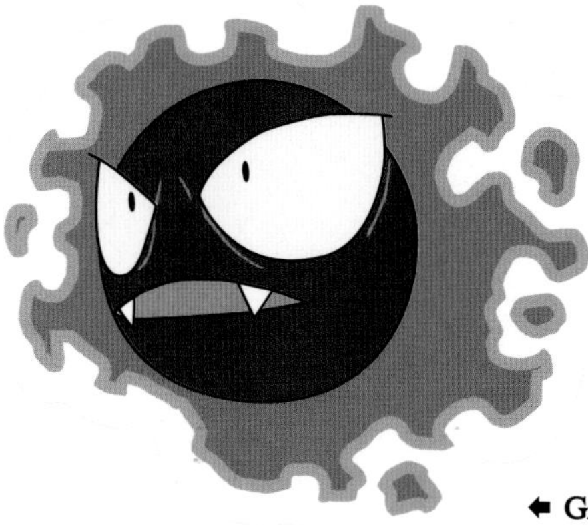

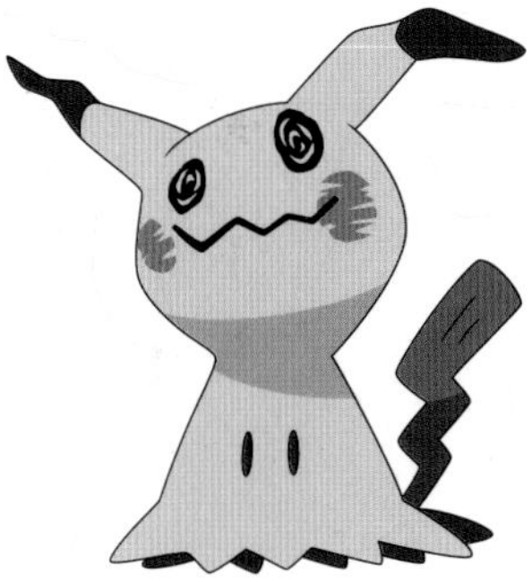

⬆ MIMIKYU

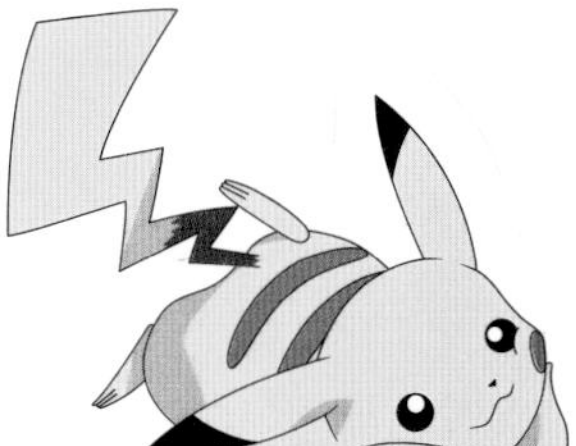

⬅ GASTLY

⬅ PIKACHU

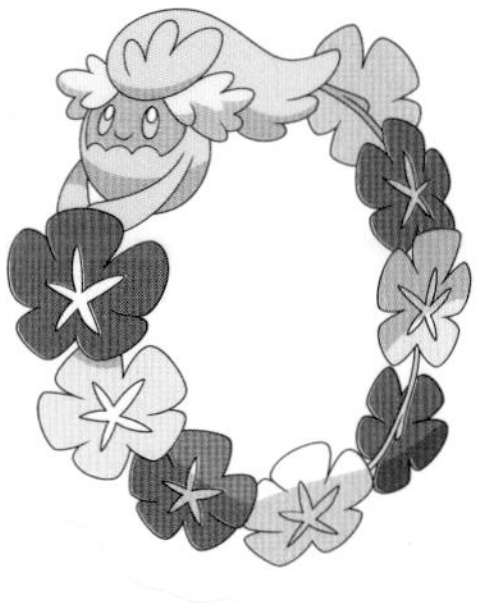

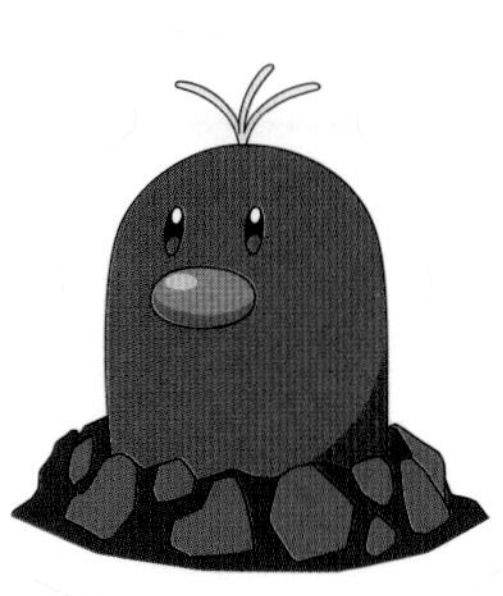

⬆ COMFEY

⬆ JIGGLYPUFF

⬆ DIGLETT (ALOLA FORM)

TROPICAL JUNGLE SCENE STICKERS

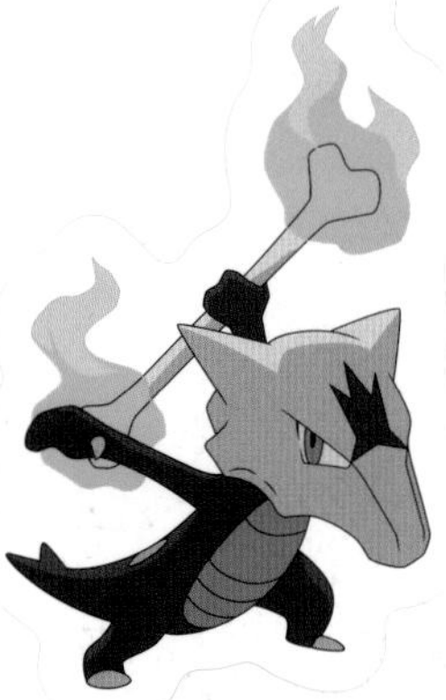

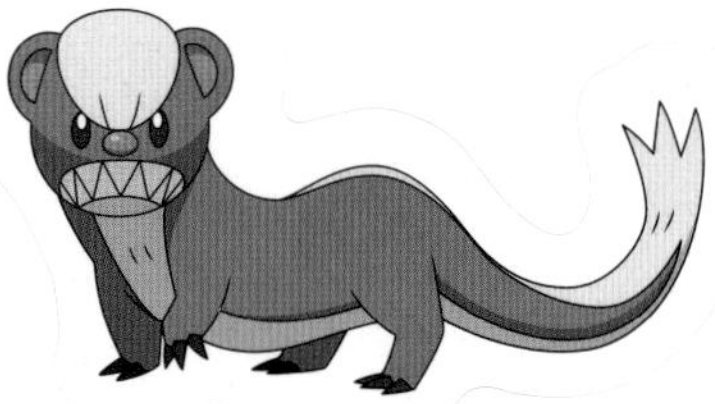

↑ YUNGOOS

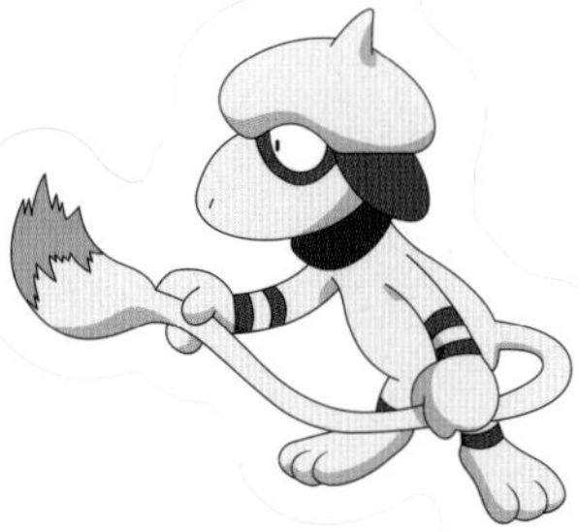

↑ SMEARGLE

↑ MAROWAK (ALOLA FORM)

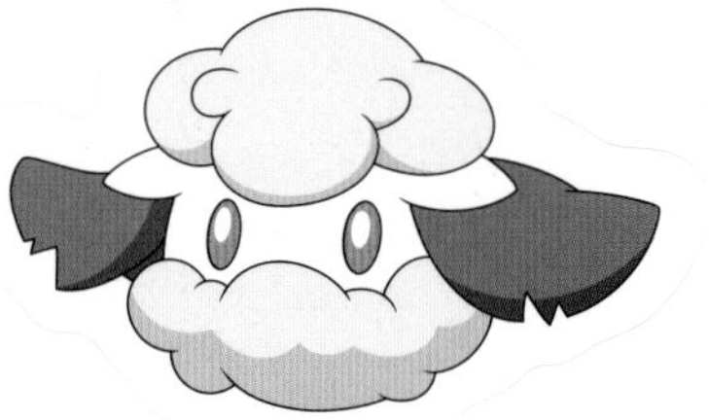

↑ COTTONEE

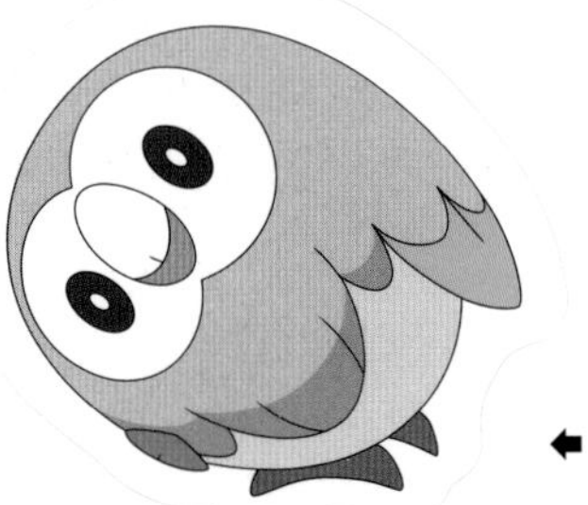

← ROWLET

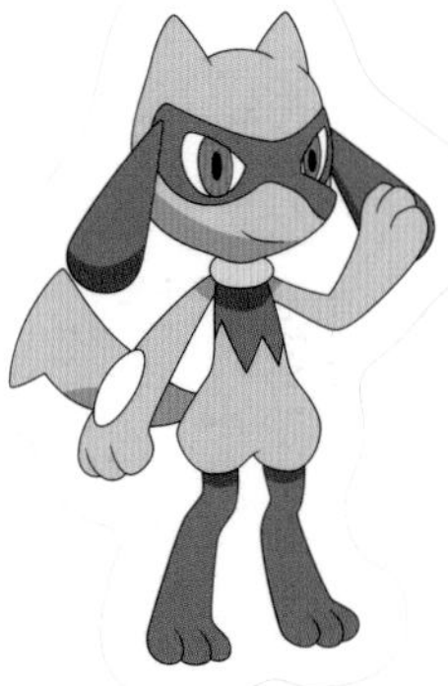

↑ RIOLU

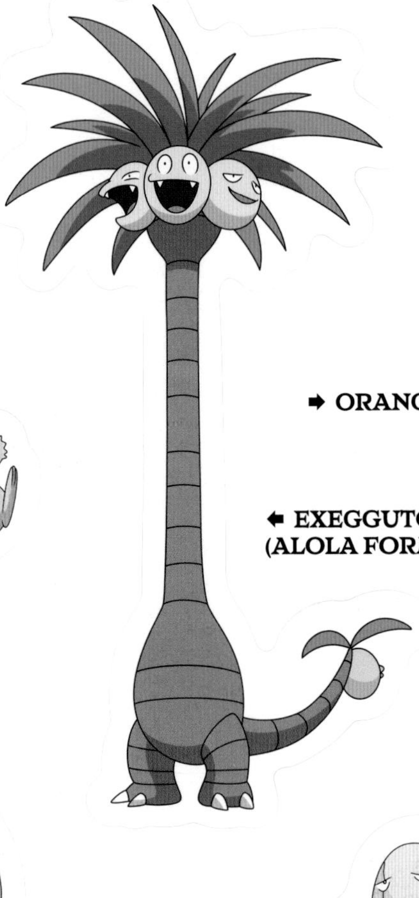

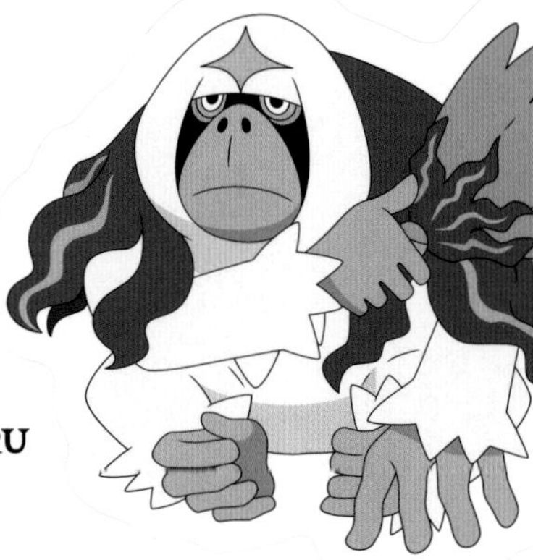

→ ORANGURU

← EXEGGUTOR (ALOLA FORM)

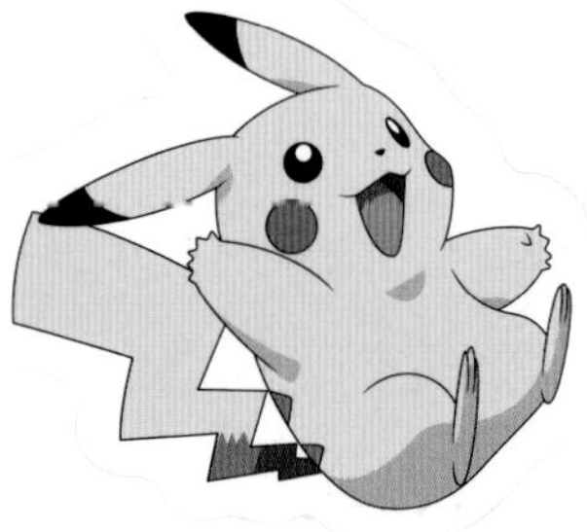

↑ PIKACHU

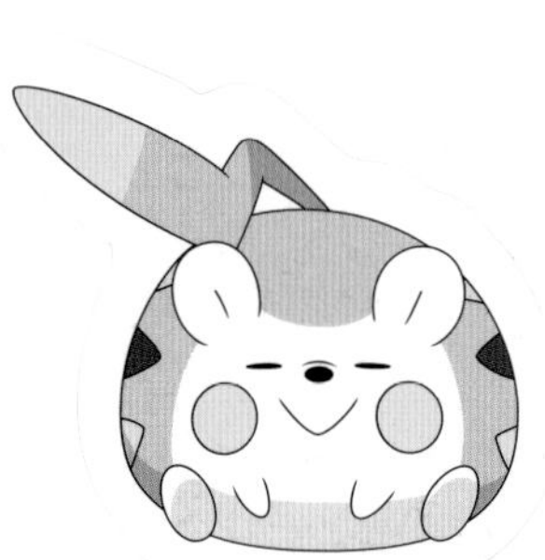

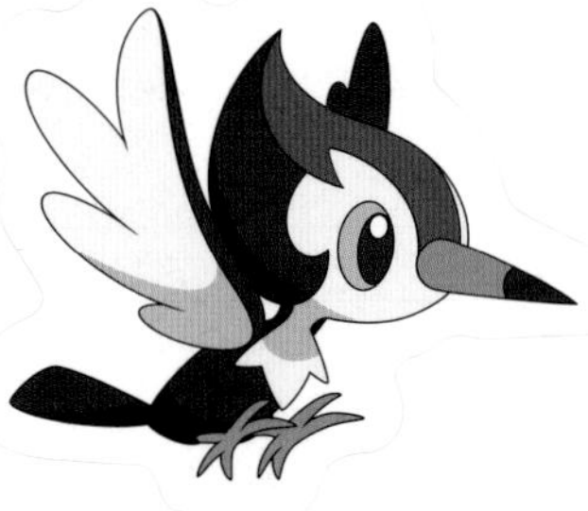

↑ PIKIPEK

↑ TOGEDEMARU

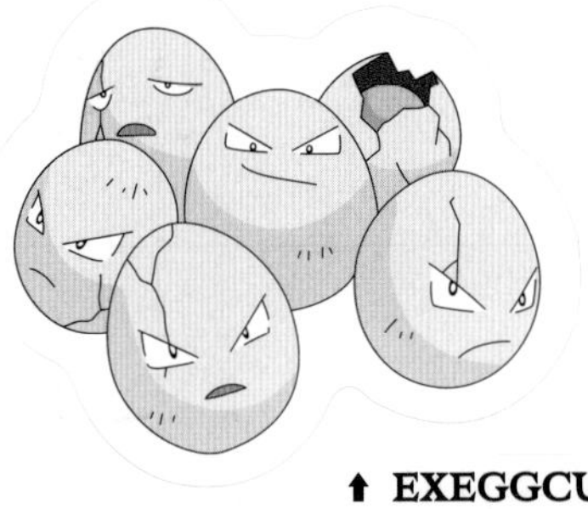

↑ EXEGGCUTE

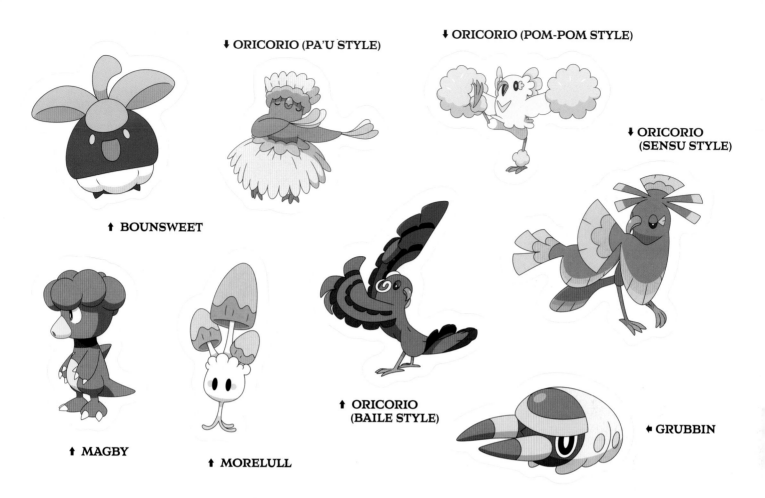

↓ ORICORIO (PA'U STYLE)

↓ ORICORIO (POM-POM STYLE)

↓ ORICORIO (SENSU STYLE)

↑ BOUNSWEET

↑ MAGBY

↑ MORELULL

↑ ORICORIO (BAILE STYLE)

← GRUBBIN

SNOWY MOUNTAIN SCENE STICKERS

↑ SANDSHREW (ALOLA FORM)

← SNORUNT

↑ MAGNEMITE

← KLEFKI

↑ DELIBIRD

↑ SANDSLASH (ALOLA FORM)

↑ SABLEYE

↑ PORYGON-Z

↑ NINETALES
(ALOLA FORM)

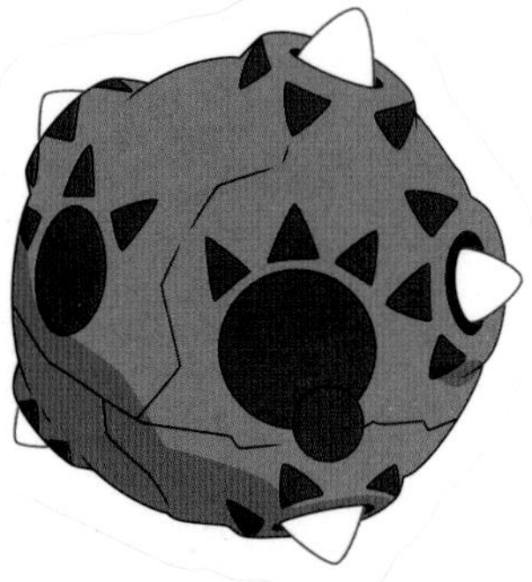

↑ MINIOR

↑ CARBINK

↑ VANILLUXE

↑ VULPIX (ALOLA FORM)

↑ CRABOMINABLE

↑ GLALIE

↑ PIKACHU

↑ VANILLISH

↑ VANILLITE

↑ GLACEON

BONUS STICKERS

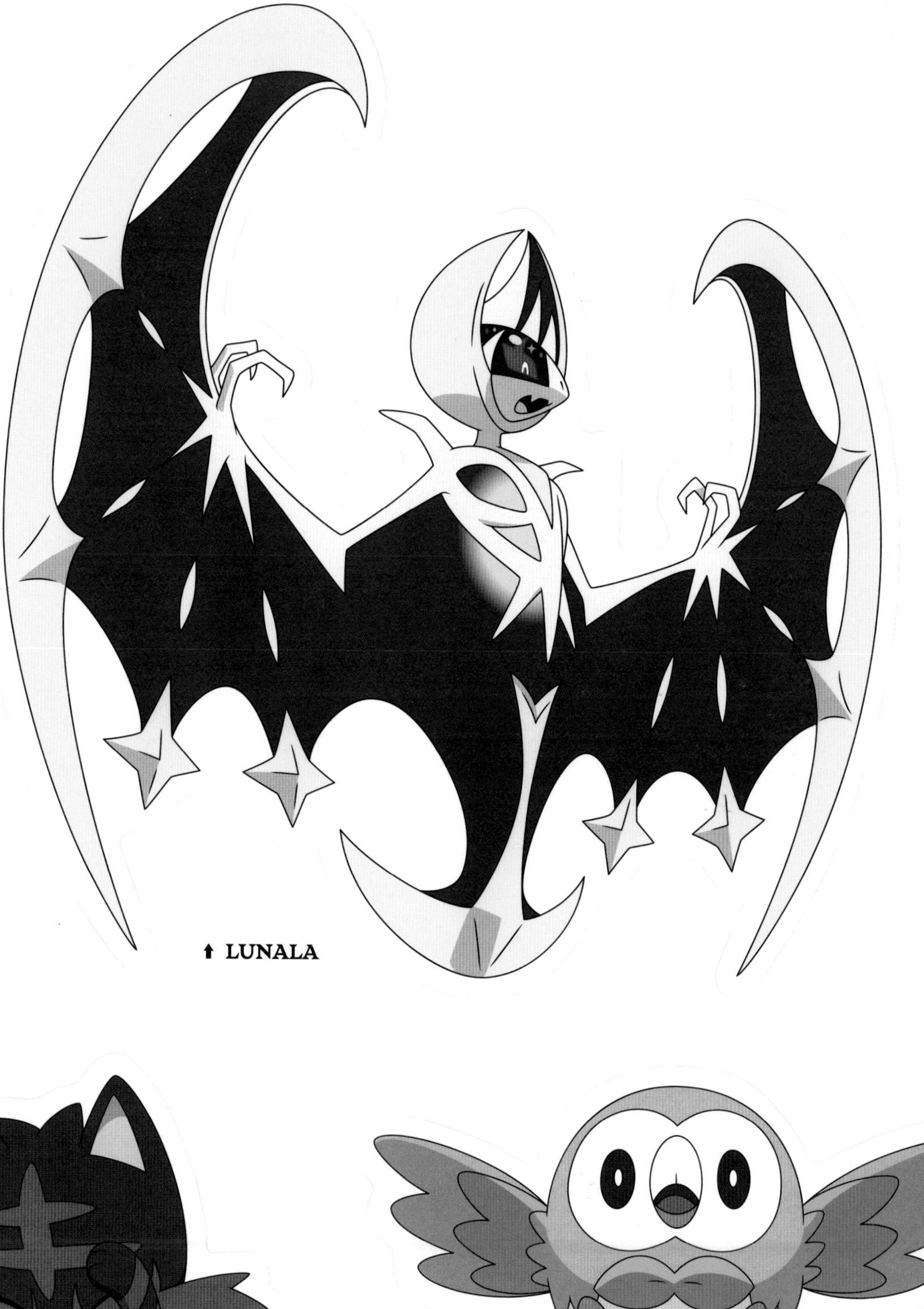

↑ LUNALA

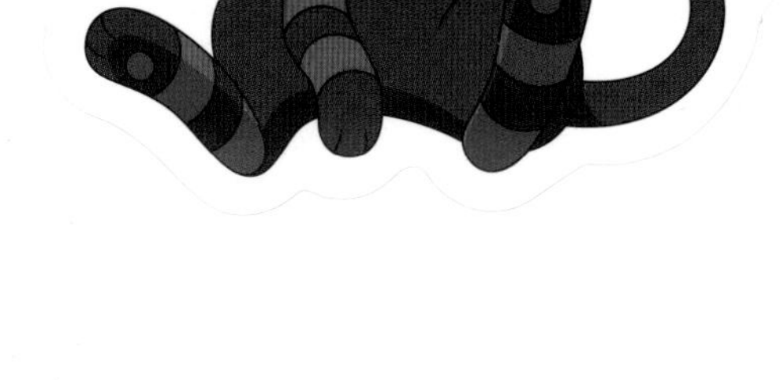

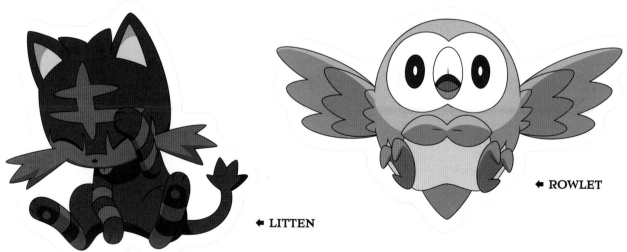

← LITTEN

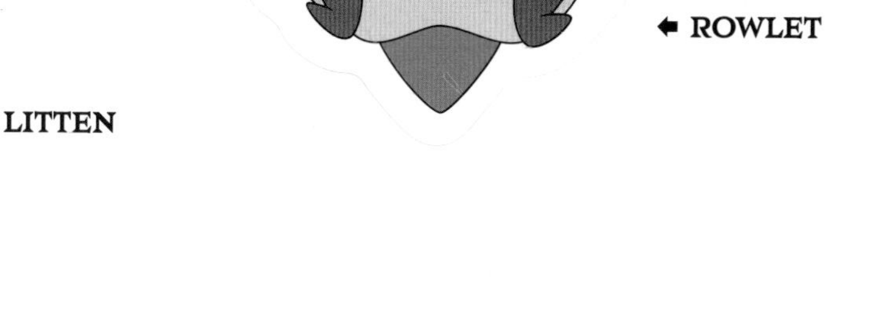

← ROWLET

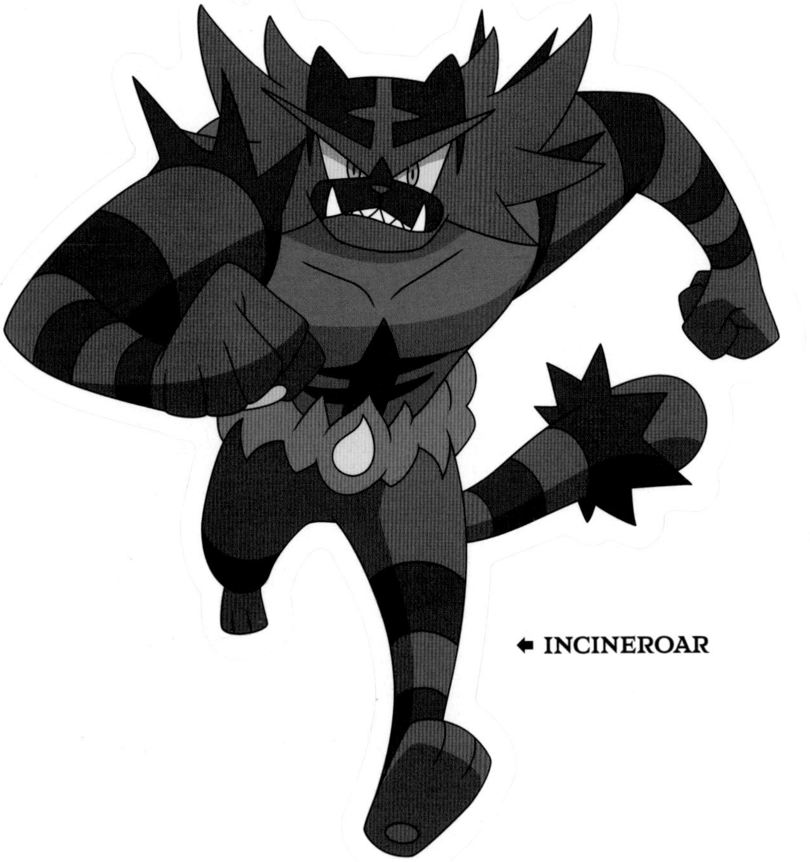

← INCINEROAR

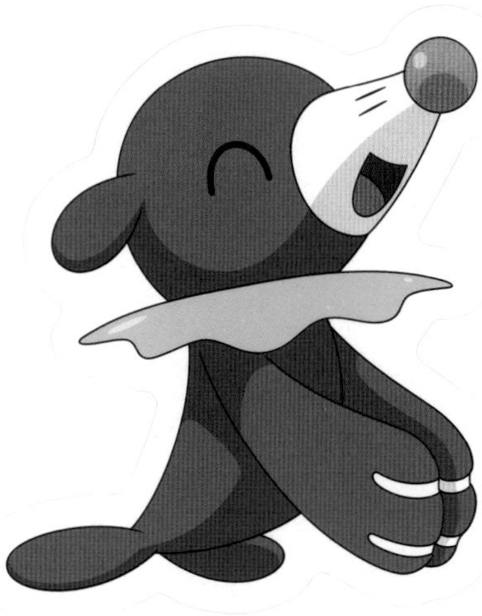

↑ POPPLIO

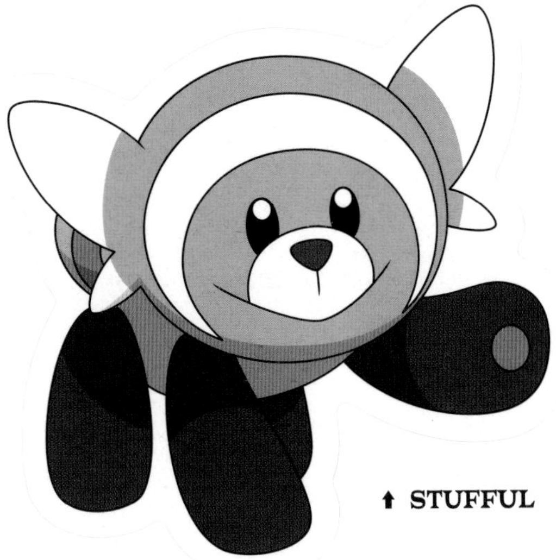

↑ STUFFUL

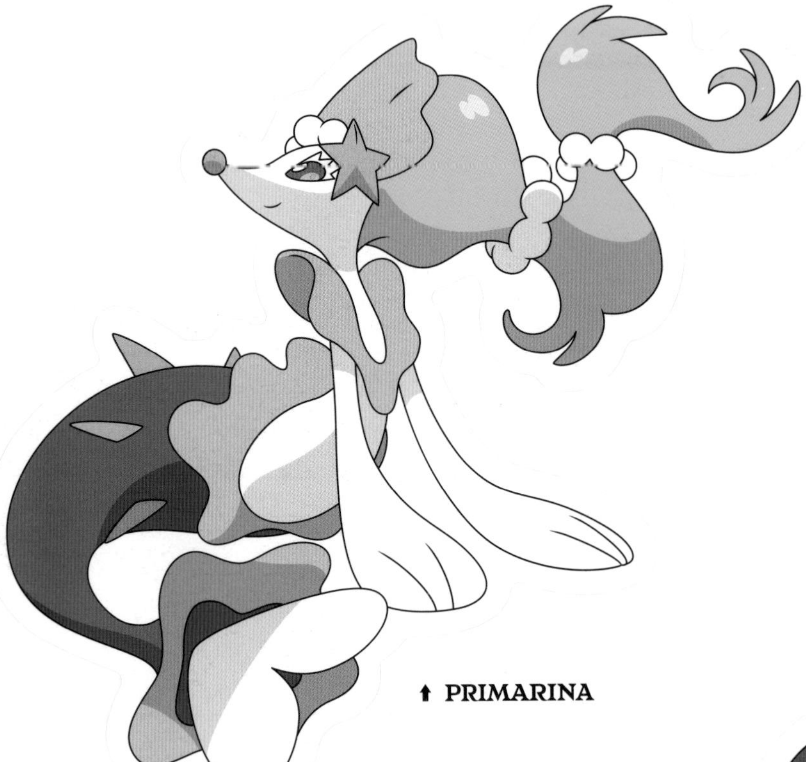

↑ PRIMARINA

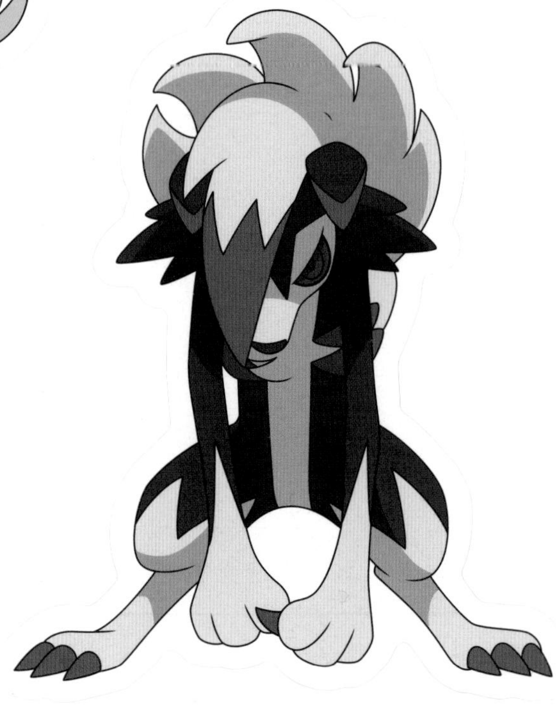

↑ LYCANROC (MIDNIGHT FORM)

↑ LYCANROC (MIDDAY FORM)

← SOLGALEO

↑ VULPIX
(ALOLA FORM)

← DECIDUEYE